INHERITANCE

NORA ROBERTS

THORNDIKE PRESS
A part of Gale, a Cengage Company

The Lost Bride Trilogy #1.
Thorndike Press, a part of Gale, a Cengage Company.

Thorndike Press® Large Print High Octane.
The text of this Large Print edition is unabridged.
Other aspects of the book may vary from the original edition.
Set in 16 pt. Plantin.

LIBRARY OF CONGRESS CIP DATA ON FILE.
CATALOGUING IN PUBLICATION FOR THIS BOOK
IS AVAILABLE FROM THE LIBRARY OF CONGRESS.

ISBN-13: 979-8-88579-480-0 (hardcover alk. paper)

Published in 2023 by arrangement with St. Martin's Publishing Group.

Printed in the United States of America
1 2 3 4 5 6 7 27 26 25 24 23

For Benita
because I still hear your wonderful laugh

■ ■ ■ ■

Part One: Betrayal

■ ■ ■ ■

He was her man, but he done her wrong.
— "Frankie and Johnny"

Inheritance

Prologue

1806

I am a bride. I am a wife.

It thrills me to know my life began today, as today I am no longer Astrid Grandville.

I am Mrs. Collin Poole.

When we met, barely a year ago, I loved. I loved not just his handsome face, his fine figure, for his twin, Connor, has the same. I loved the smile in his deep green eyes, the tenor of his voice, the dogged intelligence of his mind.

I loved his fairness, his knowledge of the world, his quick laugh, his dedication to his family and the business they built.

He is a shipbuilder, my husband, as was his father before him. I knew Arthur Poole only briefly, but grieved for him when a fall from his horse took him from this world.

Now the brothers man the wheel of the business their father established.

But not today. Today is a holiday for all in Poole's Bay, and in the home his father built there is music and dancing, food and wine, love and laughter.

On this wild cliff above the wide sea where Arthur built his sturdy stone castle, we make our home from this day, my beloved and I.

We will fill our home with children, children born of love. Perhaps we will create that first spark of light tonight. Our wedding night.

Arabelle, my dearest friend, a friend who will be a sister by law when she and Connor marry in the autumn, asked if I was nervous as I come — as she will in turn — to the marriage bed a maid.

No. Oh no, I am eager, eager to know what there is beyond the kisses that so heat my blood, so rouse my passions.

With my body I thee worship. I will keep my vows, one and all.

I look in the glass now in what will be our bedchamber, husband and wife, and see a woman so different from the girl she was.

I see the hair Collin calls sunlit silk worn up under a crown of roses with a short veil floating behind as my mother requested it. I see the white dress I worried so over. It floats as well, as I wanted, from the silk ribbon at its high waist.

I know I am not a beauty, whatever Collin tells me. But I am pleasing, especially today when the girl becomes a woman, and the bride becomes a wife.

I see the sparkle of the ring he gave me

when he asked for my hand. When he said, *I love you with all of my heart. My darling Astrid, I will never love another, but love you through all of my life, and love you even after death takes me.*

Now that sparkle, that promise, that pledge is on my right hand, and the gold band, the circle that never ends, is on my left.

The woman I am becoming will love him throughout her life, and even after death takes her.

Now I must go back after this brief moment of quiet contemplation. Back to the music, the dancing, the celebration Collin insisted on to mark this day.

I will dance with my husband. I will embrace his family as my own, for so they are. As the pipers play, I will celebrate this first day of the long and happy life we will make together.

Or so I believed.

I turn to greet her as she comes into the room. I think she looks familiar, but before I can speak, she rushes toward me. I see the knife for an instant before she plunges it into me.

Oh, the pain! I will never forget it. The shock of it as the blade slices into my flesh, once, twice. And again, again.

I stagger back, unable to scream, unable to speak when she tosses the knife at my feet.

"You will never have him," she says. "Die a bride, and know he'll come to me. He will come to me, or by your blood on my tongue, bride after bride will join you in death."

To my horror, she licked my blood off her finger. As I fall, she takes my wedding ring.

And this act is somehow worse than the pain.

"A marriage isn't a marriage until it is consummated. Only a bride, forever lost. Be damned to you, Astrid Grandville."

She leaves me there, dying on the floor near the marriage bed I will never share with my beloved. But my ring, my wedding ring. How can I leave this world without it?

The bloodstain spreads over the white of my wedding dress as that desperate need pushes me to my feet. In agony, I stagger to the door. My hands, slick with my own blood, are barely able to open it.

But I must find Collin. I must have my ring. With this ring I pledge thee. My sight dims; every breath is torment.

Someone screams, but the sound comes from another world. A world I am leaving.

I see him, only him as all else fades — the music, the pretty gowns and waistcoats, the faces blurring, the shouts going quiet.

He rushes to me, calling my name. He catches me in his strong arms as my legs give way.

I want to speak to him. My love, my life.

But the circle, the promise of a long, happy life, was stolen.

I feel his tears on my face, and see the fear and the grief in those deep green eyes.

"Astrid, my love. Astrid. Don't leave me. Don't leave me."

As it all fades away, I speak my last words, give him my promise with my last breath.

"I never will."

And I have not.

Chapter One

Present Day

Planning a wedding equaled insanity. Sonya decided that once you'd accepted that as incontrovertible fact, you could just get on with it.

If she had her way, she'd ditch the whole crazy circus. She'd buy a fabulous dress she could actually wear again, have family and close friends over for a backyard wedding. A short, sweet ceremony, then bust it all open for the best party ever.

No fancy, no formal, no fraught and fuss. And all the fun.

But Brandon wanted all the fancy and formal and fuss.

So she had a fabulous dress — that had cost the equivalent of two months' mortgage, and she'd wear it for a matter of hours before she had it cleaned and boxed away.

They'd booked a fancy Back Bay hotel for a guest list that crept over three hundred and might come close to four before the invites went out.

She'd designed the invitations — she earned her living as a graphic designer, after all. Then again, so did Brandon, so he'd had input there. Maybe the invitations had crept up to more formal than she'd envisioned, but they were gorgeous.

They'd done the Save the Date deal months before, and spent the best part of a day with a photographer for engagement photos.

She'd wanted to tap a friend to take some candid shots, casual, fun shots. And had to admit she'd resented his absolute veto there. Still, the photos were lovely.

Sophisticated. A sleek, sophisticated ad for the perfect, happy, upwardly mobile couple.

They'd spent what seemed like days going over the menu — plated and formal, of course. Then cake. She liked cake — she'd go to the ground believing something was intrinsically wrong with anyone who didn't like cake.

But Jesus, who knew building a wedding cake — flavors, filling, icing, design, tiers, topper — could become a study in frustration?

She did now.

And that didn't count the groom's cake. Or the petits fours with their initials in gold on the top.

Add the flowers, the music, seating charts, colors, themes, and despite the efficient and incredibly patient wedding planner, it all boiled down to nightmare.

She couldn't wait until it was over and done.

And that probably made her an aberration.

Weren't brides supposed to want the fuss and bother? Didn't a bride want her wedding day to be special, unique, a fairy tale?

She did want it to be special, unique, and she very much wanted the happy ever after.

But.

And those buts had been coming fast over the last few weeks. *But* it didn't feel like her day, her special, unique, gloriously exciting day. At all. Somehow, it had slipped right out of her control. When she reminded herself it was Brandon's wedding day, too, and he should have some say, it struck her he had *all* the say.

None of it reflected her vision or her wishes. It clearly reflected all of his.

And if their vision and wishes were so dramatically different, didn't that mean they just weren't suited?

If she dwelled on that, she worried. Like she worried when they spent three Saturdays house hunting and he pushed for the sleek, contemporary McMansion and she wanted the rambling old house with character.

But.

If she didn't dwell on it, if she remembered the last eighteen months of being a couple, she couldn't find anything to worry about.

A wedding day was just one day, and why shouldn't Brandon have the fuss he wanted? A house? It's what you put inside it that counted. They'd find a compromise, and make it a home.

Wedding jitters, she told herself. The Big Reality was setting in. And she had proof — literally — in the wedding invitation proof in her bag.

Accepting jitters, she canceled an appointment with the florist — couldn't face it — and headed home.

She'd have a couple of quiet hours. Brandon had some groom thing to deal with, so she'd have the place to herself until he got home.

She decreed when he did, they'd open a bottle of wine, go over the wedding invitation proof, finalize that, then finalize the ever-growing guest list. Order the invitations, and be done with it — since he'd hired a calligrapher to address them.

Something she could've done, but hey, she wouldn't complain about *not* addressing a couple hundred invitations.

She pushed through Boston's Saturday traffic with the windows down and the music up. In eight weeks, she thought, the color would have exploded with fall — her favorite season. And all this would be behind her.

She was twenty-eight, closing in fast on

twenty-nine and the end of another decade. She was ready to settle down, start a family. And in eight weeks, she'd marry the man she loved.

Brandon Wise — smart, talented, romantic. A man who'd taken it slow and easy when she'd been cautious about starting a relationship with a coworker.

He'd won her over — and she'd enjoyed being won over.

They rarely fought. He was incredibly sweet to her mother, and that mattered. He enjoyed the company of her friends, and she enjoyed the company of his.

Sure, she could think of a lot of ways they diverged. He'd go to a cocktail party, dinner party, art opening — name the social event — every night. And she needed to spread those things out, hold on to the quiet-at-home times.

He had more shoes than she did — and she liked shoes.

When he talked about buying a house, he talked about grounds crews, and she imagined mowing the grass and planting a garden.

But who wanted to marry and live with a clone?

Differences added variety.

By the time she parked, she regretted canceling the appointment with the florist. She should've taken care of it. Flowers, like cake, should make you happy.

She'd make up for it by tossing something together for dinner.

A ploy to head off a let's-eat-out suggestion? she considered as she walked to her side of the duplex. Maybe, but he'd come home to a meal in progress, a bottle of wine, and that was a good deal.

They'd eat, drink, and finalize that damn guest list.

A big check mark in the done column would lift a weight.

Weight lifted, they could spend Saturday night naked in bed.

She heard music when she opened the door and stepped into the foyer. And saw, a few feet ahead as the foyer gave way to the living room, a woman's shoe.

A red stiletto.

She set her purse on the entrance table, dropped her keys in the bowl she kept there. And slowly bent down to pick up the shoe.

Its mate lay on its side near the turn toward the bedroom, along with a white, full-skirted, strapless dress.

Music flowed out of the bedroom, a quiet, sexy score punctuated by a woman's breathless cries and moans.

Brandon liked having music on during sex, she thought dully. He made a point of it.

She'd found it endearing. Once.

Since they hadn't bothered to shut the bedroom door, she stepped over the discarded dress, kicked the man's shirt and trousers out of the way.

Who knew, she thought, that love could snuff out like a candle in a stiff breeze? And leave no trace. None at all.

She watched her fiancé's ass grind as he thrust into the woman under him. The woman whose legs were wrapped around his waist as she called out his name.

She looked down at the shoe still in her hand, looked at that naked, cheating ass.

When she flung it, when it struck, she thought: Oh yeah, that'll leave a mark.

He reared up, scrambled around. The woman managed a quick shriek and tried to drag up the rumpled sheet.

"Sonya."

"Shut the fuck up," she snapped at him. "Jesus Christ, Tracie, you're my *cousin*. You're part of the bridal party."

Sobbing, Tracie dragged harder at the sheets.

"Sonya, listen —"

"I said shut the fuck up. I'm in the middle of a goddamn cliché. Get dressed, get out. Both of you."

"I'm sorry." Still sobbing, Tracie snatched at the bra and panties on the floor. "I'm so —"

"Don't speak to me. Don't ever speak to me again. If your mother wasn't my aunt, and someone I'm very fond of, I'd kick your slut ass here and now. Keep your mouth shut and get out of my house."

Tracie grabbed the dress on the run, dragging it over her head, sans underwear, as she went. She didn't bother with the shoes.

She didn't shut the door behind her.

"Sonya. I have no excuse. I slipped, I —"

"I see. You slipped, and your clothes just tossed themselves around the room while you fell naked on my cousin. Get out, Brandon. You can get out naked or pull on some clothes first. But get out of my house."

"Ours," he began.

"My name's on the mortgage."

"Sweetheart —"

"You'd seriously dare call me that? Try it again, and I swear to God you'll leave bleeding. I said get out."

He dragged on khakis. "We need to talk. You just need to calm down so I — Where are you going?"

"To get my phone." She walked to her purse, took it out. "To call the police so they can remove you from my home."

"Now, Sonya." The way he said it took on that you're-just-adorable tone. "You're not going to call the cops."

She stood, phone in hand, studying him. Gym fit, dark blond hair tousled from another woman's hands. The smooth, handsome face, the killer blue eyes.

"If you really believe I won't, you don't

know me at all." She picked his keys out of the bowl, removed the key to the house, tossed the rest out the door. "Get out."

"I need shoes."

She opened the coat closet, pulled out a pair of his slides, tossed them at him. "Make do, and go, or I start screaming and calling nine-one-one."

He bent, picked up the slides, slipped them on. "We'll talk when you've calmed down."

"When it comes to you, to this? Consider that the far side of never."

She slammed the door behind him, turned the security bolt.

And waited for the tears, the despair, the misery. None of it, she decided, could burn through the rage.

She looked at the phone in her hand again.

Taking deep breaths, she walked to the sofa, sat. She started to send a text, realized she couldn't manage it the way her hands shook.

She called instead.

"Hey!"

"Cleo, can you come over? I really need you to come over now."

"Wedding crisis?"

"You could say. Please."

Amusement turned to concern. "You okay?"

"Not really, no. Can you come?"

"Sure. I'm on my way. Whatever it is, Sonya, we'll fix it. Give me ten."

I fixed it already, Sonya thought, and set the phone down.

On her second glass of wine, Cleo circled the living room. Long legs in tiny white shorts covered the ground. She had her mass of curling burnt-honey hair bundled back in weekend-at-home mode.

Her jungle-cat eyes flashed.

The more incensed she became, the more the traces of her Louisiana childhood flowed over the heat. And the calmer Sonya felt. This, Sonya decided, was love.

"That bastard. That lying, cheating, sonofa-bitching bastard. And Tracie? I don't even have words slimy enough. Your own cousin! And that — that miserable, big-titted *slut* was helping me plan your wedding shower."

"She ugly cried."

"Not enough. Not close to enough. Oh, oh, she's going to hear from me. You'd better believe she's going to feel my wrath. Two-faced whore-bitch."

"I love you, Cleo Fabares. You're the best."

"Oh, baby." Dropping back down on the couch, Cleo set her wine aside to pull Sonya into a fierce embrace. "I'm sorry. I'm just so sorry."

"I know."

"What do you want to do?" Cleo pulled back, looked at Sonya with her long-lidded tawny eyes. "Tell me what you want, and it's done. Murder? Decapitation? Castration?"

For the first time since she'd walked in the door, Sonya smiled. "Would you use your great-grandfather Harurto's samurai sword?"

"With pleasure."

"Let's keep that in reserve."

"Why aren't you screaming? Why aren't you kicking something? I want to kick something. I want to kick Brandon in the balls. First, I want to go buy a pair of combat boots so I can wear them while I kick him in the balls. Then I want to go buy brass knuckles so I can wear them when I punch Tracie in the face.

"But that's just me," she added, and picked up her wine again. "What do you want to do?"

"I'm doing it. I'm sitting here drinking wine and watching my best friend get pissed off and outraged for me." Sonya took Cleo's free hand. "She ugly cried; I didn't."

"If you need to, I've got a shoulder right here."

"I don't. I'm not sure what that says about me. It was like walking into a scene in a movie. The clueless bride-to-be discovers her fiancé and one of her bridesmaids naked in bed."

"You're not clueless."

"Well, I was about this, so . . . Beyoncé's 'Video Phone' was playing."

"Come on."

"Seriously."

Cleo struggled against the laugh. "Sorry."

"Don't be. When I think . . . If I hadn't canceled that appointment, if I hadn't walked in on them —"

Now Sonya pushed up to circle the room, and her legs in running-Saturday-errands cropped jeans ate up the floor. She gestured with her wineglass with one hand, shoved the other through her hair.

And dragged out the tie that held her maple-syrup-brown hair out of its long, straight tail.

"That's what gets me, Cleo. Really, fucking gets me. I'd have gone through with it. I'd have married the cheating asshole. And I'd've married him *his* way, and that kills me. The hotel ballroom he wanted, the big, slick production of it he wanted, the stupid five-tier wedding cake with the fondant and gold sugar design he wanted.

"How the hell did I let myself get lost in there?"

"Looks like you're found now. I liked him. I actually liked him, and that kills *me.* Maybe I thought the wedding was over-the-top, for you, but hell, it's the day, right? So why not? But — and before I get to the but, let me say it's good to see you found your rage again."

"Oh, never lost that. I just liked seeing yours take over awhile."

"Okay. But. You did cancel the appointment, you did walk in on them. And you're not going to marry the asshole. The fates looked out for you."

"If fate looked out for me, I'd have told him to get lost a long time ago."

"You need more wine."

"Oh, I'm going to get it. And a lot of it."

Sonya pressed her fingers to her eyes, not against tears, but sheer frustration.

"Cleo, I have to cancel everything. The hotel, the photographer, the videographer, the cake, the flowers. Jesus, the stupid string quartet I never wanted, the band. I'm going to lose the deposits. Damn it, I just picked up the proof for the invitations. When I think of the hours and hours I worked on that design."

"Keep it. We'll put a curse on it, bury it and a pair of his boxers under a full moon. And every time he thinks about roping another woman in, he'll get a chronic case of jock itch."

"That's your Creole granny talking."

"*Bien sûr.* I'll help you cancel everything, and maybe we can sweet-talk some of the deposits back. And you bill the bastard for half of the rest. I never liked that you laid all the money out."

After huffing out a breath, Cleo slugged back more wine.

"And when I think about that, and I really look? I realize I didn't like him as much as I kept telling myself I did."

"He was paying for the rehearsal dinner, the honeymoon. Doesn't matter. Lesson learned. I could really use some help with the cancellations. Oh God, the registry."

Because it jittered, Sonya pressed a hand to her stomach.

"We just finalized the gift registry. And we had appointments tomorrow to look at two houses."

"What we're going to do is drink more wine. We'll order pizza. You'll lend me something to sleep in, and we'll go over everything that needs to be done."

"You're going to stay?"

"Whenever my best friend, my college roomie, my partner in crime and sister of the heart finds her fiancé in bed with her cousin, I spend the night."

For the first time, Sonya felt tears sting her eyes. But not from sorrow or pain, from sheer gratitude.

"Thanks. Just the thought of dealing with all this makes me want to crawl in a hole. No," she corrected. "It makes me want to bury Brandon in one. I —" She broke off at the knock on the door, glanced over. "You don't think . . ."

Cleo's tiger eyes flashed. "Let me answer. I wish I had those combat boots, but a knee in the balls works."

Chapter Two

But when Cleo yanked open the door, prepared for battle, Sonya's mother, Winter, rushed in. She squeezed Cleo's hand first, then went straight to her daughter.

"Honey, baby, I'm so sorry." She wrapped Sonya tight, swayed. "Don't cry. Don't cry. He's not worth it." Turning her head, she pressed her lips to Sonya's cheek. "I know you love him, but —"

"I don't. I stopped. I don't know if it's supposed to work like that, but I stopped."

"I don't know either." Winter drew back, cupped her daughter's face, studied it. "But if it's true, I'm glad. Anybody who hurts my girl doesn't deserve love. I'm so glad you're here, Cleo." She reached back for Cleo's hand.

"How do you know about it?" Sonya asked.

"Tracie — who will hear from me — went straight to her mother. Blubbering. Can I get in on that wine?"

"I'll get you a glass," Cleo said.

"Summer called me — after she'd mopped Tracie up and read her the riot act. Sonya, you know Summer loves you, so I hope you don't blame her. She's equal parts furious, mortified, and devastated."

"I don't blame her. Of course I don't. Tracie's an adult. An adult slut."

"She — Tracie — claims it just happened. Thanks, sweetie," she said when Cleo handed her a glass of wine. "What bullshit. Landing in bed with your cousin's fiancé doesn't just happen. And in your cousin's house? In your cousin's bed?"

"Red stilettos, a low-cut white dress, and sexy underwear. Just happened, my ass. She's welcome to him."

"I can promise you he won't be welcome in my sister's house. Now, I'm going to go strip those sheets off your bed."

"I already did. I did that after I called Cleo. I thought about burning them, but they're really good sheets. I'm going to send them out for laundering because I'm not going to wash them myself. Then I'll donate them."

Winter grabbed her into another hug, swayed with it.

"That's my girl. You're really all right?"

"I'm really mad. I'm so damn mad, and furious with myself for not seeing what he was."

"I didn't see it. I think I'm a pretty good judge of character, and I didn't see it. You know what they say about hindsight. I can look back and say, oh sure, that, and that and there. I should've known. What good does that do?

"I'm going to sit."

And she did.

"I was so worried I'd find you heartbroken that I didn't have room to let the anger out. Now that I know you're not? The hell with him."

"The hell with him," Cleo echoed, and walked over to tap her glass to Winter's.

"Okay." Sonya did the same. "The hell with him."

"You need to change the locks."

"I took his key, Mom."

"Change them anyway. Where do you think he'll go?"

"Don't know." Sonya toasted again. "Don't care."

"No, really. I've got another bottle of wine in the car. And boxes the nice young man at the liquor store gave me. We can use them to pack up his things — clean sweep. And I'll take them to him."

"You don't have to do that."

"Oh, my only child, I insist." Iced fury came into her mother's changeable hazel eyes. "He'd probably go to Jerry's, wouldn't he? Best man, close friend. I can go by on my way home and dump them."

"I love you, Winter." Cleo sat beside her,

snuggled in. "I love my mama, and I love you. Sonya and I hit the mama lottery. Maybe when we're packing up his crap, some of those cashmere sweaters he's so fond of end up with little pulls and snags. And it would be a shame if a couple of his fine leather jackets somehow ran into something sharp."

"Girlfriends are the best friends," Winter said. "We could do that, or we could let that go knowing he lost the best thing he could've had in his life. I'm betting he knows it."

"I still want to bury a pair of his boxers under a full moon. Curse him with chronic jock itch."

Winter smiled. "That seems fair. Let's go get those boxes."

They packed. His two tablets, his laptop, the Alexa. His collection of watches, cuff links. Shoes. So many shoes.

Sonya remembered his luggage — Globe-Trotter, of course — so they packed those pieces with shirts, jackets, sweaters, suits, sportswear.

They boxed up toiletries.

"He's got more skin and hair products than I do." Cleo held up an unopened package of moisturizer. "Do you know what this brand costs? And he's got an unopened spare?"

"Keep it," Sonya told her. "Hell, take anything you want."

"Only if it's unopened. Anything else has

his cooties in it. Are you sure you don't want it?"

"Absolutely. I don't want any of it."

"Then I'll take it. Winter, how about we split anything that's still sealed. We've got eye gel — and eye masks — serum. I had a sample of this serum once, and it's great. I'm making a pile."

Winter just nodded, stepped back, hands on hips. She'd used one of Sonya's hair ties to pull her chin-length hair — nearly the same shade as her daughter's — back in a stubby tail. Her eyes, hazel to Sonya's deep green, scanned the now loaded bathroom counter.

"We're going to need more boxes."

"Screw boxes," Sonya decided. "I have trash bags. He has so much stuff! Where am I in this? Why didn't I notice I have half the space he did? He had the entire closet in the spare room, and more than half in the main bedroom closet. And somehow he took over the desk in the spare room for work, and I ended up using the dining room table."

"Erosion happens gradually." Winter rubbed Sonya's shoulders. "A rock's strong, but it doesn't notice how the water's wearing it away."

"You look so much alike," Cleo murmured. "The shape of your faces — that heart shape, your hair color. That peaches and cream skin that tells me I need this high-dollar skin care more than either of you."

"You have gorgeous skin," Winter told her. "Gold dust on caramel, a gift from your wonderfully diverse ancestry. My girl has her father's eyes."

Winter gave Sonya a quick hug. "He'd have kicked Brandon's ass. I don't think I'd have tried to stop him. Andrew MacTavish was a gentle man, but when roused?" She gave Sonya another squeeze. "Stand back."

Then she nodded. "Trash bags. Yeah, seems fair. More than."

"I'll get them. And order the pizza," Cleo offered. "We're closing in on done."

"She's a treasure," Winter said when Cleo went out.

"I know. She says the fates saw to it we were roommates in college."

"What do you say?"

"Luck of the draw — really lucky for me."

"For both of you. Your art, your work, didn't hurt. Now she's an illustrator, you're a graphic designer. I'm proud of both of you."

"I need to go into work Monday. So will he. I should never have gotten involved with someone at work."

"Stop." Winter turned her around. "Don't let what he did, what he is shake who you are or what you do. You loved him enough to plan a life with him. You thought he loved you enough to do the same."

"I was wrong."

"You were wrong," Winter agreed. "The mistake wasn't in loving someone. He wasn't faithful, and you ended it. You know what I haven't heard from you? *What did I do wrong? Why wasn't I enough? What did he see in her he didn't in me?*"

"I — Mom —"

"You know why I haven't heard that? Because you're too smart to fall in that ditch. You know this isn't about you. It's about him. His character. You believed in him. He proved you wrong. That's all there is to it. So clean sweep, close the book, lock the door. Change the locks," she amended, "then lock the door."

"I'll call a locksmith tomorrow. He'll corner me — or try to — at work on Monday."

"And you'll deal with it."

"I'll deal with it." She shut her eyes. "I'm embarrassed."

"Of course you are. Anyone would be, even when it's not their embarrassment. So, Sonya Grace MacTavish, make it his embarrassment."

She kissed Sonya's forehead. "That — especially to someone like Brandon? It's more painful than chronic jock itch."

They ate pizza, and while Sonya and Cleo drank more wine, Winter switched off to iced tea. Together, they made a plan. Then they carted boxes, suitcases, and Hefty bags out to the car.

On the second trip, her neighbor stepped out of her side of the duplex.

"Do you all need some help with that? Bill's home. He'd give you a hand."

Winter sent her a winning smile. "Thanks, Donna. If he wouldn't mind. We've got a couple more loads."

"No problem. Bill! Come give Sonya a hand." She put a hand on her hip, a woman with three grown children who'd downsized with her husband and had moved into the duplex just over a year before.

A nice couple, Sonya thought, neighborly but not pushy. Important qualities, in her view, when you shared a common wall.

Bill came out in a Red Sox T-shirt and cargo shorts that showed off his knobby knees.

"Moving out on us?" He grinned when he said it, making it a joke.

Sonya figured she'd had just enough wine.

"I'm booting Brandon out, or I already did after I found him naked in bed with my cousin Tracie."

Inside his scruffy goatee, Bill's mouth dropped open. On the other hand, his wife Donna's mouth thinned.

"Is that the blonde with the big boobs?"

"Why, yes, it is. You might have seen her run out of the house a few hours ago barefoot and holding her underwear."

"No, and I'm sorry I missed it. I'm sorry it happened. But I'm going to tell you I've seen her come around twice before when you weren't home. I thought they were working on some surprise for you, for the wedding maybe. But . . . I won't lie. I wondered."

"Twice before today?"

"That I saw. Last Saturday when I was washing windows, and it must've been about three weeks ago. I'd taken some cookies to Marlene's across the street. Her little boy's fond of my snickerdoodles. I was just leaving to come home. So, yeah, that's Saturday again, three weeks back."

"We went to the salon," Cleo said, "for you to try out styles for the wedding, and shoe shopping for wedding shoes."

"I remember," Sonya murmured.

"I'm sorry it happened," Donna said again. "But I'm glad you found out sooner than later. Bill, go on and get the rest of that douchebag's stuff out of Sonya's house.

"Anything else we can help you with," she added, "you just ask."

"At least three times," Sonya said when they'd loaded the last of it. "Now I have to get rid of the bed. Maybe the couch. They might've used the couch. Or God knows where else."

"No, you don't. I'm going to white sage the whole place."

She looked at Cleo. "Seriously?"

"Deadly. I might have some in my purse. Otherwise, I'll run home and get some. We are clearing him out, and her. And anyone else he might've banged in there. Sorry, Son, but maybe."

"Yeah." Though it made her a little sick, she nodded. "Maybe."

Now she needed to get tested, she realized, and that added to the humiliation. She'd need to get tested, just in case.

"Now I wish we'd sliced up those leather jackets. And I'm going to have another conversation with Summer. But first, I'm dumping all of his things at Jerry's, whether he's there or not."

Winter grabbed Sonya in another hug, a fierce one. "We're going to consider this a narrow and welcome escape."

"If he's there," Cleo said, "can you kick him in the balls?"

"I might just. I'll be here tomorrow. We'll start making those calls."

"Thanks."

When Winter drove away, Cleo put an arm around Sonya's shoulders.

"More wine?"

"Oh yeah. Can we bury Tracie's slut shoes with Brandon's boxers? Give her chronic yeast infections?"

"Now you're talking."

On Monday morning, Sonya dressed carefully. The red suit helped her feel powerful, in control. She spent time working her hair into a sleek twist, and that made her feel cool and detached.

She'd felt the opposite on Sunday when Brandon texted her — four times, before she'd listened to Cleo and her mother and blocked his number.

We have to talk. We can't throw everything away because I made a terrible mistake. You know I love you. We have to talk. You have to let me explain.

Every text had coiled up her anger. And the anger made her feel weak and stupid.

Today, she had to face him. She needed to feel powerful and cool and detached.

When she'd chosen jewelry — bold — and perfected her makeup, she went out to where Cleo sat, half dozing over coffee.

"Well?"

Sonya turned a circle.

"And that's a wow. Killer look, Son. A 'here's what you'll never tap again, asshole' look."

"That's what I aimed for."

"Direct hit. Listen, I'm going to take the spare key and your wedding binder. I'll start canceling what we couldn't reach on a Sunday."

"Cleo, you've already given me Saturday

and all day yesterday."

"And I go nowhere until the locksmith comes today to change those locks, then I'm taking the binder and the key home with me. I'm in a good place on my project to take a few hours. So I'll finish the rest of the calls. I'm guessing since there were alterations, you can't just return the wedding dress."

"No-return policy. Mom paid for that ridiculously expensive dress, Cleo."

"I know. But I bet this isn't the first time they've had this happen. So I'll call, ask them for advice. Consignment shop, eBay, who knows, maybe they have someone who'll buy it at a discount. I'm going to handle the dress for you, and what else I can. And you know you'd do the same for me."

"I would. And when this is behind us, I'm taking you for a weekend. A spa weekend. Mom, too. Yours if she can fly up. Girls' trip in lieu of honeymoon."

"I'm all in for that. Are you ready to go kick balls?"

"They're not combat boots, but they'll do."

As she drove through the madness of Boston morning commute traffic, Sonya reviewed her plan. In theory, it seemed simple.

She'd ask for a few minutes to speak with either of the co-owners of By Design — and keep that simple, too.

She'd called off the wedding after realizing she and Brandon weren't suited, and weren't ready for marriage. No further details necessary.

Due to the stress of that decision, she'd request, for the next few months, at least, she and Brandon not be assigned to the same project.

Brandon had seniority. While she'd worked at By Design for seven years, including an internship, he had nearly ten in. But they'd both climbed up the ranks, had their own offices, often headed projects, put their own teams together.

He specialized in advertising — billboards, television, and internet ads. And he was good, she couldn't deny it. He was very, very good. The dickhead.

Though digital art — websites, banners, social media — comprised the bulk of her work, she also designed visuals for companies and individuals. Created looks — consistency — in logos, business cards, letterheads, those websites, physical and digital signs.

Still, it was a small, privately owned company — exactly the kind of company she'd hoped to work for — and she and Brandon often worked on different parts of the same project.

She'd just ask for some breathing room. And promise to maintain a courteous, professional relationship with Brandon in the workplace.

Simple, she thought. Reasonable and clean.

Of course, in a small, privately owned company, there would be gossip. She'd handle it. In fact — despite Cleo's objections — she'd take the blame.

Simpler, cleaner to say she'd realized she wasn't ready, that she and Brandon had different goals in life. His being to screw her cousin, but no point in mentioning that.

And in a few weeks, the talk would die out, replaced by some other drama.

She could wait until then.

Meanwhile, she had no doubt Brandon would find some way to corner her. So she'd meet that head-on. She'd make it clear to him, in private, face-to-face, that they were done. And she'd do that calmly, dispassionately.

He'd hate the calm and dispassion, she thought, and smiled as she pulled into the employee parking of the two-story refurbished factory that housed By Design.

She went in the side door, straight into what she thought of as the Nesting Area. She'd started there, right out of college, at one of the workstations. And most who'd man those stations now, working on assignments, assisting designers, hoping to make their own mark, would be as green and eager as she'd been.

Some would move up, some would move out, others would take a leap and strike out on their own.

She'd moved up, happy with the rhythm and tone of her workplace. From production artist to graphic designer and now senior graphic designer.

She'd come in early deliberately, and walked straight through to her office.

Not big, not grand, but it had a window, and she'd put her treasured African violet, Xena, in that stream of southern exposure. It rewarded her with pretty pink blossoms and glossy green leaves.

She set her briefcase on her desk, glanced at her mood board.

She routinely created a physical as well as digital mood board for a project. The digital — easy to share, to change. But the physical meant she could stand, shift, study from different angles.

And this one, laying out the plan, the visual for a start-up company, just worked.

Baby Mine, founded by crafty sisters, created handmade baby clothes — no charge for personalization if desired. For preemies — specific to the needs of infants in the NICU — and up to eighteen months.

For the logo, she'd drawn an infant in an old-fashioned cradle with a mobile overhead spelling out the company name in softly rounded fonts, in quiet pastels.

Soft, sweet — that's what a parent wanted for their baby.

The website visual followed that tone, adding in the easy care, the lovingly handcrafted accessories, photos not just of the products but of babies wearing the products, or parents using the blankets, the burp cloths.

Various social media posts would increase those visuals, consistently. And a fresh and, again, consistent, look for the sisters' blog.

And now that they'd moved their little company out of their homes and into an actual workshop, she'd carried that design into the physical space.

A few finishing touches, and they'd be off and running.

She'd so much rather sit down and work on those finishing touches than air her personal business with her bosses.

But it had to be done.

She started out. She heard voices now, artists coming into the Nesting Area, or hitting the break room for coffee before they settled in.

She walked up the metal stairs to the second floor. It held the directors' offices — art, design, creative — and their assistants' work areas, the presentation room where designers pitched their concepts and completed work to the directors, the owners' offices, a second, snazzier break room.

Since Laine Cohen had hired her, she went there first, knocked.

"Come!"

When she opened the door, she saw Laine,

hair a sharp, angled wedge of mahogany hair, bright blue readers dangling from the silver chain around her neck, at her desk. Her partner sat on the corner of her L-shaped workstation.

The window behind her offered a view of the Boston Common on a perfect summer day. Posters of designs created in-house lined her walls. She rotated them every few months.

Sonya currently had one displayed. So did Brandon.

And she saw, when Laine and Matt Berry looked at her, they already knew.

Matt, slim in chinos and a pink polo, slid off the desk. As usual, he had his glossy blond hair pulled back in a tail. A gold hoop winked in his left ear.

"I wonder if I could have a couple of minutes," Sonya began.

"Of course, of course." Matt gestured her in. "Close the door, have a seat. How are you, Sonya?"

"I'm all right, thanks. I —"

"Laine and I were just talking about you taking a few days off."

So Brandon had beaten her to it, she thought. And in his way.

"I appreciate that, but I don't need time off. I hope to finalize the Baby Mine account today, and I hope to present some initial designs on the Kettering account by the end of the day."

The quiet sympathy in Matt's eyes, the speculation in Laine's had Sonya tossing the plan out the window.

"I take it you heard we've called off the wedding."

"Brandon called me last night." All sympathy and comfort, Matt rubbed her arm. "He's upset, of course, but he feels — I agree — you just need a little space, a little time. Planning a wedding is beyond stressful. I can still remember snapping and snarling at Wayne when we were planning ours."

"He contacted you, our boss, on a Sunday night, to tell you I was stressed over wedding planning?"

"We're not just bosses. We're family here. We hope everyone here knows our door is always open if there's a problem. Isn't that right, Laine?"

"Of course. And yes, weddings are stressful to plan. I helped plan my daughter's last year, so I know. I've also seen you handle all manner of stress, Sonya. So I was surprised when Matt told me you'd had a kind of crisis over the wedding details."

"I had a crisis?" Your mistake, Brandon, she thought, trying to draw me as hysterical. On to Plan B, designed on the spot. "I guess you could call it that."

"And nothing to be ashamed of," Matt assured her. "You take a break, pamper yourself a little. I'm sure you and Brandon will work this all out."

"That's not going to happen. I had this crisis, since we're calling it that, when I got home unexpectedly early Saturday afternoon and found Brandon in bed with my cousin. Imagine my surprise. And imagine my additional surprise when I learned that wasn't the first time.

"So there's not going to be a wedding. I don't need or want time off. I came in this morning with no intention of telling you the embarrassing details of my decision, but to let you know I'd changed my mind regarding the wedding. And to ask if, because the situation would be awkward for a time, Brandon and I aren't assigned to the same project."

"I — Are you sure about the . . . the circumstances?"

"Oh please, Matt." Laine gave him an eye roll. "I think Sonya's sure what she saw with her own eyes. I'm very sorry to hear it."

"Yes. God. I'm sorry. Do you want some tea? I can get you some tea."

"No, thanks. Thank you. I'm fine. I really am. I know it's awkward, but I give you my word I'll behave professionally in the workplace."

"We'll hold you to that word," Laine said. "And we'll expect the same from Brandon. You recently finished a project together."

"Two weeks ago. We don't have any mutual projects right now."

"We'll keep it that way, for now. Sonya, if you want a day or two, to decompress, and to handle what I know must be a slew of cancellations, notifications, you can certainly have that time."

Laine lifted her hands. "And any help we can offer."

"Thank you, really. I've got help with the details, and I'd honestly rather work. I'm sorry to bring all this in to you."

"Workplace romances." Laine smiled a little. "Who hasn't been there? The door is open, Sonya, if you decide you need that time."

"I appreciate it." She rose. "I'm going to get to work."

It didn't surprise her to find Brandon waiting between the office and the stairs.

"We need to talk."

When he reached for her arm, she stepped back. "Don't put your hands on me."

"We're not having this discussion out here." He gestured toward the door of the presentation room. "I prefer to keep my personal business private."

"Then you shouldn't have called Matt last night and lied to him." But she walked through the door.

"I certainly didn't lie." He shut the door with a snap. "I told him you'd called off the wedding. You were upset and stressed."

"You failed to mention why."

He had the grace — or the wit, she thought — to look shamed and sorrowful.

"Listen, Sonya, nobody feels worse about what happened than I do. I made a terrible mistake, and I hurt you. I was weak, stupid. I panicked."

She smiled, oh so pleasantly. "I thought you slipped."

"Please." He reached for her again.

"Touch me, and you'll be up on charges of harassment and inappropriate behavior in the workplace. Try it and see."

"I know you're hurt, you're angry. You have every right to be. What I did . . . a moment's weakness. That panic. The wedding, all the details, the decisions, it all started to weigh on me, and I panicked. Then Tracie shows up, and she, well, she came on to me. Hard. And I . . . I just gave in."

He pressed a hand to his heart. "I'm begging you to forgive me. To give me another chance to prove to you how much you mean to me."

"You slipped, you panicked, you gave in. And had sex with my cousin in the bed we shared while I was out picking up the proof for our wedding invitations. And I only know you had sex with my cousin in the bed we shared because I canceled the appointment with the wedding florist."

"It was a horrible mistake, sweetheart. I'll spend the rest of my life making it up to you.

Please forgive me. It was one horrible mistake. She means nothing to me. You mean everything. It was just sex."

She looked at him, really looked, and saw so far beyond the golden good looks. And because she saw the cheat, the liar, it made her a little sick all over again.

"I'm amazed you think this could work. I'm amazed you think I'm just that stupid."

"I'm asking for forgiveness." Shame and sorrow made a quick turn into indignant.

"How can you be so cold, so unforgiving? You sent your mother to Jerry's, for God's sake, with all my belongings. You put my things in trash bags, like we had nothing together."

"I ran out of boxes and suitcases."

"You went running to your mother with our personal business. That's pathetic."

"No, actually, Tracie went running to hers — who happens to be my mother's sister. But regardless, you got your things back, and we're done."

"It's no wonder I gave in to someone warm, someone passionate when you're so fucking cold."

"Lucky escape for both of us then, isn't it? Going forward, since you tried your end run with Matt, I've told them all of it. Not my intention, which was to simply let them know I'd called off the wedding. But I refuse to let you dump this on me. I've given my word I'll behave professionally with you, and they expect you to do the same."

Indignation snapped back, of the righteous sort.

"You couldn't wait to smear me to the bosses. I was human. Tracie ambushed me, she was all over me, and I was human."

"That one time? How about the Saturday before? Or two weeks before that? Was it just being human when the two of you romped around naked then, too?"

"You *spied* on me? That's how you handle problems, issues? By spying on me? That's contemptible."

"I didn't have to. You and Tracie didn't cover your tracks very well. We're done. I just want to get on with my life, and I suggest you get on with yours."

"If you think you'll get away with spreading this around the company —"

"I don't intend to talk about any of this. Your mileage may vary. I've canceled the venue, the band, and so on. All of it. I'll send you a bill for half the nonrefundable deposits."

"Good luck getting a dime out of me."

"I figured that. I'll just write it off as a bad investment. Now get out of my way. I'm going to work."

"You're not wearing the ring I put on your finger. I want it back."

When she smiled, when she smiled and

meant it, it felt so damn good.

"Let me echo your good luck sentiment there. Legally, it's mine. I'm selling it and donating the money to a women's shelter. You need to move, Brandon, or I call Laine's office and report you."

He stepped aside.

"You'll be sorry for this," he told her when she opened it.

"No, I won't. But I am sorry I wasted over a year of my life on someone like you."

She considered it done, finished, closed.

And she spent what she deemed a productive day finalizing the designs for the Baby Mine account. She moved forward on the Kettering account, creating her mood boards, sharing them and her pitch with her design director.

She noticed the looks — especially the ones who pretended not to look. She noticed the awkward pauses in conversations when she walked in or by.

She suspected Brandon of doing exactly what he'd accused her of planning to do. He'd twist the story, lay blame on her head, outright lie.

She wouldn't let it matter. And it would all die down in a week or two.

She made it through a week, then two, then a month. And another two weeks.

Every time she thought it had died down, he managed to resurrect it all again.

She caught wind of a rumor she'd cheated on *him.* Another went around that their wedding planner had dubbed her Bitch Bride from Hell.

He covered his tracks there, as he hadn't with her cousin, and the rumors seemed to pop up out of nowhere. And they lingered.

Someone keyed her car.

She came in one morning to find a design she'd worked on wiped off her computer, and her backup corrupted.

She spent fifteen straight hours reconstructing it, and when she finally left the office that night, she had four flat tires.

Knowing he was behind it meant nothing. She couldn't prove it. But she'd had enough.

The next morning, she knocked on Laine's door.

"I'm sorry. I need to talk to you."

"Come sit. You look tired."

"I am tired. I worked until midnight. The Happy Pet account. The design I'd worked on, had nearly completed, was gone. Wiped off my computer. My backup was corrupted. It wasn't user error, Laine. I think you know I'm more careful than that. I reconstructed it — maybe even improved it — and when I went out to my car, I had four flats."

"Oh Jesus, Sonya."

"I know you hear the rumors that come and go. Most people don't believe them. But there are always a few. I could handle that. I have been handling that. But this was my work, a lot of hard work. If I hadn't been able to replicate it in a timely fashion, we might have lost the account. My tires weren't slashed. Someone let the air out. Regardless, I had to take an Uber home and arrange for a garage to deal with the tires."

"I'm sorry. I'll talk to Brandon, believe me."

"Please don't. I can't prove any of this is on him, and I won't. He'll be shocked, appalled. Why, he's moved on. Isn't he dating other women?"

She shrugged. "But it won't stop as long as we both work here."

"Sonya, I can't fire Brandon over the possibility — I'm going to make that probability — he had some part in this."

"I'm not asking you to. I don't expect you to. I know he does exceptional work."

"He does. So do you. It's time for a full staff meeting."

"No, Laine, it's time for me to resign. I thought I could weather this. But I dread coming to work now. I loved working here, and now I dread it."

"We'll find a way to fix this, Sonya. You know we value you."

"I do know, but I don't want you to fix it. You and Matt? You've built such a good company, and I'll always be grateful to have been part of it. I just can't work here anymore, so I'm giving you my two weeks'.

Longer if you need it, but Gina Tallo? She's ready. She could move up. I could work with her for those two weeks. But I need to go, for me, Laine. I need to go."

Laine sat back. "This sucks. It just sucks."

"It really does. But, Laine, I'm so unhappy. I don't want to be unhappy in my work. I don't want to get up every morning and have a hole in the pit of my stomach because I have to go to work. I have to move on."

"To a competitor. I'm going to hate that, but Matt and I will give you bright and shiny references. We don't want you to be unhappy, and I'm furious you've been made to feel unhappy."

"I think this is what's best for me. But I don't plan on going to a competitor, at least for now. I'm going to freelance. I need the time, the space. And I need to see what I can do on my own."

Head back, Laine stared up at the ceiling. "We're going to lose accounts. I'm going to hate that."

"I won't go after By Design accounts."

"Then you're stupid. Don't be stupid. Take the Baby Mine account, they're going places. It's a gift," Laine said before Sonya could think of anything to say. "Not much of a gift, seeing as they came to you — you — on a recommendation of another account you worked on. I'm telling you that's your account, and Matt will agree with me."

"Thank you. Really, it's more than I could ask."

"You're right about Gina. We've had our eye on her. She needs a little more polish, and we'll see she gets it. Now, listen to me — on a personal level, as I've got a daughter about your age. You've got two weeks' vacation you haven't used for a honeymoon you can celebrate not going on. Take it. Take today to clear up any projects to the point they can be passed on. Then walk out of here, and be happy."

"I can't leave you in the lurch."

"You won't be. Or hell, damn right you will be, whether you leave today or in two weeks. You're a talented woman with a solid work ethic. But Matt and I will handle your projects — we still know how it's done. And we'll give Gina the polish she needs. And we'll miss the hell out of you."

Laine waved a hand in the air. "No crying. You'll start me up. Finish out the day. And keep in touch."

"I will. I owe you and Matt so much."

"Pay us back. Make us proud."

When Sonya went out, Laine sat back again, stared at the ceiling again.

And after a long sigh, said, "Fuck."

Chapter Three

She got through the day. Though she skipped lunch to focus on current projects so she could leave them in good shape for whoever took over, she chatted with coworkers in the break room.

Casual. Situation normal.

As she went through the motions, she realized in her mind, in her heart, she'd already moved on. And because she had, the stress melted away.

At the end of the day, she boxed up her things, her personal tools, her emergency power bars, spare chargers, the fluorite obelisk Cleo had given her, her African violet, and all the little things that had made her office her work home.

A single box, she thought, to sum up seven years — two as an intern — of her professional life at By Design.

The whole, so far, of her professional life.

She took one last look around her office, and Matt stepped to her doorway.

"I wanted to wait until . . . Laine said your mind's made up, and for good reasons. I feel I wasn't supportive enough, that I should've found a solution."

"No. No. It was a bad situation. An impossible one for me. I wouldn't be able to try freelancing if it wasn't for you and Laine."

"I promised Laine I wouldn't pressure you, so I won't. I want to, but I won't. Let me carry that for you."

Taking the box, he walked her out, past offices, through the Nesting Area.

"You'd better miss us."

"I already do." Outside, the fresh fall wind swept over her. It occurred to her she'd have been in the middle of her honeymoon in Paris if not for a canceled appointment.

"If you need advice," Matt told her, "a wailing wall, a drinking buddy, just call." He put the box in the car for her, turned. "I'm going to hug you."

"I'm going to hug you back."

He gave her a long, hard squeeze. "I shouldn't say this, but I'm going to. He won't last here. He's talented, and he's savvy, but he's shown himself to be dishonest, petty, and damn it, vindictive. He won't last with us."

"I want to say it doesn't matter to me, but I can't."

"Go shine." He stepped back. "And I know you will. If you ever want to come back here and shine, the door's open."

"The first time I walked in the door, as an intern my senior year in college, you were wearing a polka-dot bow tie."

"Ah yes, my bow tie period. I may have to revive that."

"And you told me if I didn't know the answer to ask the question. I always knew I could go to you and ask the question."

"You still can."

She kissed his cheek before she got in the car, and she cried a little as she drove away.

Instead of going home, she drove away from downtown and to her mother's neat two-story house with its postage-stamp yard. She'd grown up there, in that leafy neighborhood. She'd played in that yard and, when old enough, mowed the grass.

Her father had taught her to ride a two-wheeler down the sidewalk — she remembered that so well.

I've got you, Sonya. Keep pedaling, baby! I won't let go.

And he hadn't, running along beside her, until she'd shouted:

Let go, Daddy! I can do it. Let go!

He must have watched, she thought now. Had he felt twinges of pride, fear, maybe some poignant regret as she'd wobbled her way along on that little pink bike with the white plastic basket?

She could see him now, so clearly, jogging

down to where she'd stopped — flushed and thrilled with herself — at the end of the sidewalk.

The sweet spring breeze fluttering through his hair — a deep, rich blond that never had the chance to gray. A tall, loose-limbed man, in his prime, long arms and long legs, narrow hands, like hers. Artist's hands, like hers.

A man who'd die three short years later.

An accident, a tragedy. He'd started painting a mural on a building downtown. The scaffolding failed, and made her mother a widow.

She pulled into the narrow drive behind her mother's car wondering why all that flooded back now. Must be the mood, she decided. Quitting a job hardly ranked with death, but it was a sharp change.

The red maple in front of the colonial blue Cape Cod was on fire with fall. Some of the flame-colored leaves had fallen, and before long October would shake them all from the branches.

Mounds of canary-yellow mums brought sunshine to the front corners of the house. And because Winter MacTavish didn't know a holiday she didn't love, fat orange pumpkins flanked the white front door.

Her mother would carve them into jack-o'-lanterns closer to Halloween, haul out the old skeleton, the cackling, broomstick-riding witch, don a costume, and hand out full-sized

Hershey's bars to trick-or-treaters.

Sonya didn't knock — she'd never knocked on this door.

Inside, the living room smelled of the fall flowers in a vase, the woodsmoke from the fire simmering in the hearth.

One of her father's paintings hung over the fireplace, as it always had — at least in Sonya's memory.

A misty forest, deep green shadows with dappled light turning a path to shades of gold. And to the right of the path, a stream where water seemed to rush and tumble over rocks in quick falls that went from white to silver.

She'd wanted to know where the path went, and when she'd asked, he told her: *Wherever you want.*

"Maybe I'm on the path now, and I'll find out."

Knowing her mother, she started back toward the kitchen, calling out.

"Sonya? What a nice surprise."

She'd changed out of her work clothes into cozy sweats and sneakers, and greeted her daughter with a quick hug. "I was just thinking about what's for dinner. Have you eaten?"

"No. I came straight from work."

"Now I have an excuse to get the too-much-soup I made last weekend out of the freezer. Chicken veg, how about it?"

"Sounds great."

"Why don't you get a bottle of white wine out of the cooler. We'll have a glass while I defrost the soup."

"Sounds even better."

"Then you can tell me what you need to talk to me about."

Sonya got a bottle from the under-counter cooler — one of the additions when her mother had had the kitchen updated.

The only real change Winter had made to the house since her husband died.

"I can't just drop by to see my mom?"

"You can, and sometimes do. But" — Winter tapped a finger on Sonya's nose — "I know that face."

Working up to it, Sonya got out a corkscrew, the glasses.

"You know I've had some trouble at work. For the most part, I could ignore it, and for the most part, the people I work with aren't idiots. But it really hasn't let up. Again for the most part, little things. Little digs."

"He turned out to be a very ugly man inside, didn't he?"

"He's so good at it." With a half laugh, she poured the wine. "So smooth, always careful to be absolutely courteous to my face, and oh so professional. But . . ."

She took a sip, leaned back on the center island.

"Relentless, at the same time, just relentless. It's a matter of him paying me back, over and over, for what he sees as me embarrassing him. And yesterday when I came into work, a project I'd just finished was gone. Wiped off my computer."

"That's not relentless, it's vicious."

"More, my backup was corrupted. I still had my physical mood board — that would've been too blatant. But my initial sketches, gone, too. I had to reconstruct, basically from memory. I worked until midnight."

"No wonder you look tired. He's an absolute bastard. You know he did this."

"I know he did this, but I can't prove he did this. Any more than I can prove he let out the air in my tires — all four of them — while I was putting in the overtime."

"Good God, Sonya! That's criminal! Did you call the police?"

"I called an Uber, and yes, I did report it. But that's not going anywhere, Mom. I should've given him back the ring instead of selling it and donating the money. He might've let this go if I'd done that. But I wanted to rub his face in it, so . . ."

"You're not to blame for this. I don't want to hear you taking any of the blame for any of this."

"Not blame, but maybe a miscalculation. And, oh God, don't be disappointed in me."

"As if I could."

She took a breath, held it. "I quit my job."

"Oh, baby." Winter put down her wine,

wrapped her arms around Sonya.

"I thought I could handle it, but I didn't. I couldn't. I let him win."

"You stop that." Pulling back, she gave Sonya a little shake. "You didn't let him win a thing. It's not a damn scorecard. You did what was best for you. Oh, I wish they'd fired the bastard!"

"For what? Cheating on me? You're an administrative assistant in a law firm. You know that's not grounds for firing an employee. And the rest? He's too careful to leave any trail. Matt and Laine?"

Shaking her head, she walked over, dropped down on a counter stool. "They did all they could. I know they had conversations with him. And that probably made it worse in the long run. They're giving me an account, a start-up I worked on, and they're letting me take the two weeks as paid vacation instead of working it out. They didn't have to do that."

"It's not their fault. It's no one's fault but his. What do you want to do now?"

"I'm going to freelance. I've been toying with the idea for the last few weeks, and yesterday capped it off. I have savings, I have experience, I have contacts. And I have the Baby Mine account if and when they need or want what I can do. It's a great little company, and I did good work for them.

"I'll show you."

She grabbed her mother's tablet off the island, brought up the website.

"Well, that's adorable. Oh, look at the outfits! Now I need a baby to buy them for. Wait! Sylvia — from work — she's having her first grandchild in early December. A girl. I'm going to send her a link to this site."

"Please do."

"Handmade. Oh, look at the little caps. Little cat caps!"

Sonya found her mood rising as she watched her mother scroll through the site.

User-friendly, mobile-device efficient.

"Just let me send this link. You're so talented. You got your father's artist genes."

"I wish I could paint like he could."

"You paint beautifully when you want to, but that's not your passion. This is. And it's wonderful. There, Sylvia's going to love it — and your clients are going to get a big order. Now, let's have some soup and talk about your plans for your new company."

"I'm not sure a one-woman operation qualifies as a company."

"It absolutely does. And, not that I'm advocating revenge, but you know what they say about it?"

"What do they say about it?"

"The best revenge?" Winter lifted her eyebrows. "Success. And you're going to rock it."

"I'm sure as hell going to try. But before I

get in too deep, I'm taking a long weekend — a long spa weekend."

"Now, that's just exactly what you need."

"I'm taking my mom, my best friend, and her mom, if she can make it, with me."

"Oh now, Sonya, you can't afford that. Especially now."

"I'm not shopping in Paris, am I? I didn't shell out more thousands for a splashy, bougie wedding I didn't even want. I sold that damn wedding dress for sixty percent of what you paid for it. And Cleo managed to get almost eight thousand back on some of the deposits."

"She's a clever girl."

"So I'm taking my mom, her mom, and the clever girl for a spa weekend. It's a personal indulgence, and I need it. You're not allowed to say no."

"Then I won't. You'd better text Cleo so she can ask Melly."

"Starting a group text right now, then I'm going to try to book us into the Ripe Plum."

"The resort on the coast? Wow. When my girl decides to indulge, she indulges."

"Damn right. I've been so unhappy, Mom. It feels really good not to be. And this soup smells amazing."

Buoyed by the visit, the soup, the encouragement — and the fact that while weekends were booked, she'd reserved three weekday nights at the Ripe Plum — Sonya dropped into bed just after nine, and slept for twelve hours.

She woke with a new sense of purpose, and a new plan.

First step, contact the sisters at their workshop.

Twenty minutes later, she jumped up, pumped her fists in the air.

Not only were they willing to keep their account with her, but they'd given her two contacts for potential clients.

She'd worked with the sisters long enough to know their style. They'd make the contacts straight off. So she'd wait an hour — and that gave her time to work on a logo, and the design for business cards, her website, social media, and everything else.

Midafternoon, she answered the knock on her door.

"I come bearing pumpkin-spice muffins and macchiatos." Cleo shifted the takeout bag, angled her head. "And look at you. I haven't seen that look on your face in weeks. A lot of weeks."

"What look?"

"Happy. Blow-up-my-skirt happy. And here I was afraid you'd be mired in the what-the-hell-have-I-done stage."

"I know just what I've done." She pulled Cleo inside. "I've done got me two clients, and the strong possibility of a third."

"Already?"

"Already. I think I have my logo — which I need to generate contracts for said clients, to finish designing my website, and all the rest. I want your honest and true opinion. Wait there."

When Sonya ran back to her office, Cleo took the coffee and muffins out of the bag.

"Okay. Here's the ta-da — honest and true, Cleo. I want it to sing."

She flipped open the sketchbook.

She'd drawn a thick circle formed by curved petals in bold colors — red, blue, yellow, green — layered in a way that made them pop in two dimensions. Above the circle, in flowing script, she'd centered *Visual Art.* And in the circle, *by Sonya.*

"Don't tell me what I want to hear."

"I'm sorry, I have to. It's perfect. I love it. The circle — a strong symbol, and with strong colors. The petals give it dimension and interest. Using a font with a flow, going with a curve, brings it together. It's got balance, interest, a smart use of white space."

"I didn't want hard edges, or too slick and modern, but not fussy or too traditional. I didn't want to go cute or girlie, but I liked the hint of female with the petals."

"Direct hit. Holy crap, Son, you're off and running."

"I'm going to be redesigning a website for a writer — first book coming out in November.

The one she's got is absolute crap, nothing holy about it. And I'm nudging her to have me redo her social media look. Which is also crap.

"I hope her book isn't. She's sending me an advance copy."

"You'll lie if it sucks."

"You came over to give me a pep talk."

"Yeah, and that's unnecessary. But we have coffee and muffins. Can you take a break?"

"You bet. Thanks. For the unnecessary pep talk, for the coffee and muffin. I rearranged my office to make room for the wall screen I'm going to order. I can toss my work up on it. Like giving myself a presentation. Want to see?"

"Only if I get to make sure it's feng shui."

"I can accept that. Cleo, don't get pissed, but Brandon did me a favor. I don't think I'd ever have done this otherwise. And today? I really feel it's what I'm supposed to do. What I was supposed to do."

"I wouldn't go as far as favor, but we'll say his absolute assholiness gave you a push in the right direction."

"That works. Come see."

Three weeks later, she had the new website up and running for the writer — whose book wasn't crap. She'd designed holiday ads for Baby Mine, and wedding invitations (was that irony) for her next-door neighbor's niece.

By Christmas, she had three more website designs in the works, had designed two book covers and more digital ads.

She closed out what she'd expected to be the worst year of her life feeling on top of it.

Maybe the cut in salary and benefits stung a little, and the expense of shouldering the cost for her supplies and equipment stung a little more. But for a woman who'd been in business less than three months, she did just fine.

She'd have done finer without the plumbing emergency the week before Christmas, and the $1,600 that cost her.

But she did just fine.

She had to keep her prices competitive to build up her client list, her project portfolio. And, she reminded herself, she saved on gas — no commute — on lunches out, basic wear and tear on her car.

Did she miss the camaraderie of coworkers? Sometimes. Then again, she liked working solo, answering only to herself. And wearing whatever the hell she wanted.

Maybe she'd get a dog, or a cat. Since she didn't leave the house for eight or ten hours every day, she could have a dog or a cat.

Companionship.

Food bills, vet bills — with a dog, possibly a groomer.

She'd think about it, work out a budget.

Most of all, tightening her belt a little

meant nothing compared to the satisfaction of doing what she loved, and the way she loved doing it.

She wasn't worried.

Yet.

In mid-January, while Boston shivered under two feet of snow, when business had slowed — it would pick up again — she answered the door.

The man looked to be into his late forties — what she could see of him in his heavy coat and ear-flap hat. He held a briefcase in his gloved hand, and smiled.

Slow, easy, charming.

Under brows sharp and black, his eyes, soft, almost eerily blue, studied her through the lenses of a pair of glasses. The silver frames matched the tufts of hair that found their way from under the cap.

"Ms. Sonya MacTavish?"

"Yes. Can I help you?"

"I'm Oliver Doyle, attorney for the late Collin Poole. Your uncle."

"I don't have an uncle — other than my aunt's husband, Martin. I don't know anyone named Collin Poole."

"Your father's brother."

"You have the wrong information, Mr. Doyle. My father didn't have a brother."

"I believe he was unaware he had a brother. His twin. Your father was Andrew MacTavish, born March 2, 1965."

"Yes, but —"

"He was adopted, as an infant, by Marsha and John MacTavish."

"Mr. . . ."

"Doyle. I understand this is confusing, it's irregular. And I understand if you don't feel comfortable inviting me to come in and explain. I'm staying at the Boston Harbor Hotel, and would be happy to meet you where you would feel comfortable. Let me give you my card. And this."

He took a business card case out of his coat pocket, and a photograph. "This is Collin Poole. He was a close friend of mine, a lifelong friend. He died just before Christmas."

"I'm very sorry, but . . ."

She trailed off as she stared at the photo.

"That was taken nearly thirty years ago. My wife took it, of Collin and me. I've seen photos of your father at about the same age. They were twins. Not quite identical, but it's very close, isn't it?"

"I don't understand this."

"How could you? I take it you haven't done any DNA testing?"

"No."

"They were born in Maine, in the house that's been in the Poole family for over two hundred years."

She had photos of her father at this age. She could see the differences — he'd worn his hair longer. He'd been a little taller, leaner, his chin more square.

But for those slight differences, she'd have sworn she was looking at her father.

"You'd better come in."

"I appreciate it. I'm a Mainer, born and bred, but this wind cuts. You have his eyes. As I said, I've seen photos of your father, and I knew Collin very well. You have the same deep green eyes, from the Poole side of the family."

Family seemed wrong. *Family* seemed impossible. "Let me take your coat."

"Thank you."

When he pulled off the cap, she saw the black of his eyebrows running through the silvery gray hair.

"I can make coffee."

"I'd appreciate that. Just a drop of milk in mine."

She felt numb. How could her father have had a brother — a twin — and not know it? How could her grandparents not have told him? How could they have separated brothers, taking only one as theirs?

And why hadn't this uncle ever contacted her, or her father, if he'd known?

"You have questions."

Mr. Doyle stood, studying photos she had on shelves along with pretty or interesting things that had caught her eye over the years.

"I'm going to try to answer them. Can we

sit here, at the table? I also have some other things to show you, some papers."

"All right."

She set his coffee on the table, sat. "You said he died last month. Was he ill?"

"It's kind of you to ask. I'll try to explain that, too. First, I want to tell you Collin didn't know he had a brother, not for many years. That was kept from him. He learned about your father shortly before your father's death. From me. Genealogy is my hobby, a kind of passion really. I decided to research Collin's as a gift. Do an extensive family tree, as it seemed there were missing pieces — or branches, we'll say, on that tree."

He opened his briefcase. "This is a picture of Collin's father. Your father's father. This was their mother." He laid another photo on the table, smiled a little. "It was the sixties, after all."

The woman — girl, really — had long, straight blond hair. She wore a colorful band around it, over her forehead. A pretty face, Sonya thought, heavy on the eyeliner around blue eyes. A thin build in a T-shirt and low-slung bell-bottom jeans. She held up a two-fingered peace sign with a hand studded with rings.

"Lilian Crest, though apparently she went by the name Clover when this was taken. She died giving birth to the twins. A home birth that went very wrong, it seems. And a storm that knocked out power and phone for two days. The house — the manor — is a bit remote. Not inaccessible by any means, but a few miles from the town of Poole's Bay."

"She's so young."

"Only nineteen when she died. She'd left home at seventeen. She and Charles took up residence in the manor. His parents, twin brother, and his sister made their home just outside of Poole's Bay. At that time."

"Twins run in the family."

"They do. Charles was, by all accounts, devastated by her death, and I'm afraid wanted nothing to do with the children he blamed for it. He took his own life not long after. Before he did, his sister took Collin, and adopted him. Your father was placed with a foster family, and put up for private adoption. Out of state, you see. The Poole family insisted — from what I can read in the paperwork — the adoptive family have no information regarding his birth parents."

"They didn't know." The relief there came in a flood. "My grandparents. They didn't know Dad had a twin. They would have taken them both. They're good people. Loving people."

"I can't tell you why the Pooles separated the children. I know that Patricia Poole, your father's grandmother, was a very hard woman. I know that your father's uncle, Lawrence, closed up the manor again after his brother's death. and it stayed closed until Collin opened it when he turned eighteen. It came to him, you see. Legally when he turned eighteen, as his uncle died four years before without an heir.

"You make good coffee."

"Would you like more?"

"I wouldn't say no. This is a lot to take in," he said when she went into the kitchen. "And it may seem like a lot of history you don't need to know."

"I don't know any of the history, so I need to know."

"Collin and I grew up in Poole's Bay together. He was best man at my wedding — thirty-three years ago this spring. And I stood up for him at his."

"You married young."

He laughed. "Not so very young, but when you know, you know."

"I suppose."

"Thank you," he said when she brought him another coffee. "Collin didn't have much interest in his family's history, but he loved the manor. I can't tell you how often the two of us — or a gang of us — snuck into it when we were boys. It's quite haunted."

"Naturally."

At her amused tone, he looked down into his coffee. "Well. In any case, it's a storied history, but his interest was art. Like your father. Like you."

"He was an artist?"

"That was his calling, his passion. Though he was pushed into the mold of the family business. Shipping, shipbuilding. Poole's Bay is named for the first Poole who began building wooden ships, who started a mill, who founded Poole's Bay and built the original portion of the manor, in 1794."

As if catching himself, Oliver held up his hands.

"A storied history, as I said, which I hope you might find some interest in."

"He never knew any of this, my father. He never knew he had a brother, a twin."

"No, and I'm sorry for it. I want to assure you, Collin was a good man, a good friend, and if he'd had the opportunity, I have no doubt he'd have been a good brother. He'd have been a good husband and father."

"You said you stood up for him at his wedding."

"I did, some five years after he did the same for me."

"Did he have children?"

"No. Tragically, Johanna died on their wedding day."

"That's —" It closed her throat, clutched at her heart. "That's horrible."

"It was. She fell, coming down the stairs during the reception. There was nothing anyone could do. Collin was never quite the same. He rarely left the manor. He grieved,

Ms. MacTavish, deeply."

"Sonya," she murmured. "I can't imagine how awful it had to be for him."

"He spent the rest of his life mourning her, largely closed off from the world. I was allowed in, and my family, as they'd become his family. But he cut himself off from his own. As for the business, the work of it was left primarily to cousins, though his grandmother kept her hand in until the day she died. As his lawyer, I handled his financial interests in the business, and as a Poole, he retained that financial interest, but he spent his days painting and maintaining the manor he and Johanna loved. The home they'd planned to spend their lives in together.

"The home," Oliver continued, "and all it contains, he left to you."

Chapter Four

Shock was too mild a word.

"I'm sorry, what? That's crazy. He didn't even know me."

"You're his brother's only child."

"But — you said cousins took over the family business. It doesn't make sense for him to leave a house to a stranger."

"You weren't a stranger to him. You're family. And while he was a reclusive man for the last decades of his life, he had an interest in you, your career. He admired your work."

"My . . . work."

Oliver gave her that slow, easy smile.

"The manor has excellent Wi-Fi — Collin saw to that. Reclusive didn't mean ignoring technology or modernization. As I said, when he learned about your father, his brother, his twin, through my research into his genealogy, he had every intention of contacting him. Then another tragedy, another death. He mourned your father, too, Sonya, though they'd been separated only days after sharing a womb.

"You're what's left of his brother, and the only direct descendant of their biological father."

For the first time in her life, she fully understood the concept of head-spinning. "Listen, I'm going to appreciate the sentiment, even the cinematic weirdness of the inheritance from a long-lost uncle."

Oliver let out a laugh at that. "He would have liked you. I think you would have liked him."

"Maybe, but beyond sentiment and weirdness, there's practicality. I'm just months into establishing my own business. What am I going to do with a house in Maine? A house," she added, "you keep calling a manor. Which implies a big house in Maine I wouldn't be financially able to afford or maintain."

"There's a trust for that."

"Excuse me?"

"Collin established a trust for the maintenance of the manor. It's very well-funded and broad-based. I should know, as I'm the trustee. Practicalities such as utilities, taxes, insurance will continue to be paid out of the trust. Repairs, any necessary or desired changes — paint, for example, or other upkeep and personal taste options? You'll find the trustee very open, as his client instructed."

"I —"

"As his heir, you'll inherit the rest of his estate, including a five-percent interest in the Poole businesses. This percentage is a token, a maintaining of tradition. He left the rest of his interest to your cousins, and that is substantial."

Then he paused, adjusted his glasses. "Your inheritance is contingent upon you taking up residence in the manor for a period no less than three years, for no less than forty weeks per year."

"Live there?" The shocks just kept coming. "I'm supposed to just pick up and move? To Maine?

"You can contest the will. I'm a good lawyer, Sonya, so the terms are tightly knit as my friend and client wished. But you can contest it, and may prevail there. It would cost you a great deal of money and time. On a personal level, I'll tell you I wish he'd taken my advice — as his friend and lawyer — and contacted you."

"I can just say no. I could just refuse to accept any of it."

"Of course. I hope you won't." He took two thick packets out of his briefcase. "I have a copy of his will, financial data, information on the businesses, the house. Photos, an inventory of the contents of the house."

He smiled at her. "A great deal of legal nonsense, which I'll be happy to explain once you've had time to absorb all of this."

"Right now? I think that might take years."

"It's a beautiful home, Sonya. Over the many years, the Pooles have added to the original structure, maintained it meticulously. It holds so much history. Your history. It was your uncle's deep hope that you'd accept this legacy and carry it forward."

He rose. "My information, including my cell phone number, is in the packets. Please contact me, or have your attorney — which I advise you to retain — contact me. I'd be happy to meet with you and your attorney, and will be here through Thursday. I can and will come back at your convenience, or meet with you at my own office, at the manor, wherever it suits you."

She got up to take his coat from the closet. "You have to know this is crazy. All of it."

"He was of sound mind. Sound enough to make his wishes and terms clear and precise." He put on his coat, pulled the ear-flap hat over his head. "You haven't asked how much. How much the house is worth, the trust, the interest in the business, and so on. I find that very interesting."

"It's not real. Or doesn't seem like it."

"It's very real. Look through the information, take time to think, hire a good lawyer." He held out a hand for hers. "We'll talk again."

She shut the door, then just stood. Waited to wake up. But it hadn't been a dream, she admitted. No hallucination, not when those packets sat on her table.

Though she barely felt her legs, she walked back, opened one. And pulled out a many-paged, blue-backed legal document.

The Last Will and Testament of Collin Arthur Poole.

It occurred to her she'd never seen an actual will, much less read one.

She sat, and though it resulted in a banging headache, read every word.

He'd left — bequeathed — some things to his lifelong friend. A specific painting titled *Boys at Sea,* an antique chess set and board, a first-edition copy of H. G. Wells's *The Time Machine.*

Other bequests — a carnelian bowl, antique pearl earrings — to a Corrine Whitmer Doyle. Probably the friend's wife, Sonya thought.

Separate bequests to Oliver Henry Doyle II, and to a Paula Mortimore Doyle. Another painting, some jewelry.

More yet to Oliver Henry Doyle III. Son? A Louisville Slugger, signed by Mickey Mantle, eight Matchbox cars, circa 1975. To an Anna Rose Doyle, a pearl necklace.

Various monetary bequests, forty-five of his fifty-percent interest in the shipping company.

And to her shock, antique diamond-and-sapphire earrings to Winter Rogan MacTavish, her mother.

When she reached the end, she pressed her fingers to her eyes.

How was she supposed to think? How could she *absorb* any of this?

He'd left everything else to her — including a house and its land — eight-point-three acres' worth. All its contents (inventory listed in a separate document), a trust to maintain said house, property, and contents.

Life insurance policy, brokerage accounts, investments, and more she just couldn't begin to comprehend.

But rolling over all of it, her father had a brother. A twin. He'd had family he'd never known.

And so had she.

She grabbed her phone.

"Cleo, I need you to go to Mom's with me. Now."

"What happened? Is she all right?"

"Yes, she's fine. Something's happened, but I'll explain on the way. I'll pick you up in ten minutes. Please."

"Give me fifteen. Jesus, Sonya, you sound like you've seen a ghost."

"Maybe I have. Fifteen."

She dragged on boots, her coat — reminded herself of the cold and swung on a scarf, yanked on a wool cap. In five minutes, she was out the door, packets in hand.

Her mother needed to know, and not by a phone call. And she needed Cleo to talk her through it.

And hell, she guessed she'd need that lawyer.

She doubted she was coherent during the drive. God knew she didn't feel coherent. Cleo's reaction, as expected, hit shock, amazement, suspicion, curiosity, and some outrage.

"What kind of heartless excuse for a human separates brothers like that? You know your grandparents would have taken both babies."

"Exactly what I said. God, why is there always so much traffic?"

"And what you're saying tells me the grandmother, her daughter, on the Poole side, they could've kept both. They had the means."

"I don't know. I don't know why they did it, or hid it. I definitely got the sense from Mr. Doyle that the family hid it all, the real parentage, the twins. I don't know why, and I don't know what to do."

"I wonder if your dad knew. I don't mean knew-knew. But felt. Like they say twins can. And, oh, his poor brother, losing his bride, his love, on their wedding day. But think about it, Sonya. He was an artist, like your dad. They had that bond, even though they never knew.

"Where the hell is Poole's Bay?"

"I don't know."

"Let's find out." Cleo pulled out her phone, Googled. "Okay, pretty small, one of those juts of land along the Maine coast. It's probably beautiful, scenic."

"Whatever. It doesn't make any sense, Cleo."

"Sure it does. This Collin Poole didn't know about your dad, until he did. He did some due diligence, made plans to contact him. And your dad died. That's another blow."

She reached over, gave Sonya's hand a squeeze. "Think of it. You've just found out you have a brother, a twin brother your family kept from you. But before you can reach out to him, he's gone. That's devastating. But he must've felt the bond, so he left his brother's only child his home, his — well, pretty much everything from what you've told me."

"But why didn't he contact Mom, or me?"

"Maybe he couldn't face it, face the possibility of another emotional blow. What if you'd told him to stick it, or you'd been all, *Fine, what's in it for me?*"

"I wouldn't have done that."

"I know that, Son, but maybe he was just too emotionally fragile to handle it. It seems like, in the end, he tried to do the right thing. He didn't have to. You'd never have known. Or, if you did the DNA thing and found out, he still owed you nothing really."

"Here's why I called you." Some of the tightness in her chest loosened. "Why I needed you to come with me."

"When you've talked to your mom, when you're smoothed out some, you need to find out all you can about him. And about all of it."

"So I need that lawyer."

"You do. Let me Google the other one. Oliver Henry Doyle II, you said. Poole's Bay, Maine. Okay, okay, here we go. He's fifty-seven —"

"Really? I put him ten years younger even when he took the flap cap off and I saw a lot of black, like his eyebrows, in with the gray."

"Looks like his father established the firm like fifty years ago, so that's a lot. Married, two kids. Son, Oliver III, is thirty-two, daughter, Anna, twenty-eight, so our age. Everything seems solid and aboveboard. And I like that this Mr. Doyle told you to get a lawyer.

"What's the worst that can happen?" Cleo added. "You end up with a house on the Maine coast. You live there a few years — you can work anywhere, right?"

"You think I should —"

"I think you should seriously think about it. Hell, Sonya, it's an adventure, and you're due. And you'd find out more about your ancestry. Your grandparents are always going to be your grandparents. Nothing changes that. This is just more, and a chance to clear your decks, and find out that more."

Sonya pulled into her mother's drive. "I have a life here, a home here. You and Mom are here. I'm trying to establish my business."

"Working backward, you're just as capable of establishing your business there as here. Your mom and I are always going to be there for you, and Maine's not a distant planet. You have a duplex, which I know very well has always been a stepping stone for you, and right now, your life here is work."

She gave Sonya's hand another squeeze. "But stay or go, let's find out what there is to find out. And step one to all of it is telling your mom."

They found Winter putting another log on the fire.

"Well, look at this! I was just thinking about making do with a grilled cheese for dinner, now it's a party."

Then she got a good look at her daughter's face. "Something's wrong."

"Not wrong, but we need to sit down and talk."

"You're scaring me, baby."

"I don't mean to, and there's nothing scary. But let's sit down."

Sonya took off her coat, her hat. "A man came to see me today. A lawyer, from Maine."

"A lawyer? Are you in trouble?"

"No, Mom. Stop." After putting the packets

on the coffee table, Sonya took Winter's hands, drew her down to sit on the sofa.

"Dad had a twin brother."

"What? No, he didn't. Honey, this has to be some sort of con because —"

"Nan and Grandpa didn't know, and I'll get to all that. But Dad had a twin. Their birth mother died when they were born, and their birth father couldn't handle it. He ended up committing suicide."

"Sonya —"

"Just hear me out on this part, please. The family separated them — I don't know why. The aunt took one, and they put the other — Dad — up for adoption. A private adoption. You know Nan and Grandpa adopted Dad privately, and weren't given any information on the birth parents. The brother, Dad's brother, didn't know any of this, any more than Dad knew. The brother — his name was Collin Poole — found out right before Dad died, and never had the chance to connect."

"What does this man want from you, Sonya?"

"Nothing. He died last month. The lawyer came to see me because Collin Poole left me, well, pretty much everything."

"What do you mean?"

"He made me his heir — in his will. There's a house in Maine, a small percentage of the family business that's been around a couple hundred years. There's everything in the house, there's a trust to maintain the house, and financial accounts. He left you antique diamond-and-sapphire earrings."

"What?"

"I think — I guess — he wanted to leave his brother's wife something, a family heirloom. The lawyer, Mr. Doyle, and Collin Poole were friends, since they were boys. Collin never had children — his wife died — and so I'm his brother's only child. His niece."

She took out the photo Oliver had shown her. "This is Mr. Doyle and Collin Poole."

"Oh God. God! Are you sure this is real?"

"It's starting to feel that way."

"I need to —" Winter stood up, walked to the window, to the fireplace, back again.

"Your father had dreams sometimes. Recurring. One was he looked in the mirror, but the face looking back wasn't quite his. And the man looking back was talking to him, but he couldn't hear. He'd had them most of his life. A boy looking in the mirror at a boy with his face — almost his face.

"Sometimes he'd draw the dream and show me. This is the face."

"A twin bond," Cleo murmured.

"Always the same mirror. Full-length, freestanding, ornate frame. And this face looking back at him. Not dressed like him, but always the same age."

Eyes damp, she looked at Sonya. "If we'd

had a boy, he wanted to name our first son Collin."

"Do you think he knew, somehow?"

"I don't know. I honestly don't know what to think. I know he would've loved having a brother. I wish he'd had a chance to know."

"Do we tell Nan and Grandpa?"

"Oh yes. Yes, they have a right to know. They loved Drew so much, and he loved them." She sat back, closed her eyes a moment. "You say his brother died last month."

"Before Christmas, Mr. Doyle said. I didn't think to ask how."

"And he left you a house?"

"In Maine, on the coast near some little place. Poole's Bay. The Pooles started a shipbuilding company, and built the house — or the original house. Mr. Doyle said they'd expanded it over the years. He called it the manor. He said there were photos. I didn't look yet. I read the will, then I got Cleo to come here."

She opened the second packet. "Maybe in here, because the other one looks to have mainly legal stuff. The will, the trust, life insurance, appraisals."

She pulled out papers. "More of that here, too. God, it's a lot. And here, in this folder. Whoa, wow!"

She gaped at the photos of the house on the cliffs. The cobbled brown stone of many shades, the contrast of deep blue cladding, the twin turrets flanking either side with their conical tops, with a kind of half turret centered. Chimneys rose from the roof, which held a railed platform.

A widow's walk.

The bare branches of a weeping tree seemed to shiver above a white blanket of snow.

"It's gorgeous," Cleo said over Sonya's shoulder. "Gothic spooky gorgeous. Victorian Gothic. Here's one of the back. Has to be more modern additions, but fully in keeping with the Gothic gorgeous. The cladded bump out here, with that line of windows and the conical top to connect the look of the turrets. A deck over what looks like a flat-roofed addition. I love they mixed arched windows and tall square-edged ones. There's nothing ordinary.

"I'm going to have to use this someday. I just need a book to illustrate that works."

"Your dad drew this house."

"Mom?"

"I don't know if he painted it. I never saw it if he did. But he drew this house. Wait."

She stood and rushed upstairs.

"Okay, first the face in the mirror, and now this? Sense memories, blood memory. Something." Cleo laid a hand on Sonya's shoulder. "I'm going to open a bottle of wine. I'll order Chinese. I think we've got a lot to talk about."

By the time Winter came back, Cleo had the wine opened, three glasses poured, and the order placed.

"There may be more," Winter began. "I found it in these two sketchbooks, but there may be more."

She laid the open sketchbooks on the table, picked up one of the glasses.

"The first time I saw one of the sketches, I asked him where he'd seen the house. Because it's fabulous. He told me in dreams. He dreamed of it. He dreamed of it, and he'd hear the waves crashing, feel the wind."

She took a long sip.

"We laughed about it. He'd tell me he'd had the dream house dream, but this time there was a woman in a white dress on the widow's walk, or this time there'd been a party, with women in long gowns and men in old-fashioned suits strolling around the yard. He might see a man, the man from the mirror, standing at a window looking down at him."

Sonya looked at the sketchbooks again, at the photos of the house.

"How can this be?"

Winter sat. "What do you want to do?"

"I have no idea. Maybe Dad saw the house as a child, and it imprinted. It made an impression. But for him to dream of it, to draw it — and more than once — it meant something to him. He never had the chance to find out. I do.

"I need a lawyer."

"You know my boss will help you with this."

"I do, and I'm going to dump this in his lap. I want to go through Dad's sketchbooks, see if I can find more drawings of the house, and look for the sketches he made of the mirror."

"You're going to Maine." Cleo said it matter-of-factly. "Unless Winter's very smart boss advises against it, and gives you solid reasons, you're going. And you'll want to," she added, "because your dad had this visceral connection. Because that house is you, Son, right down to the ground. Last? Because you're just going to need to know."

She picked up her father's sketch pad. "I do need to know."

"I'm going to call Marshall."

"Oh, Mom, you don't have to call the boss at home. There's no hurry."

"I think you'll sleep better tonight knowing he's on top of this. I know I will. Go on up, both of you, see what you can find. I'll let you know when dinner gets here."

Her father had converted the attic into what he affectionately called his garret. Sonya remembered climbing those steep, narrow steps, coming into the space, the light, the smell of paints and oils and solvents. She remembered how he'd looked standing at an easel — battered jeans, a sweatshirt in the winter, a T-shirt in the summer. The mop of dark blond hair shining in the light from the windows, the light shooting down from the skylights.

And the focus in his green eyes that inevitably turned to a smile when he turned to her.

Let's set you up, monkey, and see what you've got.

He'd never turned her away, never told her he was too busy. And he'd taught her, as patiently as he'd taught his high school students, how to use space, color, the absence of color, how to add texture and dimension, light, shadow.

After his death — months and months after, when they could face it — she'd helped her mother store or give away his paints and tools, box up his sketchbooks.

Some of his canvases had gone to galleries, and eventually sold. Others, unfinished, were still stacked against the wall.

"I've always loved coming up here." Cleo slid an arm around Sonya's waist. "I never met him, but coming up here always makes me feel like I did."

"I know." Sonya tipped her head toward Cleo's. "When I look back, I think how much patience, how much simple good-heartedness he had to make time for me. Not just giving me time, but giving me his interest.

"When I was about ten, I showed him a drawing. For a poster for a school project. After he looked at it, he looked at me. So serious. So, so serious I thought, oh, it's a silly drawing, just dumb and silly. Then he told me to come back on Saturday. He'd get the poster board, and I could use the studio.

"And that was the moment — when he looked at me, when he said that to me — I knew I was going to be an artist. Not just play at it, or have a little fun. He changed my life that day."

Shaking her head, she brushed a hand over the easel that still stood under the skylight.

"He didn't have enough time. His art was just starting to move, but he didn't have enough time."

She moved over to one of the storage boxes that held his sketch pads. "Mom and I didn't go through all of these. Later, we talked about doing that but never did. What would we do with them? We'd never throw them out. We wouldn't sell them even if we could. She's never used this space, not even for storage."

"Some loves are forever."

They sat on the floor, each with a pile of sketchbooks. As she paged through, Sonya understood the full meaning of poignant. It hurt, and it warmed, it brushed the dust off old sorrows even as it lifted new joy.

"He was so good. Look, it's Mom holding me when I was a baby. Both of us curled up sleeping."

"Here's another one of you — what were you, about six or seven? — having a tea party in your room. Wearing a tiara! I need a tiara."

She set the book aside, picked another.

"Oh! Sonya! Look."

A dream sketch, Sonya thought. Not the manor. The mirror.

Her father, in those battered jeans, a paint-splattered sweatshirt. He held a paintbrush in one hand, his palette in the other.

In the glass, the reflection — the man, the brother — stood in rough boots, a plaid shirt loose over a tee. He, too, held a brush and palette.

Her father wore his hair back in a stub of a tail, as he did when he'd gone too long without a trim. Collin, for surely it was, wore his above the collar of the shirt.

Animals snarled and flew on the thick frame of the cheval glass. Wolves, fangs sharp; a hawk, wings spread, talons curled; a buck, with antlers tipped like razors; a coiled cobra; a two-headed dragon; a bear rearing up on its back legs; a cougar on the spring.

"He saw this, Sonya. It's so detailed. And, Jesus, that mirror is creepy. There's more in here. The same mirror, but they're wearing different clothes — and . . . different ages. Some younger, some older."

"They're just boys here. He drew these from memory. Has to be. The same mirror, but they can't be more than six or seven. Dad's holding a little car. But in this one, Collin's holding it. It's the same car, Cleo. Isn't it?"

"It looks the same. He passed it to his brother through the mirror?"

"That's not possible."

"In a dream, everything's possible."

"Dinner's here," Winter called from the bottom of the steps.

She insisted they eat at the table — like the civilized — and on plates, not out of cartons.

"Marshall contacted Mr. Doyle. Mr. Doyle is emailing Marshall the files, and they're meeting tomorrow."

"Already?"

"Marshall wanted the meeting, and Mr. Doyle — Marshall told me — was more than amenable. You'll be able to make a better decision once Marshall goes over all the documents and meets Collin Poole's lawyer."

"I'm really grateful. It takes a load off."

"See? We'll all sleep better."

Sonya didn't count on it.

"We found a sketchbook with at least a dozen drawings of the mirror dream. Some with them as boys."

"Your dad said he'd had the dream his whole life."

"The mirror's a nightmare," Cleo put in, plucking up a pot sticker with chopsticks. "Decorated with predatory birds, animals, reptiles. Nothing I'd want to use to check out how my butt looks."

"Didn't Dad have a bunch of little cars? Toy cars?"

"His beloved Matchbox cars?" Winter smiled as she ate. "You played with them when you were two, three, but lost interest. You didn't play with dolls much either. Always arts and crafts for you."

"Matchbox cars. Do you still have them?"

"After Drew died, I gave them to your cousin Martin. And apparently he took good care of them because he mentioned he put them away for when he has a kid of his own. I love knowing that. Drew really treasured those cars."

"Collin Poole left a collection of Matchbox cars to Mr. Doyle's son in his will."

"Twin synergy." Cleo lifted her shoulders. "It's a real thing."

"In one sketch, a boyhood sketch, Dad's holding a little car. In the next sketch, Collin's holding the same car. I wonder if Collin had the same dreams. No way to ask, I guess."

"You could try a séance."

At the identical stares from Sonya and Winter, Cleo gave an exaggerated shrug. "Okay, that's a bridge too far even for me. I don't think it's smart to stir that sort of thing up. But it wouldn't surprise me if he had similar dreams. You said he and the lawyer were pals since they were kids. You could ask him if he knows."

"Maybe I will. I'd like to take the sketchbook, Mom, and the ones with the house, if that's okay."

"Of course it is. I'm going to call your grandparents in the morning. Let me do this part, baby. It's going to upset them to find out Drew had a brother and they weren't told. They'll want to talk to you, but let's give them a chance to get through that part first."

"It wasn't their fault."

"No, it wasn't. One of the things I want to find out, whatever you decide to do, is whose fault it was."

Chapter Five

By the end of the week, she had her own meeting with Marshall in his office. She'd been there before, of course, and enjoyed the leathery, old-world feel of his space.

But she'd never sat in one of those deep leather chairs as a client.

Marshall Tibbets had a shock of gray-flecked brown hair swept back — dramatically, she'd always thought — from a handsomely weathered face. He tended toward classic Armani suits, tailored to his broad-shouldered frame.

He sat back now, the dull gray winter sky behind him, and studied her out of his shrewd brown eyes.

"You've had a lot of upheavals in the last six months or so."

"I think this one tops the rest."

"It ranks. Before we get started, I want to ask how you're doing. Really doing. And remember, it doesn't leave this room. Attorney-client privilege."

"I honestly don't know how I'm doing. Some days I miss my old job. Other days — and that's most days — I'm thrilled I'm running my own show. My own little show, but still mine. I have moments when I'm still incredibly pissed at Brandon, but days, even weeks, when I don't think of him at all. I worry I'm not going to be able to pull in enough work to keep a business going, but I'm doing okay. Not spectacular, but okay, and that works for me.

"Now this?" She lifted her hands. "This sort of throws everything up in the air, and I don't know where it's going to fall."

"Let me start off by saying the Doyle Law firm has a solid reputation, as does Oliver Doyle II. His father, who still practices, by the way, established the firm fully a half century ago. His handling of Collin Poole's estate? Meticulous. There are unusual aspects to his client's wishes, but the unusual is not unusual in estates. He's covered those aspects, again meticulously."

"So, that's good?"

He steepled his hands, tapped his fingertips together.

"That depends, Sonya. If you wanted to contest the terms, unusual terms, of the will . . . we could get lucky, and I have some tricks up my sleeve. But it would be a long, protracted battle, and frankly, we'd most probably lose it."

"I'm not considering contesting it. However strange it feels, these were my father's brother's wishes. I don't have any right to go against those wishes and still try to take what he wanted to give me."

"Do you understand the extent of your inheritance, if you accept it?"

"I've tried to take it in, but the appraisal on the house alone . . . it's over eight million dollars. For a house."

"The house, the land, the location, the historic value. The trust — and Mr. Doyle was shrewd there — will cover the taxes, the insurance, the upkeep."

"I got that, but I have to admit, even the idea of being responsible for a house like that? It's not just intimidating, it's scary. Then there has to be estate taxes on it and the rest."

"Which Mr. Doyle and his client factored in. Since your father's death, Collin Poole gifted you the maximum tax-free amount annually. There's a separate account in your name, well invested. In addition, the life insurance policy, Mr. Poole's investment accounts not only cover the estate taxes, but will allow you to live comfortably.

"As executor, Mr. Doyle has already calculated the taxes. In point of fact, Sonya, the payout from the life insurance covers most of it."

She understood, if she accepted the terms,

she'd become — sort of instantly — a rich woman. In all of her life, she'd never imagined or dreamed of becoming a rich woman.

And for the life of her, she didn't know how to feel about it.

"What do you think I should do?"

"That's a choice you have to make, Sonya. That only you can make. But I'd be very hard-pressed to advise a client, not yet thirty, to turn her back on an inheritance of this size. If taking up residence in the house is the sticking point, I negotiated with Mr. Doyle. A trial period. Three months. You take up residence, and if during the trial period, you decide against, you walk away."

"Three months."

"Estates, especially estates of this size, aren't settled overnight in any case. Even when they're meticulously done. For three months you'd be a tenant — rent-free — while the wheels of the legalities turn. Mr. Doyle and I agree you deserve this time to decide if the house, the location, all the rest suit you."

"If it doesn't, I say thanks, but no thanks."

"That's right. If it does, you accept the terms of the will, and it's yours."

"That's a good deal. That's a really good deal. I was going to accept it because I want — I need — to know more of my father's history. What he wasn't allowed to know. But this takes all the pressure off."

"I think you'll find a steady advocate in Oliver Doyle."

"I hope so, since he's the only person I know where I'm going to live for at least three months."

She sent her mother flowers for being wise enough to work for a sharp lawyer. Then she did a serious survey of her duplex.

She wouldn't need to take any furniture, but there were things she'd want. Her father's paintings — the two she'd chosen to keep after his death. Most of her office. Some mementos and gifts, ones that would not only remind her of home but of the people she loved.

And she realized, everything she wanted or needed to take for this trial period would fit in her car.

After weighing the pros and cons, she contacted a Realtor. She didn't want to leave her house vacant for three months. Her thought to rent it — furnished — month by month ended up with a six-month lease.

But even if she turned tail and headed home after a week, she could move back in with her mother for six months.

Safety nets, she thought. A woman needed safety nets.

But she wouldn't turn tail, she told herself. Hell, Poole's Bay was only a three-hour drive from Boston. Her mother could visit, Cleo would come. She could drive back for a weekend.

An adventure, she promised herself as she finalized arrangements, began to pack. She'd have an adventure — and at the end of it, maybe end up with an incredible house.

As she did often, she opened her father's sketchbook to study it. She liked his vision of it even more than the photos.

Could she see herself there?

Maybe. Maybe.

Wasn't it what she'd wanted when she and Brandon had looked at houses? Something with history and character and charm. Not sleek and new and shiny.

If she wondered about living there, alone, she reminded herself she lived alone now. Just in a smaller space.

She packed the sketchbooks before she went out for a farewell dinner with her mother and Cleo.

And barely slept a wink the night before her departure.

She dressed for the cold. If it was cold in Boston — and it was — it would be colder yet three hours north. She wore the cherry-red cashmere sweater her mother had given her for Christmas, black jeans, and boots.

Maybe her heart pounded when she carefully put her African violet in a box for travel. They'd both try to bloom in a new place.

She'd loaded nearly everything the night

before — because who could sleep — and now with her weekend tote and the single box, she looked around.

"It's not like I'm never coming back. But it feels like it."

She rolled the suitcase toward the door. When she opened it, Cleo stood outside, one hand lifted to knock.

"Surprise! I couldn't let you drive off without waving goodbye."

She threw her arms around Sonya. "I miss you already."

"What am I going to do without you ten minutes away?"

"We'll text, we'll call, we'll FaceTime. In fact."

She held up a bottle in a velvet gift bag. "This is champagne. The good stuff."

"Get out."

"You're going to text me and your mom when you get there. Then tonight, we're going to FaceTime and drink champagne — I got a bottle, too — while you give me a video tour."

"But you'll drive up and visit."

"You bet both our excellent asses I will. Here, take the bottle, give me the box. Is Xena in here?"

"She is. She's a little nervous."

"She shouldn't be. Hi, Donna."

"Hey there. I made you cookies for the trip, Sonya."

"Oh, that's so nice." Neighbors, she thought. There'd be no one living next door where she was going.

"I'm going to miss you and Bill."

"Likewise. I don't care if the Queen of Sheba moved in next door, she won't be as sweet as you. You have a safe trip."

"Thanks. Thanks so much."

"Don't start watering up," Cleo muttered, "and get me started. This is day one of Sonya's Amazing Adventure."

They loaded the suitcase, the box, the bottle, then just held on to each other.

"Since we met, you've never lived more than ten minutes away." Sonya pressed her face into Cleo's hair.

"Text me when you get there."

"I will. I will. I have to go before I do a lot more than water up. I love you."

"Love you right back. Embrace the change, Son."

"I'm going to try."

But she kept the image of her friend, waving with both hands, inside her head and heart and she drove away.

She'd topped off her gas tank the night before, so she wouldn't need to stop. Then stopped anyway due to a nervous bladder and a gnawing need for more caffeine.

Though her stomach churned too much to risk a cookie, she sipped a Coke and let the GPS guide her.

The landscape changed as she drove into Maine and shifted to the coast road. She had the ocean, sandy beaches and rocky ones. Little towns that struck her more as villages.

Forests, space. And, she couldn't deny, beauty.

She'd been a city or suburban creature all of her life. And though she found the inlets, the bays, the endless stretch of the Atlantic amazing, the sturdy charm of seacoast towns fascinating, she wondered how she'd manage.

No quick runs to the market. No impulsive trips to a local restaurant or bar. No friendly neighbors next door or kids riding bikes down the sidewalk.

She had to remind herself she wasn't a coward — and never had been. But the nerves kept jumping under her skin.

At just over the three-hour mark, she drove into the town (village? hamlet?) of Poole's Bay.

Charming, yes, propped on its finger of land into the bay. A bay silver under the leaden sky. Clapboard buildings — white, colonial blue, soft yellow — ran up and down what the GPS called High Street.

Buildings with covered porches and shutters, some with smoke curling out of chimneys.

She spotted a restaurant called the Lobster Cage, another called Gino's Pizzeria.

She wouldn't starve.

She spotted a bookstore, called exactly that: A Bookstore.

People moved along the skinny sidewalk in their heavy winter gear.

She was out of town again in less than a minute, and promised herself she'd explore the other side of the village, the side streets, the bay.

But for now, she was rambling along the coast and climbing.

The peaceful silver bay was behind her, and the sea made itself known crashing against a rocky beach, churning under cliffs that rose jagged and fierce enough to stop her breath.

The road narrowed until she wondered if two cars could pass without scraping fenders. It snaked so she slowed to a crawl with the cliffs and windy sea on one side, a thick forest of shadows and blanketing snow on the other.

Mr. Doyle had said remote, she remembered. And someone had plowed since the last snowfall, as the narrow, climbing, winding road was clear for the most part.

Not that she feared winter driving, but her experience there lay centered in the city. But as long as the road stayed clear, she'd be fine. And the GPS told her she'd be there in . . .

She rounded a curve and there it was, rising up, spreading out on the cliffs under the brooding sky. Astonished, she braked.

She'd thought herself prepared. She had the photos, she had her father's drawings. But there it stood on its carpet of snow, atop the rise of cliffs and over the lashing sea.

Like something out of a novel, she thought, or a classy horror movie, with its twin turrets and many windows, the deep blue cladding against stone that showed dull gold in the gloom.

There rose the big weeper, its curving branches glittering with ice. The house had the forest at its back, like a wall of green.

Smoke rose in lazy curls from the chimneys, and someone had shoveled paved walkways. One led to the wide, covered portico at the entrance.

And Sonya fell in love.

However foolish, she felt the house waited for her, and stood ready to take her in. Nerves conquered, sheer delight rising, she drove forward.

A muscular black truck was parked at the far end of the main walkway, and she pulled in beside it. She got out, simply stood in the kick of wind and studied what, through fate or lineage or the luck of the draw, could be hers.

She saw a shadow move across a window on the second floor. Someone watching for her arrival, she thought. As she lifted a hand to wave, the main doors opened.

She'd expected Mr. Doyle, but the man

who stepped out, hatless, a parka tossed over a flannel shirt, was considerably younger.

The wind caught at his hair — a lot of black hair — as he strode toward her in scarred brown boots.

She caught the resemblance quickly — the shape of the face, the blade of nose, the sharply carved lips curved in a quiet smile.

And she couldn't mistake the eyes, that wonderfully eerie blue rimmed in black.

As those eyes held hers, she smiled back at him.

"I'm Sonya. You look like your father. Oliver Doyle III?" She made it a question as she held out a hand. She'd expected smooth lawyer's hands, but his had the feel of a man who worked with them.

"Guilty. Welcome to Lost Bride Manor."

"I'm sorry. Lost Bride Manor?"

"So the locals dubbed it a couple centuries ago. How was the drive from Boston?"

"Uneventful."

"Best kind, and you beat the snow. Let's get you out of the wind, then I'll get your bags."

"I don't mind the wind, and it's not that much. But I could use a hand." She opened the trunk. "I'm going to get my purse from the front."

She grabbed it and the still unopened container of cookies.

"Is your father inside?" she asked as she

pulled out her weekender.

"No. He wanted to be here to greet you, give you the tour, but he's a little under the weather."

"Oh, I'm sorry."

"Just a cold." He hauled out her two suitcases as if they weighed nothing. "But my mother laid down the law. Is this it?" He gestured to the three boxes she'd sealed and labeled.

"That's it."

"I'll come back for them."

She nodded, looked back at the house. "It makes a statement."

"What does it say to you?"

"I'm here," she said as they carried the first load to the entrance. "I see. I know. And I'm spectacular."

She stopped, looked out. "You can see the bay, the marina, the village. Oh, there's a boat way out there. I'm surprised you can't see Greenland. I hope my room faces the sea."

He gave her a curious look. "You've got your pick, but we figured you for the master, and it does face the sea."

"God, look at these doors!" She ran her hand over the deep carving.

"Original. Arthur Poole — also the original — had the mahogany shipped over and built them himself."

"Really?" Two hundred years, she thought. She'd wanted history, and here it stood, right under her hand. "Well, they're amazing, and obviously built to last."

She stepped inside, and attributed the sudden buzz in her ears, the quick shiver of energy to excitement.

The floors of the wide foyer gleamed as they led the way to a staircase she could only call grand, as four people could have walked up abreast. A massive iron chandelier showered down light from its three tiers.

A pair of ladder-back chairs with tapestry seats flanked a long table by the wall between two doorways. It held a collection of pewter candlestands. Above it hung mirrors of varying shapes and sizes.

Across from the table needlepoint pillows plumped on a curved settee in peacock blue. The painting above it held a woman, young, her pale blond hair worn up and graced with flowers. Diamonds glittered at her ears, and a necklace of teardrop sapphires draped around her neck.

She wore a long, white, high-waisted gown embroidered at the hem and the cuffs of puffed sleeves. At first glance, Sonya thought her hands ringless. Then she saw a gold band on her left hand, a diamond on her right.

"Astrid Grandville Poole. The first bride. There's a fire in the front parlor." He gestured to the right, to the doorway beyond the portrait. "I'll get the rest of your things."

She nodded and stood where she was,

texting her mother and Cleo as she studied the painting.

You could sense the movement in the skirt, she thought — that was the artist's skill. Had he meant to paint her with sadness in her eyes? Eyes as blue as the sapphires she wore.

And the way she stood, the way she held a small bouquet down at her side, the pink and white rosebuds pointing down?

She felt that sorrow, a wave of it, as it seemed those sapphire eyes looked into hers.

She turned as he brought the last of her things in.

"How did she die?"

Shrugging out of his parka, he looked up at the portrait.

"She was murdered — stabbed — on her wedding day."

"The lost bride," she murmured. "No wonder she looks so sad."

"Her husband had it painted and hung there so anyone coming into the manor would see her, and remember."

"I take it he didn't kill her."

"No, a jealous woman. Let me take your coat."

"Thanks. Oliver —"

"Trey," he told her. "My grandfather's Ace, my dad's Deuce. I'm Trey."

"Clever." The wave of sadness passed; amusement followed. "And simpler than Oliver one, two, and three. Trey, did you know

Collin Poole — my uncle?"

"Sure. He was actually a kind of uncle to me, and my sister. He was family. I'm just going to put the coats with your things for now, but there's a closet in the front sitting room. Collin used it for coats and outdoor gear."

"There's a front parlor and a front sitting room?"

"If you're after open concept, you won't find it here. What you've got is a labyrinth. I'll take you through. Where do you want to start?"

"Might as well start here."

She turned into what he'd called the front parlor.

She found it surprisingly cozy given its size, and the fire crackling away inside an elaborate dark wood framed fireplace added cheerful.

A trio of windows offered views of the snow-covered lawn, the stone seawall, and the sea beyond it.

Another chandelier — iron again, but considerably smaller — dropped from a ceiling medallion. The sofas, chairs, all softly faded, would easily seat twenty. Like the floors, the tables gleamed. As did a piano tucked in a corner.

"Did he play? Collin."

"He did, and pretty well. Do you?"

" 'Chopsticks' is the top of my game." But she ran her hand over the piano as she wandered the room. "Do you?"

"I can fake some boogie-woogie if I've had enough beer. Most of the paintings in here are Collin's work."

He'd painted the sea in myriad moods.

"Your father was an artist."

"Yes. Their styles are very similar. I don't know if that's comforting or disconcerting."

"It's a lot to deal with."

She heard comfort in his voice, and took it. "Working on it. So, this is a friendly room. I didn't know what to expect."

"Through here's another, smaller sitting room, then the solarium."

He led the way.

"Oh! The base of the turret. It's wonderful. They didn't square it off."

The tall, rounded windows poured light into the room. It held deeply cushioned chairs in that same peacock blue, a love seat in that strong blue with rose-colored stripes. Tables she thought must be antique.

And plants. A potted tree that dripped with what looked like tiny oranges, another with lemons. Another plant with glossy leaves showcased a pair of large white flowers.

She recognized a jade plant, as her mother had one, but the one gracing a stand was fully three times as big.

"So much light even on a day like this. Now I'm terrified I'll kill the plants."

"Collin had a knack for them."

"I'm sorry." She straightened from sniffing at one of the white blooms, so fragrant it made her heart sigh. "I should've said it before. You were close, and it's a loss for you."

"Thanks. It is."

They continued on. Another parlor, another space he called the morning room, a music room with another piano — a baby grand this time, and other instruments including a floor harp, a hurdy-gurdy, a cello.

"Collected by various Pooles over the years," Trey explained. "In a lot of ways the house is a museum of your family history. Formal dining room."

"I'll say. Jeez."

A dozen tall, curved-back chairs lined each side of the massive table, while two more stood at each end. Another fireplace, fire simmering. And still the room had space enough for a pair of huge buffets. Art and mirrors ranged along the walls papered with fat white geraniums over deep blue.

She imagined that the pair of candelabras serving as table centerpieces were actual silver.

"You know, I was nervous the entire drive up here. Couldn't even eat any of the snickerdoodles my neighbor gave me for the trip."

"You have snickerdoodles?"

"I do." He made her laugh a little. "I'll share as your fee for this tour. But I want to say those nerves disappeared at my first sight of the house. Now they're back. Big-time back."

"Not a formal-dinner-party-for-twenty kind of woman?"

"More a let's-order-pizza sort. I don't suppose the pizza place I saw in town delivers up here."

"Ah . . ."

"I was afraid of that. It's a beautiful room. In a terrifying way."

He led her through another door.

"Oh. Hear my sigh of relief."

"Family dining room and kitchen. The kitchen was put in sometime in the twenties, I think. Collin updated it. A couple of times."

"But it still fits the house, doesn't it? Not in-your-face modern. And a little fireplace."

She moved past the pretty table and its sensible eight chairs into a kitchen with dark wood cabinets, some with pebbled glass fronts, against walls that reminded her of the forest shadows. The white appliances kept it from looking too sleek. He'd contrasted the dark cabinetry with cream on the island. Counters of pale gray covered it, and ran alongside a deep farm sink.

"He was a hell of a good cook."

"Really?"

"Oh yeah. He and my mom — also a hell of a good cook — used to exchange recipes. You cook?"

"That depends on your definition of *cook.*"

"Yeah." He slipped his hands into his pockets. "I fall into that category. Fortunately, my friend's the head chef at the Lobster Cage in the village, and I can mooch off my parents, my grandparents. Anyway, we stocked the fridge and butler's pantry."

"There's a butler's pantry." Overwhelmed, she blew out a breath.

"With a dumbwaiter."

"Get out!"

She turned into the ell of the main kitchen. More cabinets, another sink, a wine cooler and ice maker under the counter.

Trey opened one of the lower cabinets.

"He had it updated, but wanted to keep the original feel. It goes down to what was the original kitchen."

He pressed a button, and the bottom lowered with a mechanical hum.

It made her laugh. "It's my first dumbwaiter. What did he use it for?"

"He renovated some of the servants' area." After pressing the button to bring it back up, Trey closed the cabinets. "He made use of a lot of the space."

"He must've loved the house. Thanks for stocking me up. I didn't expect you to do all that."

"No problem. Especially since I'm going to bum a Coke."

"Bum one for me while you're at it." She walked back into the kitchen, to the window over the sink. "So a deck over the — is it a basement?"

"Not the actual basement, no. Collin added that, a kind of apartment. Self-contained. He had a couple — housekeeper, handyman — living here until about six, seven years ago, I guess. They retired, and he never had anyone else live in. Want a glass?"

"No, the bottle's fine."

"I've got a list of names for that kind of thing. Cleaning, repair, yard work."

"Oh, I wasn't thinking about hiring anyone."

"It's a big house," he pointed out. "You'll probably close some rooms off, but it's a big house. You've got a snowblower and a lawn tractor in the little shed, but it's a lot of work."

"I'll think about it."

They wound their way back to the front of the house. Another powder room — she'd made use of the first they'd come to. A den — and the first television she'd seen in the place.

"Did he game?" she asked, noting the system.

"Not really. He put that in for me and my sister, our pals."

"You spent a lot of time here."

"After his wife died . . ."

"Another lost bride."

"Yeah. Before, Dad says Collin was outgoing. He liked to travel. You've seen some of his art is of Europe, or out west, all over. But after, he closed in. He liked having us come — my family, and some of my friends, Anna's. But he hardly left the house, the grounds, especially in the last few years. If he wanted to go somewhere, he'd go on the internet. That's what he used to tell me. He used this as his office."

She could work here, Sonya thought as she stepped in. A good desk, space for her mood boards, a fireplace for warmth and cheer. Decent light — or it would be on clear days. What she assumed was a closet for storing supplies.

Then she saw it, over the fireplace.

The manor in the magical glow of a full moon. Moody and brilliant, the subtle light, the deep shadows, the gleam against glass in the turrets.

"That's my father's work."

Her voice felt tight in her throat as she moved closer.

"Are you sure? I don't see how —"

"I know my father's work. This is his signature. MacT— that's how he signed his work. Bottom left corner. It's right there."

"I see that. I never noticed before." As he spoke, Trey laid a hand on her shoulder. "I always assumed Collin painted it. I didn't read thoroughly through the inventory."

"When did he get this? How long did he

have this?"

"I don't know. As long as I remember. My father may know. I'll ask."

"He had dreams of this place," Sonya murmured.

"Dreams?"

"My mother told me, recurring dreams. She told me after I showed her the photos of the manor. He did sketches. I have them with me. But she didn't remember him ever painting it.

"But he did." She said it quietly. "He did, and it's here. Right here."

She took a step back. "Comforting or upsetting? Somewhere in between."

"I didn't know about your father either, or you, until Collin died. But I have to think he kept that painting in here — his private space — because it mattered. He wanted you to have this, because it mattered."

As simple and true as that, she thought, and nodded.

"I can wish he'd reached out to us before he died, but that doesn't change anything. I guess . . . let's see the rest."

He took her through the rest of the first floor, then picked up her suitcases. "In your room?"

"Yeah, thanks." She took the weekender. "It's a lot." She breathed out. "It's just a lot."

He paused on the landing, pressed a hand to the wall.

It opened.

"What! Secret passage?" Sheer delight poured back. "Well, hot damn."

"Not exactly. Back when for the servants. The kitchen, their dining hall, their work spaces, downstairs. Their living quarters were up on the third floor, north wing."

"Wing," she murmured. "The place has wings."

"You can get more of the history from my father, but I'm pretty sure they stopped using it for that purpose in the thirties. Collin put a media room down below."

"A media room."

"He liked movies, and the dumbwaiter came in handy there. There's a gym down there, too. He kept fit. Upstairs is either closed off or used for storage. The Pooles collected a lot over a couple hundred years."

He gave her that quiet smile. "I thought seeing this would cheer you up."

"Good call. I'm not sad — not really. A little overwhelmed. Bullshit. A lot overwhelmed. What am I going to do with all this space?"

"Use what works for you, close off the rest."

"A practical man."

"Mostly. So, second floor, bedrooms, including the main, with its own bath — Collin again. A couple of the other rooms have their own baths, and there's another full one, a sitting room. And my personal favorite."

He opened a set of pocket doors to what she knew would be a turret room. And she gasped.

Chapter Six

Under a soaring ceiling, a two-story library had bookcases on its rounded wall full of books. Over the massive stone fireplace, the thick, carved wood of the mantel held candlestands of varying height. Centered between them, a mantel clock, its oval face framed in wood, ticktocked the time.

Stairs wound up to the second story. Through the arched windows she saw a light snow had begun to fall.

Window seats offered cozy nooks for reading, deep chocolate–colored leather sofas a place to sprawl with a book or take a nap.

Centered in the room, a big, beautiful old desk, gently curved, sat on a round carpet of muted pinks and greens.

"It's — it's *everything.* I could live in here, and I just found my studio."

"Graphic art, right?"

"Mmm. Maybe it's anachronistic to set a computer on that amazing desk, but that's just what I'm going to do. I love everything about it. The — what do you call it — millwork? All thick and carved and dark, the soaring ceiling. Jesus, counting the second story, it's as big — probably bigger — than my entire house. I need a big screen. Not on the wall. I wouldn't touch these walls. I'll get a stand."

"There's a big-ass flat-screen upstairs."

"Get out!" She ran over and up. "This is *it*! I figured on taking one of the bedrooms or parlors or maybe Collin's office to set up. But this?"

Grinning, she looked over the rail, down at him.

"Is it?"

"It is. I'll make this work. I can make this work. Your favorite?" She turned a circle before coming down again. "My favorite. By a mile."

"That's how you looked when you got out of the car."

"How's that?"

"Happy. Alive with it."

"I fell in love. Boom. When I saw the house. Now I've fallen all over again."

"There's still more."

"Nothing's going to top this."

Her bedroom — in the twin turret (yay!) with its sweeping view of the sea — came close.

Her own sitting room, which made her wonder why people sat so damn much, opened into the bedroom with its big four-poster, another window seat. A fireplace simmered. A pair of atrium doors opened to the little balcony with a curved wall. The soft blue walls held art — the quiet sort of misty forests, blooming meadows.

Fresh flowers sat on the dresser with its oval mirror reflecting the room.

"It's just lovely."

"My sister switched some of it out. She said it was too much a man's room."

"It's perfect. Thank her for me."

"That's a fainting couch — according to Anna." He gestured to the curved sofa in soft blue-and-gold stripes at the foot of the bed. "In case."

"If I swoon, I'll try to hit that. The bathroom's like the kitchen."

"First I've heard that one."

"It's got the modern but maintains the character. Claw-foot tub, but a big glass shower. The sweet little washbasin stand, but this old cabinet or dresser converted into a vanity with double sinks. And the tile looks like stone, the sconces like, well, sconces.

"Collin Poole had really good taste."

"He loved this place, you were right about that. I hope you know he left it to you because he loved it."

They toured the rest of the bedrooms, and up to what he told her had once been a ballroom — imagine that — now used for storage.

More storage in what had once been the servants' wing — imagine that, too.

She climbed to the widow's walk, stood hugging herself against the cold while the snow fell just a little thicker.

"On a good clear day, when you're not freezing your butt off, you might see whales sound."

"It doesn't seem real. It's starting to not seem real again."

"Hey, what's the problem? You found out a few weeks ago your father had a twin brother, separated at birth, who died and left you a big old house on a cliff, a big pile of money — not to mention antiques and art. Only hitch is you've got to pack up, move, and live in the big old house where you don't know anybody."

He shrugged.

"Happens every day."

Laughing, she rubbed her arms. "Well, when you put it like that."

"Come on, you're freezing."

She went in, and he showed her more. The apartment, the media room and gym. And the middle turret room where, so like her father, Collin had done his art.

But it all started to blur.

"You're about to zone out," he observed, "but I really need to go over some practical things with you before I take off and let you settle in. How about we go over those things in the dining room? Not the scary one."

"Okay. I think I need a cookie. Do you want cookies?"

"I trust no one who answers no to that question."

She got the cookies, and the champagne.

"From my friend Cleo. We're going to Face-Time later, drink champagne while I give her a virtual tour."

"Tech keeps the world close," he said as he picked up a soft-sided leather briefcase that looked, like his boots, as if it had put in plenty of miles.

"You still don't look like a lawyer," she said as they walked back to the family dining room. "Your father didn't either, not really. My mother works for lawyers."

"So I'm told."

"They look like lawyers. Armani suits and Hermès ties. Tag Heuers and Rolexes."

Not just a slow smile, she thought, but a quick grin when he wanted. And it was a zinger.

"In court I wear a tie with my flannel shirt. To show respect."

"I bet it looks good on you." In the kitchen, she opened the fridge to put the champagne in, goggled. "Holy shit. You seriously stocked."

"Doyles do nothing halfway."

"I think I need coffee." She stared at the coffee maker. "I have no idea how to work this machine."

"Happily, I do. Collin really liked a good cup of coffee." He set down the briefcase. "Watch and learn — consider it the first on the practical things."

She watched his wide-palmed, long-fingered hands work their magic. And sincerely hoped she learned.

They sat at the table with coffee and cookies.

"On the snickerdoodle scale, these hit a solid ten."

"They're her specialty. They're wonderful neighbors. I hope the tenants moving into my place appreciate them. And it suddenly occurs to me I've never not had neighbors."

"You can consider everyone in Poole's Bay a neighbor. No, we're not next door, but" — he hitched up to take a card case, leather and battered, like the briefcase, out of his hip pocket — "that's got my cell and the office numbers. Just a call or text away."

"I appreciate it."

He opened the briefcase, took out a folder. "More numbers."

He handed her a paper with a list of names. "Hal Coleson, chief of police. The manor's considered part of Poole's Bay. Also the number for the county sheriff. You've got Ace, Deuce, and Trey on here, too, along with names and numbers of a plumber, electrician, a general handyman, cleaning service, yard service, a mechanic and towing service if you have car trouble. John Dee'll be plowing your road, clearing off your deck, walkways. You can expect to hear him out there before dark, and again in the morning if we get enough to warrant it.

"He also likes a good cup of coffee if you're open to it."

"I can be."

"You've got the names of restaurants, the grocery, the pharmacy, laundry and dry cleaning. The mail carrier, if you get any, hits up here around noon most days. Doctors — we've got two in the village — same with dentists. And there's a small urgent care. The two local banks. The one Collin used is bolded. There's Jodi's Salon — they do hair and nails."

"Oh." Instinctively she reached for her hair. "I've used the same stylist for five years."

"That's what my sister said you'd say. But it's on the list. Liquor store. Collin had a nice collection of wine, and there's sipping whiskey and so on. Butler's pantry.

"Cable company," he continued. "Service can be iffy up here in a storm."

He took out another sheet. "Wi-Fi password — you can change that."

"LBManor," she read. Lost Bride Manor. "This is fine."

"Password for Collin's computer. The combination for the safe in his office."

"Six-twelve-nine-six."

"The month, day, and year his wife died. Johanna."

"You'd have been too young to remember her, or that day."

"I was about four. I was there, so was my sister. She'd have been a newborn. But no, I don't really remember."

"It's terrible. On such a happy day, a wedding day. Just a stumble, a trip on the stairs, and —"

Somewhere in the house, a door slammed.

"You'll have this."

"I guess. Old house." Sonya rubbed her arms at the sudden chill. "I thought, when I first saw it — in person — it looked like a house in a classy horror movie. And, of course, I thought I saw someone at one of the upstairs windows."

He said nothing for a full beat.

"Do you spook easily, Sonya?"

"I don't know. I don't think so." She tried a smile. "It's the kind of house where things go bump in the night, isn't it?"

"It's all that. You've got my number if you need it."

She angled her head. "Your father said it's haunted."

"That's right."

"That's right he said that, or that's right

it's haunted?"

He gave her a long look and that quiet smile. "Both. I've never known any . . . entities, we'll say, in the manor to be more than sort of playful."

"Playful. You're serious. You actually believe in ghosts?"

"It's more what you believe, or don't. You strike me as someone who decides for herself.

"So . . . Collin never put in a security system — never saw the need. But we can arrange that for you if you decide you want one."

"A lot of good that'll do if I'm going to need Ghostbusters." Then she shrugged. "I'll think about it."

"Have another cookie."

"Do I look like I need one?"

He surprised her by reaching over to squeeze her hand. "Have another cookie."

Then he took a cigar box — an actual cigar box — out of his briefcase.

"Cookies and stogies?"

"If only. Keys."

When he opened the box, she sat back. "Oh my God, there are so many."

"They're labeled, color coded. See — exterior doors. Front, south side, north side, back, apartment. The little shed. I didn't take you out there. You've got the lawn tractor, the snowblower, shovels, chain saw, various tools.

"There's a generator out there. Power goes out, it comes on. You won't be in the dark."

"Hallelujah."

"Door opener for the detached garage. And the key fob for the truck."

"What truck? There's a truck?"

He took another cookie himself, studied her as he bit in. "Did you read the inventory list?"

"I got lost in it."

"You've got his Ford F-150."

"What is that?"

"It's the same model I've got."

"That big, burly thing?" Horrified didn't quite cover it. "I've never driven a truck in my life."

"Your Hyundai's got all-wheel drive, but you're not in the city now. Even with John Dee, you might find a big, burly thing useful."

She pushed up, walked to a window.

Everything outside held quiet, all sound muffled by the gently falling snow. It was a picture, a painting, a postcard.

And her nerves had boomeranged back.

"You said there was wine."

"There is."

"I think I could use some. Do you want some?"

He rose. "What kind of man would I be if I let you drink alone? What kind do you want?"

"It doesn't matter. It really doesn't matter."

"Leave it to me."

"It feels like I'm leaving a lot to you," she said as he walked into the butler's pantry. "And you're being pretty damn patient. Is that a lawyer thing or just part of the package?"

"Could be both."

"It's snowing, and you probably want to go home. Maybe to your beautiful wife and two adorable children."

"I need a time machine for that. The wife — and that would be gorgeous — and two adorable — and you forgot brilliant — children are in the future."

"Maybe they're hanging out with my handsome, sexy husband and three adorable, brilliant children and our lovable yet frisky dog."

"Three, huh? What kind of dog?"

"To be determined. Then there's the cuddly kitten. And we all live in this wonderful old rambling Victorian — which was never going to be as big as this — my handsome, sexy husband and I will be renovating for the rest of our lives. But we love it."

"Sounds pretty good. But I've already got the dog."

"You have a dog?"

"Mookie. Lab/retriever mix."

"Mookie?"

"For Mookie Betts," he said as he came back with two glasses and a bottle of wine. "Multiple Gold Glove winner. Played for the

Red Sox. They traded him to the Dodgers in 2020, but you can't hold that against him."

"I won't, and I'm from Boston, so I know Mookie Betts. Thanks," she added when he handed her a glass of straw-colored wine. She downed half in one go.

"Wow. Kudos."

"Okay." She let out a breath. "Why didn't you bring the dog?"

"I didn't know how you felt about dogs. I'll bring him next time."

"Good. I like dogs. I was thinking about getting a dog before . . . all this, because I wasn't spending all day in the office. He's probably a nice dog, Mookie, since you seem to be. I'll like him. I like you. I like your patience and how you don't actually look like a lawyer. Less intimidating. And I think I have a thing for blue eyes. I almost married a guy — asshole — with blue eyes. They weren't as good as yours."

"That's a story I'd like to hear."

"Maybe next time. Keys." She sat again. "Jesus, so many keys."

He went over them with her, then closed the box, nudged it aside.

"I don't see any reason you'd lock up most of the interior doors, but you've got keys for the ones that lock. Collin kept a couple of files in his office of instruction books, warranties for the appliances. For everything. But if you need help with any of that, just ask."

"Okay."

"Fireplace in the master and other bedrooms are gas, but most of the fireplaces are wood-burning. Have you ever handled wood-burning?"

"Yeah, I'm good there. My mother has one. I grew up there."

"Good. There's the rack just outside, and it's full of wood. You've got half a cord stacked back by the little shed."

"That sounds like a lot. Is it a lot?"

"Maine winters are long. If you need more, you tell me or John Dee. You've got a log splitter, but you're going to do me a favor and not mess with it."

She swiped a hand over her heart. "I can give you my solemn oath on that one."

"Anything I didn't cover you want to know? Anything I did you have questions about?"

"I'm hoping I don't forget half the things you went over, but I think I'm good. Or good enough. But I do have one question. Your father didn't tell me how Collin died."

"He fell down the stairs. The same stairs Johanna fell down nearly thirty years ago. He'd taken a sleeping pill. Just one according to the coroner, but enough to make him woozy. And some over-the-counter cold meds. He'd caught a cold, and it lingered. For whatever reason, he got up in the night, and fell. My mother had made him some chicken soup, and I stopped by to bring it and check on him."

"You found him."

"I did."

For a moment she thought she caught the scent, just a hint of the aftershave her father had worn. Then it faded.

"That was hard for you."

"He was family. So the way it comes down, Sonya, makes you family."

"I understand he was family to you, and you to him. I don't understand why he left all this to me instead of to you and your family."

"He wanted you here," Trey said simply. "Now you are. Personally, I think you'll stay."

"Why?"

"The manor weaves a spell. I've been watching it weave one on you. I'm going to leave you to settle in." He got to his feet. "You need anything or have any more questions, you know how to reach me."

"Take half the cookies. You more than earned them." She took a handful out, gave him the tin.

"That's more than half."

"So share."

She walked with him to the front door. "It's snowing pretty good now. I hope you don't have far to go."

"I've got the third floor over the law offices. It's not very far."

"Handy. No commute to work. I've gotten

used to that myself."

"You're going to hear John Dee and the plow before long. He might wait to blow off your walks until morning."

"Either way, I'll have coffee. Thank you for everything, and tell your father I hope he feels better soon."

"You're welcome, and I will." In his parka, still hatless, he took her hand. "You'll be fine."

"You sound sure."

"Because I am. Welcome home."

"Trey," she said as he opened the door to the wind and blowing snow. "Just one question. Have you ever actually seen a ghost?"

He gave her a long look and that quiet smile. "Yes."

"In the manor?"

"That's two questions. Same answer. She was on the widow's walk dressed in white."

He left her shivering in the doorway. She waited until he'd started the truck, backed out of the drive.

She closed the door, leaned back against it. And looking at Astrid Grandville Poole's portrait, said, "Well, shit."

The best thing to do — the smart thing to do — was go up, unpack, give that champagne time to chill.

She'd FaceTime with Cleo, call her mother.

She'd make something to eat — God knew, from the look of the fridge, the Doyles had supplied her with enough for a month.

She walked up the stairs, trying not to think two people had died on them, and down the long hallway into what was now her bedroom.

She walked to the window. And the view simply entranced her.

The blowing curtain of snow with the steel-gray sea behind it. That curtain hid the bay and the village. It closed her in.

But the fire offered warmth and light; the room smelled of fresh flowers.

She would be fine, she told herself. And she could be happy here if she gave herself a chance to be.

Opening a suitcase, she began the task of making the room hers. Clothes tucked in drawers, hung in closets. Cosmetics and creams in the vanity drawers, to be organized later. Her tablet sitting on a nightstand, charging. Her great-grandmother's old silver-backed brush and mirror on the dresser along with three pretty little bottles she'd found antiquing with Cleo. And a fourth holding the perfume she'd indulged in post-Brandon.

More hers now, she decided.

In the morning, she'd set up her office in that fabulous library. She'd hang her father's paintings there.

He already had one hanging in the manor, she thought. How had Collin come by it? That's a question she wanted answered.

Halfway down the stairs she felt a wave of cold air and turned, half expecting to see someone behind her.

"Old house," she muttered. "Drafts expected."

She went into the kitchen, slapped a sandwich together with the provided bread and cold cuts. She ate it over the sink, watching the snow.

And felt a ridiculous lift when she heard what had to be John Dee and his plow.

A quick hunt scored her a lidded mug and she filled it with coffee. She'd watched and learned.

Gearing up, she took it outside to meet another neighbor.

When the shadow moved at the window, she didn't notice.

Chapter Seven

After the drive, the tour, the unpacking, a somewhat more abbreviated tour FaceTiming with Cleo, and the consumption of the best part of a bottle of champagne, Sonya called it early.

By ten she lay in bed in a dark so complete it seemed the world had flipped a switch. Eyes firmly shut, she listened to the crash of waves, the wail of the wind, the moans and groans of an old house settling.

Two minutes later, she switched on the bedside light, got up, turned the fireplace on low.

A person could walk into a wall, she told herself — or, obviously, fall down the damn stairs.

Not that she was afraid of the dark, she assured herself as she climbed back in bed. But there was dark, and there was *dark*.

Satisfied with the quiet flicker of light, she turned off the bedside lamp.

She'd pick up some night-lights, plug one

in the bedroom, another near the landing. Maybe . . .

She drifted off.

Somewhere in the night she dreamed. Music drifting, voices murmuring. The woman in the portrait danced with a dark-haired man. He wore a high, starched-collared shirt and jacket, and like in a costume drama, close-fitting breeches.

They laughed into each other's eyes; their smiling lips met in a sweet kiss.

Even in death, we will not part.

As they danced, red spread over the white dress. The music became a dirge, and shadows smothered the light. In those shadows she lay, the white dress soaked in blood. And he hung over her, a rope around his neck.

Throughout the house, a clock struck the hour. One. Two. Three. For a moment, the low fire boiled up, snapped, snarled, then quieted again.

In the foyer, the portrait wept.

When Sonya woke, sunlight streamed through the windows. Blinking against it, she sat up.

"Here I am. Day two."

She rose, and after turning the fire up, walked to the window.

Winter sun sparkled on the fresh snow as if someone had tossed tiny diamonds over the ground. A bird swooped onto a white-flocked branch of the skeletal weeper and sang its heart out.

The sea held a strong blue under a sky where the wind had whisked the clouds away.

She decided to take it all as a good omen.

Ready to start her first full day, she grabbed her tablet and went down for coffee. It amazed her how still and quiet the house was, and how filled with light.

The dark had been *dark.*

No street noises, no dog barking in a neighbor's yard. Just the roll and thrash of water against rock, depending on where she was in the house.

She stood now, looking out over another blanket of sparkling snow. The wall of green woods had snow draped on branches. And something moved in its shadows, she realized as her heart tripped up to her throat.

Then a deer stepped out, its coat dark and shaggy for the season, its steps slow and dainty. Delighted, Sonya watched it stand in the sunlight, scent the air, before it slipped back into shadows and vanished like a ghost.

Maybe she'd use some of Collin's canvases, some of his paints and brushes. Inspiration lay everywhere. Why not amuse herself trying a few landscapes?

Not her passion, no. Her mother had been right about that. But it might be fun when she could make the time.

Work came before fun, and she had plenty of that ahead of her.

Setting up her office, number one. She might be living rent-free for the next three months, but that didn't mean she didn't need to work.

She had one job to complete — and she needed to generate more.

At some point she should go through the storage areas and see exactly what was what. And she'd need to go into town, become familiar, make some contacts.

She didn't mind living alone, but she'd never been a hermit.

After she settled in, settled down, she'd have the Doyles over for dinner. That seemed the gracious thing to do — with the added benefit of finding out more about the house, its history, who'd lived there.

Who'd died there.

With a second cup of coffee, she scrambled up some eggs, and hearing her mother's voice in her head, sat at the island rather than eating standing up.

She checked her email, as relieved as pleased to find her website had generated a new inquiry for a quote.

A caterer, just starting up. A web design to include menu, prices, service area, and so on.

"I love a start-up, so let's hit it."

She answered on the spot, posing a list of questions that would help her, and the potential client, make some decisions. Added a few careful suggestions to test the waters.

That done, she dealt with the dishes, then went up to take the shower she'd been too tired for the night before.

Hot water flowed generously from the rain showerhead in a shower double the size of hers in the duplex.

"I miss shower sex." She lifted her face to the water. "I miss sex altogether. Oh well, priorities."

And it wasn't like she had a lot of candidates for shower sex anyway.

It made her smile to remember her conversation with Cleo when Cleo had demanded three words to describe Trey Doyle, then John Dee.

Patient, personable, and hot for Trey.

Cheerful, married, and gay for John Dee.

She started to imagine shower sex with Trey, then shoved that aside. That way, she decided, lay madness.

Plus, he probably already had someone (or someones) in his life. And though she missed sex, she didn't miss relationships. Not yet. And she didn't feel ready for sex without the relationship end.

So scratch that entirely for now.

She stepped out of the shower, reached for a towel. And frowned at the bathroom door.

She'd thought she'd closed it — out of habit — but it stood open. She closed it now as, alone in the house or not, an open bathroom door made her feel exposed.

After wrapping the towel around her body, she wrapped another around her hair. Opened a vanity drawer and frowned again when she saw her skin care supply neatly organized.

She thought she'd just dumped it to sort out later, but . . . Had she been in that much of a daze when she'd unpacked?

Apparently.

After using what she wanted, she hung the towels to dry, bundled into the robe she'd hung on a hook.

Because her mother's voice nagged in her head, she went in to make the bed. And found it already made, pillows fluffed.

Dazed, she told herself. She must have made it on autopilot.

Since she'd spend the morning setting up her work area, she decided sweats equaled the uniform of the day.

She walked to the dresser, started to open a drawer.

This time a chill sprinted up her spine.

Her three pretty bottles lined up in front of the mirror; the silver-backed brush and mirror lay together on the left with the vase of flowers dead center.

She'd arranged the bottles near the corner, in a kind of triangle, to balance the flowers on the other side, with the brush and mirror off-center between them.

She was sure of it.

Too much champagne? she wondered.

But she hadn't had any before she'd unpacked. Obviously, she'd moved them after that, probably when she'd gotten ready for bed.

She moved everything around the way she wanted them. Gave the display a determined nod before taking out sweatpants and her beloved Boston College sweatshirt.

After pulling her wet hair back in a tail, she put on sneakers and considered herself ready for the day.

She switched off the fire before she left the room, then went straight to the library. After plugging in her tablet, she programmed music. Quiet was nice, but *quiet* could be a little much.

Next order of business: light a fire.

The Doyles made it easy, she noted. Wood right there in the rack — she'd bring in more — a starter log, the long matches.

Pleased when it crackled to life, she stood and admired it.

Now, she thought, decisions.

She could set up down here, then if and when she needed or wanted her work on the big screen, take her laptop up. Or she could just set everything up there.

"Easy choice, because this room really is everything."

She opened the boxes she and Trey had carted up the day before, and got to work.

It took time, but she had plenty of it.

With her computer set up and — yay! — running, her sketch pad within easy reach, she made use of the desk drawers for supplies. Pencils, markers, rulers, extra sketch pads, client files.

Since she had the space, she thought she'd use the computer in the office on the main level, do her personal business in there. A nice way, she decided, to separate her business.

She put Xena in a south-facing window.

"We're going to bloom here."

When she opened a free-standing cabinet, she found decanters inside — whiskey in one, brandy in the other, according to her sniff test. Lowball, highball glasses and snifters stood on a pair of shelves.

She could clean it out, use it for more supplies, but she could so easily see the man with her father's face sitting by the fire with a book and a glass of whiskey.

She didn't have the heart.

Neither did she have the heart to set her printer next to that gorgeous desk. No question she'd find a sturdy table or stand somewhere, but it would just ruin the look of the room.

She could network with the printer in the office, but . . . inconvenient.

Wandering the room, she looked for options. Set another log on the fire, then went up the curving stairs.

More books, another killer view, a smaller, more feminine desk, a big wine-colored leather sofa. The big flat-screen, and a cabinet under it.

She opened one of the doors and found a DVD player, along with an impressive collection of DVDs. Add these to the ones she'd seen in the media room, and yes, Collin had loved movies.

All sorts of movies, she mused as she browsed through them.

Books, movies, art, antiques. Children? He'd put in a gaming system for his friend's kids, so yes, children.

"So much like Dad. Really, I think you were a lot alike. And I think . . . I think you'd have enjoyed each other. You should've had the chance to find out."

On her tablet below, the music stopped, then started again with what she recognized as The Byrds' "Turn! Turn! Turn! (To Everything There Is a Season)" because her father had often played it and, to her, other ancient records on his old turntable in his studio.

"I guess that suits the moment," she muttered.

But more to the point, she could make room in the cabinet, set up her printer, her letterhead, a ream of paper.

Of course, that meant hauling the printer — and its considerable weight — up those curving steps. So that could wait, as much as it pained her to admit, until she had someone with more muscle and a strong back to carry it up.

By early afternoon, she'd done all she could do both personal and professional office–wise.

Time for a break, she thought, and debated grabbing something to eat or cleaning up a bit more and venturing down to the village.

Before she could decide, a trio of bongs all but boomed up the stairs. By the time her heart stopped jumping and she realized it had to be the doorbell, they sounded again.

"Okay, Jesus!" Hoping it was Trey or John Dee — muscles, strong backs — she jogged downstairs to answer.

A woman with a varicolored knit cap over short black hair stood on gorgeous knee-high boots in the portico. She held a cake carrier.

"Hi! I'm Anna. Anna Doyle. Welcome to Poole's Bay."

"Oh, thanks." She should've noted the resemblance, but the eyes were more blue-gray, the face more heart shaped. "Come in."

"I hope you're not working. Trey said you'd probably be working or setting up your work area."

"I just finished setting up. Or enough."

"This is for you. Coffee cake. I bake when I'm thinking."

"I eat when I'm thinking. Can I take your

coat?" The fabulous red suede coat.

"If you don't mind me pushing in for a few minutes."

"I don't. At all."

Anna handed over the coat, the hat, and the amazing scarf of butter-soft wool.

Beneath she wore a winter-white tunic and chocolate leggings that set off the boots Sonya wanted for her own.

Tall and leanly built like her brother, with a short, sleek cap of black hair and flawless skin, she looked like she'd just stepped out of a fashion magazine.

"Are you settling in?" Anna asked as Sonya took the coat to the closet to hang. "It's such a spectacular house."

"I'm making headway."

And needed to make friends and contacts, she thought.

"Why don't we take this cake back to the kitchen and try it out? I'll make coffee."

"I'd love to — if you could make that tea for me. I've had my one miserly cup of coffee today." She laid a hand on her belly as they walked. "That's all we're allowed."

"Oh. Well, congratulations."

"Thanks. We're thrilled. I've hit my second trimester, and got the all clear. So other than my family, my husband Seth's family, and a few select friends, you're the first to know."

She paused outside the office. "Trey said the painting's your father's work."

"It is."

"I've always loved it. I'm so sorry Collin and your father never had a chance to be brothers."

"So am I. I was just thinking they'd have liked each other. They had a lot in common, I'm finding out. My friend calls it twin synergy. I think I saw tea in here."

Anna gestured to a cabinet. "I helped Mom stock you up. Do you mind?"

"Go ahead. I appreciate all your family's done to make this easy on me."

"Can't be easy." Anna opened the cupboard, selected a tea from what Sonya noted were half a dozen choices. "Finding out you had an uncle, and finding out the way you did. Relocating, adjusting to a place like this."

She filled a copper kettle as she spoke, obviously at home.

"We were Collin's family, so we want to do what we can. We hope you'll stay, first because he did."

She got out two dessert plates, a cake knife, forks.

"And next because my dad and my brother both liked you. I thought I'd take a chance and drop by, see if I did."

If Cleo asked for three words to describe Anna Doyle, Sonya would have said fresh, free, and gorgeous.

"How am I doing?"

"You asked me in. That's a good start."

"I asked you in even though you look like a glossy ad for casual chic, and I'm in old sweats. I should get more points."

"You would, except you look good in the old sweats. It's a wash." She cut two generous slices of cake marbled brown and gold. "Plus, I brought cake. And I'm willing to gossip if you have any questions about Poole's Bay. Trey's more discreet."

"I'll take you up on that when I've met more people. I did meet John Dee."

"A hunky sweetheart, and his husband's adorable. Kevin owns and runs the shop where I sell my pottery. Or the shop in Poole's Bay where I sell some of it."

"You're a potter?"

When the water boiled, Anna poured it over the tea bags in two cups. "I am. It started out as a hobby, and grew. How's the cake?"

"You could be a baker."

"Baking's a thinking-time thing for me, or a relaxing thing. But it's damn good cake. I don't know anything about what you do. Graphic art, graphic design. So I checked out your website. It's impressive."

"It better be, or I'd be out of work."

"You worked for a company before."

"In Boston, yes. I've been freelancing a few months."

"It's a little scary, having your own business. I admit I've got a cushion. Seth's family owns the Bayside Hotel. Small but classy," she added. "We're not Bar Harbor here, but we do get tourists. Nevertheless, it's still a little scary trying to have my own business."

She sipped some tea. "After I saw your website . . . I have another reason for coming by. I wonder if you'd take on another client."

"You?"

"My website is . . . It's just not good. I know if I had a stronger website, I could build a stronger internet presence, build up online orders. As it is, I'm lucky if I sell one or two pieces a month."

Sonya took her phone out of her pocket. "Plug it in."

"Oh, it's going to be even less than not good on a phone."

"If you want traffic, your site has to work well on mobile devices."

Anna's shoulders hunched, then fell. "And it doesn't."

"I'm set up in the library."

"Oh, good choice."

"Let's go take a look."

"Really? You don't mind?"

"I had cake. I need clients. And I really hate when a website's not good."

"I think you'll probably have to start from scratch." Anna pushed up as Sonya did.

"We'll see, but that's probably what you're going to want anyway. Fresh start, fresh look. Is the business on social media?"

"Sort of. In a half-assed sort of way."

"We'll fix that. I'm going to show you another client I designed for. Ground up. Baby Mine. Infants to toddlers, clothes, gear, stuffed toys. It's going to suck you right in."

"It doesn't seem fair to taunt me with baby stuff."

"If we do this, I'll be taunting them with your stuff."

"I'm going to join Dad and Trey in liking you. Isn't this the most fantastic room?" she added when they stepped into the library. "And your monitor on the desk just adds to it, I think. Where's your computer?"

Sonya tapped a small box beside her keyboard.

"That little thing? That works? If it does, I want one."

Sonya woke the computer up. "Give me the website."

Sonya typed it in, looked at the page with its square banner reading *Pottery by Anna* in a swirly font, the pale colors. She clicked on the Shop tab.

Waited.

"It takes too long to load."

"I've heard that."

When it finally loaded, she studied the photos.

"You did the vase in my room."

"Yes! Good eye."

"And the candleholders on the mantel in the front parlor."

"Very good eye."

"I like your work — the photos are good, show it off, but it's not organized, and they come off a little muddy against your background colors. You've got vases — and I love this one." She hovered the cursor over it. "You've got them mixed in with bowls, platters — baking dishes," she continued, and waited while it brought up the next page. "Pots with mugs and wine coolers and so on. I can fix this."

Already seeing it, Sonya nodded.

"You and your work aren't pale and muddy. You need something more striking, more arty. And you need a much better format. It needs to load fast — people have no patience. Revise the Shop tab," she muttered. "We'll add an About the Artist tab. We should have some photos of you making pots and stuff."

"Throwing. You throw pots."

"That. At least one piece from, what, a hunk of clay, through the stages to complete."

"Oh, I like that."

"Facebook, Instagram?"

Anna made a noncommittal sound, shrugged.

"I'll fix it. Do you have business cards?"

"No."

"I'll fix it. Brochures. Small, colorful trifolds, I think, you can leave at local businesses — and there's your husband's hotel. That's a built-in right there. Here's what I'm going to do.

"I'm going to do a mood board, a template — an inactive website, the shell of one. No charge."

"Listen, your time's —"

"Consider it a very sincere thanks for helping stock my kitchen. You'll look that over, and if you like what you see, we'll go from there. If you don't, no obligation."

"I have a feeling I'll like it."

"I'm good at what I do."

"So am I." Hands in pockets, Anna studied the computer screen. "And you're right, it doesn't show well, at all."

"Let's sit down in what I've just decided is my consulting area." After picking up her tablet, she gestured to the leather sofa facing the fire. "First, let me get your contacts so I can send you some options."

Once they'd settled and Sonya put Anna's information in her contacts list, she moved to the next phase.

"First, I'm going to suggest a name change for your business."

"Really?" Obviously dubious, Anna hedged. "I don't want anything cutesy, you know? I want to keep it simple, so it's about the art, the pottery."

"Exactly. Your pieces can be displayed, as art, but what I've seen on your website, and here in the manor, you create the usable, art with purpose. Practical Art."

She brought up her drawing app, and using her stylus, wrote that out giving the first letters in each word a sweep, keeping the rest of the words in clear, concise cursive.

"That's really good."

"Just a first pass, but it says what it is, so simply. It says you can have something beautiful you can use. I'll play with the font, but something like this, in a strong color, has impact."

"I thought using quiet colors would be more friendly."

"It can be, but in this case, the pastels don't say: *You'll use this, it's beautiful, and it's going to last.* The personality of the artist should come through in the design. You're not pastel."

Anna sat back, nodded. "Keep going."

Sonya spent an hour, asking questions, answering them, toying with a logo, and getting a feel for the needs of her newest client.

"I've got enough to get started. I'd print some of these basic ideas for you to think about, but I still have to find a way to get my printer upstairs. There's a cabinet up there where it can be out of sight."

"The DVD cabinet, sure. Can I help you with that?"

"Even if you weren't pregnant, no. It's a monster."

"You should give Trey a call."

"I imagine he has enough to do. I'll figure

it out, and meanwhile work up those options for you. If you like, we'll move forward."

"I already like. You had me at Practical Art. I got a lot in exchange for a coffee cake." She rose. "And wait until the soon-to-be grandmothers get a look at Baby Mine. Now I'm getting out of your way so you can work."

"I should have something for you in a day or two," Sonya said walking Anna downstairs.

As they reached the first floor, the music Sonya had turned off when she answered the door started again.

"Well, that's . . . weird." Sonya looked up the stairs. "I must've jostled the app or something."

"Or something. I don't think I know the song."

"More weird." Sonya got Anna's coat. "It's one of my mother's favorites. Apparently Dad had it playing when she was in labor with me. 'All for Love' — an oldie."

"They must like you." Anna spoke casually as she put on her coat.

"They?"

"The lost brides, and the rest. They picked a song that has personal meaning for you."

"You don't actually believe in ghosts."

Anna just pulled on her hat and smiled. "Ask me again after you've lived here for a week. Thanks for taking me on. I realize now I need you more than I thought I did. Talk soon."

When she closed the door, Sonya stood staring up the stairs as the music flowed down.

A technology glitch, she told herself. They happened; ghosts didn't.

It may have taken her a few seconds to push herself up the stairs again, but she went up. And got to work.

Chapter Eight

1828

I am, I believe, first a sensible woman. I have been educated, speak French fluently, play the pianoforte quite well indeed as well as being more than competent on the harp. As the oldest daughter, I have learned how to run a household, as I would, of course, one day make a fine match.

Above all this, I am pleased to say, my father instructed me, from a young age, on the workings of the family business. Some would say a young woman has no need to understand business matters.

I do not find those who say that sensible.

My father, the younger of twins by seven minutes, inherited the manor and his brother's share of the Poole family business when, in the autumn of 1806, my uncle died by his own hand soon after the tragic death — by murder — of his bride of only hours.

My dear parents, already betrothed at the time, married the following spring. I was born ten months thereafter.

I have two brothers and two sisters. Though I am the eldest, I must accept that the manor will one day pass to my brother Horatio, as is Poole family tradition.

This is of no import as, with that fine match, I will have my own household.

Being a sensible woman, I did not — as my flighty sisters do — subscribe to Jane Austen's novel's entertaining but unrealistic view that romantic love must, can, or should factor into a match.

Like minds, mutual respect, and of course social standing are much more important to a successful marriage.

I found all of that in William Cabot. To my surprise, I found love as well.

Our courtship began with those like minds, and a mutual attraction that, I admit, added a thrill. That attraction bloomed into love.

The day I accepted his proposal of marriage, and my father gave his blessing, was the happiest of my life.

Until our wedding day.

I, a winter bride (we do not wish to wait!), take my vows. I, a sensible woman, wear white silk, embroidered with stars at the hem and trimmed in ermine, sashed at the waist in satin.

Given the season, the sleeves are long and gathered, with stars forming the poof at the shoulders.

I have never thought myself beautiful (though William tells me I am), but I feel beautiful in my wedding dress, with my hair swept high under my veil and my grandmother's pearls around my throat.

And William, in his black tailcoat, so handsome as he looked in my eyes and put the gold band on my finger.

I return to the manor a wife, to celebrate this match that is all my heart desires. I dance with my husband, with my father, my brothers. I embrace my mother and kiss the happy tears on her cheeks.

As we will wait for the spring crossing for our honeymoon in Europe, we spend our wedding night in my girlhood home. And I become a woman in William's arms.

He shows me love well into the night, and I find nothing sensible here. It is all feeling and discovery, and awakened passions.

And I think I dream when at last we sleep. I dream of wandering my childhood home in my nightclothes, holding a candle aloft to guide my way.

I see the great doors my grandfather built standing open. I walk through them into spring, into flowers madly blooming in the sunlight. I, a sensible woman, laugh and toss my candle away, where it gutters out in the snow I neither see nor feel.

I walk through the snow, through the wind blowing wild, and feel only soft grass and balmy breezes.

I see a woman at the seawall, beckoning to me.

When I reach her, I see a stranger who looks at me with mad eyes. She grips my hand, so hard, and I feel then the bitter bite of cold that has seeped into my flesh, into my bones.

She speaks.

"He chose death rather than me. He chose death to stay with her. Be damned to them, and now to you. Walk with them, Catherine Poole. Forever a bride."

I try to run, but the wind batters at me. I stumble in the snow. I hear her laugh, more bitter than the wind, as I fall, drag myself up, fall again.

The world is white now, and swirling. The wind a screaming gale that blows my desperate calls out to sea.

I think of William, sleeping in our marriage bed, and cry out for him to save me.

I reach up toward the manor, my home, but it is lost, lost in the snow that covers me in icy blankets. I see my hand, raw and red, nearly purple. The ring William put on my finger is gone.

I drift away, drift to sleep in the cold and the snow.

And die.

Sonya worked through the dinner hour, took

a break when she realized lack of fuel was making her light-headed.

Down in the kitchen she told herself no on making a sandwich. Instead, she heated up a can of soup, put a salad together. While she ate, she played with a few more ideas on her tablet.

She answered a text from her mother.

Everything's good! Pretty much set up, and been working most of the day. Met Anna Doyle — lawyer's daughter — and I'm pretty sure new client. Big cheer! She's a potter — a good one. I'm having soup and a salad, so I'm not starving. Planning on getting into the village tomorrow — next day latest — so I won't be a hermit. Love and more love.

They texted back and forth a few times, and when they signed off, she sent a text to Cleo.

Hey! Met Trey's sister, Anna. More gorgeous. She's a potter who needs a design package, so woo to the hoo on that one. Texted with Mom, and she's hoping to come up for a day soon, maybe spend the night. You have to come visit!

And because she knew just how to tempt her friend, she added:

Not only is the manor amazing, they're saying it's haunted. Portrait of a Poole bride from the early 1800s in the foyer, murdered on her wedding day. Spooooky!

The response came quickly, as Sonya knew it would.

Ghost bride! You know I'm there. Give me a couple weeks to clean up some work. I'll come for a weekend. We'll go ghost hunting.

Yeah, sure, Sonya thought, but gave Cleo a thumbs-up emoji.

After she tidied the kitchen, she went back to work for another hour. Too early for bed, she thought, but had to admit her brain had worn down.

She'd go over it all again in the morning, and if it still looked good, she'd send the options to Anna. And drive into the village, get out of the house, and explore a little.

But right now, too tired to work, too wound up to sleep, she decided on a glass of wine and a movie. After all, she had dozens of DVDs to choose from and a big screen right upstairs.

She settled on a romantic comedy, something fun, she mused, frothy and fun, and sprawled on the big couch.

She made it through most of the glass of wine and most of the movie before she drifted off.

The clock chiming three woke her. Her heart pounded as she lay, confused and half dreaming. She heard music, piano music. Something wrong with her tablet, she thought, and rubbed at her eyes.

She thought she heard someone weeping.

She must've turned the TV off before she fell asleep, she decided. And turned the lamp on across the room. And pulled down the throw currently tucked around her.

Just more tired than she'd thought, and still adjusting to a strange house and all its strange spaces. Still groggy, she groped for her phone to take with her and charge overnight.

Or what was left of the night.

It wasn't on the table. Yawning, she pushed her hands into the pockets of her sweats. Instant panic struck when they came up empty.

Jumping up, she shook out the throw, began searching the cushions of the couch.

She told herself she wasn't one of those people whose life depended on her phone, but . . . Her life was on that phone.

She got down on the floor, hunted under the couch, under the table.

And noticed the wineglass, the remote weren't on the table.

Had she gotten up before she'd fallen asleep?

She yanked open the drawer of the coffee

table, and there sat the remote, exactly where she'd found it.

"Okay, I put it away. That's something anybody might do and forget when they're half-asleep."

She pushed up, walked to the railing and looked over.

The fire simmered — shouldn't it have gone out by now? — and she clearly saw her phone on the desk, on the charger. The tablet with it, also on charge.

Relieved, she turned to the steps.

The music stopped, and for whatever reason, the sudden silence had her nerves jumping.

She left the tablet where it was, grabbed her fully charged phone to take with her to her bedroom.

Where the bedside light glowed, and the duvet and sheet were smoothly turned down.

"Sleepwalking? Anxiety might bring that on, and I'm feeling pretty anxious."

After putting the phone on the bedside table, she climbed into bed, still in her sweats. But left the light on.

A precaution, she thought. Just a precaution.

As she closed her eyes, she heard — thought she heard — a door softly close.

For the first time in her life, Sonya pulled the covers over her head.

■ ■ ■ ■

When she woke in the light, she convinced herself she'd imagined things. Just anxiety, she thought again. She hadn't allowed herself to admit how much stress this move entailed.

Enough she'd slept in her clothes.

No big deal. She'd get coffee — and some of that coffee cake — check the work, fuss with what needed fussing with. Then she'd shower, spruce herself up a bit, and drive into the village.

She needed to get out, stop at the bank and open an account, visit some of the shops, take a close-up look at the bay.

She went straight down to the kitchen. And saw her wineglass standing beside the sink.

"Okay, that's it. No more crashing in front of the TV."

After she made coffee, sliced some cake, she took both up to the library. She'd go over the work while she ate.

Since she only planned to work an hour or so, she didn't bother with a fire.

She spent a little more than two, but knew when good was good.

And this was damn good.

Let it sit, she told herself. It was still shy of nine, so she'd let it sit, get that shower, change, then take one more look before she sent it off to Anna.

When the doorbell bonged, she nearly jumped out of her ancient slippers.

"Jesus! I've got to ask if I can change that thing."

When she went down and opened the door to Trey, her first thought was: Why? Why hadn't she showered and changed first?

"Morning," he said. "I hear you have a printer that needs moving."

"Oh. Anna shouldn't have bothered you about that." She stepped back to let him in. "It's not urgent."

"I'm heading out to see a client, so it's not much of a detour. Where's the printer?"

She had a moment to think he smelled good — fresh, outdoorsy good. And she almost certainly didn't.

"First floor in the library. I'd like to set it up on the second floor. Can I get you coffee?"

"That's okay, I'll be getting some. The client drinks it by the gallon."

Wishing she'd at least taken a brush to it, she shoved a hand at her hair. "How's your dad?"

"The boss cleared him to work today, so he's good."

"The boss being your mother."

"You got that. Anna said you're redoing her website."

"I'm working on a design I hope she likes." She walked upstairs with him. "I networked with the printer in Collin's office to get started, but that's not really practical day-to-day. It's helpful to print out some of the design, add it to my mood board."

"Mood board." Then he nodded when he walked in, saw hers. "Okay, I get it. That's a major change for Anna."

"Too much?"

"I like it, if that matters."

He hooked his thumbs in his front pockets and studied the board.

Really studied, Sonya noted. Took time.

"Yeah, I like it. She had a college friend do most of the one she's got now. It didn't have much, ah, bang, I guess, and was a pain in the ass to load and navigate. This looks like it'll have the bang."

"It'll also be quick to load, easy to navigate."

They stood, elbow to elbow, studying her work.

"Is this a logo? She doesn't have an actual logo."

"She should. That's one option for it. She wants simple, so I thought a sketch of a vase and candle holder, strong colors. Different shapes, but both her style. I thought a sketch rather than a photo, but we can try that, too."

"You've gotten a lot done in a short time." He glanced around. "This is a good setup for you. You don't want the printer down here? Easy access?"

"See that thing?" She pointed to it. "Efficient but unattractive. This room's too wonderful to have that monster sitting here. There's a cabinet upstairs."

"Yeah, DVD cabinet. We'll haul it up."

He started to lift it, shot her a look that made a laugh tickle her throat.

"I said monster. Look, it can wait. Maybe I can get John Dee to help you haul it up sometime."

"Now you're impugning my manhood."

He took off his coat, tossed it on her chair.

No flannel shirt this time, but a navy sweater and black trousers.

She actually gripped her hands together when he picked it up.

"It's so heavy. We really can wait until —"

"I've got it."

When he hauled it up the stairs, she followed him.

"Which side?"

"The left." She rushed to open it. "Everything else is on the other side now, and the power strip's right there. God, thank you."

"Let me plug it in. I'm down here anyway."

While he did, she glanced over at the couch. The throw, folded, draped over the back.

"Want it on?"

"What?"

"The printer. Do you want it on?"

"Oh. Yes, please. You're stronger than you look."

When he straightened, he smiled at her. "How do I look?"

"Well, lanky. More like a runner than a weight lifter."

"You can do both."

"Apparently. Are you sure I can't get you coffee? Or coffee cake?"

"Anna's coffee cake's tempting, but I've got a client."

"I really appreciate you taking the detour."

"No trouble," he said as they started down. "How's it going for you? Figuring things out, sleeping okay?"

"Slowly figuring, and sleep hasn't been a problem, as I've conked early two nights running. A little off, I guess, moving things around when I'm half-asleep."

Watching her, he shrugged back into his coat. "Really?"

"Like not remembering putting my phone on the charger, but hey, there it is. Absent-minded stuff, which tells me I need to get out. I'm going into the village today, try to get my bearings there."

"Good idea."

He looked at her, she thought, as he had her mood board.

Taking time.

"If you're up for it, you could come by the office, meet with Dad. He'll want to follow up with you."

"I could." Should, she amended. "I'll call

for an appointment."

"I've got that." Trey pulled out his phone. "His schedule's on here, since Ace and I would handle his appointments if the boss didn't clear him. He's got eleven-thirty, one-thirty, and three open."

"Ah, well . . . three?"

"You're in. We're on Bayview, a block off High Street, north side of the village."

"Thanks. Really."

"You're welcome. Really."

The minute she shut the door behind him the music started.

"Are you serious?" "Hooked on a Feeling," she thought, rolling her eyes as she started upstairs. She hadn't known she'd put it on her playlist, only recognized it from the *Guardians of the Galaxy* soundtrack.

"And I'm not hooked on a feeling just because he's got those blue eyes, and the rest. Plus, I'm going to stop talking to myself. Right now."

Calculating the time, she decided to start a fire after all. She could take a couple hours, print out what she wanted, go over the work for Anna one more time, then send it off before she cleaned up and drove to the village.

And when she went to the fireplace, she saw a nicely shoveled-out hearth and wood stacked for burning.

"When the hell did I do that?"

She tried thinking back, going over her steps, but just couldn't remember.

"Doesn't matter," she muttered. "Just being efficient."

She lit the starter, and caught herself rubbing a chill from her arms as she stepped back.

"Adjusting. I'm just adjusting to a lot of everything. And why shouldn't I talk to myself? Who the hell cares?"

She went back to the desk, printed out the templates for the projected brochure, business card, a design for a potential ad.

Once she'd retrieved them, added them to her board, she sat again. She brought up the inactive website on her computer screen, on her tablet, on her phone.

"Really want those photos, from clay to finished piece. A timelapse video. Oh yeah, wouldn't that be cool?"

It wouldn't hurt to have some visuals of the village on the About tab, she considered. She'd take some with her phone when she got there, upload them, see how they worked.

The bare bones of it looked good on a mobile, she thought as she scrolled through on her phone. The typography, the color, the shapes. Of course, there would be photos to load, the shopping cart to build, but yeah, good bones.

Satisfied, she wrote the email to Anna and sent the links.

If she didn't like it, well, she'd be wrong, but she was entitled.

She turned her tablet off, left it charging. Taking her phone with her, she crossed to the bedroom.

Where the fire simmered.

She didn't remember turning it on. She sure as hell didn't remember making the bed.

Pressing her fingers to her eyes, she did her best to breathe through the sudden crash of nerves.

She just needed to get out, get some fresh air. Walk outside.

She felt steadier after a shower, and decided on a dark green sweater, a grey wool vest, and pants. She took her time with makeup because she planned to meet shopkeepers, locals, and first impressions mattered.

Better, definitely better, she thought. She looked friendly, professional. And sane.

Deliberately — making a mental note of it — she turned off the fire.

Downstairs, she got her coat, a cap, fussed a bit with the arrangement of her scarf. Not just for warmth, she thought, but style.

As she reached for her gloves, she heard a door creak open — or closed. Ignoring it, she grabbed the house keys and left.

The air hit fresh — and cold — with a brisk wind blowing in from the water. It filled her, she realized, that endless view, the wonderfully fierce sound of water surging against the rocky shore.

She needed to get out like this — even just for a walk. She crossed the pavers to her car, and sent a thanks to John Dee for clearing them and her car after the snowstorm.

The road wasn't bad either, she noted as she carefully navigated the curves. At some point, she needed to check out the garage and the truck in it. But her car held its own just fine.

She had a solid ninety minutes before her appointment, so she'd make good use of it.

She liked the hints of the bay, the village as she drove down, and noted the white, red-capped lighthouse on the far point beyond it.

Something worth another visit — maybe in warmer weather. Today, she'd find a place to park, pop into a few of the stores. Meet some people, buy a little something, as supporting local shops mattered.

Maybe grab some lunch. She wondered if the pizzeria served it by the slice. She'd like a slice of pizza.

She'd drive down to the bay, take some photos. Potentially for Anna's website — hell, maybe her own. But also to send to her mother, to Cleo.

As she drove into the village, she let out a happy sigh. Just what she needed. People, places, movement. After only a couple days in the manor, she'd begun to understand how easy it would be to become a recluse — as her uncle had.

With everything right there — the space, the views, winter roaring outside — why not stay in the warm and the quiet?

And talk to yourself, she thought.

Whoever took charge of street cleaning had done the job, and she parked at the curb in front of the bookstore.

She'd make a note of town businesses, check their websites, their online presence.

A woman with a two-story library hardly needed books, but to Sonya's mind nothing held the pulse of a community like a bookstore.

She studied the sign — well done, good graphics — then climbed the trio of steps to the covered porch. Chimes rang as she opened the door.

It smelled of books, coffee, and fresh orange peel.

The long counter to her left held the coffee station, a checkout station, and a workstation with a monitor. To the right, books lined freestanding bookcases, made clever stacks on tables. Along with them stood spinners of bookmarks, greeting cards.

A woman with streaky brown hair worn in a bouncy tail looked up from the monitor. "Hi, welcome to A Bookstore. Can I help you find anything?"

"I thought I'd look around." She walked to the counter, held out a hand. "I'm Sonya

MacTavish. I'm living up at the manor."

"Collin Poole's niece." The woman pushed off her stool, took Sonya's extended hand. "It's great meeting you! Diana Rowe. Everyone's been wondering when you'd come into the village. How about some coffee, tea, hot chocolate? On the house."

"I'd love some coffee."

"The white chocolate mocha's our flavor of the month."

"Who am I to say no to that? It's a great store."

"There's more in the back. Books, of course," she said as she went to the coffee station. "And sidelines. Soy candles made locally, T-shirts, book bags. Feel free to look around. Here's my partner. Anita, it's Collin Poole's niece, Sonya."

"Oh! I see it. You've got your uncle's eyes. Welcome to Poole's Bay."

"Thanks."

Anita had a thick, soft fall of light brown hair and a firm handshake.

"Are you settling in? The manor's an amazing place."

"It is. I'm starting to settle."

"The library," Anita said in tones of reverence.

"My favorite room."

"Collin was a big reader." Diana brought the coffee around the counter, offered it. "He used to come in at least once or twice a month. Not so much in the last few years."

"He'd call in an order," Anita continued. "Deuce Doyle — I know he's handling the estate, so you've met him — would pick them up and take the books to him. Or Trey would — Deuce's son — if he couldn't make it."

"I know you never met him," Diana said, "but he was really well-liked. We just loved him, didn't we, Anita?"

"We did, and we miss him. Why don't we show you the rest of the store?"

When the door opened, bells chiming, Diana waved them off. "I've got this."

"You're a graphic designer, isn't that right?"

"That's right. Oh, this is wonderful."

Two cozy chairs faced an electric fireplace. More books, a section for kids with some pint-sized chairs. An open corner cabinet displayed the local candles, diffusers. Another held colorful T-shirts and book bags.

"You've got more space than I thought from outside. And you've managed to make it cozy." After a sip of coffee, Sonya lifted her eyebrows. "Where's this been all my life?"

"Diana's got a knack. The coffee's locally roasted. Poole's Bay supports Poole's Bay. Have you met your cousins yet?"

"No."

"You've barely had time to unpack. The Pooles still build the best wooden sailing ships in Maine — in my opinion. Fiberglass boats and so on, too, but they keep up the founder's tradition.

"I'll let you browse. Just call on me or Diana if you need anything."

The woman with a two-story library ended up leaving with three books, two bookmarks, and a pretty bag to carry them in.

She got her slice of pizza — solid A — and sat at the counter chatting with the man on duty who tossed dough to the approval of the lunch crowd.

She stopped in the gift shop that carried Anna's pottery, had yet another conversation about her uncle with the assistant manager, who sold her one of Anna's pots. An actual pot that would display Xena perfectly.

Another stop netted her a hand-knit scarf she didn't need but was oh so soft and pretty. Plus, another contact, another conversation before she drove down to the bay.

She stood in the winter wind, taking pictures, watching boats and buoys bounce in the waves. And she marveled at the sight of the manor high up on the cliffs to the north.

And to the south, with the lighthouse above, the weathered brick buildings that housed Poole Shipbuilders.

Another day, she thought — maybe. How could she be sure how her "cousins" felt about her inheritance?

She'd give that some time, give them some space.

Maybe Oliver Doyle could give her a little

better feel for that, and them.

She glanced at the time on her phone.

And no time like the now to find out.

In a fresh gust of wind, she walked back to her car to drive to her appointment.

Chapter Nine

The beauty of small towns, Sonya discovered, was you'd have to work hard to get lost.

One block west across High Street, and she was there.

The law office stood on the corner inside another Victorian.

Not with the size and scale of the manor, she noted, but absolutely charming.

They'd gone a sagey green for the cladding, cream for the trim on the fanciful three-story. A covered porch stood on one side of the entrance doors and an angled turret on the other.

Peaked roofs, a pair of dormers, what she thought of as kind of a half turret on the far side of the third floor.

Trey's apartment, she thought, and it would have a wonderful view of the bay, the point, the lighthouse.

They'd provided a space for parking, but since it seemed nearly full, she pulled up to the curb and wound her way up the path to the short stairs with their twin rails to the entrance.

No doubt it had once been a home, and if it remained one, she'd have knocked. But thinking business, she tried the door.

And walked into the hum of an office.

The requisite fireplace crackled with light, and the generous windows offered more.

They kept it homey, she supposed, yet dignified with the dark millwork, a waiting area with chairs upholstered in burgundy and navy. A woman somewhere in her fifties sat at a desk. From just a few days at the manor, Sonya thought she recognized it as an antique.

The woman had a short cap of steel-gray hair, a sharp-jawed face, and cheaters perched on her nose.

The fingers flying — no other word for it — over a keyboard paused. "Good afternoon."

And there, Eve thought, was the down east accent she'd wanted to hear.

"Hi. I'm Sonya MacTavish. I have a three o'clock with Mr. Doyle. The second Mr. Doyle."

"You've got the look of him. Poole green eyes. Could use a little more meat you don't want to get blown off in a nor'easter. Have a seat, I'll let Deuce know you're here."

"Thanks."

Sonya chose a chair, noted another desk —

currently empty — sat across the room.

"Collin's niece is here. Ayah," the woman said so Sonya had to bite back a smile.

She hung up the phone, and when she rose, Sonya assumed she'd sat on cushions, as she barely topped five feet.

"I'll take you back."

"Thanks. Did you know my uncle?"

"Of course I did. Went to school together, didn't we?"

She led the way down a wide hallway, paused at a set of pocket doors.

"First boy I kissed. No spark on either side, but you don't know till you know." She opened the doors.

"You don't get coffee unless you drank that tea I made you. And I'll know if you lie."

Deuce pushed his glasses back up his nose. "I drank it, Sadie, and it's every bit as nasty as I remember from last time."

She stood in the doorway, eyeing him. Then nodded. "All right then, I'll get you coffee. How do you take yours?" she asked Sonya.

"Actually, I just had coffee at the bookstore, so —"

"Water then. Keep hydrated."

Deuce rose as Sadie marched off. "Sadie runs my life here; my wife runs it at home. What I need is a hunting cabin." He crossed the room to take both her hands. "I'm sorry I wasn't there to welcome you to the manor."

"I'm glad you're feeling better."

"Just a cold, but between the two women running my life, you'd think I had the plague. Sit, come sit. Tell me how you are."

He took one of the two wing chairs facing the desk.

"I'm told you're working up something for Anna."

"Yes, I sent her some options before I came into the village. I want to thank you, your family, for everything you've done."

"Collin would've done the same for mine. What do you think of the manor?"

"It's a cliché, but truth. The pictures don't do it justice. My father's painting . . ."

Now he reached over, laid a hand over hers.

"I honestly didn't realize it was your father's work, and don't know how that slipped by me. I assumed Collin had painted it."

"Their styles were similar."

"I wish I could tell you how and when Collin acquired it, but I don't know. We were in our twenties when Collin moved into the manor. Honestly, I don't remember that painting not being in his office once he set it up."

Sadie came in with a mug of coffee and a glass of water.

"Sadie, Collin, and I went to school together."

"I tried them both out. No spark. Turned out I like girls."

She went out, closed the door.

Deuce shook his head. “She marches to her own — and drums you right along with her. I couldn’t manage without her. She and Maureen have been together nearly thirty years, I’d say. They’d be among the few who spent any real time with Collin the last four or five years, so may be able to fill in some blanks if you need them filled.”

“She’s a little scary, but I may risk it.”

“Oh, she’s a lot scary.” He said it with a laugh. “And she was fond of Collin. So. Trey gave you information on the local banks, doctors, and all of that. Do you need any guidance there?”

“I’ll open an account this week. I should’ve done that today, but I wanted to just . . . look around. I decided I’ll use the bank my uncle used. It seems simpler.”

“I think that’s a good choice. You set up your office in the library! Another good choice. It’s a marvelous room.”

“It is. Everything is. I don’t know how to handle it. What I mean is, I didn’t expect to love it. And I do, and at the same time it’s so intimidating.”

“That sounds like how I feel about Sadie. Are you worried about being up there alone?”

“Not exactly. I like the quiet, and being alone will help me focus on getting my business running, hopefully expanding. I did want to ask about the Pooles — the cousins — if there’s any problem with them — with me —

the inheritance. It's not just the house, which is a lot, but the money."

"Collin left them all but the five percent of his share of the business, and it's substantial. None of them, or their attorneys, have questioned the terms of the will. Owen — I know him very well, as he and Trey are friends — runs the business here. The hands-on business, you'd say. Believe me, I'd know if he had any issues. His cousin — and yours — handles the PR, and another the business of the business, another the design, and yet another lives in London and handles that end.

"Your share in Poole Shipbuilding is minimal, Sonya, and changes nothing for any of them."

"All right. I don't want any resentments. I think I should know more about the history — the family history."

"I can certainly help with that. I made Collin a book — that's in his office. And there should be a digital copy of the family tree on his computer. Also a family Bible, in the library, but it's not completely accurate." He gestured toward her. "As you prove by being here."

"Why would they have done it? Separated the brothers?"

"Patricia Youngsboro married Michael Poole, and like some converts became a fanatic regarding the Poole name. Though she refused to live in the manor."

"Really?"

"To my knowledge, she never stepped foot in it. She was a hard woman, Sonya. I expect she took Collin, placed him with her daughter simply to keep the line intact. She had no reason to keep both children, not in her mind."

"But there had to be people who knew."

"Money can obfuscate very well. The story put out, and one Collin spent the first decades of his life believing, was he was born out of wedlock, and his father died in Vietnam before he and his mother could marry. Gretta was a dutiful mother."

"Dutiful."

"Cowed by an overbearing mother. She never married. Collin was raised in his grandmother's house, where he and his mother lived. His grandfather had little interest in the business, but Patricia more than made up for that. Michael spent his time traveling, indulging in what did interest him. Women, drink, adventure. He flew planes — and jumped out of them — raced boats, scuba dived, climbed mountains. He died at fifty-eight, in a climb of Denali in Alaska."

"Mr. Doyle —"

"Call me Deuce. Mr. Doyle or Oliver can get confusing around here."

"Deuce. You said before she — Patricia — refused to live in the manor, closed it up for years. Why didn't she just sell it?"

"For the simple reason it wasn't hers to sell. Michael left it to his son Charles, and he, in turn, to his brother, Lawrence."

"All right. I'm going to take a good look at that book, and the family tree. Is the daughter — the woman who raised Collin — still alive?"

"She is, but she's not well. Alzheimer's, which spawned dementia. She's in a memory care facility in Ogunquit. Though she no longer knew him, Collin visited her twice a month. She was a dutiful mother," Deuce said again, "and an unhappy woman, one who suffered from depression, migraines, and as she grew older, extreme social anxiety.

"Patricia Poole cast a long shadow."

"I can see that."

Just as she began to see a troubled, tangled family dynamic.

"I'm grateful for all you're doing, and for trying to help me understand what's obviously a complicated family history."

"You're my closest friend's niece. I'm more than willing to answer any questions I can. As I did with your grandfather."

"I'm sorry?"

"Your father's father contacted me. He and your grandmother are understandably upset to learn their son had a brother, that they weren't informed at the time of the adoption."

"Angry, too. I know."

"Also understandable. But more, at this point, my sense is their concern's for you. That you're safe here, and looked after."

"Oh, well —"

"I'm going to have my first grandchild." He beamed when he said it. "So I have a glimmer of that concern. We had a productive conversation. All in all, Sonya, I think your father was the more fortunate brother. I don't think you'd describe your grandmother as a dutiful mother to her son."

"No, I wouldn't. Loving and supportive, of him, of my mom, of me. I'll call my grandparents when I get back to the manor." She got to her feet. "I need a little more time to find my bearings, but I'd like to have you — your family — come to dinner one night."

"We'd enjoy that very much."

"Possibly. I'm not much of a cook, but I'll figure out something. Oh, and one more thing. I need to find those bearings, but if I stay, I think I want to get a dog. I like the quiet, don't mind being solo, but sometimes it'd be nice to have some noise and companionship. Is there an animal shelter, or an animal rescue in the area?"

"There is. Trey's dog is a local rescue. I can get you that information."

"I appreciate it." She held out a hand. "I really do."

"You took a leap, Sonya. I appreciate that."

When he walked her out, a man sat at the

second desk. About her age, she judged. A very cute man in a sports coat and sweater, his black hair in short twists.

Another man stood looking over his shoulder, and there was no mistaking the resemblance. This Doyle looked like a lawyer from the top of his full mane of hair — white as fresh snow — to the tips of his polished Oxfords. He wore a very sharp gray, three-piece, chalk-stripe suit.

"Now, that's what we're after, Eddie!" He gave the man at the desk a slap on the shoulder.

He looked over, pushed his black-framed glasses back up his nose, and gave Sonya a long look.

"You must be Sonya MacTavish." He strode over, grabbed her hand in a quick clutch and shake. "Ace Doyle. You're a looker, aren't you?"

She'd never thought of herself that way, but felt her smile spread. "You sure are."

He laughed, a big boom of one. "Quick, too."

He had those blue eyes, no less gorgeous behind bifocals, with those sharp black brows over them. He had to be in his late seventies, maybe early eighties, but as with his son, she'd have cut a decade off.

"How are you liking the manor? Everybody up there treating you all right?"

"I like it very much, but it's just me."

He winked at her. "It's never just you in Lost Bride Manor."

"Ace."

And just grinned at his son. "Hell, ghosts are just people who aren't ready or able to move on or recycle. You can bet I'm going to haunt this place after my time comes." He pointed at Sadie. "Get used to it."

"You already haunt this place."

At her dry response, he let out another boom.

"You give me a call next time you're coming into the village. I'll take you to lunch. I like taking pretty girls to lunch. Keeps me sharp. Eddie, say hello to Sonya, Collin Poole's niece. Eddie's my latest victim."

He said, "Hello," and grinned at her. "Ace, you've got that conference call in five minutes."

"Work, work, work." He gave Sonya's hand another clutch and squeeze. "Don't you be a stranger."

He strode out on a wave of energy.

"Well," Sonya began, "he's —"

"A character?" Deuce finished.

"I was going to say amazing."

"And another falls under his spell. Be careful. He'll end up getting your life story and deeply buried secrets out of you inside of five minutes."

"I bet he would. Thanks again. I'd better get back to my haunted manor."

She realized as she went out that she'd only been half joking. And that she'd better shake that off.

After checking the time, Deuce walked back, past his father office, past his son's assistant's office where Jill clicked away at a keyboard, and into what had been the kitchen when he'd grown up in the house.

Now, transformed, it served as his son's office, with a view of the backyard through the windows. Trey sat at a desk Collin had given him when Trey passed the bar. A desk from the manor's attic, and one Trey had lovingly refinished himself.

Trey held up his index finger as he talked on the phone, so Deuce took a seat. As he did, the dog dozing beside the desk got up, stretched heroically, then walked over for a pet.

Even as he scratched the dog between the ears, he could see his mother at the old stove, stirring up oatmeal she claimed would stick to his ribs before he walked to school. See himself sitting with his father at the kitchen table having his first (legal) beer.

See himself and Collin sneaking cookies from the jar on the counter.

Now where the counter had been, a shelf held law books.

A good old house, he thought, and as a good old house should be, full of memories.

It served a new purpose now, made new memories now, and had for nearly as long as his son had been alive.

And he was glad of it.

Trey hung up, puffed out a breath. "Heidi Gish got another speeding ticket."

"Lead foot."

"She wants to take it to court and sue the state trooper who clocked her doing ninety-four because, she claims, he was rude. She's going to have her license suspended this time. She doesn't want to hear it, or that, this time, it's going to cost her more to try to fight it than to suck it up.

"Anyway. How's your day going?"

"I just met with Sonya."

"Right." Trey looked at the time. "Forgot."

"I can't fault the way she's handling this. But I find myself annoyed with my dead friend for not reaching out to her, talking her through it, answering her questions before he died."

"He might have down the road. He had to think he had plenty of time left."

"Did he?"

Trey sat back. "Dad. There's nothing that says it was anything but an accident."

"Nothing but hindsight. The last conversations we had." Absently, he patted the dog's head when Mookie laid it on his knee. "I told you, he'd bring her up, ask me to be sure to convince her to come, to take over the manor.

He wasn't sad, and I never thought suicidal, but he was . . . absent somehow. As if he'd already left. Still, I couldn't convince him to contact her. He'd just smile, tell me he would when the time was right."

"Which goes back to him thinking he had that time."

Deuce just nodded. "Ah well. You'll keep looking after her."

"I wouldn't call it that. I'm betting she wouldn't like calling it that."

"You're right there. Just check in on her now and then." He cupped the dog's face, rubbed. "Take this one. She's thinking about getting a dog. You should send her the information for where you got this mutt right here."

"I can do that."

"Good. I'll let you get back to work."

"Dad," Trey said as his father rose. "She strikes me as a capable, self-reliant woman."

"Yes. And she'll need to be."

Sonya's phone rang just as she pulled up to the manor. She pulled it out as she parked, held her breath as she saw Anna Doyle on the ID.

"This is Sonya. Hi, Anna."

"I was working, so I didn't get to the phone. Then when I did, I had to look at everything, then look at it again. And again. I love it. I love it all. You're a genius."

Sonya let out the breath. "That's true, but it's always nice to have my genius recognized."

"I want Option One — the whole package. I love the use of color, the streamlined style that still manages to be friendly. And! How it looks on my phone!"

Sonya shook a fist in the air, as she'd hoped for Option One. "Putting you on speaker so I can get the bags out of my car."

"Oh, I can call you back."

"No, that's fine." She hauled the bags out of the back seat of her car, juggled them and the phone while she dug for the house keys. "I need all the photos and descriptions to build the shopping pages, then the shopping cart. We need to finalize your bio and so on — that list I attached — and we're ready to —"

She broke off as something drew her eye up. As on the first day, she saw a shadow at the window. She'd have sworn the curtain moved. Then she shifted a bag, and it was gone.

"Ready to?"

"Sorry, distracted." Just the way the light hits the window at this angle, she decided, and walked to the portico.

"Ready to launch your social media."

"Yeah, that's my hitch."

"I can get it up and running, and keep it updated for you. As long as you give me those updates. But you need that presence."

She unlocked the door, dumped the bags.

"Let's start with the photos," she said as she took off her coat. "And the bio."

"I dragged my mother into my studio today to take pictures of me at the wheel, and moving a piece through to firing. She's a really good photographer. Some of her work's at the same shop mine is."

"I was in that shop today. I bought one of your pots."

"Hooray."

"Send me the pictures." After hanging up her coat, she went back for the bags to carry them upstairs. "We'll start there, and I'll finish the design for the brochure."

When she walked into the bedroom, she caught the scent of perfume. Her new perfume, since she'd tossed out what Brandon had given her for Valentine's Day the year before.

The bottle stood with the three decorative ones, and not beside the hand mirror.

"Sonya?"

"Sorry, I missed that."

"Could be because I'm talking so much and so fast. Send me the contract. I'm in for the works, and I'll get you the pictures. I'm going to ask my guy to help with the bio. He writes a lot of the publicity stuff for the hotel."

Deliberately Sonya walked over to the dresser, moved the perfume bottle back where she wanted it. Groggy this morning, she thought. She'd been groggy.

"I'll send it this afternoon. You should have one of your three handsome lawyers look it over. I can take care of getting your business cards printed if you want."

"I've got a source through the hotel, so that's no problem. This is all better and easier than I expected, Sonya. And a whole lot faster. I really do love everything."

"You'll love it more when it's fully built. Send me the pictures you have. We'll need one of the piece you made today when it's finished."

"Sometime tomorrow for that, but I'll send the rest. Talk soon."

"Talk soon."

After a quick happy dance, she unwrapped the bowl she wanted for the table on the second floor of the library, the candle she'd bought for the bathroom counter.

She pulled out one of the books, set it and a bookmark on the nightstand. After draping on the scarf to put away downstairs, she took the other books and the bowl into the library.

Rather than put the books on a shelf, she put them on a table by the sofa, and since she'd work, laid some logs in the hearth, lit a fire.

She took the bowl up, admired the way it looked, then walked down again to get a Coke out of the kitchen.

"Stairs, lots of stairs in this place. I probably don't need to try the gym if I keep going up and down all these flights every day."

The part of her that wanted to explore in what she still thought of as secret passages warred with the part that imagined getting stuck down there. Somehow.

"Maybe tomorrow. I'll have my phone, so if I do get stuck, I can call somebody to get me unstuck. I'll feel like an idiot, but so what?"

Plus, she needed to take a good look at what she had in storage spaces.

Over the weekend, she told herself. Just like a professional. Workweek, weekend.

"I'll begin the going down there, going up there on Saturday."

As she started upstairs to do that work, the music came on.

Elton John, shouted out: "It's getting late, have you seen my mates? Ma, tell me when the boys get here."

"Oh, for fuck's sake!"

After jogging up the rest of the steps, she turned into the library. Sir Elton sang away on her iPad.

"What's wrong with you? And that's too damn loud."

She lowered the volume, and shaking her head, sat.

Fine, just fine, she'd have turned on the music anyway.

First, she downloaded the photos Anna had

just sent.

"Okay, yes, yes. These are very good. In fact, perfect. Exactly what I want. Nice work, Anna's mom. So here goes."

She brought up the contract, sent it, then went back to the photos.

As she worked on layout, she caught herself singing along with the music. "Saturday, Saturday, Satur—"

She broke off, looked back at the tablet.

"That's weird, isn't it? Kind of weird that I was thinking about Saturday, and this starts up."

As her belly jumped, she rubbed her hands on her thighs.

"It's just a song, a song and a glitchy app. I'm going to work now. I need to concentrate."

And this time she couldn't be sure if she talked only to herself.

That night, a clock struck three. And she dreamed she walked the long halls of the manor where somewhere echoed the sound of a woman's weeping.

She dreamed she stood before a mirror framed with predators that seemed to snap and snarl. But rather than her own reflection in the glass, she saw another.

She dreamed of a woman with hair the color of roasted chestnuts falling nearly to the waist of long white nightgown.

As she watched, the woman walked out of the great doors of the manor and into a snowstorm. In the dream Sonya heard the crash of the waves, the feral howl of wind, but the woman, smiling, trudged through the snow in bare feet.

Another female waited at the seawall, in a black dress the wind didn't seem to touch, her dark hair falling in waves.

They spoke, but Sonya couldn't hear the voices. She only saw the fury in the second woman's eyes, and the fear in the one with chestnut hair when the dark woman grabbed her hands.

Now, the woman in the nightgown shuddered in the cold, tried to run back to the manor on feet that must have been frozen.

The manor that stood, shadowed against the whirling snow, its grand doors firmly shut.

She fell while the other watched. Her lips going blue as she struggled up, fell again.

Her eyes, green, Poole green, shed tears that went to ice on her cheeks.

She fell a final time with the snow falling over her like a shroud.

In the dream, Sonya walked the long halls, slid back into bed.

She thrashed in her sleep. And wept.

Chapter Ten

By morning, the dream faded from her mind and memory. She woke eager to work.

She began her routine with coffee, sitting at the counter with her tablet.

A check of her email netted her another inquiry: a recommendation from — bless them — Baby Mine.

Fingers mentally crossed, she answered.

Next she found an email from Trey with information on the rescue organization.

> They have photos, what they know of the history of the dog. This one's just dogs. Ages, temperament, breeds — or the best they can determine breeds. Mookie and I found them pretty terrific. It's county-wide, but Lucy Cabot works with the county group, and fosters dogs in her home in Poole's Bay. Let me know if you want/need more.
>
> Trey

She hovered the cursor over the link, nearly pressed it. Then pulled back.

Thanks. I'm not going to let myself look yet because I'm weak, and I still need some time to organize myself before I bring home a dog. Which I now find I want desperately. I hope I last a week without peeking.

Also, I mentioned to your father that I'd like to have your whole family to dinner. I can't guarantee the quality of the meal, but want to start on the right foot. Are any of you vegan or vegetarian, or does anyone have a food allergy or an extreme aversion to any particular dish? No rush. Need time before that, too. More thanks.

Sonya

She took coffee with her upstairs to change, and stopped short when she saw the neatly made bed, and the fire burning low.

"I didn't do that. I know damn well I didn't do that."

Because the mug shook in her hand, she set it down.

"I wasn't groggy. I can't be that forgetful. Can I be that forgetful?"

What were the choices? She had a bed-making intruder, she'd done it on autopilot, or the place *was* haunted. With bed-making ghosts.

"I'm taking door number two. That's it. Making the bed's a habit. Thanks, Mom."

Because suddenly changing made her uneasy, she decided to work in her pajamas. Not a thing wrong with that.

Taking the coffee and tablet, she walked down the hall, past the staircase, and into the library. After plugging the tablet in, she crossed over to start a fire.

In the clean hearth with logs already set.

Could whoever once cleaned for Collin slip in, do some chores?

And that, she admitted, hit the ridiculous scale as much as bed-making intruders or ghosts.

Autopilot.

She lit the fire, took a steadying gulp of coffee. As she turned to go to her desk, her tablet hit a disco beat with "She Works Hard for the Money."

After a burst of involuntary laughter, she shuddered.

One more door, she thought. Someone was trying to scare her. Maybe Deuce was wrong about the Poole cousins. Maybe they wanted her out of the house, wanted her to forfeit the inheritance. And they'd found a way to pull some tricks.

"It won't work. You're just pissing me off. I've got work to do, so back the hell off."

She grabbed the fireplace poker, took it with her to lean on the corner of the desk.

Just in case.

The work soothed. Here she felt confident, creative. She spent the morning on the layout for Anna's pottery, organizing by type, by purpose to coordinate with the drop-down menu she'd added to the Shop tab.

She tested, adjusted, tested again. And began to build the shopping cart.

"That's how it's done."

She broke, went down for a Coke and an orange. When she came back, already planning the next steps, her tablet signaled an email.

> I peeked. You're sunk.
> As for dinner, thanks in advance. We're all ravenous carnivores, no food allergies or aversions. Name the date; we'll be there.
> FYI, Anna showed me the website in progress. You hit it dead-on. Nice.
>
> Trey

> I'm not peeking — yet.
> I'll think of something suitable for ravenous carnivores, and try to make it edible.
> Glad you liked the in progress. More glad that Anna did, but you count. If Doyle Law Offices ever decides to get an updated web presence, you know who to call.
>
> Sonya

Another email came in as she sent the first. Anna sent photos of the tall vase she'd thrown the day before, after what she called the bisque firing. She'd send more, she wrote, of the glazing process, the completed glaze.

And after the final firing, she'd send photos of the finished piece.

Along with it, she'd sent a bio, with an invitation to edit, if necessary.

"Excellent."

Sonya answered just that, and told her client to give it ninety minutes, then check the Shop and the About tabs on the website.

"Now, let's see what we've got and what we'll do with it."

Halfway through the ninety minutes, she texted Anna to make it two hours.

She wanted it perfect.

After she tested it on all her devices, she sat back.

"It's good. It's really good. Time to leave it alone, then fine-tune."

A log fell in the fire, made her jump.

She'd toss another on, then go for a walk. Ten minutes out in the air. She figured she knew Anna well enough to be sure it wouldn't take her much longer to look the site over.

When she rose, she saw snow falling outside the window. Not a blustery snow like before, but soft and pretty.

She could walk in that.

After she'd added the log, she remembered she still wore her pajamas. Since she considered pajamas outside a bridge too far, she switched to a sweater and winter-weight leggings. Downstairs she pulled on her old reliable UGGs and the rest of her outdoor gear.

Rather than take the house key, she unlocked the front door. And stepped out into the wonderland.

Snow fell, soft as cotton, to cling to branches. It lay thin, for now, on the walkways, drifted over the seawall. The wind only murmured as she kept to those walkways and circled the house.

She smelled smoke from the chimneys, and the chilly freshness of snow, the sharp sting of pines.

The woods looked like a painting, green and white and deep. She imagined the deer she'd spotted before, but saw no sign of it.

If she got a dog, they'd walk there, just wander together in the quiet. She climbed the steps to the deck on the flat roof of the apartment, and just looked.

She recognized a long swatch of hydrangeas, their old wood like bones gathering flakes. What she thought were azaleas, tall and wide enough to rise above the floor of snow.

She'd need to learn more about plants, since most of what she did know applied to Xena. Or she'd need to give in and go with a grounds crew.

She walked down, continued on to make a circle, and told herself she'd make new habits.

Trips to the village, strolls outside — longer ones, she hoped, once spring broke through. She loved her work, and work was necessary, but she'd take time for this. Take time to go through other parts of the house.

She'd put that off, she could admit that. Because it felt so big, so overwhelming, and keeping to a handful of rooms just less so.

The house deserved better. Hell, so did she.

For another moment she stood, looking out to sea, listening to the waves.

Maybe time for some hot chocolate, she thought. Hopefully the Doyles had stocked some instant. Hot chocolate by the fire on a snowy afternoon sounded glorious.

She turned, pressed the tongue on the iron handle of the front door.

It didn't budge.

She tried again, again, and felt the first tickles of panic in her throat.

She'd unlocked the door. Unlocked it, then checked to make sure. Now she yanked at the handle, nearly pounded on the door.

The wind came up, sudden, frigid, blowing what felt like needles of ice in her face. And with it images blew into her mind — walking barefoot through a blizzard in a nightgown. Walking toward a woman standing at the seawall.

She looked over her shoulder, half terrified she'd see a figure standing there. A woman in black.

But she saw only the snow and the sea behind it.

Shaking now, she pulled her phone out of

her pocket. She'd call Trey. Embarrassing, yes, but —

Even as she started to punch in his contact, she heard a thunk. Like a lock turning.

And when she tried the door again, it opened smoothly.

She rushed in, slammed and locked the door behind her. As she leaned back against it, heart pounding, she knew her eyes were wide and wild.

Deliberately, she closed them.

"It was probably stuck. Just stuck. I unlocked it, and it was unlocked, so it jammed for a minute. That's all. And the rest, stupid panic."

She pulled off her boots, carried them to the closet, carefully hung up her coat, unwound her scarf. Though she'd lost her yen for hot chocolate, she followed the agenda.

No handy packets of Swiss Miss in the cupboards, or in the butler's pantry. She did find a fancy canister with instructions, so she got out a pan and followed them.

No handy canister of Reddi-wip either, but a small carton of whipping cream.

She was not going that far, so she'd take her hot chocolate naked.

Feeling better, she went up to the library. For whatever reason, that room felt like hers. She sat by the fire, sipped hot chocolate.

Then pulled out her phone when it signaled a text. From Anna.

Somehow I've got to not work when you're doing a big reveal. I'm flabbergasted! And I don't flabbergast easy. The shopping pages are a kind of miracle. I know you haven't finished, but everything looks wonderful, and it works so smoothly. The About page makes me impressed with myself. I love the way you used the photos my mother took yesterday.

Great. Now get me a video, with audio. I'm going to do a widget.

And, Sonya thought, use it to launch you on TikTok at some point — but no need to scare you off.

I don't know what a widget is, but I'm for it. I'll work on it. When this is all done, I'm taking you to lunch. I swear, if I wasn't married and pregnant, I'd marry you and have your baby.

While that's tempting, we'll stick with lunch. I'll get your social media up sometime within the next ten days, so watch for that heading your way.

I will. TY. Anna

A good day, Sonya thought. In spite of a stuck door, a good day.

As she put her foot on the coffee table, her tablet played Michael Bublé's "Home."

"Fine. Whatever."

In the evening, she decided to spend some time with the Poole family tree, a glass of wine. Then maybe she'd start one of the new books she'd bought or switch over to another movie.

As Deuce had told her, she found the book in Collin's office. A coffee-table style, bound in brown leather.

A caring friend, she thought as she carried it and the wine back to the library.

She read the forward where Deuce explained his interest in genealogy, and his hopes that the book would provide a connection to those who came after with those who'd come before.

It opened with the family tree, meticulously documented on a two-page spread. It started in the early 1600s.

"Holy shit, they had eleven children! Two died in infancy, another before he reached five, and another at sixteen. How do you get through that?"

She followed it down, but would look at details later. And there was her father and his twin brother. Her mother's name and the date they'd married. The date her father died.

The woman Collin had married — that date and the date of her death the same.

And there, her name, connected to her parents.

So many on those branches, she realized. She'd never thought about it. The only child of an only child — so she'd believed — on her father's side. One aunt and three cousins on her mother's.

Now there were so many more.

"Dad would have loved this," she murmured.

Engrossed, she didn't notice when her tablet played "We Are Family."

So many births, she mused, with twins running through them. So many deaths.

She turned the page.

Deuce had gone deep into his research, she realized after spending more than an hour reading through the ancestors in the seventeenth century. There had been lords and ladies, soldiers and farmers in her ancestry, and their share of triumphs and tragedies.

By the time she got to the next century, she decided to make tea — a rarity for her — and take that and the book into bed with her.

Tucked up, fire simmering, she worked her way through to the Arthur Poole, from Liverpool, who'd made his home in Maine and founded the family business. An adventurous man, she thought as her eyes began to blur.

Making his way across the sea at the age of seventeen. Heading to a brave new world and leaving the one he knew behind. A shipbuilder by trade, after years of apprenticeship.

And by the age of twenty-four, he'd started his business, and had married a wealthy young heiress, one Leticia Armond, and begun building what would become Lost Bride Manor.

Love for Leticia, she wondered, or money?

They'd had twin sons followed by three daughters, and had been married for nearly twenty-five years before he died.

A fall from a horse.

So his son Collin inherited the manor. Continued his father's expansion of the original structure while he and his brother ran the business.

A few months later, Collin Poole married Astrid Grandville.

And tragedy.

As she felt herself fading, Sonya closed the book, set it aside. She switched off the light and dropped instantly into sleep.

The clock chimed the hour of three, and the music, soft and sad, drifted into her dreams. She studied herself in the mirror, the young, happy bride in her long white dress. Music, quick and lively, echoed up from the main floor where her husband — ah, such a word, *husband* — hosted family and friends in celebration. Through the open window, the spring breeze came to flutter at the curtains.

On the other side of the mirror, Sonya smiled at her. You look beautiful, she thought.

The bride smiled in return.

"I will always be beautiful. Young and beautiful. A bride to my groom, a wife to my husband. A mistress of the manor. And I will always return to this day when I held true love and joy in one hand, despair and grief in the other."

It happened so fast, the woman with the knife rushing in. On the other side of the mirror, Sonya shouted, but the sound couldn't penetrate the glass. As the knife plunged, she pushed and beat on the mirror to try to get through somehow. But she could only watch in horror as the blood spread red over the long white gown.

As the young bride fell, and the woman cursed her. The murderer took the ring from the dying bride's finger, put it on her own.

For a moment, an instant only, darkness flooded her, swept through the room.

And she was gone.

The bride, blood seeping through the fingers she pressed to her belly, staggered to her feet. Through the glass, her eyes met Sonya's.

Again and again, over and over, year by year, and bride by bride. Find the seven rings. Break the curse.

Like the woman in black, she was gone. The

music, the soft and sad, the lively and quick, went with her.

With the dream having faded, Sonya woke just after first light to the sound of the snowblower. Remembering her duty, she went down to make coffee and took some out to John Dee.

A bear of a man with a brown beard and eyes to match, he grinned at her.

"Get ya up?"

"I'm a working girl. I need to start my day, too. That's a seriously blue sky."

"Yep. Should have a stretch of clear days coming. Only got about six inches with this last one."

They stood, drinking coffee, him in his bulky navy coveralls, her in a coat tossed over her pajamas.

"Heard you ventured into the village."

She had to laugh. "Is that news?"

"Most everything is in Poole's Bay. That was my brother's wife sold you a scarf. Friend of my mother's daughter's who makes them."

"It's wonderful work."

"You oughta be wearing it. It's a cold one." He polished off his coffee, handed her the mug. "Appreciate it. How about I stack some more wood by the back door for you? You're going through it."

"Oh, that would be great. Thanks."

"Happy to. I've gotta get back to it." He

winked at her. “I’m a working boy.”

“Here’s to the workers of Maine.”

She’d unlocked the door, and put the keys in her pocket as backup. As the snowblower started up again, the door opened smoothly.

“Okay then.”

A working girl did best with routine, she decided. Hers began with a quick breakfast, a check of emails and texts. Yesterday’s inquiry moved to a consult. Fingers crossed, she scheduled one for late morning.

A shower, sweats, her water bottle.

She refused to think about the neatly made bed as she dressed.

Not today; today she’d focus.

She took the Poole family book into the library to set on the coffee table before she started the fire.

The rack by the hearth was full. As John Dee said, she’d gone through it, so it shouldn’t be. The logs in the hearth, neatly laid, waited only for a match.

Maybe she’d look up what supplements or herbs — something — helped with memory.

But she wouldn’t think about it. Not today.

Not even when her iPad pumped out the Beatles’ “Good Morning Good Morning.”

She sat down, began refining Anna’s website design.

She broke for the consult, and did a shoulder wiggle, chair bounce as they moved from consult to contract.

Just after noon, Anna sent the final photo and — bonus — a sixty-eight-second video.

Anna at the wheel — and looking good — holding some sort of thin blade to the turning clay, and explaining she'd have a new piece, inspired by the last snowfall, on her website in a few days.

Smart, Sonya decided.

She added it to the inactive website, tested it.

When she broke again, she geared up and took a walk, this time venturing down to the seawall under those clear blue skies.

With the PB&J she'd made — always hit the spot — she sat on the stones and watched a couple of boats glide along. Fishing boats, she thought, doing their cold, hard work.

She nearly dropped the sandwich as, far out, the sea parted and a whale rose up, its massive body spearing toward the sky. Water spewed up, streamed down as it sounded, as he gleamed with it in the strong sun.

When he dived again, the sea rippled and rippled. And stilled.

"I saw a whale. I'm just sitting here eating a PB&J, and I saw a whale."

Then she cursed herself for not grabbing her phone and getting a picture.

"Next time."

She slipped a hand into her pocket, closed it around her phone in case it happened again. She waited until she had to admit it was just too cold to sit on a rock wall hoping to see another whale.

She didn't see the shadow at the window again, and the door didn't give her any trouble.

"Progress. Settling in." She studied the portrait as she took off her boots.

"I read about you last night. About you and your Collin, and the crazy bitch who stabbed you. Hester Dobbs. Killed him, too, when you think about it, since he hanged himself, apparently because he couldn't live without you."

As she went to hang up her coat, Taylor Swift's "Lover" played in the library.

"I'm getting used to that."

She spent the rest of the day on Anna's project, shifted briefly to start on a mood board for the next client.

And the evening reading a bit more Poole family history.

It seemed Hester Dobbs escaped from her cell shortly before she was to be hanged for Astrid Poole's murder, only to leap to her death from the seawall at the manor after Collin Poole's suicide.

Various tools of witchcraft were found in her cabin.

"That's cheerful."

She turned to Connor, Collin's twin, who'd inherited the manor at his brother's death.

And by all accounts had lived a happy life,

from childhood, through his own marriage — with a big ugly murder and suicide in there. He, too, had expanded the manor, and the business, while producing five children.

One of which, she noted, had died on her wedding day.

Just creepy.

Yet he'd died at the age of seventy-two, in his own bed, surrounded by his wife, their surviving children, and his grandchildren.

She decided to end the night's reading on that happy note.

She then binge-watched three episodes of a new Netflix series and called it a night.

"Situation normal," she murmured as she slipped into bed, and into sleep.

The clock chiming three didn't wake her, nor did the creaks of doors, or the drifting music, or a woman's heartbroken sobs.

■ ■ ■ ■

Part Two: The Manor

■ ■ ■ ■

All houses wherein men have lived and
died are haunted houses.

— Henry Wadsworth Longfellow,
"Haunted Houses"

Chapter Eleven

She rolled through the next few days. Maybe she used tunnel vision more than once, but she rolled through. And with the start-up catering company having signed the contract, she had plenty to roll through.

On a Saturday morning, armed with her phone and a flashlight — just in case — she went through the servants' passageway. The stairs creaked on the way down, but the light showed the way, so she stuck the flashlight in her back pocket.

She couldn't imagine herself sitting alone in the media room. Not that it wasn't nice, she observed as she wandered it. Cozy in its way, with big, comfortable chairs and a huge screen.

He'd even put in a little bar. Maybe he'd stocked it with drinks and snacks.

Had Collin sat there, alone in the big, empty house, going into the worlds on-screen? Had he laughed at comedies, felt his pulse quicken at a thriller?

Had he munched on popcorn and watched old favorites as she often did?

So odd, she thought, to have never known him, and see clearly they'd had things in common. A love and talent for art, a love of stories — books, movies. An appreciation for rambling old houses steeped in history and character.

Would the brothers, if they'd had the chance, have bonded? Would there have been shared holidays? Family jokes?

The longer she lived in the house, the more she thought yes. She'd never know for certain, but she felt yes. They'd have become family, even if they'd met as grown men.

She moved from the media room into the gym with its rack of free weights, a treadmill, and a recumbent bike. And yet another wall screen.

The man had seriously liked TV.

Hooks held exercise bands and yoga straps. He'd had a stability ball, medicine balls, even a pull-up bar. So he'd been serious about fitness, too.

Idly, she picked up two dumbbells, faced the mirror, and did some curls.

She could probably talk herself into using this space. She missed her membership at the gym — a gym she'd given up, as Brandon went to the same one.

She could stream workouts on the screen, get back into the habit.

"No time like now," she decided, and spent the next thirty minutes reminding herself how much she hated squats.

Rubbing her ass because she *felt* it, she toured a storage area, found holiday decorations. Halloween, Christmas, Fourth of July.

"You and my mother would've gotten along, too."

She found another set of stairs leading down, peered into the dark.

"The basement basement," she concluded. "I just don't think so."

It gave her the boiler room from Stephen King's *The Shining* vibe.

And she shut the door.

She wandered more, and to her delight found a panel of bells. Maybe she didn't have her uncle's full passion for movies and TV, but she'd seen this sort of thing in period pieces.

Each bell connected to a room, and signaled the staff to respond. No connection now, of course, but they'd kept that old communication in place down here.

She rang one.

"Mr. Poole must want his elevenses in the morning room."

She shook her head and thought, What a life.

Up and down the stairs, she thought as she started back up. In and out of the passageways so the family or their guests didn't have to see you.

Did it make a good life or a bad one? she wondered.

Had there been a warm bed at night, a full belly, decent pay?

Would someone have been pleased to work here, or had it been sheer drudgery?

As she started to the third floor, the bell, far below, marked the Gold Room rang.

But she'd walked into another storage area, and didn't hear.

She found furniture — tables, desks, chairs, what she thought might be a cabinet for sheet music. She discovered an old Victrola — and a stash of the thick old records that played on it.

For the fun of it, she cranked the Victrola, chose a record at random. Billie Holiday — she'd heard the name, didn't know the music.

After carefully placing the needle, she heard a few seconds of scratchy, jazzy piano and a horn.

Then magic.

"Okay," she mumbled as the music, that voice filled the air. "I get why I've heard the name when you recorded this about sixty years before I was born."

Ms. Holiday, the Victrola, and all of it, she determined, needed to find a home in the music room. Once she figured out how to get it down there.

When she opened the first of a treasure

trove of trunks, she actually squealed, then sighed in pleasure as she ran a hand over the lace and silk of the top dress.

Careful packing layers of tissue and the cedar lining had helped preserve the deep green material. She didn't have a clue what era it represented, only that it was gorgeous.

Afraid to disturb it, she lifted an edge, saw more dresses beneath, just as meticulously packed.

They should go to a museum, she thought. She needed to have someone who knew fashion and eras come in, go through them.

"Maybe keep a few," she considered. "This would *kill* at a costume party. And if the manor isn't the spot for a killer costume party, where is?"

Sitting back on her heels, she realized it hadn't taken three months. It hadn't taken three weeks.

She'd already decided to stay.

One by one she opened trunks. More clothes — for the lady and the gentleman. Shoes and hats, all lovingly wrapped.

A museum, she thought again. Or if they weren't worthy, at least a vintage shop.

"My great-great-whatevers wore all this stuff. They need to be seen, admired, worn again."

She stood up, looked around.

On impulse, she chose another record. "In the Mood," because she sort of knew it, and, well, she was in the mood.

Was it odd, she wondered, for her to stand here with the old music playing on the old machine while surrounded with so much from the past?

Her family's past.

She didn't think so. She thought it struck just the right note.

Sheets, white as ghosts, draped over most of the furniture. Not too much dust yet — and she could thank the Doyles and the meticulous inventory for that.

But too much stored away, hidden away, that could and should be used and appreciated. Heirlooms, yes, but . . .

Maybe the cousins wanted some of it. Or at least a select piece or two. And her mother . . . Yes, her mother should have something.

It wasn't a matter of selling it. Selling it didn't seem right somehow. And some, maybe most, should be kept for future generations.

Family history, in wood and glass, in silks and satins, in thick old records.

It would take her days — more realistically, weeks and months — to go through it all. Going down the inventory list simply didn't do the job of seeing, touching.

Feeling, she admitted.

"Okay then. This goes on the handle-it list. So does hiring a cleaning service, because I really can't maintain this place the way it needs to be maintained by myself."

She made notes of the pieces she wanted to move downstairs, added finding a consultant on vintage clothing, picking a cleaning service.

The practical thing, she thought as she wandered, would be to close off most if not all of the third floor, the attic. After she'd opened that door to the cousins, her mother. A seasonal cleaning should work there.

She walked into the half turret, Collin's studio. Light poured in from the windows on three sides, spilling onto the polished wood floors.

He'd kept his supplies on shelves on the rear wall, and a worktable. A couple of easels stood folded there, but another stood in that semicircle of glass.

"What do I do with your things? Maybe I'd use some of them eventually, but . . ."

She trailed a finger over the brushes in one of the brush easels. Brushes for oils, for acrylics, for watercolors. Color shapers, spatcher blades. Palette knives on a rack of their own.

Sketchbooks, pencils, charcoal.

Her father had had nearly the same setup.

And had used the same brush washer, the cold-pressed linseed oil, the mineral spirits.

It would've smelled the same in here as in her father's studio, and the thought of it made her eyes sting.

"I don't have the talent for this, or the time.

Or — Mom was right — the passion. But what do I do with your things?"

One of the cousins again? Or Cleo?

Unsure, she opened the door beside the worktable.

And lost her breath.

The full-length portrait stood framed in simple dark wood. Though not as large as the one of Astrid Poole, it had the same impact.

The woman stood, again in a long white dress.

Not the same dress, but unmistakably a wedding gown, with its off-the-shoulder sweetheart neckline, the full frothy skirt. The woman in it wore a headpiece of rosebuds with a trailing ribbon over auburn hair that tumbled in waves to her shoulders. Joy radiated out of summer-blue eyes.

In her right hand, where a diamond glinted on her finger, she held a bouquet of blue hydrangeas and airy greenery. On her left, she wore a platinum band sparkling with more diamonds.

The sea spread at her back.

"You're Johanna. You have to be, and I'm not leaving you shut away in here."

As she reached for the canvas, the closet door nearly slammed shut behind her.

"And I'm not getting shut away in here either."

She took a nearly full jug of mineral spirits off the shelf, used it to brace the door open.

She maneuvered the painting out, then carried it over to set it on the easel.

"For now. I actually like you in the simplicity of this frame. No fuss, no carving, and I'll find a place for you. I don't know why he didn't."

She sucked in her breath as a door slammed, then a second, then a third.

Suddenly cold, she hurried out.

"Closing off the third floor," she told herself. "Making sure all the doors are shut, and closing off the storage areas as soon as possible."

Her thought to make coffee — to warm up — flew out of her head when she reached the kitchen.

Every cabinet door stood open.

"That's just enough." Maybe her voice shook, but she said it again. "That's just enough." And shut every door with a snap.

She started to rush to the coat closet, grab her things, get out. And as she reached for her coat, she knew if she left now, left when her hands trembled, she might never come back.

"It's my house. It's my damn house."

So she'd make coffee, and work awhile. Before she worked, she'd take something out of the freezer. Maybe chicken. And later, she'd make a meal that wasn't a salad, a sandwich, or canned soup.

"I'm going to work here, and sleep here,

and eat here, and live here. Because it's my damn house."

That evening, she gave the Poole family history book a pass. She FaceTimed her mother so they had dinner together, and her world seemed back on track.

"Let's see, your first dinner party at the manor." Winter considered. "You're in Maine, in the winter, a good-sized group of meat eaters. Pot roast."

"That sounds — complicated."

"It's not, trust me. You can do it. You need a big Dutch oven, with a lid. And I'm going to give you a list of ingredients, send you the recipe. You put it together, baby, and it does the rest."

"If you say so."

"I do. Write this down."

The longer the list, the more she considered the idea of just taking the Doyle family out to dinner.

"Don't even think about that. You're going to invite them into your home and make them a lovely meal. Remember how the house smelled when I made pot roast?"

"Yeah — amazing. But that's you."

"You've got this."

Maybe, Sonya thought when they'd said goodbye, and she took another look at the — long — list. But she wouldn't place any bets on it.

She'd make tea — something she'd discovered added a soothing note in the evening — get in her pajamas, and start the novel by her bed.

She had her agenda for tomorrow already laid out in her head. An early start, she thought, a midday walk, then back to it.

She paused by the music room, studied it with tea in hand.

Yes, definitely the Victrola, the music cabinet. She could arrange them in there.

"And you know what else? That still life's a little formal for me. Johanna could go there. Maybe she played an instrument. Note to self: Ask Deuce."

She walked up to her room, felt her stomach clutch. The fire simmered, and the bed was turned down. And this time, a fresh pair of pajamas sat, neatly folded, on the space between the pillows and the turned-down duvet.

"I have to talk to someone about this. How do I talk to someone about this without sounding like a crazy woman? Maybe I am a crazy woman. I don't feel crazy."

But she felt uneasy enough to shut the door and turn the lock.

Sonya spent the beginning of the week with her head down, her blinders on, and her mind on the work. If doors creaked open or slammed shut, she ignored them. When her iPad greeted her with a song, she shrugged it off.

By Thursday, she started the final testing cycles for Anna's website, her social media, the works.

Incredible, Sonya thought, what she could accomplish with long hours and few distractions.

But today, she cut her work time short. Cleo would be there tomorrow — she couldn't wait — and she actually needed to go to the market.

And since that meant a trip to the village, she'd take care of opening that bank account. The Lobster Cage had a terrific takeout menu, so she'd order something and bring home dinner for herself.

On her way to her car, she detoured to the garage, used the remote to open it.

As she'd suspected, Collin's truck appeared every bit as big and intimidating as she'd imagined.

That, she determined, she could sell without guilt.

She eyed the pair of snow shovels that, thanks to John Dee, she'd yet to use. A big, red, freestanding tool cabinet stood next to a workbench; a man's twelve-speed bike hung on the wall. What she thought might be a compressor sat in the far corner.

She closed the door again.

She'd figure out what to do about the truck,

at least, then she could park her car in the garage.

The bank took longer than she'd imagined. Not just the paperwork, but conversations.

It turned out the assistant bank manager was a very distant cousin — the Oglebee side, stemming from George Oglebee, who married Jane Poole, Hugh Poole's daughter, in the late eighteen hundreds.

"I'm Mary Jane." She adjusted her red-framed glasses. "I go by M.J. Everyone was very sorry about Collin. But we're very glad there's a Poole in the manor again. I just hated to see it closed up and empty like it was for a time after Charlie Poole died back in — what was it? — sixty-five or sixty-six, I think. My mother would know exactly. She knew Charlie Poole."

"I'm just starting to learn about the family history."

"Isn't everybody! Nobody had any idea Collin had a twin brother, or that they were Charlie's. My mother claims she's not a bit surprised, but she will say that. It's just sad, if you ask me, that your dad and Collin never had a chance to know each other."

"I feel the same."

"And poor Gretta Poole, living with that lie all her life." Tsking, M.J. shook her head. "Her mother ruled that roost, you'd better believe."

"Do you know her? Gretta Poole?"

"She did her banking here — or Collin did it for her, for the most part. She hasn't been well for, oh, a dozen years or more. But he took care of her, good care."

She filed it all away as she finished setting up her account — just before the bank closed for the day.

She had her market list on her phone — fresh salad makings, fresh fruit, more eggs and milk, more coffee, butter. In and out, she promised herself.

But in the market, she added bagels, chips. And because she didn't know her way around yet, added more.

Gauging her time, she placed her order at the restaurant. But since the market stood only steps away from a little florist, why not?

Flowers for Cleo's room, her own, the front parlor. What the hell, the library. Didn't she spend most of her time there?

Plus, contacts, she reminded herself, and chatted with the florist on duty.

Who happened to be a friend of Anna's.

"You're updating Anna's web page, I hear."

"More of a new build, but yes."

"She tells me what she's seen and approved is terrific."

"I think so."

"You know, we have online ordering, and we deliver to the manor."

"I didn't know. Do you have a card?"

"Yes. Do you?"

They exchanged cards, and when Sonya walked out, loaded with flowers, she thought: Maybe.

She drove to the Lobster Cage, followed an arrow that said PARKING, and pulled in by what she recognized as Trey's truck.

More conversation, she thought, but good. She had some questions for him. Unless he was on a date. Though it seemed early for a date.

Even if he had a date, she'd say hello, and potentially meet someone else. This trip had netted her a banker, a grocery clerk, and a florist.

She walked into a bar area, cozily rustic with a brick wall behind the bar, a scatter of dark high and low top tables. Though the wide opening that led to the dining area showed that room was largely empty, the bar area did a lively business.

She spotted Trey at the long bar with a beer in his hand as he talked to the man beside him.

He spotted her, smiled, and swiveled on his stool.

"Buy you a drink, cutie?"

"Tempting, but no. I'm doing takeout and have stuff in the car."

"Take a minute. Meet your cousin Owen."

"Oh."

Owen turned, looked at her with eyes a lighter green than her own and flecked with amber. His hair, a deeper brown than hers, fell unruly around an angular face carrying a couple of days' worth of stubble.

She supposed, if she looked hard enough, she'd find a resemblance.

"It's good to meet you."

He took the hand she held out in one as hard as a wood plank.

"Yeah. You're a surprise."

"You, too. Actually, I was hoping to meet you. I went through some of the storage areas over the weekend and wondered if you'd want anything."

"Want what?"

"There's so much stored away. So much altogether really. I thought you or the other cousins I didn't know I had might want something."

"I can't think of anything offhand, but . . . thanks."

"And there's his truck."

"You want to get rid of Collin's truck?"

"Not get rid of so much as . . . I've never driven a truck."

"You should learn." He looked at Trey. "She should learn."

"Yeah. Maybe don't rush into that, Sonya. And, Owen, you should go on up there sometime, take a look at what's stored away. I see where you're coming from," he said to Sonya. "It's a shame so much is just closed away."

When Owen shrugged, she pressed.

"I wish you would. I'm there most of the time. I work right there. You could just let me know." She dug out a card. "And tell the others."

"Sure. I'll pass it along."

"Good. And, Trey, do you know anybody who could move a few things? I did find a few items I'd like to move down. And there's a painting I want to switch out."

"You've got two able-bodied men right here. Why don't we run up there this weekend, Owen? Two birds for you."

He shrugged again.

"It's not a lot. Just a couple of pieces and the painting of Johanna on her wedding day."

Trey took a slow sip of beer. "What painting of Johanna?"

"The one I found in the closet of Collin's studio. It's beautiful, and it shouldn't be shut up in there."

"In the closet, in the small turret?"

"That's right."

"Okay." Eyes on hers, Trey sipped his beer. "How about Saturday?"

"It'll have to be after three," Owen said.

"After three on Saturday?"

"Perfect. And much appreciated. I need to pick up my order. I'm glad I met you, Owen."

"Don't get rid of that truck. If you want it out of the way, I can park it down by the dock."

"Thanks. Maybe. See you both on Saturday."

Owen watched Trey watch her walk away. He took a sip of his beer. "She might not know your poker face, but I do. There wasn't a painting in that closet, was there?"

"Not as of a few weeks ago, and I'd remember if there'd been a wedding portrait of Johanna Poole in the inventory."

"Well, somebody wants her to have it."

"Apparently."

Idly sipping his beer, Owen watched her leave with her takeout bag.

"Do you figure she'll last up there for the three years?"

"I wouldn't bet against her."

"She's your type."

Surprised, amused, Trey swiveled back. "Since when do I have a type?"

"Since she walked in."

"Huh. Maybe. Still need to keep it light."

"Because?"

"Not only because she's dealing with a lot right now, but she was engaged — weeks from the wedding — just last summer."

"Huh back. She didn't strike me as the flighty type."

"Don't think she is."

"Could be she has bad taste in men. That gives you a shot."

Trey met Owen's smirk with one of his

own. "Let's order some nachos and another brew."

"I'm for it."

When she got home, Sonya carried half the flowers and half the groceries into the kitchen, then went out for the rest. She'd bought too much, obviously. But maybe it wouldn't be too much if she talked Cleo into staying a couple extra days.

She hauled in the last, shut the door.

The tablet she'd left on the desk upstairs started up with Ariana Grande's "Thinking Bout You."

"Maybe you shouldn't," she muttered.

And when she walked into the kitchen, all the cupboard doors stood open.

She dumped the flowers and groceries on the island.

"Fine! I surrender. The place is haunted. Happy now?" After yanking off her coat, she tossed it on a stool. Pulled off her hat, tossed that, then dragged her hands through her hair.

"Losing my mind," she muttered. "Just losing my mind."

She put the groceries away, closing doors as she went.

"Okay, vases."

She heard it, the little creak from the butler's pantry. She eased that way, saw the pair of upper doors over the sink open.

"I'll deal with it." She snagged the flowers, marched in. "I'm not going anywhere, so you deal with that."

After choosing vases, she focused on arranging flowers.

She'd live her life, she told herself. Her normal, productive, reasonably sane life. In the big haunted manor.

To prove it, she'd warm up the shrimp scampi takeout, eat dinner, have a glass of wine. She'd take the flowers upstairs that went upstairs, make sure the room she'd earmarked for Cleo had everything ready for her.

Put in an hour, maybe two on work. Then settle in for the night with her book.

Normal.

"This is my house now," she said as she poured the wine. "So get used to it."

Late in the night, pounding woke her. She pulled herself out of sleep, tossed the covers aside. Someone pounded on the door, the front door, she thought. She heard it still, over the howling wind, the thrash of the sea.

As she rolled out of bed, she saw the snow — fast, thick, whirling — outside the windows.

A storm had come up, and someone needed help.

She rushed out, grateful for the night-lights she'd plugged in down the hallway.

Someone stuck in the blizzard. An accident, a breakdown.

As she hurried down the stairs, she thought she heard them cry out for help. But the noise — the wind, the waves — stormed through the air.

Breathless, she twisted the dead bolt, pulled the door open.

To a cold, calm, clear night.

No storm raged; no desperate traveler stood calling for help.

Shocked, she nearly stepped out. But remembering the stuck (locked?) door on her first walk, she pulled back.

Not a raging blizzard, but bitterly cold. She wouldn't risk getting locked out of her own house in the middle of the night.

Shuddering, she shut the door. Maybe by morning she'd convince herself she'd dreamed it all. But now, it was all too real.

Had Collin heard pounding at the door? Had he rushed to help and fallen on the stairs? Fallen to his death?

That leaped a long way, a hell of a long way, from playing music, opening doors, making up the bed.

Now, as she stood alone in the foyer, the house stayed silent around her. As if it waited.

"I'm pretty steady on my feet. And I'm not going anywhere."

Her voice seemed to echo back to her as

she walked to the staircase. As she climbed, the clock struck three.

Chapter Twelve

In the morning, it remained real. She knew she hadn't dreamed it all.

She'd seen what she'd seen, heard what she'd heard.

And she'd handle it.

Because she wanted to live here. She wanted to work in the library, and wake to sunrises over the sea. She wanted to watch whales sound and spot a deer coming out of the woods.

She toasted a bagel, made coffee, and with her tablet sat at the table answering emails and texts.

A check on her weather app told her they'd likely see snow — two to four inches — by midafternoon.

Hopefully, Cleo would arrive about noon, as planned.

After filling her water bottle, Sonya went back up. She'd shower, put on actual clothes, then work until Cleo got there.

The made-up bed and fluffed pillows barely

gave her a jolt this time. Ignoring it, she went into the bathroom, firmly closed the door.

She needed to talk to Cleo, she thought as she showered. If anyone stood wide open to . . . ghosts, spirits, poltergeists — whatever the hell — it was Cleopatra Fabares.

Or maybe just having someone else in the house for a few days would . . . disburse things.

Somehow.

She hooked a towel on, started to reach for another to clear the steam from the mirror. And stared at the message written in it.

7 lost

"Seven what?" Annoyed as much as shaken, she wiped it away. "I don't do cryptic."

Since the patchy sleep after three a.m. showed, she used makeup to disguise it. She dressed in jeans, a sweater, even added earrings.

And decided she looked fine. Cheerful and sane.

In the library, she set her tablet on the desk, walked over to start the fire.

The tablet greeted her with Steve Holy's "Good Morning Beautiful."

"That doesn't win you points after last night."

The fire caught with a crackle. Snow might come later, but for now, the sun beamed.

After yesterday's tests on Anna's website and social media, she wanted to make a few minor adjustments before she ran another round.

Then she wanted Cleo's eye on the project.

She lost herself in it, working straight through the morning.

When the doorbell sounded, she jumped, cursed herself, then shoved out of the chair. She rushed downstairs, swung the door open.

And locked her arms around her friend.

"You're here! I'm so glad you're here."

"It took me about ten minutes to shove my eyes back in my head after I saw this *house,* but I'm here. You okay, Son?"

"Yes, yes. Just really glad to see you."

Sonya pulled her, her suitcase, and her shoulder bag inside.

"Well, oh my God, wow."

"I know, right?"

"It bears repeating. Wow. This is like . . . No, it's like nothing else. Look at that staircase! The chandelier! The floors, the every-freaking-thing. I know I had a video tour, but holy crap, Sonya, actually seeing it."

"I felt the same way. I think I'm sort of getting used to it, then I realize, no. Not really."

"I want to see it all." Cleo pulled off her hat, and her gorgeous hair sprang free. "Every single inch. And this is the murdered bride. Oh, Sonya, she's so young and beautiful."

As she took off her coat, Cleo stepped

toward the portrait.

"He must have loved her, really loved her, to have this painted after."

"And hanged himself as soon as it was finished," Sonya added.

"Which is awful. Tragic all around. But she's still here, isn't she? Young and beautiful. So, where do we start?"

"Turret sitting room. Coat closet."

She hadn't started a fire in there, or in the front parlor. But in both rooms fires burned cheerfully as she guided Cleo through.

"I have to come up with better than *wow*, but I'm sticking with it for now."

"Let's take your bag up so you can see where you're sleeping. We can go through the rest down here later. I picked out your room," Sonya continued as they started up, "but you can pick another if you want. We got plenty of 'em."

"You'd have to in this place. The library! Oh yeah, it's just perfect. What a work space. I'm crazy about it."

"Me, too." Or it was making her crazy. Take your pick. "I'm on the other side, end of the hall."

"Let's start there, work our way back. Jesus, the length of this hallway! The color, that incredibly rich rose, the arches. Is this his art?"

"A lot of it," Sonya said as they walked. "But apparently art runs in the family. I've found some signed Arthur Poole, Jane Oglebee — who was a Poole — a Leticia Poole Bennett, and so on."

"Talent in the genes. And you've got double doors. Pretty freaking grand."

Cleo nodded as she wandered Sonya's room. "Collin Poole knew how to honor the history of this place, and live well while he was at it. And the view. I'd stand here and picture myself as the heroine in one of those old Gothic novels. You've got your own sitting room, which is both classy and adorable, and this very classy bedroom with a changeable painting for a view."

She turned, grinned. "Score. Let's see where you put me."

"You've got choices." Sonya led her back down the hall. "But I started with this."

"A sitting room? Oh, look at the wallpaper." Cleo traced a finger over a bluebird in flight.

"This is listed as Bluebird. The rooms have names."

"Of course they do. This is just gorgeous. The little curved divan, those sweet lamps. And the bedroom. I've got a canopy bed! And a view."

The sea view opened to a room of rich blues and deep roses with a fireplace, where Sonya had started a fire in anticipation, facing a bed with an open canopy draped in the same tones.

The white lilies and pink rosebuds Sonya

had arranged in a slender cobalt vase sat on a long dresser with carved curved legs.

"I'm going to feel like a celebrity. A celebrity Gothic heroine. With her own adorable bathroom."

"There's another I thought about — it faces the forest, which is wonderful in its own way. So —"

"Uh-uh." Smile dreamy, hands on her hips, Cleo turned in a circle. "This is mine. I stake my claim."

To prove it she flopped onto the bed, stared up through the canopy at the ceiling.

"I can help you unpack."

"Oh, the hell with that. Later. I want to see more." She sat up. "Is there a creepy basement?"

"There is."

"I want to see that, too."

"You're on your own with that. I really, really missed you, Cleo."

"I missed you. I swear, it feels like months instead of a couple weeks." She popped up. "Come on. Show me more. Then let's pick a room and open a bottle of wine."

Sonya showed her more, and felt even the dregs of anxiety drain at Cleo's delighted reaction to everything. When they stood shivering on the widow's walk, the snow began to fall.

"Imagine standing here, looking out, and not knowing when the person you loved would come home."

"The Pooles not only built ships but sailed them," Sonya said. "So I guess more than one stood here looking out and wondering."

"I see what you mean about the forest. It's magical. It's all magical." She wrapped an arm around Sonya's waist. "My best friend fell into magic. I love this, Sonya. I love it for you.

"Let's go have wine."

They went down, opened a bottle. For now, Sonya noted, the iPad stayed quiet. And the cabinets in the kitchen remained closed.

If she'd imagined it all, maybe she needed to see a doctor.

They took the wine — Cleo's pick — into the solarium to sit in the warm among the plants and watch the snow fall.

"Now." Cleo settled back. "We're just into our second decade of knowing each other. What's worrying you?"

"Not nearly as much with you here. I think all this alone time in this big house started making me a little crazy. I love it, and didn't expect to. I didn't expect to be so determined to stay. I miss you. I miss Mom. Sometimes I miss living in the city. But I want to be here."

"It's yours, Son. And it's not just a house, it's your history, and generations of family. You're making it your home. I can see pieces of you all around. Not just the library, though that's all you now. You don't love it just because it's amazing, and it is. You love it because it's you."

"I'm a big old house on the coast of Maine?"

"Not the location necessarily, but yeah, the rest. You always wanted this." Lifting a finger, Cleo ticked it in the air. "I'm not wrong there."

"I did. It feels sort of strange to know I did want this."

"When that asshole whose name I won't speak unless it's in a curse wanted to look at houses, you wanted something just like this. Smaller scale, for sure, but a house with history, with character, with quirks. All he wanted was a big fancy box with *status symbol* all over it."

"You're right about that."

"I'm here until Monday morning." Settling back, Cleo toasted both of them. "I know your mom's coming up in a few weeks. And I'll come up again. Trust me on that because I miss you. Plus, I love this place, too."

"You could stay."

"I've got a meeting Monday afternoon, so —"

"No, I mean stay-stay. Move in."

Cleo's topaz eyes widened. "Move in . . . here?"

"Why not? You can work anywhere, just like me. It's only three hours to Boston to have meetings if you can't do it by remote. Your family can come and stay anytime. At all. You can have that bedroom. Or you could take the apartment if you want more space."

The words tumbled out in a rush.

"You know we can live together. We did it for four years in college. And it's such a big house. We could go days without seeing each other if we wanted to."

"Well, holy shit, Sonya." More than stunned, Cleo pushed a hand through her hair. "And here comes another wow."

"You could think about it, couldn't you? Just think about it. The village — it's not Boston by any stretch, but it's charming, and there are some restaurants, some shops. Have some more wine," Sonya said, almost desperately now, "and just think about it."

"You're serious about this?"

"I'm serious."

And wanted it more than she'd let herself admit.

"You fell for Collin's studio during the video tour, and when we just walked through again. It's yours. Or you could set up anyplace you want, but you know you could work there. And have the space and the time to paint more. You really only paint in the summer now, outside, because your apartment doesn't have the light or space. You'd have it here."

Eyes narrowed, Cleo pointed a finger. "You're playing dirty with that turret space."

"It's made for you. You have to at least think about it."

"It's hard to think of anything else right now."

"Good. That's good." Bracing herself, Sonya took a long sip of wine. "Because I need to tell you either I'm having some sort of a breakdown, I've got a brain tumor, or the manor's haunted."

Cleo said nothing for a moment, then picked up her own glass. "Those are words I never expected to hear coming out of my most sensible friend."

"I know. I know. But —"

Cleo held up a hand. "You're not having a breakdown, you don't have a damn brain tumor. And of course the manor's haunted."

"I don't know how to . . ." As she stared, Sonya's breath hitched in, hitched out.

"How do you know it's haunted? They haven't done anything since you've been here."

"Well, Jesus, Son, because they're *here.* Because I felt them the minute I walked in. At least one of my wows was for them." Cleo angled her head.

"What do they do?"

"They — they — God, I can't sit down." She pushed up, paced around the plants. "They open doors, shut them. Move things. Music starts playing on my iPad. Sometimes they open all the kitchen cabinets. They clean out the wood-burning fireplaces and set the logs — I think they bring logs in, too. They make up my bed in the morning, and turn it down at night."

"Do you thank them?"

Sonya goggled. "Thank them?"

"If someone made up my bed and turned it down for me, I'd thank them."

"No, I haven't thanked them, or it, or . . ."

"Because you didn't want to believe they exist."

"Why would I?" Exhausted by the rant, Sonya dropped down again. "Why would anybody want to believe they might be living in a haunted house? Last night . . ."

She closed her eyes, breathed deep.

"Last night, someone pounded on the door. The front door. It woke me up. And when I looked out the window, I swear, Cleo, there was a blizzard. Snow, howling wind. I went down. I thought someone had an accident or their car broke down. But when I opened the door, there was nothing. No snow, nobody, no howling wind. I didn't dream it."

"Okay." With a nod, Cleo took another sip of wine. "It'll take me two or three weeks to get everything together and move up here."

"You —" Sonya covered her face with her hands and burst into tears.

"Aw, come on, Son. Come on." Rising, Cleo shifted seats and wrapped around her friend. "It's okay. We'll be roomies again. In really big rooms. You don't think I'd let you have a haunted house all to yourself."

"I love you so much."

"I love you right back."

"You're sure — not about loving me, but moving here?"

"Absolutely sure. And I hope whoever's in charge of housekeeping turns down my bed, too."

"If they don't, I will."

With a laugh, Cleo drew back. "We're going to have some fun. Anyway, if loving my best friend and the ghosts hadn't done it, that turret studio did. I've been obsessed with it since we FaceTimed."

"Do you want the apartment?"

Laughing, Cleo gave Sonya a little shove. "Do you think I'm giving up the beautiful Bluebird? No possible way. Come on. Let's go get me unpacked."

They unpacked, then finished the wine in one of the sitting rooms by the fire. They made canned tomato soup and grilled cheese sandwiches for dinner — a college-days staple.

Over another bottle of wine, they huddled on the sofa in the front parlor, sharing a bowl of popcorn and making plans.

When they finally went upstairs, Sonya pulled Cleo into her bedroom. "See! Do you see? You know I haven't been up here. But the fire's on, the bed's turned down."

"Say thank you."

"Thank you? I —"

"Now let's go see if I got the same service."

When Cleo walked in, saw the gas fire glowing, the bed turned down, her reaction was to clap her hands together and laugh.

"All right! That's so sweet. Thank you!"

"There are parts of you I'll never fully understand."

"Born in the bayou," Cleo sang.

"But you weren't."

"My grand-mère was. I'm going to sleep like a queen. See you in the morning."

Sonya might have shaken her head as she walked back to her room. But when she slipped into bed, she smiled knowing Cleo slept just a few rooms away.

"Sonya! Wake up!"

With the stage-whisper voice in her ear and the hand shaking her shoulder, Sonya shot from dead asleep to wide awake with a single wild jolt.

"What? What?"

"Ssh! Listen!" Cleo gripped her shoulder now.

The piano music seemed to float upstairs. "Do you hear that?" In the dim light of the fire, Sonya clutched at Cleo with both hands. "Tell me you hear that."

"Of course I hear it. It's why I'm waking you up at three in the morning. We have to go check it out."

"We have to go check it out," Sonya repeated, struggling against dread as she got out of bed.

"Do you know the song?" Still whispering, Cleo tugged Sonya out of the room. "It sounds familiar. Sort of familiar."

"I thought I dreamed it."

"Unless you and I are having the same dream at the same time while we're walking out of your sitting room, that's a no."

As they approached the staircase, the music came clearer.

"Wait." Sonya dashed into the library, arrowed toward the fireplace. She grabbed the poker.

"Son, I don't think a piano-playing ghost is looking for a fight. Plus, what are you going to do with that? Kill them?"

Gripping the poker with both hands, Sonya sent Cleo a don't-argue-with-me glare.

They crept down the stairs, and when they reached the base, Sonya nodded toward the music room. Light flickered there, as if from candles or flames in a hearth.

The song played on as they approached. Then came a long, distinctly human sigh, and it faded away.

Armed with the poker, Sonya rushed the doorway. She saw nothing but shapes and shadows in the dark. Cursing, she groped for the light switch.

Under the glitter of the chandelier, no one sat at the piano. But for the instruments, the furniture, the room was empty.

"This is bullshit. I saw light in here, and I can still smell candles. They heard us coming and took off."

"Sonya, we were almost at the door when it went dark and the music stopped. Nobody could've gotten by us without us seeing them."

"There could be a passageway. Another passageway, like for the servants." Determined, she put the poker down to search along the walls. "The wainscoting, the — what do you call it? — chair rail. There could be a button or pull worked in."

"I'm going to do reverse *X-Files.* You don't want to believe."

"Of course I don't want to believe." Her voice pitched up two full registers. "Especially at three in the morning I don't want to believe some ghost got the urge to play the damn piano. Help me look."

Obliging, Cleo took the next wall. "You'd rather believe someone's sneaking around the house, opening doors, moving things, and so on, and playing the piano in the middle of the night? This person can also blow out the candles and zip into a secret passage in about two seconds?"

"At least I could give them a good smack with the poker and tell them to get the hell out of my house. So yeah, I'd rather believe that."

She stopped, scrubbed her hands over her face. "And no, I don't actually believe that. Before you got here today, I was torn between accepting there's something in the house or accepting I was going crazy. Hallucinating. Maybe that brain tumor."

"Well, I am here, and I can tell you you're not crazy or hallucinating." Cleo walked over, wrapped an arm around Sonya's shoulders. "There's more than one something in this house. And the one playing the piano's a female."

"The sigh. I heard it, too."

"She's sad."

"I don't think many people are happy to be dead."

"Maybe it's Astrid. Getting murdered on your wedding day's bound to make you sad. The song . . ." Wandering to the piano, Cleo tried to pick it out. "Sort of like that, right? The basic notes. I really think I've heard it before, but I can't place it."

"And that's the most important element in this scenario?"

"Could be a clue." Cleo brightened. "It's like we're Nancy Drew and this is *The Case of the Haunted Piano.*"

"I'm going back to bed."

"Good idea. The candle wax is still a little soft in these tapers," she said as she poked a finger in one.

"You're not the least bit freaked out."

"Not yet. Right now I'm freaking fascinated. Hey, don't forget your poker."

"Ha ha. You'd've been glad I had it if we walked in here to an axe murderer."

"That would be the axe murderer who takes time out to play the piano? The axe murderer who sweetly turns down the beds at night? That one?"

Sonya let out a sigh of her own and took Cleo's hand as they walked upstairs. "I'm glad you're here."

"I'm gladder of it every second. Oh, when I was falling asleep, I had this thought."

"Don't tell me if it involves calling in Paranormal R Us."

"Not that. When the lawyer and the cousin come tomorrow to move those things you wanted, can I ask them to move anything else if I see something?"

"I don't see why not. Did you see something?"

"We went through before we talked about me staying, and working in that fabulous turret space. I could look, pay more attention, with that in mind. Anyway, tomorrow."

They paused at Cleo's door.

"There's a desk, a great desk. The one you use now, it's serviceable, but you could have better. And you need some seating."

"Got a mental list going on it, and a couple

other things. Tomorrow," Cleo repeated. "We've got men coming, so I need sleep so I don't look like a hag."

"And that happens never."

"If you hear something and I don't, come get me."

"Count on it. Good — I hope — night."

Sonya expected the same restless, patchy post–three a.m. sleep she'd experienced the night before, but she dropped off in seconds.

And woke to soft morning light.

Since she expected Cleo would sleep at least two more hours, she went to make coffee. She'd squeeze in a little work, then they'd do a kind of brunch before they went on a hunt for what Cleo could use in her studio — and anywhere else she wanted.

The idea that her friend would live there gave her such a boost. And it didn't hurt, really, to know she hadn't imagined things, forgotten things.

Optimism ruled the day as she sat at her desk.

Even her tablet deciding to play "Come Saturday Morning" didn't dim it.

Just after eleven, Cleo came in.

Her hair fell in perfect corkscrews. The lids on her long, amber eyes showed just a hint of bronze. She wore snug black jeans with an ombré sweater that went from the palest of lavender to the deepest purple.

"You're all duded up."

"Company's coming. Male-type company." She struck a pose. "First impressions are first. Plus, my best friend bought me this sweater because she knows what I like.

"Working?" she added. "I can get scarce."

"I was working until you got up." She checked the time. "They're not coming until after three, so I've got time to put myself together."

"I hate you can look like that before putting anything together. I've always hated you for that, but my love's stronger."

On cue, the music switched to Queen's "You're My Best Friend."

Cleo laughed in delight. "You've got like a ghost DJ. You know that's cool."

"I'll shut down, and we'll go have a girl brunch."

"Don't shut down yet. Let me see what you've got for the potter. We didn't get around to that last night."

"I'm running tests. I'm going to have it up and running next week."

"That's fast."

"Plenty of time to work here. First, here's what she had."

Cleo came around, looked over Sonya's shoulder. "Okay, I like her work. The site's not horrible."

"Load times are, and it didn't work worth shit on mobile devices. You saw the mood board there. And this is what I designed, she approved, and I'm testing."

Cleo cackled, gave Sonya a light punch on the shoulder as the website came on-screen.

"Okay, baby, that sings. Classy but approachable. Arty but down-to-earth. Strong colors, more impact. Good call on the little video. Can you enlarge it?

"Yeah, yeah. She's got a face — great bones — the hair shows them off. I may have to sketch that."

Sonya clicked on the Shop tab.

"And I change *like* her work to *love.* Your new format really shows it off."

"Xena's new pot's Anna's work."

"What?" Cleo walked over to the window. "How could I not have noticed her new outfit? Love it. And Xena looks happy with it."

"She's got some new buds coming in."

"So I see."

"Enough work. I've been up since eight, and I'm starved."

"I want to eat in that major dining room."

"Really?"

"Absolutely. We'll be completely bougie. You've got a big house, pal, let's use it."

"Boy, did I need you."

"And we'll talk about some terms."

"Terms?" Sonya shut down. "You're not paying rent, Cleo. I don't pay rent so you don't."

"I get that. I do, and it's appreciated. But I

will contribute. I'll do the grocery shopping — we'll make weekly lists — and buy the food. I'm a better cook than you, which isn't saying much about either of us, so I'll handle dinner — let's say five nights a week. Roughly."

"We'll work it out."

"Yeah, we will." Cleo grinned as they started downstairs. "It's what we do."

Chapter Thirteen

At Cleo's insistence, Sonya "duded up" after brunch. It seemed wasteful, since she'd probably help move furniture, but at that point in time, if Cleo had asked her to do handsprings in the foyer, she'd have tried it.

So in rust-colored suede pants and a stone-gray turtleneck she guided Cleo through storage areas again.

"This desk." Sonya had to maneuver her way back to it while Cleo cooed over a floor lamp shaped like a mermaid holding a crystal ball.

"I want this lamp in the studio."

Sonya swiped at her hair, nodded. "I should've known that."

"She's perfect. I'm doing a book on mermaids."

"Did I know that?"

"I haven't started yet. It's the Monday meeting. An adult book." She circled the lamp. "Coffee-table, illustrations depicting various lores, various cultures."

"That's your wheelhouse."

"It is. The desk. Oh, oh, oh!" She danced to it.

"It's going to weigh a ton," Sonya predicted. "And it'll take some work to get it down there, considering the L-shape extension."

"Where there's a will. It's gorgeous." Reverently, Cleo ran a hand over the surface and its leather insert. "I wonder what kind of wood it is."

"No clue. But drawers for supplies, room for your monitor, and you could use the extension for hand sketching."

"Well, I want it, and the mermaid. I can bring my own desk chair, it works for me. Same with my desk lamp. I could probably use a small couch, settee, divan. Something curved would be nice, considering the shape of the studio. At least one chair for when my best friend hangs out up there."

Laughing, she looked around. "God, Sonya, it's like shopping for free in a fabulous antiques shop."

A board creaked overhead.

"Attic space," Sonya murmured.

"I remember — the trunks of clothes and more. Let's go see."

Hedging, Sonya slid her hands into her pockets. "It's pretty chilly up there."

"I remember from yesterday. I didn't really get a good look."

They went up now, and Cleo pointed.

"I wanted a small, curved sofa, and there it is."

"You know that was covered with a sheet yesterday — and when I went through before that."

"Well, it's not covered now, and it's just right." Beyond delighted, Cleo circled it. "I love this deep royal blue color. It's velvet, and look at the hearts carved in the frame. So sweet! It'll really work in there. A chair, a couple tables, and kaboom, a sitting area, a work area, that view, and room to paint when that mood strikes."

"Use Collin's supplies. They'll go to waste if you don't. Later on — when it's not as cold up here — we should go through everything. Take the sheets and tarps off, and go through it all."

"Then we will." After one more circle, Cleo nodded. "You know, I think we could get that little sofa down there."

Sonya studied it. "Won't know unless we try."

It proved heavier than it looked, but small enough to maneuver down steps and hallways.

When, a little out of breath, they set it in the curve of windows in the studio, they fist-bumped.

The doorbell bonged.

"Now I know why it's so freaking loud. Well, let's go let the manly men in, and hope they're up for it."

They went down, opened the door to the two men. And two dogs.

"It's Mookie!" Since the big blond swished his feathery tail, Sonya crouched down. And was rewarded with more wags and a nuzzle. "And who's this?"

"That's Jones," Owen told her.

Sonya cooed over the scrappy-looking black dog with an eye patch over his left eye.

"What happened to his eye?"

"He lost it in a bar fight with a Doberman."

Hands busy petting two at once, Sonya looked up. Owen shrugged.

"That's the story I got."

"I bet the Doberman got the worst of it." Cleo stepped back, gestured. "Bring them on in out of the cold."

"Yes, sorry. Cleo Fabares, Trey Doyle, Owen Poole."

"Nice to —" Trey broke off. "Mook!"

The dog, already heading into the front parlor, glanced back.

"He tends to make himself at home."

"Fine with me. Let me get your coats. First, we really appreciate the help, and second, full disclosure. We've found more stuff to move."

Owen handed Sonya his coat. "Got beer?"

"Yes."

"Then we're good."

"You're a tough little guy, aren't you?" Cleo bent to scratch Jones between the ears, along his square jaw. He huffed.

"He doesn't think of himself as little."

Giving her hair a toss, Cleo shot Owen a quick, side-eyed smile. "Well, it's the size of the fight in the dog, isn't it?"

"Jones has plenty of it. Where's the accent from?"

"Louisiana. Lafayette." She gave them both the regional pronunciation.

Sonya glanced in the parlor as Mookie sniffed his way around.

"Hunting for treasure," Trey explained. "Collin used to hide a dog biscuit or rawhide bone, so Mookie could . . . I guess we missed that one," he said as Mookie nosed under a chair cushion and came out with a dog treat.

"Well, hell." Owen dug into a pocket of the coat Sonya still held. He took out a small biscuit, tossed it to Jones, who fielded it with a quick snap. "Fair's fair."

"That's it. I'm getting one."

"We're getting a dog?" The idea had Cleo slapping her hands together. "We need a cat, too, Son. This place is made for a faithful hound and a good, slinky cat."

"More disclosure." Sonya carried the coats into the closet. "Cleo's going to move in. That's okay, isn't it, Trey? I mean, it doesn't break any terms, does it?"

"Yeah, it's okay, and no, it doesn't. It's good. Welcome aboard."

"Thanks." Cleo spread her arms. "I don't

know who could resist a place like this, but I'm not one of them."

From the library, Cyndi Lauper rang out with "Girls Just Want to Have Fun."

"And that," she said with a laugh, "is only one more reason why. Did everybody but Sonya know the place is haunted?"

"She had full disclosure there." Trey hooked his thumbs in his jean pockets. "She wasn't buying it."

"So that's not unusual?" Sonya asked. "Cuing up songs on my tablet?"

"They like music," Trey said simply.

"And you." She pointed at Owen. "No reaction?"

"I'm more into rock than pop, but Lauper's always cool."

"My friend's a realist." Cleo gave Sonya a one-armed hug. "So this is a little tough for her. I'll balance that out."

"Let's not keep these men and their dogs standing in the foyer. We've got things moving from there to here, and here to there. If any of it's too much, that's fine. But I have beer."

She led them up to start with the Victrola.

"That's a nice piece." Owen ran a hand over the wood cabinet. "In damn good shape, too."

"I meant it, Owen. If you want something, it's yours."

"He can't have the mermaid."

Interest flickered as Owen turned to Cleo. "What mermaid?"

"She's in another section — a floor lamp — but you can't have her. She's already mine. I'll negotiate on the desk in case it has any sentimental meaning. I'll go as far as rock, paper, scissors on the settee we already moved, but I stand firm on the mermaid."

"Anything but the mermaid," Sonya qualified. "I want to move the Victrola down to the music room. Unless you want it, Owen."

"I'm good."

They hauled it down, then the cabinet for sheet music while Sonya and Cleo carried boxes of old records.

The dogs trailed up, trailed down. Then sensibly wandered into the library to nap by the fire.

"That's where I want to put Collin's painting. Johanna's portrait. I can find another place for the still life. If you need a break —"

"Sonya." Trey set a hand on her shoulder. "We carried two pieces. I think we've got more in us."

"We've got the mermaid, and a big desk. Cleo's taking over Collin's studio."

"You paint?" Owen asked as they started back up.

"Now and then. I make a living illustrating."

"What's the difference?"

"How much time do you have?"

"Dumb it down."

"Okay, condensed version." She gestured to a painting as they walked. "Stands on its own, eye of the beholder. An illustration is connected to text, to serve a purpose, and — hopefully — they enhance each other."

"Okay."

They wound their way up, and to the mermaid.

"Okay," Owen said again, with reverence. "Okay, she's a beauty."

"Mine."

Ignoring Cleo, he ran his hand over the carving, the long fall of windswept hair, the knowing smile, the smooth breasts.

"She's solid mahogany, Trey." He glanced at Cleo. "What's her name?"

Cleo had already given him points for helping Sonya, had added more for Jones. With the question, she doubled them. "Circe."

"That works. Circe's no lightweight."

"The desk won't be either," Sonya warned.

"All right." Rubbing his hands together, Trey nodded. "A challenge."

"Somebody got it up there, so somebody can get it down." Owen worked his way to it, crouched down to test the drawers. "Cherrywood, pristine. The wood's a little thirsty. This and the mermaid need a good buff with paste wax. Don't be using any supermarket spray shit on these pieces. Any of them. You can do the lemon oil, orange oil between, but once, maybe twice a year, you buff with a good paste wax."

"We'll get some."

"None of my business." Owen straightened, turned to Sonya. "But do you figure the two of you can maintain all this furniture the way it needs to be? Keep it dusted, protected? Not to mention the acres of wood floors?"

"No." Sonya huffed out a breath. "No, I have to swallow getting a cleaning service. It's on my list for next week, or the week after. I wish you'd take something, Owen. More than one something."

As she spoke, a sheet slid slowly to the floor. Sonya gripped her elbows.

"That's creepy. Come on, that's just creepy."

"Little bit." But Owen walked over to the chest of drawers with the sheet now pooled at its feet. "Needs a little work. Got a handle missing. The bottom of this drawer's cracked. Looks like some dog chewed on the front leg here. I'll take it."

"Really?"

"I can fix it. And maybe you'll stop feeling so damn guilty."

And with that, he earned more points on Cleo's scoreboard.

"Look at the back, Owen." Trey crooked a finger and grinned. "Somebody — probably a kid — carved his initials down at the bottom. ODP. Owen David Poole. Your initials, too."

"Yeah, well. Like I said, I'll take it. Let's tackle the desk first. It's going to be a bitch."

It took some muscle, some geometry, and some inventive cursing. Sonya hugged one of the drawers to her chest as the men turned it, braced it, eased it into the studio.

"You deserve a lot more than beer."

"Oh, oh, look at the way the light hits it! Can you put it over there?" Cleo ran ahead of them, spread her arms, swooped them down. "Right here, angled this way. Look how it's already coming together in here. I'm going to name my firstborn Collin Oliver Owen."

"You should put a painting on the easel, Cleo, when you're not working there. It just adds. But," Sonya added, "Johanna goes downstairs."

Trey walked over to the portrait. "You said you found this in that closet?"

"Yes. Maybe it made him sad to look at it, so he put it away, but —"

"Sonya, I can't count the number of times I've been in this studio. And I went through this space myself after Collin died. I've never seen this portrait before. And there wasn't a painting in the closet. He stored blank canvases in there."

"It was in there."

"I believe you."

"That's Johanna." Owen stepped over to stand by Trey. "I've seen pictures. Collin didn't paint people much. Landscapes and that sort of thing."

"That's a shame," Cleo said. "Because he had the talent for it. She's beautiful. His use of light and lines and movement? Beautiful." Sighing over it, Cleo tapped a hand on her heart. "He loved her. It shows."

"It was in the closet," Sonya said again.

"Then I'd say he wanted you to have it." Trey turned to her. "Let's get the rest of what you want moved, then we can talk about it over that beer."

Sonya pressed her fingers to her eyes. "Are you always this calm?"

"Mostly he is," Owen told her. "But if you push the wrong button, step back."

It took well over another hour, then an outdoor break for the dogs, before they gathered in the kitchen.

"That took a while." Cleo got a bottle of wine while Sonya poured beer into pilsners. "And we owe you more than the beer. I don't suppose anyone cooks."

"He cooks better than I do," Trey replied.

Considering, Cleo looked at Owen. "You cook?"

"Somewhat above average."

"That's about where I hit, which is a full step up from Sonya. I can make a pasta thing."

"I could eat a pasta thing."

"All right then. I'm going to see what we've got around here."

"I am going to cook — for the Doyles." Decision made, Sonya thought. "How about next Friday night? Or Saturday?"

Trey took out his phone, studied his calendar. "Friday looks clear. Anna and Seth have a thing Saturday."

"You have everyone's schedule on there?"

"He's an organizer." Owen took a counter stool. "Whether you want him to be or not."

"Just avoids scheduling conflicts. I'll pass the word."

"Let me know if that works for everyone. I think seven's good. Owen, you're more than welcome."

"I'll let you have this Doyle thing, but thanks."

"There's a chair at the table, and possibly an edible meal if you change your mind. Now." She picked up her wine, turned to Trey. "Can we talk about the invisible elephant in the room?"

"Why don't you tell us what's been going on? Besides the song list."

"Okay." Sonya paced along the island as Cleo hunted up what she wanted. "Doors open, doors close, boards creak. I can — could — dismiss that. Old house."

"And solid as the rock it's built on," Owen pointed out. "The floors — ruler level. Sure it's settled, but you're not going to have doors open and close on their own."

"I get that. I'm not pulling a Scully. Not anymore. The day you moved my printer for me, Trey? I'd watched a movie the night before upstairs in the library. I woke up, and I had a throw over me, the TV was shut off, the remote back in its drawer. And when we went up with the printer? The throw was folded again."

She paused, sipped. "I need to start documenting. I use the fireplace in the library every day, and every day it's cleaned out and set. I'll come down and make coffee in the morning, and when I get back, my bed's made. And at night, turned down like a hotel maid service."

"I could use one of those," Owen commented. "Who wouldn't go for one of those?"

Taking a moment from her search, Cleo glanced back at him. "I know, right?"

"I thought I was just losing it, forgetting things. Oh, the things on my dresser, they're in different places than where I put them."

"Piano music," Cleo reminded her as she began to mince garlic.

"Middle of the night. I thought I dreamed it, or imagined it. But we both heard it last night, and went down. There was light — like candles make — in the music room. Until we got there, and no light, no music."

"I can't place the song." Closing her eyes

to bring it back, Cleo waved a finger. "Da-da-da-da, da-da-da-da."

" 'There was a young maid dwelling'," Trey sang in a clear, easy tenor. " 'And every youth cried well-a-day. Her name was Barbara Allen.' "

"That's it! Plus, he sings."

"An old folk song. The lyrics change depending, but the tune's the same."

"I've heard it," Sonya murmured. "It's sad."

"He's dying, but she turns away. He dies brokenhearted, she dies out of guilt and sorrow. So yeah," Trey agreed. "Pretty damn sad."

"I think it's Astrid." Cleo added the garlic to the pan where she'd melted butter. "Murdered on her wedding day. Doesn't get much sadder."

"I've come in here, and all the cabinet doors are open, and one day — maybe it was stuck — but I went out for a walk, unlocked the door, but I couldn't get back in. Not at first."

"You didn't tell me about that one."

"I forgot. And the night before Cleo came, I heard someone pounding on the front door. It woke me up. When I got up, there was a blizzard. I could hear the wind just howling, and see the snow flying. I thought, someone's had an accident or needs help. But when I went down, opened the door, no one, and it was a clear night. No howling wind, no flying snow.

"I nearly stepped outside, then I remembered getting stuck out there. So I didn't."

"That's not playful. That's on the mean side." Trey exchanged a look with Owen. "That's something I haven't heard before."

"No, me neither."

"Maybe I pissed them off. I don't have any experience in this area."

"But you're sticking," Trey pointed out.

"I'm sticking. Sometimes, like that night, I don't know why. But I want to be here. Another I forgot. I got out of the shower, started to wipe the steam from the mirror, and it was like someone wrote on it. Seven — the number. Seven lost."

"There were seven brides," Trey told her.

As she stirred in tomato paste, Cleo glanced back. "Like the musical?"

Owen looked blank; Trey laughed.

"No. Seven lost brides. Astrid was the first. Didn't you read the book?" he asked Sonya.

"I started it. I read about Astrid and Collin, and about his brother, Connor, and . . . Arabelle? And Hester Dobbs. I started on Connor and Arabelle's children."

"Keep reading."

"It read like Connor and Arabelle had a good, long life here. A bunch of kids."

"One of their daughters was the second bride. Don't sugarcoat it, Trey. Is that vodka?"

Frowning, Owen pointed toward the stove. "You're putting vodka in there?"

"It's essential for pasta in vodka sauce."

When Owen got up to take a look, Trey pointed to a stool. "Why don't you sit down?"

"Do I need to?" Sonya sat, reached down to pet Mookie when he walked to her.

"Her name was Catherine. She married William Cabot. They spent their wedding night at the manor with plans for a honeymoon, early spring, in Europe. She went outside that night, or early that morning. In a blizzard. She froze to death."

"She went out in her nightgown, just her nightgown," Sonya murmured, "and bare feet. She — she didn't feel the cold. She didn't feel it. There was a woman in a black dress by the seawall. And she walked all that way in the snow, in her bare feet. The woman took her hand — took her ring? Wedding ring? Then she felt the cold. She said something — the woman in the black dress. I couldn't hear. And Catherine tried to get back, but she was so cold, and she kept falling. Then she didn't get up again.

"I dreamed it." Pressing a hand to her bouncing heart, Sonya rubbed it there. "How could I have dreamed it?"

"I'm going to give you creepy on this, Sonya." Cleo went to her, hugged her hard. "That's a horrible dream. It's horrible. Is that what happened?"

"No one could explain why she went out in the storm. But when they found her the next day, she wasn't wearing her wedding ring. They never found it."

"Hester Dobbs's curse, according to local legend." Owen stirred the sauce. "A bride every generation dies — on her wedding day, or within the year. At the manor. I'm not sure about the ring thing."

"Johanna would be the last? Now there's me?" On an expelled breath, Sonya picked up her wine again. "Good thing I'm not a bride."

"I never bought into the legend. Some, like Lillian Crest, died in childbirth. Unfortunately, not that uncommon. Especially back then, and carrying twins. I'd have to refresh my memory," Trey added. "But I think one, at least, died choking on some food. Also not that uncommon in the nineteenth and early twentieth centuries. And you had others, like Connor and Arabelle, who lived long lives here."

"But seven, like on the mirror."

"Someone wanted you to know." After another squeeze, Cleo went to get a pot to cook the pasta.

"Collin wanted you here. He wanted to give you this. I knew him all my life. He'd never hurt anyone."

"He was a good guy," Owen agreed. "He cared about family. You're family."

"You're family."

"Yeah." Leaning back on the counter by the stove, Owen looked Sonya in the eye. "And he gave me what I wanted, what I needed. It's appreciated. I wasn't sure what I'd think of you — long-lost cousin from Boston — but I figure Collin had his reasons for wanting you here. And you'll figure it out.

"How soon is this ready to eat?"

"It needs another twenty."

"I'm getting another beer. Don't let the witch scare you off."

"My grand-mère's a witch — so she says. I'm going to ask her for advice. I'll be back here to stay as soon as I can."

"This pisses me off."

"Here comes the stubborn." Cleo carried the pot of water to the stove.

"Determined. I like *determined.* So no, I'm not going to let some dead, murderous witch scare me off. It's not her house. It's mine. I don't believe in curses, but if I did? If you can cast one, you can break one."

Cleo picked up her wine, toasted. "That's damn right."

"It's easy to say that when I'm sitting here with three people and two dogs, but I mean it."

The music rang out. "It's Gonna Be Alright."

"The Ramones." Owen walked in with a beer for himself, another for Trey. "Now we're talking. You've got Trey's number in your phone?"

"Yes."

"Give it." He held out his hand. "I'll put mine in. You're freaked, you call."

Trey laid a hand over hers. "You're not alone, Sonya."

Sonya glanced toward the music. "That's for damn sure."

Chapter Fourteen

Monday morning, Sonya stood in the foyer with Cleo.

"You've got two capable men who'd come if you needed them. You'll have company for your dinner party on Friday."

As she spoke, Cleo took Sonya's hand, glanced around. "Your mom's coming the next weekend. Then I'll be back."

"Don't worry about me. If you have worry to spare, save it for the innocents subjected to my first, very likely only, attempt at pot roast."

"It'll be great. When you set your mind to something, Son, you get it done. Maybe that's why you're here. Houses need people, don't you think, or they're just walls.

"I think, seeing you here, you needed this house. And it needs you."

She wrapped Sonya in a hug. "I've got to go make that meeting. I'll send some of my stuff with Winter when she comes. Just shove it out of your way until I get here."

"See you in a couple weeks."

Sonya watched Cleo walk to her car, load in her weekend bag. After a final wave, she watched her drive off.

The minute she closed the door, her tablet sang out with, "I Think We're Alone Now."

"I am not amused."

To her surprise, the track stopped, then picked up with Joel Corry's "Sorry."

Sonya just shook her head, and went upstairs. Before she started work, she decided she'd start documenting "incidents."

She backtracked as best she could and found something solid, even logical in making an organized list of the illogical.

Satisfied, she focused in on the Practical Art project.

For three hours, she worked undisturbed. The fire simmered, the house — and whatever inhabited it with her — stayed quiet, and the tests she ran, ran smooth.

"It's ready to go live," she told herself.

She texted Anna to give her a heads-up — and a request to send any desired changes asap.

She'd switch over to the caterer's project, she thought as she got up to add a log to the fire. That would give Anna time to review.

She'd barely settled down again when she got Anna's return text.

It's perfect! It's all perfect. Go!

"Okay then. Here we go."

She activated the website, the new social media, sent the blast she'd prepared to Anna's contact list — and the contacts she'd added to it.

Obsessively checked it all again on her desktop, her phone, her tablet. Shook her fists in the air, then texted back.

You're up, and you're beautiful!

Queen's "We Are the Champions" rocked out.

"I'll allow it," Sonya decided.

And singing along, she went down to get a celebratory Coke. Then got back to work.

The day passed productively and so well she had to talk herself into taking a break and fitting in that daily walk.

While she stood at the seawall hoping to see another whale, she got a text from Trey.

Excellent work on Anna's web page. Do you have any time this week to talk about doing the same for Doyle Law?

"Boy, do I!"

But she answered more professionally.

Absolutely. I can easily work around your schedule.

Wednesday? Four-thirty? Okay if I come to you?

That'll work. As long as you bring Mookie.

He's counting on it. See you then.

"All right. I will get this job." She turned, looked at the house. She saw the shadow in the window. Not a trick of the light.

Someone — something — stood there, watching as she watched.

Maybe it made her heartbeat shake its way up to her throat. Maybe it made her skin go cold. But Cleo was right.

She needed this house. Nothing and no one would push her out.

She went back in, but instead of going to work, she finally allowed herself to open the file Trey had sent her on dog rescues.

Twenty minutes later, she had an appointment and was on her way out the door again.

"This doesn't mean I'm bringing a dog home," she told herself as she drove to town. "It just means I'm starting the process of bringing a dog home. At some point."

In town, she made the turn away from the bay and followed the directions into a neighborhood of Cape Cods and Tudors with roomy lawns. As instructed, she pulled into the driveway of the third house on the right of Mulberry Lane.

The house had a covered front porch with a pair of benches and a welcome mat that read:

WIPE YOUR PAWS.

A calico cat sat in the front window; barking sounded before Sonya lifted her hand to knock.

The woman who answered wore a tie-dyed sweatshirt over black leggings. She had a dish towel over one shoulder, and her sunny blond hair was scooped back in a tail.

She shoved a pair of blue-framed glasses back up her nose as a trio of dogs danced around her feet.

"Sonya?"

"Yes."

"Lucy Cabot." She stuck out her hand. "Nobody bites."

"Good to know."

"Come on in. Settle down," she ordered, and the dogs more or less obeyed. The biggest, with fluffy white fur, thumped his fan of a tail as he sat. Another, sleek and brown with a pointed face, whined softly and sniffed at her boots.

And the third, the one whose photo had pulled her here, danced in place as he stared up at her with big brown eyes.

"Solo," she said, pointing at the biggest. "Lando. My boys are Star Wars fans. We're calling this little sweetie Yoda. We've only had him for a few days."

"Can I . . ."

"Of course. Lando! Sit, stay. Yoda is about ten months old," Lucy said when Sonya crouched down to pet him. "And he really is a sweetie. He's housebroken, current on his shots. He — as you can see — gets along just fine with other dogs, with cats — we have two — and people. He's great with kids — I have three."

Sonya heard it all, but vaguely, as she felt herself falling as the dog nuzzled her hand, then lifted both his front paws onto her knee.

"A prize-winning Boston terrier got seduced by a dachshund mix," Lucy explained. "So he's got the brindle terrier face and coloring and the stubby legs and slightly elongated body from his dad. He's no show dog, so they didn't want him."

"Aw," said Sonya, and felt her heart melting.

"But they kept him until he was weaned, I'll give them that. And when he was about four months old, gave him to a couple who ended up getting a divorce a few months after that. Neither wanted him, poor little guy.

"He likes you," Lucy observed. "But then, he likes everybody. Have you ever had a dog?"

"Yes." Sonya gave up, sat on the floor, and let the dog crawl into her lap and kiss her face. "When I was growing up. When I lived in Boston, worked in an office, I wasn't home enough to have a dog. It didn't seem fair. Look at you. Look at those ears."

"You're up at Lost Bride now."

"That's right, and I work from home."

"Planning on staying then?"

Cuddling the dog, Sonya looked up. "Yes."

"I'm asking because he deserves a stable home. He's been passed off twice already. I'd keep him myself because, well, he really is a sweetheart. But I made a deal with my husband we wouldn't have more animals than humans, and we've got two dogs, two cats, and a guinea pig."

Sonya ran a hand over the smooth, tiger-striped brown fur. "I'm making a home here. I can make a home for him. I was only going to look today." Sonya cupped the dog's face in her hands. "But here he is. Yoda's a good name."

"Is it?"

"What did they call him — the divorced couple?"

"Stubby."

"Oh, well. It's cute, I guess, but it's not dignified, is it? Yoda's dignified and wise. He looks wise. And Yoda was small but powerful."

"My boys'll be happy to know he's going with someone who knows her Star Wars."

"I can adopt him?"

"Looks to me like he's already adopted you.

Have you got supplies?"

"Not a thing," she said cheerfully. "We'll go shopping on the way home. If you can tell me the brand of food he likes, and the vet you use. We need stuff," she told Yoda. "We need to get you bowls and a bed. We need toys and treats."

At that all three dogs sent up a howl.

"You said the *t* word." Lucy laughed. "That's fine, treats all around. And you get an adoption package to get you started after we do the paperwork. You can take the bed he's been using because it'll comfort him. And because I like you."

"Thanks for that. I like you, too. What you do is just lovely and loving."

"Come on into the kitchen. We'll get those *t*'s, and the paperwork. My husband works for your cousins."

"At Poole Shipbuilders?"

"That's right."

"I met Owen this weekend, and Jones. And there's Mookie, so Yoda will have some friends."

"Trey Doyle's dog." Lucy nodded as she passed out treats. "Would you like some coffee?"

"If you're having some."

"Let's have some coffee, deal with this paperwork. Then you can take your boy home."

Since Lucy loaded her up, Sonya skipped

the shopping. Anything she needed she could pick up when she got the dinner party supplies.

On the drive, Yoda jumped into the back seat, planted his front paws on the window, and watched the world go by.

"I need to warn you, odd things happen at the manor. But we'll look out for each other. And look, just look at it. Is that the coolest house ever? I'm going to put your leash back on. We'll walk around. Lucy said it's smart to find a place for you to do what you need to do, then you'll mostly go there to do it."

She snapped the leash on, cuddled him again.

"Let's walk around our domain. I think around back's the best place for doing what you need to do."

She got out with him, and though she'd worried he'd pull on the leash, try to run, he just trotted along beside her.

"How could those people let you go? You're such a good boy."

He sniffed — a lot — trotted, then, to her delight, did what he had to do.

After rounding back to the car, she got the adoption basket. Made the second trip out for his bed before unleashing him.

The iPad played "Every Dog Will Have His Day."

He wandered and sniffed, but stayed close while she hung up her coat. Then followed her when she took the basket into the kitchen.

"Let's take your bed upstairs so you know where you sleep."

For the next hour she showed Yoda around, took pictures to text to her mother, Cleo, sent one to Lucy, and, after some mental back-and-forth, to Trey.

For that one she added the comment:

Presenting Mookie's new pal, Yoda. It's your fault. Thank you.

"Okay, there's a lot more house, but you don't have to see it all at once. We've hit the main places I live — for now. And I really need to squeeze another hour in on this project."

She cupped his face, kissed his nose.

"So you could maybe take a nap by the fire."

For the first nap, in any case, he preferred under her desk. But she got her hour in, even with pauses to answer Yoda texts.

Since the dog seemed content, she put another hour in before shutting down to make them both dinner.

After a successful post-dinner walk, they settled down by the library fire. Yoda curled beside her while she read another section of Poole family history.

"In 1864, Hugh Poole's wife of nine months, Marianne, died in childbirth delivering twins. Owen and Jane. He remarried — Carlotta — in 1866, had three more kids. One son died in infancy. And how awful is that?"

She closed the book. "That makes Marianne the third bride, if we're counting."

After taking the dog out for one last round, she settled in for the night. Yoda appeared to find his bed by the fire more than acceptable.

She didn't wake at three when the clock sounded, or stir at the drifting music. But the dog's ears pricked up. He wandered out, wandered down.

And tail wagging, walked through the candlelight to the piano to sit.

When invited, he perched his front paws on the bench and nuzzled the hand that stroked him.

In the morning, Sonya started her new routine. She made coffee, put on her outdoor gear, leashed the dog, and walked him outside.

She had hopes that, in time, he'd handle the early-morning and late-night session on his own.

He ate his breakfast while she ate hers and checked her emails.

"Gotta go to work," she told him.

He followed her to the stairs, started up with her. Then stopped by the hidden door, wagged his tail.

"Something in there?" She shook off a chill. "Maybe, but we're not going in there. Not today."

In the bedroom, she let out a long breath at the bed — freshly made, pillows plumped. Yoda's dog bed had been nicely smoothed out.

"Okay. Okay, thanks. It's not necessary, but thank you. Fine."

After she'd changed into sweats, Yoda walked with her to the library.

He took his place under the desk; she put her mind into the work.

Twice she heard doors closing. So did he, as he lifted his head.

"It's not me," she muttered, and kept working.

She decided to consider walking-the-dog time as thinking time. The catering project had some challenges. The packages, the à la cartes, all the images, the pricing. And she wanted it appealing but streamlined so potential clients wouldn't have to wade through everything.

By the time she shut down for the day, she'd rejected two designs before settling on one that hit appealing and streamlined.

And because Yoda paused by the damn hidden door every time she went up or down, she opened it.

"You want to see, we'll go see. I'm supposed to work out anyway."

He did a lot of wandering, and occasionally stopped, wagged at nothing. At least nothing she could see.

He seemed entertained by the poor excuse for a workout she managed before she just wanted out.

This time, as she passed the bells, she heard one ring.

"The Gold Room. Which one is that? I think that's on the third floor. It's closed off."

She steeled her spine.

"We're going up."

She picked Yoda up as much for comfort as to spare his little legs the steps. She wasn't sure of the room, but she'd start where she had a blurry picture of a large room papered in deep gold. One of the important suites, she thought she recalled.

When they reached the third floor, she set Yoda down.

"It's cold up here. Colder than it was before." She opened doors one at a time. Draped furniture, floral wallpaper or creamy panels.

And as she reached for the knob of the door at the end of the long hall, Yoda growled.

She looked down to see him standing stiff-legged, his teeth bared.

"I won't let them hurt you. Or it."

Though her stomach clenched, her heart pounded, she pushed open the door. She swore the air flowed like ice. The drapery over the furniture shook with it. At the threshold, Yoda barked like a mad thing.

"It's my house." She scooped him up. "It's our house."

But because the dog trembled — or she did — she shut the door again.

"It's all right." As she walked away, she kissed Yoda's head. "Everything's all right. Let's go downstairs. You can have a treat."

He didn't manage a howl, but more of a whine. Still, she took it as a good sign.

In the kitchen, all the chairs at the small table lay on their backs on the floor.

"Somebody's trying to scare us, but they won't."

She put Yoda down, righted the chairs.

Then rewarded the dog with a treat, and herself with a glass of wine.

The dog brought comfort, a sweet little warm body to share her space. After their last-round walk, she decided to skip Poole family history for a night, and went back to her novel with Yoda curled in his own bed by the fire.

And slipped into sleep with the book sliding out of her hands.

Did she dream?

She stood in front of the mirror, the mirror from her father's dreams. The predators framing the glass seemed to snap and snarl.

But rather than her own reflection, she saw a room beyond, shadowy movements, as if the glass was a window and not a mirror at all.

The shadows began to shift, and the light grew brighter.

Firelight, candlelight illuminated a bedroom.

Hers?

Not the same bed, no, and the walls were covered with full-blown flowers with pink-tipped petals over a field of the palest gold. But she recognized the room she'd claimed in the manor as her own.

A woman lay on the bed, obviously in labor. Though Sonya had never seen a live birth, what she saw through the glass was unmistakable.

Two women attended her — midwives? — one bathing her face, the other kneeling between her legs.

And through the glass, Sonya heard voices, cries, muted at first, then growing louder and more distinct.

Not now, Sonya thought, through the glass wasn't now. The woman who stood at the head of the bed wore some sort of cap on her head, a long gray dress with a kind of apron over it. And she could see the button-type boots on the woman who knelt on the bed.

A dream, it had to be a dream, she thought as she lifted a hand to the glass.

And passed through it like she would a doorway.

They took no notice of her, the three women, as all their focus and energy centered on the work of bringing life into the world.

"The babe's coming! You must push! Draw up your strength, Mrs. Poole, and push!"

The woman in bed braced on her elbows. Her face a mask of exhausted pain as she bore down. Her scream, so primal, so fierce, lanced through Sonya's bones.

"There's the head, and a bonny one. One more push, dearie. One more now."

As the mother sobbed, the midwife turned the baby, drawing its shoulders free so the rest of him slid into her hands.

"You've a son, Mrs. Poole. A fine lad. Here we are, here we are now," the midwife said as she used a cloth to clean the newborn's face.

He let out a whimper, then followed it up with an insulted cry that had Sonya clutching her hands to her heart.

So beautiful. She hadn't known it could be so beautiful.

"I want him. I want my son."

The new mother, her long, dark hair matted with sweat, held out her arms. And as she wept, she laughed, and took the baby into her arms.

"He's Owen. I have a son. Ah, God! Take him, take him. The pain!"

"Take the young master, Ava. There's another yet to come. Don't push yet, dearie. Do the panting now, pant while I see to this."

"God help me."

So the beauty became pain with the midwife dripping sweat, and the mother begging it to stop.

So much blood. Should there be so much blood?

Sonya knew what she dreamed now. Marianne Poole, the third bride.

The daughter — Jane, Sonya remembered — was born in blood, her mewling cries like sorrow as her mother lay dying.

"I have to stop the bleeding. Fetch more towels. Fetch the master."

But it wouldn't stop, and as it flooded the sheets, Marianne lay pale as death. "Jane. My daughter is Jane. Owen David, Jane Elizabeth. My children."

Sonya's breath caught when Marianne's eyes, glazed with shock, met hers across the room. "My children. You come from them."

He burst into the room, a man with her father's eyes, her father's build, in a loose white shirt and black trousers. He rushed to the bed, took his wife's limp hand in both of his.

"Marianne, my love. I'm here."

"We have a son. We have a daughter."

"They need their mother. Stay for them." He pressed his lips to her hand. "Stay for me."

"I'll stay for them. I'll stay for you. I'll just . . . rest now," she said, and slipped away.

He wept, her hand clutched in his.

While the sobs racked him, the woman in black came in. She walked to the other side of the bed and took the ring from the dead woman's finger.

"No!" Sonya stepped forward to stop her. "You can't do that."

With madness and power in her eyes, Hester Dobbs said, "I can. I have. I will." She slipped the ring on her finger where another two glinted in the candlelight. "Do you think you can stop me? Stop what I forged in fire and blood? You're the ghost here."

Furious, Sonya lunged forward.

And woke standing by her own bed with the dog whining at her feet.

Shaken, she sat on the side of the bed, then gathered the dog up to comfort them both.

"It's okay. I had a bad dream. Just a bad dream."

But she could smell blood and candle wax.

She could hear the sound of the voices in her mind. The slight Scottish burr of the midwife's, the exhaustion in Marianne's, the grief in Hugh Poole's.

And the hard, vicious edge in Hester Dobbs's.

Why had she woken up standing by the bed instead of lying in it?

She'd fallen asleep reading, she remembered. But the light was off now, the book closed and on the nightstand. The mug of tea she'd brought up was nowhere to be seen.

She knew she'd find it washed and put away in the kitchen.

So someone looked after her, doing little kindnesses and household chores.

And someone wanted to scare her.

Just how many were there in the house with her? And who were they — or had they been?

She glanced at the clock. Three-twenty-two.

No piano music, no banging on the door.

Apparently it was over for the night.

But when she got back in bed, she took the dog with her.

"I saw it all so clearly. The mirror, then the room on the other side. The people in it. I think I could draw them. Not my strongest skill, but I think I could draw them.

"I watched two babies being born — the first so beautiful, the second so tragic — but I saw, and heard, and felt. I saw a woman die, a woman who fought so hard to bring her babies into the world. I saw her just . . . fade away."

She stroked the dog, grateful for that sweet, warm body against hers.

"I saw Hester Dobbs. I saw that bitch take Marianne's ring while her husband grieved. And she saw me. She saw me, spoke to me. Marianne saw me, spoke to me as she died. But no one else did.

"I was the ghost there. Hester Dobbs had

that right. On the other side of the mirror — or whatever the hell it is — I was the ghost."

Chapter Fifteen

Considering the night she'd had, she might have slept through the morning. But she dragged herself out of bed for the dog. A walk in the brisk wind did a lot to blow the cobwebs away.

Determined to stick with routine, she sat down at her desk — a little late, and in her pajamas — but she sat down at her desk.

The first order of business: adding the mirror dream/incident to her log.

Once done, she got out a sketch pad and did her best to draw the figures in that dream/incident.

She didn't have Cleo's skill with illustration, but she thought she managed decent likenesses.

Then she set them aside.

"A girl and her dog still have to eat," she said, and got to work.

Nothing and no one disturbed her. She no longer counted the musical iPad greetings, as she'd grown used to them. She shut down at three-thirty.

"I'm not meeting Trey Doyle — man and/or potential client — in my pj's and with a naked face." She tapped Yoda's nose and made him wag. "Gotta be professional. Plus, he always looks so damn good. You haven't met him yet," she added as they walked over to her bedroom, "but take my word on it."

She stopped short at the sight of the short, sort of sassy red dress laid out neatly on her bed.

"Okay, that's new — not the dress, but the gesture. And, ah, thanks? But this is more for date night than client meeting. It's a great dress though."

And now, Sonya thought, she talked to ghosts as well as to herself.

Holding it up, she turned this way, that way in the mirror. "And who knows when I'll have a reason to wear it again. But not today."

She hung it back in the closet.

She hadn't thought of wearing a dress, but she could. Client meeting and all that. But not anything suit-y. Something casual.

She pulled out a slim ribbed knit dress in a dark, deep green. Simple lines, long sleeves, and the midi length looked good with booties.

"And done."

When she'd changed, she studied herself in the mirror again. "Okay, this works. It's like I take my work seriously, but I'm still friendly and easy." Amused, she pointed at Yoda. "Not that kind of easy.

"Although, God, I do miss sex. No thinking about sex during a client meeting," she told herself, and went into the bathroom to deal with makeup.

Same rules applied. Professional, but casual and friendly.

As she debated just the right eye shadow, she asked herself if she really intended to carve in a six hour–plus round trip to visit her longtime hairdresser.

The sensible thing? Give the local salon a try. If they screwed it up, she'd never return.

She added earrings — just studs — and took a last look.

"I think I hit the mark, and it only took me three times as long as it would have if I'd tossed on jeans and a sweater like I figured I would. But this is better."

Her iPad let out with Roy Orbison's classic "Oh, Pretty Woman."

"Thanks. I'm getting pretty comfortable here, despite everything. It doesn't hurt to remember how to take some time. The whole self-care thing. Now, I should make coffee."

She'd use the coffee service in the butler's pantry, set it up in front of the library fire. Or would the kitchen suit better?

No, the library.

"I'm thinking about it too much. And not," she admitted to the dog, "just because he's a potential client. He's just so damn attractive. The way he looks, yeah, but also the way he is. What I know of the way he is, because I hardly know him really.

"And this has to stop."

She made the coffee, then carried the tray up.

Professional, she thought. A woman running her own business.

She plumped the pillows on the sofa, added another log to the fire.

And decided: Perfect.

The dog let out a series of barks and raced out of the room seconds before the doorbell sounded.

"No one's going to sneak in from outside anyway."

She went down, pointed at Yoda, who danced in place by the front door. "You behave. This is business."

She opened the door and there he stood, tall, handsome, with his big, adorable dog.

"Right on time. Come in. Meet Yoda."

"Hey there." Inside the door, Trey crouched right down and gave the dancing Yoda a good rub. "You've got Yoda eyes, all right. What do you think, Mookie?"

In answer, Mookie slapped a long tongue kiss straight up Yoda's face, which caused the smaller dog to spin in circles.

"We brought a homecoming gift." Trey pulled a tug rope out of his back pocket.

"Show him how it's done, Mook."

In five seconds flat, the dogs were playing tug-of-war and fake growling.

"You know the big guy could drag the little guy all over the house with that."

"Yeah." Trey just grinned at him. "And he probably will."

"Let me take your coat."

As she went to hang it up, Sonya shut her eyes.

He'd brought a present for the dog. How was she supposed to resist that?

"So, I'm set up in the library, with coffee."

"Appreciate the coffee, and you making the time."

"I took a look at your website," she said as they went upstairs with the dogs behind them. "It's very serviceable."

"I think that's a dig."

"Not at all. Or, okay, not much of one. I can make it better, but we'll start with what you're looking for."

"It feels dated. Poole's Bay's small-town, but we do have clients outlying. We're family run. I want to play that up. We've got people who've worked for us for decades, and we do internships."

"And there's the office itself. The house. The family house. It has a feel. A you-can-trust-us-to-look-out-for-you feel."

"There you go."

"Have a seat."

Sonya poured coffee while the dogs played tug.

She made notes as he laid out what he thought they needed. More as she asked questions and he answered.

By the time the dogs settled down by the fire, she had the gist.

Sharing a house with ghosts might have her questioning her sanity. Feeling — no question about it — a sexual buzz for a potential client definitely had her wondering what to do, or not do, about it.

But when it came to the work, confidence ruled.

"You want clean, simple, traditional, with an emphasis on the history of the firm. Nothing fancy, no big hype. Doyle Law Offices is an institution in Poole's Bay for a reason. I'd use a photo of the offices as a banner. It says: When you come into our house, we're going to help you. Right now you just have the name of the firm. This would warm it up. Doctors and lawyers are very personal choices. So make it personal."

"I can't argue with that."

"Add a tab for the staff — photos and short bios. And since you take on interns, another for that. With your success stories. *Julie Smith went on to Harvard Law,* that sort of thing. And you need a page for each of you. Ace, Deuce, Trey."

"I like it, but it doesn't sound simple."

"My job's to make it simple — for you, and for the potential client shopping for a lawyer. Take your business cards. The one your father gave me is slightly different than yours. They should all have a look, a consistent Doyle Law Offices look. And instead of black on white, I'd suggest a warmer color. Ecru maybe."

"Ecru." His lips curved in that slow, easy smile. "That's not a word you hear every day."

"You do in my line. Coordinate your business cards, letterhead, the works. One cohesive look for one cohesive firm. Right now, your website's a white background with bright blue font, blue backgrounds on the photos. It's too staid."

"Staid."

"And you're not. None of you are. Let it reflect who you are and what you do. Your father traveled to Boston, sat at my table, and changed my life. And he was so kind, so patient. You came here on your weekend and moved furniture for me."

"Neighbors do for neighbors. And Collin was family. Family does for family."

"Yes." She beamed at him. "Exactly. You're the neighborhood law firm. You're the people a family can trust to take care of them."

"You're good at this."

"I am."

"Can you work up a proposal?"

"I can. And if you decide against, no harm

done. You'll be making a mistake, but that's on you."

He laughed, sat back. "Anna's over the moon."

"I'm really glad."

"She told me she's sold more since the new site went up than she had in the previous month. What I'm looking for isn't really to generate more business — or not primarily. It's to keep up."

"You're not looking for slick. You're looking for a fresh look that reflects the firm and the people in it."

"That sums it up. So that's done. How are things going here? Any problems?"

"A lot of what's become the usual. I've started documenting, just to have a record. There's the in-house DJ, but that's gotten to be almost entertaining. Hell," she admitted, "it is entertaining. There's doors opening, closing. And Yoda hears that, too, which is oddly comforting. Something on the third floor."

The thought of it had her rubbing a chill from her arms.

"The dog kept stopping by the servants' door on the landing, so I finally went in with him. I'm trying to talk myself into using the gym anyway."

To keep her hands busy, she poured more coffee. "Do you work out?"

"Little bit."

"I had a routine in Boston. Went to the gym three times a week. But, well. Anyway, after a poor excuse for a workout, Yoda's sniffing around. And those bells — the ones people used to signal one of the staff to a room? One of them rang. The Gold Room. Third floor. We went up to check it out, but I couldn't remember exactly which room it was. So we walked down the hallway with the bedrooms — everything's shut. We open this door, look, move on. Then we're at the end of that hall, and Yoda starts growling at the door. Serious growling, and I swear his hair's standing up. When I opened the door — This is going to sound crazy."

She had his full attention. "I doubt it."

"It's crazy to me. It wasn't just chilly because that area's closed off. It was frigid, and . . . It was like a wind going through an open window. I could see the sheets over the furniture moving. Like . . . rippling. I could see it. And Yoda's barking like a maniac, growling, snarling. I was afraid he'd run in there, so I shut the door. I brought him down to the kitchen, and all the chairs at the small table were lying on their backs on the floor."

"Why don't I go up, check it out?"

"Now?"

"Sure." He pushed up. "Give me a couple minutes."

The idea made her throat go dry, but . . .

"No, if you're going, I'm going." She stood

up. “I have to live here. I want to live here,” she corrected. “And, well, all these weird rooms are mine to figure out.”

He smiled at her. “I think Collin knew what he was doing when he left the manor to you. Looks like the troops are with us,” he added when the dogs stood and stretched.

“Have you heard anything up there since?” he asked as they started up.

“No. But I want to say, whatever I did hear or feel wasn’t benign. Not like the invisible DJ or housekeeper. I think — and here comes crazy again — I think it’s Hester Dobbs.”

“The half-assed witch who killed Astrid Poole.”

“Killed her, and took her ring. And lured Catherine, the second bride, out into a blizzard on her wedding night. And took her ring. And —”

She broke off when they reached the third floor. “Do you mind?” She reached for his hand. “Yeah, that’s better.”

“Dobbs died a couple decades before Catherine.”

“Yeah, I said crazy, but I *know* it. Don’t reach for the straitjacket, but I saw it. I dreamed it — or think I dreamed it. Everybody dreams, but these were so lucid. Then last night . . .”

“Last night?”

“Let’s do this first,” she said as they reached the door at the end of the hall. “Look at the dogs. They're not growling, but they're braced, aren't they? Like they sense something and don't like it."

Trey shifted — a subtle move that put him between Sonya and the door. When he opened it, both dogs made warning sounds in their throats.

But inside, nothing moved.

"Feels colder."

To Sonya's dismay, he released her hand and walked inside. Skirting draped furniture, he checked the windows.

"Nothing open, but it's definitely a cold spot. Easily ten degrees under the hallway."

"We walked through all of this the first day, and I went through with Cleo. It wasn't like this."

"Nope. It is now."

Steeling herself, Sonya started to step inside. The door slammed in her face.

And the dogs went wild.

As they barked, and Mookie leaped at the door, she grabbed the knob, turning, tugging when it refused to move. Giving up, she pounded on the door, shouting for Trey.

Inside, Trey stood as the temperature dropped enough for him to see his breath. Around him, the drapes over the furniture fluttered and snapped.

Under its white sheeting, the bed began to shake, then hammer against the floor. The drawers on the covered bureau flew open, slammed shut as wind roared down the chimney.

His hands wanted to ball into fists to fight what he couldn't see. Instead, he tucked them into the pockets of his black trousers.

"Is this all you've got? A bunch of noise and cold air? Even dead you're still a half-assed witch."

On a shriek, the pale gold damask wallpaper split open like wounds. It bled.

"Right. I could do this all day, but the lady's waiting."

He walked to the door, paused to look back. "This isn't your house. It never was your house, it's never going to be your house. You want this room, you've got it. For now."

As he put his hand on the knob, the air stilled and warmed. The walls healed.

When he opened the door, he found his arms full of Sonya, and a pair of dogs leaping and licking.

"Are you all right?" Sonya ran her hands over his face, his shoulders. "The door wouldn't open. It slammed shut and wouldn't open. I couldn't hear anything."

"You couldn't hear anything?"

"I mean, yes. The dogs were barking and jumping at the door. I pounded on it, called you, but you didn't answer."

"I didn't hear any of that." After a last look inside, he shut the door. "That's interesting."

"Interesting? *Interesting?* I have to sit down."

She did, on the floor in the hallway. Yoda scrambled into her lap and Mookie leaned on her shoulder.

Trey hunkered down so they were at eye level. "Let's go on down. And it's probably best to stay out of that room until we figure it out."

"Oh, you think? Staying out of the evil, scary room? There's an idea."

"The room's not evil, Sonya."

"Right." She pressed her hands to her face. "Full panic. I don't know if I've ever hit full panic mode before, but now I'll know what to expect if I ever do again."

Dropping her hands, she reached for his again. "I didn't know what was happening in there, to you. What happened in there?"

"Somebody put on a little show. Not all that impressive, but I think you may be right about Hester Dobbs, so let her have the room, for now. And we'll figure it out."

"What show? Be specific."

Rising, he brought her up with him. Then shifted to put his arm around her shoulders to lead her away. "The room got meat-locker cold. The bed bounced some, drawers opened and slammed. The best trick was making the walls bleed."

She stopped dead. "The walls *bled*?"

"She couldn't keep it up," he said, and

nudged Sonya forward. “As soon as I touched the doorknob, it all stopped. Situation normal.”

“Your situation normal and mine don’t exist on the same planet.”

“You’re cold. Let’s go back in the library, and you can tell me about last night.”

“How are you so calm? I mean it. How?”

“Mostly calm’s my crisis mode.”

Giving in, giving up, she leaned against him as she worked to get her breath back.

“Well, Jesus. I guess that’s a good thing, even though it’s completely baffling.”

In the library, she dropped down on the couch, Trey stirred up the fire, added another log.

“They’re still bringing them in, by the way. I haven’t filled the wood rack since I’ve been here.”

“That wouldn’t be Dobbs.”

“No,” she said as he sat beside her. “And I don’t think whoever — whatever — is making up my bed, washing my teacups is the same as what’s playing music on my iPad, and the piano player’s probably something else.”

“She’s outnumbered. Hester Dobbs.”

She hadn’t thought of it that way, but now that she did, some of the knots in her shoulders loosened.

“I suppose that should inspire calm crisis mode.”

"Last night," Trey prompted, and took her hand.

"Last night. I fell asleep reading in bed. Then I woke up — or didn't. If it was a dream, it was incredibly detailed. I was in front of a mirror. My father dreamed of the same mirror — one with the glass full-length. Predators carved into the frame. Owls, foxes, hawks, bears — all on the hunt. But I didn't see me, I saw a room through the glass. So clearly, and I walked through the mirror like it was a door."

"Really?" Obviously fascinated, he kept her hand in his, and those deep blue eyes never left her face. "Where did you go?"

"It was Marianne Poole. She'd be bride number three. I think it was my bedroom, but the walls were papered, and she was in a different bed. She was birthing her twins."

She told him, the details still fresh and clear in her mind.

"When she was dying . . . I've never seen anyone die, but I knew, I'd have known even if I hadn't read it in the Poole book, she looked at me. She saw me, Trey. No one had seen me, but as she was dying, she did. She said she had a son and a daughter, and I came from them."

Sonya swiped a tear away. "She'd fought so hard to bring her children into the world, and she was leaving it. I saw Hugh Poole rush in, and I watched him grieve when she died.

He loved her — that was real. God, I could feel his grief. Then I saw her — Hester Dobbs. She just walked in. He didn't see her, but I did. She took Marianne's wedding ring."

After a calming breath, she continued, "I said no, you can't. You can't do that. And she looked at me. She saw me. She said — and this is verbatim because I'll never forget:

" 'I can. I have. I will. Do you think you can stop me? Stop what I forged in fire and blood? You're the ghost here.'

"She put the ring on, and she already wore two others. Wedding rings, I'm sure of that. And I woke up, or came out of it, whatever the hell it was, standing in my bedroom with poor Yoda whining and shaking."

She laughed a little. "I guess I whined and shook some, too."

"Why didn't you call me?"

"At three-something in the morning?"

"Yes."

She looked at him, those oh-so-appealing blue eyes filled with concern.

"You actually mean that. Most people who say call anytime don't actually mean at three-something in the morning." She gave the hand still holding hers a quick squeeze. "Who are you?"

"I can't claim I always say what I mean. I'm a goddamn lawyer. But if I tell you to call anytime, I mean it. You were afraid, and had a right to be. You don't have to be alone."

"It helps having the dog. I know that's silly, but —"

"No, it's not."

"No," she agreed, "it's not. And it helped telling you all of it, and you believing me. Hold on."

She rose to get her sketch pad.

"I drew them — the midwife, Marianne, everyone I saw."

He took the sketchbook. "These are great. I didn't know you could draw like this."

"I'm much better at graphic art than fine art, but —"

"Don't diminish your talent," he murmured, and paged through the sketches. "You'd have a portrait of Hugh Poole in the inventory."

"There's a picture of his portrait in the book, and another of Marianne Poole — younger, I think, than she was when she died. But none of Hester Dobbs."

"And this is her."

She'd drawn the face from two angles, and another full-length with Dobbs holding up her hand with three rings.

"As close as I could manage."

"I didn't imagine she was beautiful."

"She is — was. Really striking, the black hair, the milk-white face, the dark eyes. Her voice is . . . throaty. Sultry. She has crazy eyes. I don't think I quite captured that."

"Close enough. And this is the mirror?"

"Yes. My father drew it, too. He dreamed about it, my mother told me. He dreamed he saw — it must have been Collin — reflected in it. From boyhood and on."

"I don't remember anything like this mirror in inventory, and I think I would. But I'll check."

"I did; it isn't. But I saw it, and my father saw it. So . . ." She shrugged. "I can't explain it."

"Collin never mentioned it, or anything like the room on the third floor. At least not to me. I'll ask my father."

He closed the sketchbook.

"Got any plans for dinner?"

"Dinner?" She glanced at the time. "Oh, this has taken a while, hasn't it? I could toss something together — not like Cleo does, but I can toss something together."

"So can I, but let's try this. Let's go out."

"Out?"

"You know, to dinner. Where someone with a lot more skill cooks food that you get to pick off a menu. When's the last time you went out for dinner since you moved in?"

"That would be not at all."

"Eating out alone can suck. Don't make me eat alone. Let me take you to dinner. You can meet my friend who cooks at the Lobster Cage. She's got mad skills."

"You don't have to —"

"Let me take you to dinner," he repeated.

"You look too good to toss something together."

And the iPad on the table played Childish Gambino's "Heartbeat."

"Stop that," Sonya muttered. "Honestly, I don't know about leaving the dog alone in the house."

"Why don't we give them dinner — if Mookie can join in there. I'll take them out for a walk before we go, and Mookie will hang with Yoda until we get back. Take a break."

Why be stupid? she asked herself. Why be stubborn?

"I could use one. Thanks."

Not a date, she told herself as they went downstairs to feed the dogs.

Just two people going out to dinner after a shared scary experience, she thought as she excused herself to dash upstairs and check her makeup and hair.

She supposed she had the sexy red dress ghost to thank for inspiring her to do better than jeans.

When she came down, Trey slipped his phone back in his pocket while the dogs played tug. "Got us a table."

"Great."

"I'm going to grab my coat, take these guys out."

"Oh, I'll go with you. I'm keeping Yoda on

a leash outside until I'm sure he won't run off."

"He looks like a boy who knows when he's got it made. And he loves you."

"He does." Knowing it made her heart swell a little. "It was pretty much love at first sight, on both sides."

"You got him from Lucy, right? Lucy Cabot," he said as the dogs trailed them to the front of the house.

"I did. She's terrific."

Another cold, clear night, she thought as they went out. Maybe the calendar said spring was creeping closer, but it sure didn't feel like it.

"You don't leash Mookie?"

"In town. He accepts it's the law inside town limits. Otherwise, he doesn't need it. He's a good dog."

"Did you get him from Lucy?"

"I wasn't so much as thinking about getting a dog, and one day she brought him into the office. She'd just taken him in. She told me, 'This is your dog, Trey.' And he was."

"She knows you well then."

"I dated her niece back in high school. You'll meet her tonight. Bree's head chef at the Lobster Cage."

"Oh. You go back."

"We do."

"And still friends after the high school sweetheart era?"

"Friends after that, and the drama of the breakup, the very brief reconnect the summer of our junior year in college, and the far less dramatic parting. And her marriage to a restaurant guy in Portland, her divorce."

"Divorced. Could lead to another reconnect."

"No. Too much friends now. Friends who know they really don't suit otherwise. I'd say this is mission accomplished out here."

They went back in, and she unleashed Yoda.

"You listen to Mookie, and be a good boy. No third floor. I'll be home soon."

Since the tablet played "How Can I Miss You If You Don't Go Away," and the dogs were back on the tug rope, she decided everyone would be fine.

"I already appreciate you talking me into this."

He opened the truck's passenger side door for her. Of course he did.

"I do go into town," she continued when he got behind the wheel. "But maybe not as often as I should. Still, priorities."

"What are they? Your priorities."

"The first has to be the work. Doing good work that leads to satisfied clients that leads to establishing a solid business. I liked working in an office, working with a team, working up to managing one. Freelancing's a whole lot different. It's just me."

"I bet you're tougher on yourself than your

boss was."

"Maybe." She shifted. "You run your own business. You, your father, your grandfather. You have a team, but the three of you are in charge. And obviously good at it or that team wouldn't stay in place."

"Are you looking to put a team together when you're established? Where you want to be?"

"I don't know. Right now it's one day at a time, one project at a time. I'm good with that. Was it always law for you?"

"Other than dreams of pitching for the Red Sox or being a rock star, yeah. It was always the family business."

"A rock star?"

"Owen and I and a few other friends had a garage band back in high school."

"Really?" And here, she realized, was another layer that fascinated. "What did you play?"

"Covers mostly — Foo Fighters, Green Day, Van Halen, some Bon Jovi, a little Aerosmith. Like that. And some really bad originals."

"You wrote music?"

"I wouldn't exactly call it music."

"And what instrument?"

"Rhythm guitar. Never could fully master the G major ninth. Owen was lead guitar. He's got the hands for it."

"This is fascinating information. A whole

new side to the village lawyer with his rescue dog and pickup truck. Do you still play?"

"Play at," he corrected. "Now and then."

"I'd like to hear you play. God, I'm relaxed," she realized as they drove into town. "I wasn't sure what it would take to relax again after the Gold Room."

He shot her a look of mild surprise. "You're resilient. I figured that out in five minutes after we met. It's a very attractive quality."

He pulled in to park.

Resilient, she thought as she got out of the car.

She'd take it.

Chapter Sixteen

The hostess, who might have been old enough to buy a legal beer, greeted Trey with a quick, flirty smile.

"Heard you were coming in." She flicked Sonya a look caught between wistful and envious. "With a friend."

"Sonya, this is Halley."

"Sonya Poole?"

"MacTavish," Sonya corrected.

"Right. I meant you're up at the manor. Wow. Welcome to the Lobster Cage. Your table's ready." She picked up two menus, the wine list, then escorted them through the dining area to a corner table for two. "Ian will be your server tonight," she continued as Trey helped Sonya with her coat. "Enjoy. Oh, Trey, my dad really appreciates your help with the . . . you know."

"Give him my best."

"I will. Ian will be right with you."

"She's crushing on you."

"She's twenty."

"And still. She's a very pretty girl, so you get points for not flirting back."

"She's twenty," Trey repeated.

Their server, short, wiry, with orange-streaked dark hair twisted into a topknot, arrived with a cheerful smile. "Hi, Trey. Welcome, Ms. MacTavish. I'm Ian, and I'll be taking care of all your culinary hopes and dreams tonight."

"How's it going, Ian?"

"Going good." Grinning, Ian made a check mark in the air with his finger. "Aced it."

"I never had a doubt."

"That makes one of us. Can I start you off with drinks? A bottle of water for the table?"

"Wine?" Trey asked Sonya.

"That's a yes."

He skimmed down the wine list. "We'll take a bottle of the sauvignon blanc. If that works?"

"It definitely does."

He added a bottle of water before Ian walked off.

"So, since you know everybody, what did he ace?"

"Short version. Ian's dad got sick a couple years ago, so he dropped out of college to come home and help out. Got his degree online, and now he's working on his master's."

"In what?"

"Environmental engineering. Ian's bright

and committed."

"On behalf of planet Earth, I'm grateful. His dad?"

"In remission."

"That's good."

A busser delivered the water, and had a quick word with Trey before Ian brought the wine.

"The lady'll taste it."

"Trey tells me you're working on your master's in environmental engineering."

"Yes, ma'am."

"I did some graphics work for Green Engineering and Environmental in Boston."

Ian lit up as he drew the cork. "That's one of the best. Tops my list when I'm ready to send out résumés."

"When you're ready, you could let me know. I'll put in a word."

His jaw dropped a full inch. "Seriously?"

"I can't promise it'll have weight, but it can't hurt."

"I — wow. That would be awesome."

When he poured the wine, she sampled. "And this is perfect."

Ian ran through the night's specials, then backed off to give them time.

"First, you made his night. Possibly his month. Second, you'd put in a word for a server you just met?"

"You said he was bright and committed, so he is. He put his family first, which shows loyalty and heart. If we're going to save the planet, we need the bright, committed, loyal, and plenty of heart."

"We're on the same page there."

"Now, let's get down to immediate priorities. You eat here all the time. What should I order?"

"I'm thinking the lobster ravioli."

"I could go with that."

"No, you can't. How can I mooch off your plate if you get what I get? And vice versa?"

"I see." Considering, she perused the menu. "I feel a pull toward the crab-stuffed lobster tails."

"Surrender to it. You won't be sorry. You should go with the mashed potato puffs with that. If you want a starter —"

"How am I supposed to eat the main, potato puffs, and the lemon grilled asparagus if I have a starter?"

"Fine. But you need the jalapeño hush puppies. I have to be firm on that."

"Deal." She closed her menu. "My plans — loose as they were — included opening a can of tomato soup and making a grilled cheese sandwich."

"One of my personal staples. I'm a grilled cheese master."

"Is that right? I've never met a grilled cheese master."

She leaned forward. "Tell me more."

"Pepper jack cheese, sourdough bread, and

chili oil. You'll thank me later."

After Ian took their order, she sat back, picked up her wine. "So, lawyer, grilled cheese master, teenage rocker. What else should I know? How about where you studied law?"

"Cambridge."

On a laugh, she leaned forward again. "You went to Harvard Law?"

"Guilty."

"I dated a Harvard Law student once for about five minutes. It wasn't you, was it?"

"I'm pretty sure I'd remember."

"I didn't think so, because he was full of himself. Which is why the five-minute relationship. If you were full of yourself, you'd have found a way to work in Harvard the first time we met."

"I dated an artist once. It was more like ten minutes. Inexplicable abstracts and a weird obsession with Virginia Woolf."

"Definitely wasn't me. I'm more thrillers, fantasy, and a side of romance where the bad guys get what's coming to them, the world is saved, and love eventually conquers. I like the spooky, too, but I'm giving that a pass for now. Considering."

"Probably a good idea. You said you fell asleep reading last night. What were you reading?"

"It wasn't the book's fault. We'll lay it on a long workday and the Gold Room. *Rabbit*

Hole — new author to me. I've only just started, but it's really good."

"I just read it last week. It's going to get even better."

They talked books and ate lobster, segued into movies as Sonya became a passionate fan of the jalapeño hush puppy.

She couldn't remember the last time she'd had such an easy, wide-ranging conversation with a man over a meal.

"That was amazing. Now I have to work out tomorrow, which is totally on you."

"You're all right going down to the gym?"

"It's my house. She's got one room, and that's temporary. But it's my house. I'm thinking of asking Cleo to talk to her grandmother about a juju or mojo or whatever the hell it is."

"Is that a serious thing?"

"Cleo's grandmother's serious about it. I met her when we spent an amazing spring break in New Orleans. She's fascinating, and spooky. Fascinatingly spooky, not scary spooky. She read my palm, my cards. Tarot."

"What did your future hold?"

"Some of it's more a reading into who you are and what you're looking for. She was pretty damn accurate, but I put that down to her reading people well, and knowing me through Cleo. Then you get to meeting the tall, dark stranger or going on a long sea voyage. And . . ."

She trailed off as Ian came back with dessert menus.

Pulling herself out of the memory, she smiled at him. "Just where would I put it?"

Between the two of them, they talked her into a cappuccino and the signature house bread pudding.

"And?" Trey prompted. "You thought of something before."

"It's strange. I haven't thought of any of it for years. She said I'd face a betrayal, which would hurt but provide a fortunate escape and open opportunities. I'd be wise to take both. And that I'd make my home in a house of history and secrets overlooking the sea."

She picked up her water glass. "Looks like she was pretty damn accurate on that part, too. Spooky," she repeated, and drank. "I never believed any of it; any of the, well, spooky stuff before I came here."

"How do you feel about it?"

"Yet to be determined." She shrugged. "Or partially. I love that house, Trey. Like Yoda, it was love at first sight. Which I also didn't believe in before I saw the house or Yoda."

"Practicality or cynicism?"

"Maybe a little of both. And I insist on maintaining at least some of both."

"That and your resiliency will help you deal with what's in the house."

Charmed, simply charmed, she shook her head. "You're not even the tiniest bit, we'll say cynical, about the manor."

"I grew up with it, and to some extent in it. You've had about a month."

He glanced over as a woman with short, boldly red hair arrowed toward their table. The white chef's coat gave her away.

"Interrupting. Mind?" She snugged into the booth beside Sonya. "Bree Marshall."

"Sonya MacTavish. Trey told me you were a wonderful chef. He didn't say you were a goddess in the kitchen."

"I like you. I like her," she said to Trey.

Ian brought the coffee and dessert.

"Can I get you something, Chef?"

"No, I'm only on a short break. We're winding down, thank Christ and all his followers. I just need Trey for one quick minute. It's not private. Eat," she added, and waved at the dessert plates. "Manny," she said to Trey.

"Manny? What about him? I had a beer with him a week or so ago. He's fine, right?"

"Sure. Right. Manny and me."

"Manny and you what? Oh." Now Trey sat back. "When did this happen?"

"It hasn't yet. Completely. Just around the edges. You know me, you know him." She turned to Sonya. "We all go back. High school. Trey and I had a thing in high school. Don't worry about that."

"I wasn't."

"Good. Confident. Like her even more. We — Trey and I — had not even what you'd call a thing a few years later. Not to worry there either."

"I won't."

"Bree." Trey managed to infuse the single syllable with deep frustration, mild embarrassment, and endless affection.

"Right. Back to it. Manny and me. A friend — you know Marlie — talked me into going over to Ogunquit a couple weeks ago. Rock Hard had a gig. Rock Hard's Manny's band. He's a drummer. I don't know if the name's a reference to the Maine coast, the music, or woodies, since they're an all-male band."

"Jesus, Bree."

"Sorry." As Trey rubbed his face, Bree turned to Sonya again. "Was that offensive?"

"Not in the least. Sounds to me like it could be all three."

Bree jabbed a finger at her. "Bet you're right. Anyway, Manny used to drum for Trey's band back in the day. Head Case."

"Head Case?" On a rolling laugh, Sonya picked up her cappuccino. "I love it."

"They weren't bad. So I went to Manny's gig — they're solid, Trey, you've heard them. And Manny and I hung out some, and things clicked. Not that way. What do you take me for?"

"I said nothing."

"You thought it. Then he came in the other night, hung around until closing, and more clicked. Still not that way. But. So, what do you think? Yes or no."

"If I say yes and things go bad, you'll be pissed. If I say no and it's what you want, you'll be pissed. So I'm going to say you're both friends of mine, both all grown up, and don't need anyone's permission to . . . click."

"I screwed up before."

"Bree, no, you didn't. You got out of a bad relationship because you're not an idiot."

"My ex-husband turned out to be a scum-bag who cheated on me with my sous chef."

"I caught my ex-fiancé banging my cousin in our bed a couple months before the wedding."

"Okay, you win. I like Manny. I've always liked Manny. I don't want to mess him up."

"Then you won't," Trey told her.

"Then I won't." She nodded, pushed out. "I've got to get back to the wars. Bring her in again. I like her."

As Bree arrowed away again, Sonya spooned up some bread pudding. "I can see why you had a thing with her. Twice."

"The second time wasn't really a thing."

"I can see why. So, if I take a vow of silence, will you tell me what you think about Bree the chef and Manny the drummer?"

"I think I wonder why it took him this long. He's had a soft spot for her for years."

"That's nice. And it's nice you didn't tell her that. It keeps things balanced between them. So." She took another bite of bread pudding. “Head Case?”

Nearly three hours after they’d driven away from the house, he parked beside her car.

“I didn’t know how much I needed this. You did.”

“Everybody needs a break.”

“The lamp’s on in my bedroom,” she noted as she got out of the car.

“I’ll go up and check.”

“No need, really. My . . . chambermaid? I don’t know what to call her. I assume her. She does that every night when she turns down the bed, puts the fire on. And from the sound of it, the dogs are on guard.”

The barking stopped the minute she opened the door. Both dogs greeted them as if they’d been separated for months.

“I’ll walk them around.”

“I could use the walk, too.” Instead of getting the leash, Sonya pointed at Yoda. “I’m trusting you to stick to the program.”

It didn’t take long to realize he’d not only stick to the program, but very close to Mookie, his new best friend.

“Thanks, for every bit of this,” she said when they walked back to the door. “Please don’t expect anywhere near the same level of cuisine on Friday.”

“We’re looking forward to it. All of us. Call,” he insisted. “Anytime. No bullshit on that, Sonya.”

"Message received." She knew when a man was about to kiss her, and he wasn't. So she scooped up the dog and opened the door. "Thanks again, and I'll see you Friday. Good night."

Inside, she snuggled the dog, leaned back against the door.

Tonight's music choice, Peter Gabriel's "In Your Eyes."

"It wasn't a date."

The next afternoon, she bundled Yoda in the car. Armed with her mother's shopping list, she drove to the market for the supplies needed for the dinner party she now feared more than the room on the third floor.

She took Yoda into the flower shop, much to the delight of the florist.

She sent flowers from Yoda to his foster family.

And left with flowers and the possibility of another client, thanks to the work she'd done on Practical Art.

Another stop at the bookstore netted her more candles, and a book Trey had recommended over dinner.

Since she'd be cooking — a lot — the next day, she made one more stop for a takeout pizza.

After bringing in the flowers, bookstore bag, and pizza, she let Yoda walk off his time in the car before hauling the groceries in.

When she shut the door the last time, her in-house DJ greeted her with the Moody Blues and "Lovely to See You."

"I can't say the same because, big laugh, I can't see you."

When she carried the groceries into the kitchen, the flowers and pizza were gone, the bookstore bag neatly folded with her new book on top.

"What the actual fuck."

As she dumped the groceries, she saw the warming light on the oven glowed red. And found her pizza inside. Dragging off her knit cap, she turned. There, on the big dining table, her flowers spilled artistically out of a low oval dish, with the new candles arranged — just as artistically — on the mantel.

"Should I be thankful that might be better than I could've done, or just a little pissed off?"

She decided she could be both, and went in to put away the groceries before somebody else did it for her.

"You know," she said to the dog, who was busy gnawing on his new chew bone, "I was going to hire a cleaning service. But somebody else already keeps it all cleaned and polished."

She decided to work through the evening, so had pizza at her desk with the fire she hadn't lit crackling. She completed the proposal for the Doyles, worked up another for the florists.

As an experiment, she deliberately left her plate and empty glass behind when she shut down for the night.

A light snow fell as she walked the dog. He amused her by leaping at it, turning in his happy circles. When she rounded back, she noted the lamp glowed against the glass in her bedroom.

No doubt the fire would glow as well, the bed turned down. No light in that third-floor room, but she wondered if the glass held darker there than all the other windows.

Back inside, she walked up, turned first to the library.

No plate, no glass on the desk.

And in her bedroom, a turned down bed, a low fire, and the quiet light to guide her way.

She planned out her dinner party day not like a general prepping for battle but like a lowly recruit who'd been inexplicably field promoted.

Stage one, marinate the giant slab of cow, then say a desperate prayer she hadn't screwed that up.

Stage two, work until noon, and pretend she had no other tasks.

Stage three, put on an apron, line up all the ingredients, and face the music. Literally, as her tablet played Lil Wayne's "No Worries."

"Easy for you to say."

Twenty minutes later, she FaceTimed Cleo.

"Hey, hi!"

"Can you take a break?"

"Sure. Is everything all right?"

"I'm cooking. I'm afraid. Mom said to brown the hell out of the roast, so I did. Does this look right?"

She turned the screen so it showed the roast resting on a platter.

"I guess. This is above my pay grade. No one would pay me to cook, so it's definitely above my pay grade, but it looks right. Is it done? This early?"

"No, no, I'm peeling potatoes and carrots, and I've got to do celery and onions. I need moral support."

"I'm here for that."

"Then talk to me. How's the purging and packing going?"

"Purging's harder than I thought. Not the big stuff, but all my pretty little things. I don't want to part with my pretty little things."

"Then don't. We've got the room."

"I'm boxing some up to send with Winter next weekend. And I'm having a yard sale — your mom's lending me her yard — for the big stuff. Son, you look stressed."

"I'm cooking!" She said it as if she were hacking her way through a jungle full of sound and snakes.

"I have to do all these vegetables, then sort of stir them around in the meat juices. Herbs!

I need to do the herbs. I'm supposed to scrape up all the brown stuff. What does that mean? Look at the size of this pot."

She turned the screen again, then attacked the pot with a wooden spoon. "Oh! There is brown stuff. Look at that!"

"Magic. Listen, everything's smooth here. Jess is taking over the apartment."

"Jess and Ryan? Your place is a lot smaller than theirs."

"They broke up. Bad breakup, and she's moving on."

Jess and Ryan, and Boston in general, seemed a world away.

"When did that happen?"

"About three weeks ago, and he's already seeing someone else. Since she moved in with him, she moved out. And she's already moved some of her things in here. Trust me, I'm ready to get out. Send vibes for the yard sale. If it works, I can pack up the rest in two, maybe three days. And then I'm heading to Maine. Where's our puppy?"

Sonya stopped long enough to hold the screen down. Yoda angled his head back and forth as Cleo cooed at him.

"I need to tell you about the room on the third floor. The Gold Room. I need to tell you before you do that yard sale and pack the rest."

"What about it?"

Sonya started at the beginning as she

quartered potatoes, chopped herbs.

"Sonya, why didn't you call me?"

"Now you sound like Trey."

"You should have called him. He's a lot closer than I am. Just . . . stay away from that room."

"Trust me. But you have to know there's something there, Cleo. Not like the rest. I think it's evil. I hear myself saying that and want to roll my eyes, but I do. I think it's evil."

"Then we'll get rid of it. We'll find a way. I'm glad Trey was there to, well, experience it. There are more of us, Sonya."

"He said something like that. That Dobbs is outnumbered. He's so damn steady. He took me out to dinner after."

"What?" On-screen, Cleo threw up her hands. "That was days ago, and I'm just hearing about it? You had a date with the sexy lawyer!"

"It wasn't a date."

"I'll be the judge of that. Tell all."

"Hold on. I have to put everything in this pot and stir it and cook it for a few minutes."

"Cook and talk."

"In a second. Oh God, there's so much! Is it too much? I can't think about it. I'm just stirring. We went to the Lobster Cage. I met his ex."

"Awkward."

"No, not. I liked her. You'd like her. She's

the chef there. And I'm getting ahead of myself. Plus, I forgot to tell you about the red dress."

"You wore the red dress! That's a date dress."

"I didn't, but one of the . . . inhabitants laid it out on the bed before the meeting. I wore the green midi."

"That looks great on you. So dinner."

She went through it, felt the tension drop as Cleo laughed at the band names.

"I already like the chef — especially since she's smart enough to like you."

"I wouldn't mind having her here now. I think this looks like it's supposed to. I have to put this big slab of meat on top of everything. And pour in an entire bottle of red wine."

"A whole bottle? I wish I was there now because I bet that's going to be amazing. And because I wish I could tell you in person, Sonya, you had a date with the sexy lawyer."

Because she had to admit she wished it had been, she shrugged. "He didn't make any moves."

"Did you?"

"No. But he may be a client, and I'm already sort of a client. And he's being such a good friend. I don't want to mess that up. And God, Cleo, he's so attractive, so appealing, so just, well, yum. I don't want him to be the rebound guy. He deserves better than rebound guy."

"Sonya, you broke it off with the cheating asshole over six months ago. Seven, over seven months ago. You're way past rebound territory."

"Do you think?"

"Absolutely. And you weren't in love with the cheating asshole."

"I thought I was. I was going to marry the cheating asshole."

"Which would've been a mistake, because cheating asshole, and you didn't love him. He didn't break your heart, Son. He broke your trust and insulted you, and that's way, way different. The client thing? Neither of you has a position of power over the other, so toss that one. If you want to make a move, make a move. If you want him to, let him know you're open to it. You know how."

"Maybe. First I have to get through tonight. It's all in there now. All in the biggest pot in the universe of pots."

"What happens now?"

"I put the lid on it, put it in the oven, and according to Winter MacTavish, I forget about it. For hours. Leave it alone. For hours."

"Then your work is done."

"Mostly. Mom gave me a recipe for biscuits, but I bailed there and bought Parker House rolls."

"There's no shame in the store-bought Parker House roll."

"Good, because my nerves couldn't take the biscuits. And Anna texted me earlier in the week. She's bringing dessert. Thank tiny baby Jesus. And you, for holding my hand, virtually, through this process."

"Next time, we'll hold each other's in person."

"Wow, this is really heavy. I think I made enough to feed most of Poole's Bay. And now it's in there. Done. Don't peek. Hours."

"Now go for a walk with our sweet Yoda."

"Good idea. Yard sale vibes heading your way."

"Text me later, let me know how tonight goes. See you inside two weeks. Cleo, out!"

After she disconnected, Sonya caught herself reaching for the oven door.

"No, I'm not going to peek in under a minute. Let's clean this disaster up, Yoda, and take that walk."

As she started to deal with the unquestionable mess she'd made, she heard a mechanical hum.

"What the hell was that? Did you hear that?"

With Yoda at her heels, she followed the hum into the butler's pantry.

"That's the dumbwaiter, isn't it? Oh shit, that's the dumbwaiter. I . . . I think it's coming back up now. Coming back up from downstairs."

She clasped her hands together while the dog sniffed at the cabinet.

He didn't growl, not even when she heard a soft thunk and the humming stopped.

"I have to look, don't I? It's my house, fuck it all, so I have to look. Then I have to deal with . . . I don't know until I look."

She stepped forward and, after a long breath, pulled the cabinet door open.

Inside sat a large serving platter with painted copper handles and rim. A dozen star-shaped flowers circled that rim, with a single one centered.

Carefully, as if it might explode at her touch, she lifted it out.

"Well, it's beautiful. It sort of has a blue luster, right? It looks old, and . . ." She turned it over. "Jesus, it's Limoges. This is hand-painted. Look here, it was a wedding gift. It's painted on the back. For Lisbeth on her wedding day. June 12, 1916.

"She was one of the brides," Sonya murmured. "I remember her name from the book. On the family tree Deuce did. I guess someone thinks I should use it."

As carefully as she'd taken it out, she set it on the counter in the butler's pantry. "And I guess I could. It's too beautiful to just sit down there in storage."

From her tablet, David Bowie sang "Right."

Sonya pressed her fingers to her eyes.

"Gotta overlook the creepy. I don't know how, but I really have to do that. So, we're going to clean up this mess, then take a walk. A nice long, quiet walk. And if that damn pot roast doesn't completely fail, we'll use Lisbeth's platter."

Chapter Seventeen

After dealing with the mess, after the long, calming walk with Yoda, Sonya peeked a couple of times. But what amazed her was the scent. And the scent permeating the house was gorgeous.

It boosted confidence when she moved to a new stage. Dress for dinner.

She went with a navy cowl-neck paired with tights and booties. Then spent far too long working her hair back into a French braid. Which reminded her she had to make the firm decision about a stylist soon.

Doors slammed on the third floor loudly enough to make her jump and for Yoda to snap out a series of barks.

"She's just trying to get us upset. So we won't be. We're going down. I'm going to make a nice charcuterie board. I'm good at that one."

Picking up the dog, she rubbed her cheek to his as she walked. "We're going to set a really pretty table. Something else I'm good at."

As she reached the landing, the slamming became a pounding. Her heartbeat matched it, but she continued down.

"It's like a tantrum, that's all. A bitch fest."

Outside, the sound of the sea became a roar, and a sudden, vicious gale hurled rain and sleet against the windows. In her arms, the dog whined and trembled.

She clutched him tight, maybe a little too tight as her pulse jumped and raced.

"It's not real. It's like the night with the blizzard that wasn't there." And still goose-flesh popped out on her arms.

Not real, not real, she repeated over and over in her head.

Something pounded against the front door, so hard she thought, for a moment, she saw the wood bow.

"She's pissed, she's pissed because I'm opening the house to people. But it's *my house*!" She shouted it, and strode back to the kitchen.

On the counter, the iPad played "Don't Worry Baby."

Warmth filled the room, and what felt like . . . a presence.

She turned, half expecting to see someone behind her. Yoda stopped trembling, yipped, then wiggled to leap out of her arms. He danced in place, turned his circles, then sat and lifted a paw.

To nothing she could see.

"That's supposed to be comforting. Reassuring. Maybe it will be when I've got my breath back. I'm going to set the table."

Once she had, the pounding stopped.

Had she given up for now? Sonya wondered. Either way, the quiet soothed.

Confident there, she arranged the charcuterie, then slid the board in the fridge while she dealt with her mother's final instructions.

Yes, it smelled amazing, she thought, and looked damn good when she put the meat on the Lisbeth's platter. But.

Carefully, she sliced half of it, then one more small, thin slice.

"We're going to sample," she said to the dog, who sat hopefully at her feet. "Half for you, half for me."

She laughed when he licked his lips, then fed him half. Though he all but inhaled it, licked his lips again, she took a careful bite.

"Oh, jeez! It's good. I think it's good. No, that's all," she added when he whined for more. "For now."

She arranged the medley of vegetables around the roast, tossed on some sprigs of fresh rosemary. Grabbing her tablet, she took a picture. All but dancing in place herself, she texted it to her mother, to Cleo before hauling the platter into the second oven to stay warm.

"I'm supposed to thicken all this juice into a smooth, thin gravy. I wish I didn't have to, but if it doesn't work, we toss it out. Nobody has to know."

She thought she managed it.

She opened a bottle of red wine to let it breathe, added a pitcher of spring water. Pretty little plates and napkins for the appetizers she'd serve in the kitchen.

Friendly.

She started to go in and light the candles in the dining room, but somebody had beaten her to it.

He, she, they were just trying to be helpful, she told herself. And the assist was worlds better than banging and pounding.

At seven, she set out the charcuterie and turned down the volume on her tablet.

"Music's fine," she said to whoever listened, "but we're going to keep it nice and low. Background."

She took off her apron, hung it up, then look a long look around.

"It's going to be fine."

Still, Yoda's barks and race to the door just before the sound of the doorbell made her jump.

"Showtime."

When she reached the door, she pointed at Yoda. "Friends." Then opened it to Anna and a man a full head taller holding a cake carrier.

Anna moved straight in for a hug. "I just missed you in town yesterday. In the market. And this is Yoda. Hello, handsome. And this handsome's all mine. Sonya, Seth, Seth, Sonya."

With his oak brown hair, sculpted features, and hazel eyes, he earned the *handsome.*

"Nice to finally meet you. Even though you're partially responsible for Anna working longer hours."

"Sales are up!" Anna said.

"I think that's the art and artist's fault. Let me take your coats."

"At least one of us was close behind. Saw the headlights. Oh, it's a convoy of Doyles. We're never late for dinner."

Doors slammed upstairs.

"I'm sorry about that."

Seth glanced up as Anna laid a hand on her belly.

"I visited Collin with Anna a few times, but never heard . . ."

"I hope you can ignore it. I'm so glad all of you could come."

Ace and Paula came next, bearing flowers. They made a striking couple, he with his flirtatious smile, she with her easy elegance and short, sleek swing of white hair. Then Deuce and Corrine, who offered a bottle of wine.

Corrine, with eyes of blue steel and silver-streaked black hair, nearly matched her husband's height.

Then Trey — more flowers — came in behind them, and it occurred to her she should have invited him to bring a plus-one.

But found she couldn't regret not doing so.

Besides, he'd brought Mookie, who made Yoda delirious with joy.

Within minutes, the kitchen filled with people, voices, flowers, wine.

Something slammed hard overhead.

"Someone's at it again," Corrine said easily. "Does it worry you?"

"I'm learning to live with it."

Corrine nodded, popped an olive. "Can I say — well, I'm going to — the house feels different with you in it. Not like a widower too often alone, but younger and fresher. And sexist or not, just a bit female. So here's to you. The lady of the manor."

"Thank you," Sonya said as glasses lifted. "I love it. I'll love it even more, I think, when my friend moves in."

"The illustrator." Paula nodded and smiled. "We hear all there is to hear."

"Know all there is to know." Ace wiggled his eyebrows. "And I know something in here smells good enough to eat."

"Let's hope so. I'm not much of a cook." She gestured toward the dining room. "Ace, please take the head of the table. Trey, could you give me a hand? It's a big platter."

When she opened the oven, he took one

look, then gave her a long one. "You made that?"

"Through my terror, yes. I'm going to open more wine, and get the gravy. And the rolls. Almost forgot the rolls. And I thought I could lure the dogs into the living room with a couple of chew bones."

"I already did that. They're settled."

She glanced around, realized no dogs roamed underfoot.

When Trey carried the platter in, she heard Ace's "Now, that's what I call a roast!"

She brought in the rest.

"It looks magnificent," Paula told her.

"Let's hope for good enough. It's a really big platter, so I'd like to plate everyone at the table."

She moved to Paula. "A little bit of everything, thank you."

"No need to be stingy with me. You can load me up," Ace told her.

"Now that you've had some time," Deuce began as she worked her away around the table, "how are you liking Poole's Bay? Not just the manor, but the village, the area."

"I like it very much. I never really expected to move out of the city, or far from it in any case. It's a big change, but it feels right for me. I like everything."

She sat, then looked up at another slam. "Or almost everything."

Seth looked up with her. "I'm not sure I

could get used to that."

"I'll let you know if I do. Right now I'm trying to figure out how my mother's going to react when she's here next weekend." And since no one made gagging noises as they ate, Sonya concluded she'd done well enough on the meal.

"I'm sure she'll be delighted to see you." Corrine sipped from her water glass. "And where you're making your home. Does she know the history of the house?"

"I've given her bits and pieces. I've been reading the book," Sonya said to Deuce. "The Poole family history. And I've been documenting the . . . incidents."

"That shows a practical nature," Corrine commented, then took another bite of beef. "That would be helpful in a move like this. Poole's Bay and the manor are a world away from Boston. A good quality for a woman building her own business, I'd think. Honesty would be another key, wouldn't it?"

"If you're not honest with a client, you'll lose the client."

Corrine nodded as she ate. "Honesty in business, and in personal matters, is essential to building relationships. And yet, you weren't honest with us."

"I — I'm sorry?"

"You said you weren't much of a cook, and I'm finding myself just a little irked that your pot roast is better than mine. It is, isn't it,

Deuce?"

"I take the Fifth."

"And we all know what that means." Now she picked up her wine, and those steel-blue eyes shifted to Sonya. "I think false modesty's just a dangling hook for compliments."

"I think you just gave me one," Sonya said as Anna didn't bother to smother a laugh. "And on my first attempt at pot roast."

"This is your first? And to think I was disposed to like you. Well, I want your recipe."

"It's actually my mother's but —"

"Check with her. She may not want to share outside of family. But if she will, I'll trade my pound cake recipe for it, which I don't offer lightly."

"She does not," Deuce confirmed.

"You'll sample that for dessert, if anyone has room after this meal. Anna made it for tonight. Do you bake?"

"I put frozen pizza in the oven. That's the height of my baking skills. Wait, I warmed up these rolls without burning them."

Corrine smiled. "I expect living up here you'll learn enough to get by."

"I'm hoping my friend Cleo handles most of that end of things."

"An illustrator," Paula said. "It's so nice to add more artists to the community."

They talked art and food, local events and impressions. And with conversation, the fire simmering, second helpings, and a fresh bottle of wine, Sonya put her first dinner party at the manor in the success column.

"I thought we'd have coffee and dessert in the music room."

"What a lovely idea. It's one of my favorite rooms," Paula told her.

"Would you play, Grandma?"

She smiled at Anna. "I could be persuaded."

"Why don't we let the younger generation deal with that." Corrine rose. "And I'll start persuading. We know the way," she said to Sonya.

Sonya got busy with the coffee. "I wasted a lot of nerves on tonight. You've got a great family."

"We do, and the meal didn't hurt. It was better than Mom's, and if you tell her I said that," Trey added, "I'll sue you for slander."

"Lips sealed. Oh God, Anna, that cake's gorgeous."

"Tastes even better," Seth told her. "Do you want me to start on the dishes? I have experience."

"And I may call on it before we're done. But let's leave all that for later, and keep this party rolling."

As music drifted in, she glanced toward the doorway. "She really can play. It's the first time I've heard the piano when I know someone's playing it."

"You hear piano music when there's not?"

She shrugged at Seth. "Sometimes, late at night."

A rich baritone joined the piano.

"That's Ace." Obviously familiar with the kitchen, the butler's pantry, Anna got out cake plates, coffee cups, and saucers. "They're a hell of a pair."

Together, they loaded up the dessert cart — a first for Sonya.

When they rolled it into the music room, she saw dogs piled together at Deuce's feet. Ace stood with his hand on his wife's shoulder, singing "One for My Baby."

When they finished, she applauded. "You're hired!"

"Do you play, Sonya?"

Sonya shook her head as Paula played some sort of trill. "My mother plays — not like that, but she plays a little. When she tried to teach me, we both agreed my talents lay elsewhere."

"Do one more before dessert," Anna insisted. "Do 'Embraceable You.' "

"Are you up for a duet, sweets?"

Paula glanced at Ace over her shoulder. "I could be persuaded."

"I asked them to sing this at my wedding. Our first dance."

"I've still got the moves." Seth turned Anna into a dance.

"It meant the world to them to sing at Anna's wedding," Corrine murmured.

"Their voices just mesh, don't they?"

"They do. Deuce grew up in a musical household. He can play, and he has a strong voice. I have no musical talent."

"Yours lay elsewhere. In your photography, your family."

"They do. Johanna played."

Glancing over, Sonya saw Corrine studying the portrait. "You were friends."

"We were. Trey told me you'd found her portrait. Seeing it? It's like time stopped. They'd like that you put her in here. This was one of her favorite rooms, too."

"It felt like the right place."

"Because it is." She surprised Sonya by linking their hands for a moment. "She'd never hurt you."

"Do you . . . Do you think she's here?"

"We'll talk sometime. I'll help with the coffee. I know how everyone likes it."

Since she felt she had to leave it at that, Sonya sliced cake.

And considered the idea of post-dinner in the music room a perfect choice when Anna sat down to play and dragged a clearly reluctant Trey with her to add his voice.

Anna stopped abruptly, and with wide eyes, pressed a hand to her belly.

Seth had already shoved up from his chair when her face lit up like the sun. "I felt him move! I felt the baby move!" Though she gripped Seth's hands, she looked at her mother. “Mom.”

“You’re okay?” Seth pressed his hand over hers. “I don’t feel anything.”

“Too early for you to feel,” Corrine told him as those steel-blue eyes went damp. “Right about on time for Anna.”

“It’s normal?” Trey gripped his sister’s free hand. “It’s a good thing?”

“It’s a normal, lovely thing.”

“When do I get to feel him?”

“A few more weeks, Daddy.”

Because it seemed like a family moment, Sonya slipped out. She’d give them a few minutes, and get the dishes started.

She walked into the kitchen and found it spotless. The dishwasher hummed, the sink sparkled, and when she checked the fridge, she found the leftovers — a fraction of what she’d feared and expected — efficiently tubbed.

“I — oh jeez — I appreciate it. You didn’t have to do all this.”

She still stood, at a loss, when Trey came in.

“No way you’re this fast on KP.”

“No, not me.”

“Well, okay. I think everyone’s going to head out. I was going to stay and give you a hand with all this. But no need for that.”

On cue, the tablet played “Stay.”

She heard the nerves in her own laughter. “Somebody likes having you around.”

Yoda came in, danced, whined.

"Oh, you want to go out. Of course you do. Give me one minute."

"I've got him. Mookie's going to want to go out with him. And when I say they're about ready to head out, it always takes a while for them to actually get out."

He wasn't wrong.

"Seth, be a good boy and take the cart back to the kitchen for Sonya. Ace and I should take our old bones home. As Corrine said, we'll leave the younger generation to help with the cleanup."

"It seems someone from what must be a much older one already took care of that."

"You're not kidding?"

Anna patted Seth's butt. "Come on. I'll go with you. I'll protect you and get my cake carrier."

"I ain't afraid of no ghosts," he said as he wheeled the cart away.

"Myself, I wouldn't mind an invisible maid. But," Corrine added, "it must be disconcerting."

"A time and energy saver, and yeah, *disconcerting*'s one word for it. I have, by my current count, the maid, a house disc jockey, a firewood hauler, the door slammer, the piano player. At least one of them likes dogs because they taught Yoda to shake. I need to write all that down, too."

"When you do, if I could see it? With what

I know of the family and house history," Deuce told her, "I might be able to help identify some of the . . . occupants."

"Sure. I'll send it to you once I get it together."

"You're a sturdy young woman." Paula offered a hand, then closed her other around Sonya's. "And we had an absolutely wonderful evening. Thank you so much."

Sonya got coats as Trey brought Yoda back. "I put Mook in the car. They wore each other out."

He lingered in the foyer as his family left. "You're okay?"

"Yes."

"And if you're not?"

"I'll call."

"This was great, and I think you're what the house needs. I hope it's what you need."

She felt her heart flutter, just a little, as he stood close with his eyes direct on hers.

"It feels like it."

"Good. I'll see you soon."

She closed the door behind him.

"He was thinking about it. I'm not wrong about that. He was thinking about making a move." She looked down at the dog. "Should I have made the move? I'm gun-shy, that's what it is. I have to get over it. But tonight, I'm pretty worn out, too.

"Let's go to bed, Yoda."

■ ■ ■ ■

She dreamed someone played the piano, but not in the music room. In the front parlor Astrid played something lively and quick. An older woman sat by the fire, working with a needle and an embroidery hoop while she tapped her foot in time.

In the grate, a log fell; embers flew.

Collin Poole stood beside Astrid and turned the page on her music.

Someone had pushed the furniture back, so three couples formed two lines, weaving back and forth as they danced.

She recognized what had to be Collin's twin, Connor. And the way he looked at his partner, she knew her for Arabelle, the woman he'd marry. The doomed Catherine's mother.

But young now, all of them, except the woman by the fire, and she saw the man sitting nearby, smiling, sipping his whiskey as he watched the dancers.

Astrid's parents, she thought, not certain why she felt so sure of it. She moved through the room, a ghost among ghosts.

She smelled the flowers — roses from the hothouse. The candle wax made by a family in the village, the woodsmoke from the logs a servant named John split and stacked.

It was early April — she knew it — only

weeks before Astrid Grandville would marry Collin Poole. The first bride to marry at the manor.

The first to die there.

When the dance ended, Collin took Astrid's hand, brought it to his lips.

It all froze.

Astrid turned her head and looked at Sonya.

"We were so happy this night. A prelude, Collin said, to all the parties we would host, with friends, with family. We had everything ahead of us."

"I'm so sorry."

"Find the rings. You're the last who can."

"But I don't —"

"Play, won't you, Astrid?"

"Of course."

The six dancers stood in their two lines. Collin stood at Astrid's shoulder.

She played the same song, exactly as before. Everything moved, exactly as before.

The old woman plied her needle and tapped her foot. The old man smiled and sipped his whiskey. Collin turned the page while the dancers wove.

In the grate a log fell with a shower of embers.

And Sonya woke standing beside the bed.

The dog slept on, so she hadn't disturbed him. She moved quietly out of the room, down the stairs, into the parlor.

The furniture stood exactly as it should. Then again, she thought, it hadn't been the same furniture in the dream. Or experience.

No fire burned, no candles flickered, no oil lamps glowed.

She wandered the room, but the only scent she caught came from the Asiatic lilies she'd bought the day before. At the piano, she ran her finger lightly over the keys.

Then she walked into the foyer, looked up at Astrid's portrait.

"I heard you. I don't know what it means or what to do about it, but I heard you."

But the house, and whatever walked in it, stayed silent.

In the silence, she walked back upstairs.

In bed she closed her eyes and waited for sleep.

Chapter Eighteen

In the morning, she documented every detail she could remember. Afterward, she held herself to half a day of work — in her mind to more or less make up for the time she'd taken for personal things during the work-week.

She put an extra hour in compiling a list of invisible companions. Considering her experience the night before, she included Astrid as the second bride to have seen her, spoken to her.

That left her free to handle the few domestic chores her invisible housekeeper left for her. Since the sun beamed, and with weekly laundry in the machine, she took a long walk with Yoda. The thinning blanket of snow lured her and the dog to the edge of the woods.

Then a few steps in.

She couldn't deny the wonder of it, the mystery of bare-branched trees, the deep green of pine. The light wind stirred pine needles to a kind of rustling, and from deeper in came the sounds of chirping and chittering.

Yoda scented the air just as she did, but the snow lay thicker there where the sun didn't quite reach.

And she was reasonably sure she saw hoofprints or paw prints, or some sort of animal tracks. While she'd enjoy crossing paths with a deer — getting a closer look — she doubted she'd enjoy crossing paths with anything less benign.

They'd just leave the woods, for now, to whatever wildlife wandered there.

"I'm a city girl, Yoda. And that's a fact."

Instead, they walked back to stand at the seawall. Now the wind stirred through her hair and blew cool across her cheeks. With it came the fresh, adventurous scent of the sea.

And under the clear sky, the sea held boldly blue to the horizon. Waves crashed below, and out on that plate of blue, boats glided.

To her delight, she spotted her second whale, even picked up Yoda hoping he'd share the thrill.

But he only wagged and licked her chin.

"This is it, doggie," she murmured. "This is it for me. Times like last night I get a little shaky, but this is it. Water and woods and whales. Who knew?"

When she took the dog back in, she swore she caught the scent of fresh orange oil.

"She keeps busy," Sonya muttered, and

hung up her coat.

Very busy, Sonya decided when she found her delicates hanging on the rod in the laundry room. A check of the dryer showed it empty, so she had no doubt she'd find what she'd tossed in it folded and put away.

Just as she'd found the dishwasher empty, and the dishes all put away when she'd checked that morning.

How would it feel, she wondered, to spend your afterlife — if that's what it was — cleaning up after someone else?

However ridiculous she found it, she took a long breath.

"Thank you very much. Please don't feel obliged."

The iPad played Kid Rock's "God Bless Saturday."

"Okay, fine." She couldn't stop the laugh. "Message received."

Clear skies gave way to thick, heavy clouds, and a solid six inches of snow fell overnight. Sonya took it as an excuse to indulge in a lazy afternoon. She took John Dee coffee, added a generous slice of pound cake. Then she snuggled in for the day.

Games of tug with the dog entertained both of them. Cuddled on the sofa on the second level of the library, she streamed whatever appealed.

She FaceTimed her mother, then Cleo. She

watched the dog romp through the fresh snow.

As normal a weekend, she supposed, as she could ask for. To cap it off, she and Yoda settled down by the library fire, he with a chew bone and Sonya with the book Trey had recommended.

He wasn't wrong in that plug, as she gobbled half of it down in one sitting.

She walked the dog under a pure white globe of moon that shed pale blue light on the new snow. And felt perfectly content, and absolutely home.

1892

I look like a queen. No princess am I, as I am a woman grown. My lover, my groom, my husband is a man of stature. As I stand in the chapel for all to witness our union, I stand proud, I stand regal in a gown by Worth.

I would accept no less than the best on this day.

I am blessed with an hourglass figure, and it is displayed to perfection in the heavy white satin with its long, lovely train. Its fluidity enhances my waist — a waist so small Owen can span it with his hands.

And he has.

The bodice of lace clings to my breasts and is layered with sheer gossamer to a deceptively modest high neck. I have eschewed the popular leg-o'-mutton sleeves — far from flattering on me — for slimmer and ruched.

My veil — precisely the length of my train — is topped with a diamond tiara I know sparkles in the light streaming through the windows of the chapel.

Under it, my hair, black as a raven's wing, has been styled in a smooth, high Gibson. It suits, very well, I'm told, my face and features, to which I added — discreetly — a bit of rouge on my cheeks and lips.

Owen has my hand as we take our vows. He is the most handsome of men in his high, starched collar and formal morning coat.

His eyes, so deep and green, smile into mine as he slips the ring on my finger. The gold band with its five diamonds he had designed for me by Cartier.

The vow, the kiss — soft, sweet, though we have shared more passionate kisses in private — and we are wed.

I have become Agatha Winward Poole. Mrs. Owen Poole. We are the Pooles of Poole's Bay.

And I know as we walk from the chapel, as people cheer and throw their rice, we make a fine match.

We hold the same rung on the social strata, and come to each other with respected family names and fortunes. Our looks complement each other's, so I expect to give him handsome sons and lovely daughters.

We will travel. This I have insisted upon. While we will make our home in the manor above the sea, we will not be chained to it. A pied-à-terre in New York will be essential to taking and holding our place in that society.

We will, of course, make a crossing to Europe for our honeymoon, where we will spend three months at the best hotels in Paris and Rome and London.

I will be the wife he needs as he is the husband I deserve.

People of the village tip their hats, their caps, toss flowers as the carriage rides through.

Owen, a generous man, tosses coins to those who line the roads.

I will also be generous. I lift my hand to acknowledge those who toil on the sea, in the fields, in the shops and cafés. And of course those who work for my husband and his family.

We will make a generous donation to the school in Poole's Bay to commemorate our wedding.

But today is a day of feasting and celebration. Though I could not include Jane, my husband's twin, in my wedding party, as she is heavy with her fourth child (and I find her so very dull and ordinary), I embrace her when we arrive at the manor.

We are sisters now, after all.

Of course, the servants are well prepared and serve our guests champagne. Soon, there will be dancing in the ballroom.

We will have music and wine, food presented from the menu I prepared. The manor is filled with flowers I selected and approved.

I am filled with joy as I embrace my dear mother, kiss my dear father.

All is a glorious blur.

I sweep up the grand staircase on the arm of my husband.

There is food beautifully presented in the dining room for those who grow peckish from dancing. I have arranged for two small buffets near the ballroom as well.

And wine, champagne, music.

I dance with my husband, with my father, and with my father by marriage, my brothers. With cousins, with friends.

We are lively on this day, and I drink champagne.

Because my husband asks it of me, and I am dutiful, I sit awhile with dull Jane. She speaks of her children, of course, as if the world revolves around them on this, my day.

Someone brings me a plate — so considerate. I nibble a bit, and find the cook and kitchen staff have outdone themselves.

I know I am radiant as I watch couples waltz, and see Owen, a kind man, take his niece — barely seven — around the floor.

Something sticks in my throat, and I reach for my glass. I am suddenly short of breath, dizzy. Too much champagne, I think, but now my throat is closed. I can draw no air.

My heart, my heart is palpitating. I cannot breathe!

The plate slips to the floor, and so do I. I am flushed with heat, fighting for breath as the world spins.

I hear voices. Who are they? Who are they?

I see Owen. Am I in his arms? I cannot speak. I would reach for him, but my arms are so weak.

I know fear, such terrible fear that clings to me as I die in my Worth gown on the ballroom floor.

I seem to be standing aside, watching and fearing as Owen holds me. I see the woman in black walk in. Why don't they see her? I would call out, but I have no voice.

She takes the ring from my finger, the beautiful wedding ring designed only for me.

She puts it on her finger where she wears three others.

She looks at me, and I am so afraid. She looks at me and smiles a terrible smile, and I am more afraid still.

Then she is gone, as I am.

Sonya spent the early part of her workweek ignoring the occasional bangs and slams, the bell ringing when she pushed herself down to the gym.

She sent proposals off to the Doyles and to the florist, and made what she considered solid headway on the caterer's project.

Midweek, she took a call from her old boss.

"I waited until noon," Laine told her, "hoping I'd catch you on a lunch break."

Lunch was usually half a sandwich or some cheese on crackers, maybe an orange at her desk. "It's good to hear from you, Laine."

"How are you doing, Sonya?"

"Really well, thanks."

Her iPad blasted out "R.O.C.K. in the USA." She swiped it off.

"How are you, how's Matt, and everyone?"

"We're good. Situation normal, so, you know, controlled chaos. Sonya, we got a call from Burt Springer. Ryder Sports."

"I remember Burt, sure."

"Ryder's opening another branch in Portland, Maine. They'll still have their three Boston stores, including their flagship."

Puzzled why Laine would contact her about an account, Sonya answered cautiously. "Business must be good."

"Must be. They want to refresh everything with a major campaign. It's a big expansion for them. Keep the logo, but with an update. Burt asked for you specifically."

"Oh." Torn between pleasure and regret, Sonya reached for her Coke. "That's flattering."

"You did good work for Ryder, and Burt knows it."

"I had a team."

"You did. And I'm going to be honest. I

told him you were no longer with us, and we could certainly handle the project. I also gave him your contact information. Matt agreed with me on that."

After the quick jolt, she struggled to keep her voice even. "That's more than generous of you, both of you."

"Fair's fair. He'll certainly contact you. In the meantime, we're going to work up a proposal and presentation."

"Of course."

"We're fond of you, Sonya, so I'm going to tell you, take the shot only if you're sure you can hit the target."

"That's damn good advice, and I'm going to take it."

When she hung up, she drank some Coke and tried to think. She got up and paced, and tried to think as Yoda took that to mean time for a walk outside.

She took him out, let him do what he had to do, let him romp through the snow. And thought.

She could hit the target if she got the shot. Yes, she'd had a team working on the designs — the signs, the ads, the beefed-up web page, on all of it. But she'd headed that team.

And an update, a refresh wasn't an overhaul like Burt and Ryder's had wanted four — no, five, five years ago. Nearly six, she remembered. The first time she'd headed a team on a major project.

She was better now, she told herself.

Yeah, damn right. If she got the opportunity, she'd take the shot.

She started to call the dog, then heard someone coming up the road. And recognized Trey's truck when he rounded the last turn.

Surprise.

Of course she wasn't wearing makeup. When would she learn? And had tossed an old jacket over older sweats.

He looked so damn perfect when he pulled up, got out. Leather jacket instead of a parka, as the temperature had inched up a bit. Jeans, boots, sweater. His hair just the right amount of windblown.

He'd smell good, too, she thought. He always did. Like . . . easy-going man. Nothing specific, nothing overt, just, well, mmm.

"Looks like I didn't interrupt after all."

"No. We're just on our afternoon walk. No Mookie?"

"He's with Owen and Jones. I had to go by there — business — and he ditched me." He bent down to rub Yoda into delirium. "Next time. I'm on my way to meet another client, had a couple minutes."

"Come on in."

"No, really, a couple minutes." As he rubbed the dog, he frowned up at her. "Is everything okay? Did something happen? You look a little stressed."

No makeup, old sweats, gorgeous guy she'd

really like to sink her teeth into, potential big, big job.

"No — well, a work thing — possible work thing. Oh yeah, I did meet Astrid the other night."

"Met? Astrid? The Astrid from the portrait?"

"I really think so, yes."

"I want to hear about that, and have to figure it'll take more than the two minutes I've got right now. If you don't have plans later, why don't I come back? I can pick up a pizza."

"I — sure." Why did he have those eyes? she wondered. Those glorious blue eyes. "If you don't have any plans."

"Now I do." He straightened. "Give me your toppings."

"Dealer's choice, except for anchovies. That's a firm no. Mushrooms are okay if you must."

"Got it. And I've about eaten up my two minutes. I wanted to come by in person to tell you, you're hired."

"Yes!" In triumph, she gave his chest a light tap with her fist. "You're not making a mistake."

"That's unanimous. You even got the nod from Sadie, and she's tough. I've got to go. I should be able to get back, with the dog, by six, six-thirty if that's not too early."

"You're bringing pizza. There's no too early

or too late. If you have another half a minute, can I ask if you think Bree would give me a recipe for something nice but easy?"

"I'm bringing pizza."

"Not for you, for my mother. She'll be here early Friday evening. I don't want to do takeout after she's worked most of the day and driven up from Boston."

"I've never asked Bree for a recipe, so I can't say for sure. But you should give it a shot."

She was going to take that shot, too, and pulled out her phone. "Can you text her, give her my number? If she's willing, she could text me. Remind her she likes me."

"No problem. See you tonight."

Which, she thought as he drove off, for her own purposes, she'd consider a date. "But now his firm's a client, so no taking a shot there unless I'm absolutely, positively sure.

"Back to work, Yoda, so I can close it down in time to make myself presentable. Casually appealing," she added as they started toward the house. "That's the goal."

She planned to knock off at five sharp.

But she got the go-ahead for the florist job.

Then had a long conversation with Burt Springer.

Grateful the conversation wasn't via Zoom so he couldn't see the nerves, she took detailed notes. In the end, she'd agreed to work up a proposal and presentation.

When she hung up, she sat very still.

"I can't blow this. What if I blow this? I can't blow it."

Her iPad played the *Rocky* theme and broke her panic with a laugh.

"Okay. It's okay. I've got ideas. I just have to pick the right one and make it shine. And oh shit, it's almost five-thirty! Shit, shit, shit!"

She shut down, then dashed over to her bedroom.

The red dress lay on the bed.

"No, no, no. It's pizza in the kitchen! Face first." She raced into the bathroom, took a breath. "Not too much. Just a little this, a little that."

Not too much still took time, especially since she couldn't decide on a happy dance or dropping her head between her knees.

She had three new projects — and one was a whopper. She still had one to finish, a client to satisfy.

"So we're rolling. We're busy, productive, and very, very nervous."

When she walked back into the bedroom, the red dress had been replaced by stone-gray jeans and a red sweater. "Okay, that's a very nice choice. We'll go with it because I don't have time to think about it."

She changed, decided her wardrobe assistant had made the perfect choice. As she tossed the sweats in the hamper, Yoda let out a bark and tore out of the room.

The doorbell rang.

"Okay. Here we go."

Yoda danced at the door, and when she opened it, the dogs immediately greeted each other with canine joy.

"A man, a dog, and a pizza. Jackpot!"

"You have to pay for it with a ghost story."

"No lack of those around here. Let me take your jacket."

"I've got it." He handed her the pizza before heading to the closet.

From the library, the iPad played "Welcome to the Party."

"They never quit. Come on, boys. And man."

"From what I've heard, your DJ has eclectic tastes."

"They lean toward rock or pop, spanning eras. And . . ." Sonya glanced back as they walked toward the kitchen. "They're quick. How did things go with the client?"

"Outside of privilege, I can say good enough. I'm also going to say, that alone?" He pointed a finger up. "Would send a lot of people heading back to Boston."

"I like music." After setting the pizza box on the counter, she peeked inside. "Pepperoni and black olives."

"I hear that's your go-to."

"No secrets in Poole's Bay."

"Oh, more than a few."

"I guess a lawyer would know. Want a beer?"

"Thanks." His brow lifted when she pulled one out of the fridge. "Sam Adams."

"I hear that's your off-tap go-to."

"So it is. Bottle's fine, I don't need a glass."

She handed him the bottle and wine for herself. "Has Mookie eaten?"

"I picked him up too early for him to mooch off Jones."

"Then he can mooch off Yoda."

She fed a couple of hungry dogs, got plates before they settled at the small table. Trey slid a slice on each plate before tapping his bottle to her glass.

"Did you get a chance to text Bree?"

"I did, and she grilled me some. Food allergies and all that. I just said you didn't mention any. She wanted your skill level."

"Did you tell her nil?"

With that slow smile, he shook his head. "Sorry, cutie, the pot roast ruined you there."

"That was a one-off."

"I hope not. Anyway, she said she'd send you something. She's tight with her mom, so you got points for wanting to make dinner for yours."

Sonya's eyes laughed over a bite of pizza. "And Manny? Is she tight there, too, by now?"

"Don't know, didn't ask. Don't really want to think about it. Pay up." He gestured with his beer. "Astrid."

"Astrid. I think I went through the mirror again."

"The mirror from your father's sketches."

She nodded, drank some wine. "I don't remember that part, but it felt like it. Which is impossible to explain."

"You don't have to."

"I don't know if it was a dream or real, but it felt real. I was in the front parlor," she began, and told him.

"I woke up, or whatever I did, standing by the bed again. But Yoda was still sleeping. Maybe because it wasn't scary this time, or not scary and tragic like seeing Marianne Poole die.

"But she saw me, Trey, and looked at me, spoke to me. No one else in the room did. I think she's the piano player. She doesn't play in the parlor now, and I'm wondering if it's because she's sad. And that night, the night I saw, everyone was happy."

"You didn't call me," he pointed out.

"It wasn't scary, not like before. I admit, I'd actually feel better about it if I thought I'm hallucinating. But I'm not."

"I can go through the house, try to find the mirror."

"I don't think you'd find it. I honestly don't think anyone will until it's ready to be found."

"You're ascribing a will to a mirror."

She put a second slice on each plate. "And that's the strangest thing about all this?"

"Got me there."

"I've thought about it, a lot. I think these — I'm calling them dreams — are a positive. I'm seeing and hearing and learning. Not just names and pictures in a book. And it's not like a movie, because I'm in it somehow. Like I step into that time, that moment."

Brows lifted, he studied her face. "You're adding time travel to hauntings?"

At that, she could only shrug. "And if I'd thought or said any of this a year ago, I'd have raced to the nearest shrink."

"You're about as stable as they come," Trey said half to himself.

"So I always thought. I always found Cleo's crystals and white sage, and her easy acceptance of, let's say woo-woo, just charming and harmless. Now I'm going to be particularly glad when she's living here and has that viewpoint."

"How soon?"

"She hopes another week or so. She had a yard sale at my mom's over the weekend, and told me she sold a lot. She's packing up some things, and my mom will bring what she can. And she's already got someone who'll take over the apartment. Bad breakup.

"The thing is, I'm not afraid here."

He looked her in the eye. "Ever?"

"All right, there are times. The Marianne dream, the business with the Gold Room, the banging, and the blizzard that wasn't. But now I have Yoda."

At his name, Yoda pranced over. Mookie followed.

"That's right, I've got you. And you, too, when you're around." She rubbed both dogs. "And I should let them out."

"I've got it. Are you trusting him on his own?"

"I've let him out a couple times. Watched him like a hawk. He stays close."

"And he'll stick with the Mook. He doesn't wander off."

Trey opened the door, but watched while the dogs played in the snow.

"Yoda sees them — or someone I don't — now and then."

Trey glanced back at her. "Mookie did whenever I brought him over to see Collin. Jones, too."

"You said you saw a woman on the widow's walk. A woman in white. I didn't believe you then. I do now."

"It wasn't Astrid. She was blond, and the woman I saw had dark hair. I couldn't really see her face. My father says I used to babble at ghosts when I came here as a toddler. I don't really remember."

Because she hoped he'd linger, she topped off her wine, got him another beer. "Anything else?"

"I was five. I know that because I'd just started kindergarten. I remember — it's a little blurry, but I remember seeing this guy in Collin's office. Wearing a tux. I knew it was a tuxedo because Owen — well, his parents — had a dog, and his markings looked like a tuxedo. It's why they called him Tux. Anyway, he was sitting there with a glass in one hand and a fat cigar in the other.

"I could smell the cigar smoke. He blew smoke rings and laughed. 'Young Oliver,' he called me. He said I was a good boy for visiting a lonely man. And to watch out for the witch or she'd gobble me up."

He glanced back. "I said that witches were for Halloween, and he said: 'Not around here.' I mostly remember because that one sent me running back to my father to tell him. And that's how the story goes."

"Did they check it out?"

"Apparently I wouldn't have it otherwise. But no one was in there. I'm going to let the dogs in the mudroom. Got an old towel?"

"There's one in there."

She rose to go with him, grabbed a second towel so they dried off the snow-coated dogs together.

"Kids and dogs then, I guess."

"I guess. One other time, and this I do remember." He straightened to lay the towel over the rod. "I was about twelve, and just taking up the guitar. Dad and Collin were in the game room — the one just beyond the library — playing chess. I didn't then nor do

I now have any interest in chess."

"He left the chess table and pieces to your father."

"Yeah, he did."

The dogs followed her back into the kitchen, where she got them both treats.

"I was bored, so I went down to the music room. Collin told me I could practice on the guitar in there anytime. I knew how to strum a few songs. Didn't have any fingering down, but I could strum a couple."

He picked up the beer. "So I'm working on it, trying to play Tom Petty's 'Free Fallin' ' — an oldie, but Tom Petty, and the chords are pretty basic. I tell myself I'm jamming it, and I look up, and there she is. Really hot babe."

He took a swig of beer.

"My twelve-year-old system's a lot more jolted by really hot babe standing there, smiling at me, than where the hell did she come from."

"Did you recognize her?"

"Not then." He shook his head. "Long blond hair, waterfall long and straight. She's wearing these jeans that ride low and tight on the hips and flare out below the knees, and this little white top, short enough that I can see — holy shit — skin."

He grinned as he waved a hand in front of his stomach. "It's got these flowers like embroidered up here, where it rides pretty low again, so oh my God, boobs are happening right under there. She's got beads — lots of them — hanging where I'm trying not to look. Pale pink lips, eyes that have all that stuff — liner and all that — thick, catlike so they just sing a song to a boy's libido."

"That's a lot of detail you've remembered on this one."

"It imprinted on my brain and my balls in that moment. 'My man,' she said, and I might have drooled a little, 'you can handle that axe.' At twelve, I didn't know axe meant guitar, so I think I said: 'Huh?' And she told me Petty was great but to try learning 'Satisfaction' because the Stones were gods. Then she shot me the peace sign, and she tapped those two fingers on those pale pink lips and blew me a kiss that left me a quivering puddle of hormones."

He lifted his beer in toast. "And she was gone."

"That's some story."

"I never saw her again, and Owen and I both looked. That is, until I saw her picture in Collin's book. I had my first real crush over the ghost of Lilian Crest, who called herself Clover."

That struck Sonya like a lightning bolt. "My father's birth mother."

"Don't hold it against me. I saw a hot babe, and she'd have been about eighteen. Actually, except for the pale pink, you've got her mouth."

"Oh." Instinctively, she pressed her fingers to it. "That's so strange to hear."

"It's a really nice mouth. So those are my experiences with the haunted and haunting — that I remember."

"But did you learn to play 'Satisfaction'?"

"Oh yeah. I like to think she heard me when I whacked away at it in the music room."

"I'm not a music history buff, but I don't think Tom Petty was around — professionally — in the sixties."

"No, he didn't hit until . . ." With a frown, Trey trailed off. "Now, why didn't that come home to me before?"

"Twelve-year-old hormones." Impossible, Sonya admitted, to ignore the fact that the man who currently had her hormones humming had once crushed on her biological grandmother.

In spirit, she supposed.

"She kept up, somehow."

"Must have. Collin liked music. You saw his vinyl collection."

And with a second lightning bolt, Sonya raised a hand. "Trey, maybe she's the DJ."

"Having that same thought."

On the counter, Sonya's phone played ABBA's "That's Me."

"Holy crap." She grabbed her wine, took a gulp. "Give me a second, because this is good. Unsettling for a minute, but good."

"That's your biological grandmother."

"Okay, back to unsettling. But it's good. We have an identity, and that has to be positive. I'm not calling her Grandma. I mean, when you think about it one way, she's younger than I am. I wonder if Collin ever met . . . his mother."

"I don't think he ever mentioned that to my father. I didn't tell my dad or Collin. I told Owen, because hot babe."

"Is it odd that I'm going to feel easier knowing who she is?"

"I think it would be odd if you didn't. She isn't trying to scare you. She wasn't trying to scare me. She was, and is, making a connection."

"She died here." And it hurt Sonya's heart to think of it. "She had to be afraid, in pain, but she plays music for me. I got a chance to bid on a major account today, and she played happy music for me."

"What major account?"

"Oh." Distracted, she pushed a hand at her hair. "Do you know Ryder Sports?"

"Sure. Based in Boston. I've bought plenty of their stuff online."

She smiled. "What did you think of their website?"

"Sucks you in, easy to navigate. Your work?"

"I headed the team that designed it. They're expanding, putting a store in Portland, and want to update. I'm going to be competing for the job against my old company. Which is . . . let's go back to *unsettling.*"

"Not for long." He said it so matter-of-factly, he gave her a boost she hadn't known she needed. "You're confident in your work for a reason."

"They're a strong, innovative company. But I've got the chance, and I'm taking it. And as you're a client, I'll say this in no way means I won't give your firm exactly what it needs and wants."

"Never doubted it. And speaking of clients, I've got a little work to do for the one I saw before I got here."

"We've still got pizza."

"No breakfast tops the breakfast of cold pizza."

"On that we agree. We'll split it."

Chapter Nineteen

It would help, Sonya thought as she took two slices for a plate, if she didn't like him so much. His looks, his manner, that easy way. She wasn't a puddle of hormones, but she could definitely feel them pulsing whenever he came around.

It was either get over it, or make that move and see.

A casual goodnight kiss at the door, she decided. And she'd know if they equaled hang-out buddies or had the potential for more.

He reached for the pizza box just as she turned. Bodies bumped. For one humming second, eyes locked.

"Sorry." He took a full step back.

No casual kiss at the door then, but . . .

"Are you sorry because you are or because you think you should be? If it's the first, I'll stop wondering. If it's the second, I'd like to know why."

"I'm sorry I think I should be."

"All right, sort of. But that doesn't answer the why."

"First off, the firm represents Collin's estate."

"Your father represents the estate, and my interests."

"We're a family firm."

"Okay, but . . . I kind of looked it up."

The faintest hint of a smile came into his eyes, then curved his lips. "Did you?"

"I thought it might, possibly, become an issue. My take is, I'm not actually your client, and even if I were, you'd continue to represent me competently. And, at your father's advice, I hired a lawyer in Boston. I'm not going to date him."

"Good policy."

"Especially since he's my mother's boss. But you said first off. If you're not attracted that way, then —"

"You're not a stupid woman, by any measure. But that's the beginning of a very stupid statement." He slid his hands into his pockets. "The way I see it, you've had a lot of major upheaval in less than a year. You called off your wedding."

"That's right. I think that's the sensible thing to do when finding your fiancé in bed with your cousin, don't you?"

"Sensible doesn't mean you weren't hurt."

"I was pissed. Shocked, and that still grates because it makes me a fool. And pissed, which is better. But I'm a little ashamed to admit I wasn't as hurt as I should have been. As I would have been if I'd loved him the way I thought I did. The way I should have loved a man I was going to marry. But he wasn't the man I thought he was, and *that* makes me a fool."

"You're not —"

Fire snapped into her eyes as she jabbed a finger at him and stopped him cold.

"I knew something wasn't right. I knew it, but I kept telling myself it was wedding jitters. I don't generally get jitters, but, well, I never planned a wedding before. And he wanted exactly the opposite of what I did. I wanted lovely and intimate and romantic, and he insisted on . . ."

She waved her arms in the air. "Big, fancy ballroom in the big, fancy hotel with a few hundred of our not-so-close friends, top-shelf open bar, and on and on. We looked at houses, and I wanted something like this. Not this scale, but I wanted a house with history and character, which is why this place had me at first sight. And he wanted sleek, modern, new, important neighborhood. I kept giving in, which isn't like me either. Why did I keep giving in? Because I'd said yes, and I thought I loved him.

"Fuck!"

After grabbing her wineglass, she circled the kitchen while he stood and watched her.

While both dogs sat and watched her.

"I'm shelling out ridiculous amounts of money for deposits because I'd said yes. Because it felt like we had more in common than not, and the sex was fine. So don't tell me I'm not stupid, don't tell me I wasn't a fool when I was. On the day, the very day I walked in on him and Tracie, I canceled an appointment with the breathtakingly expensive florist because I just couldn't take it. I needed a break, all the while telling myself it was just wedding jitters."

She glugged some wine. "My ass! And there they were, their clothes scattered along the way to the bedroom. And if I had loved him, it shut off just like that!"

She snapped her fingers. "All I felt was pissed off and disgusted. I kicked them both out of *my* house. Both of them mostly naked. That was satisfying."

She drank more wine. "With him claiming it didn't mean anything, she came on to him, he just slipped. And that was it for me, but he wouldn't leave it alone. He went to our bosses and strung them some bullshit about me having a little breakdown when I had no intention of telling them what he'd done. But he's going to lay it all on me? Just hell no. So I told them, and we thought we'd worked it out. I loved working there, and they'd see to it we didn't work on the same projects. He obviously didn't love me, so he'd get over it, and we'd both move on.

"But no. He found little ways to get under my skin, and I ignored it. Then he found bigger ways. He keyed my car, he let the air out of my tires so I had to call an Uber at midnight. Midnight because he'd sabotaged my work, just wiped my work off my computer, my backup, so I had to stay late and put it back together. I couldn't prove it, but come on, who else? They couldn't fire him, no proven cause, so I had to quit."

She jabbed a finger at Trey. "You're not rebound guy because I'm not rebounding. And that was a lot. Wow. I'm still pissed."

"Done?"

"Yeah, sorry." More than a little appalled at herself, she dragged a hand through her hair. "That was way beyond where I meant to go."

"We're going to back up a little." He picked up the second beer he'd only half finished. "Why did you pay the deposits?"

"He was going to pay part of the balance, and for the honeymoon — mostly. Traditionally, the bride's family pays . . . because I'm an idiot."

"Stop it. You're not."

He didn't jab a finger at her — not his style — but held up a hand and just as effectively cut off her response.

"He manipulated you, and it sounds like he's damn good at it."

"I suppose. I got some of it back — more

than I expected, largely due to Cleo. She took some of it on, and she's got this way of talking and talking, all calm and reasonable." As it hit her, she took a slow sip of wine.

"A lot like you."

"Good. Now let's talk about him keying your car, giving you flat tires. Did you file a report?"

"Yeah. What were the cops going to do? Nobody saw him. What could the bosses do? And if they'd fired him, I think it would have made it worse. I did what was right for me, and found out I like working freelance. I like being in charge of, well, all of it."

"Has he bothered you since?"

"Not really. Then I moved here. And this is the most I've thought of him since I have."

"I want to know if he does."

She frowned at him. "You're mad," she realized. "It hardly shows, but it does, a little."

"Of course I'm mad. We'll put aside him screwing your cousin. That's just the move of an asshole who thinks cheating's no big deal. He manipulated you into pumping out money for something you didn't want, and if you hadn't caught him, you'd very likely be living in some slick house you didn't want. That would've been your mistake."

She opened her mouth, then shut it again. Because truth was truth. Her mistake.

He set the beer down again. "But the rest is vindictive, mean, petty, criminal, and dangerous. So yeah, I'm mad, and I want to know if he comes at you, in any way, again."

"All right." The fact she could see the mad not only calmed her but gave her another boost she hadn't known she'd needed.

"Will you punch him in the face?"

"That's always satisfying, in the moment. But you can prolong the moment by maneuvering him into doing the punching, in front of witnesses. Then he's got an assault charge to deal with."

"I bet you could do it, too." She let out a breath. "Now, the whole point of that unhinged rant was to say yes, I had an upheaval, but it unleashed rage — pretty obviously — and didn't leave me with a broken heart, weeping into my caramel ice cream while watching sad movies."

"You made your case there. I figured you'd quit your job because it was too awkward to work in the same office. So, moving from there, you still have upheavals. Learning your father had a twin, Collin's will, packing up your life in Boston to come here. Add what you're dealing with here."

"I love this place. It surprises me how much. Still, I understand you might not want to get involved, on a personal level, with a woman who goes on an unhinged rant about a man she broke things off with months ago."

"You didn't."

"I didn't?"

"You went on a rant about a situation and your reaction and responses to it. Which, in my opinion, you're taking too much of the blame for. But you'll get over that."

"I will?"

"Because you're really not stupid, Sonya. But he did hurt you. Even if it was only your pride, your ego, your sense of trust, he hurt you."

"Cleo said about the same. Maybe I should try to fix you up with Cleo."

"I like her, but I'm interested in someone else."

"After all that?"

"More after all that, actually."

He took a step toward her. The phone jammed out with "Let's Do It Tonight."

When she laughed, he drew her in. Slow. In a kind of glide that had her heart bounding into her throat, then dropping down to her toes.

He watched her as his hands slid from her shoulders, down her arms. Watched her as he eased her just a fraction closer. Watched still as his lips brushed hers, just brushed.

She lost her sense of time and place as he took the kiss deep. Slow, sumptuously slow and deep.

Her knees didn't go weak. She thought they might have dissolved, but the hands on her hips kept her upright as his mouth woke every nerve in her body.

"Oh. Well," she managed. "I was hoping that would work."

"I'm good with taking things slow if you want some time."

"I really don't."

With a hand at the back of his neck, she drew him down to her again.

"If we keep this going, we'll end up on the kitchen floor." He nipped his teeth at the side of her throat and sent those awakened nerves snapping. "And the dogs'll be all over us. I can let them out or we go upstairs."

"I vote for bed." Wanting him, wanting her hands on him, she tugged him from the room. "It's a really nice bed. The dogs can share Yoda's."

He stopped, twice, driving her a little more crazy each time. The dogs trotted up ahead of them.

"You said sex with the dickhead was fine."

"I did?"

"Yes. Do you want to retract or amend that statement?"

"I can wish I hadn't said it, but no. It's accurate."

He circled her into the bedroom. "I can do better than fine."

"You already are. I might be a little rusty, but I'm pretty sure it's all going to come back to me."

Linking her arms around his neck, she pressed her body to his.

"It already is."

In the flickering light of the fire, the low light of the lamp, he ran his hands under her sweater, up her back. He took his time learning the body he'd imagined far too often over the last weeks.

Something about her. Something.

Now she hummed low in her throat as his hands roamed. Now he felt her skin warm under the trail of his fingers.

"Nice sweater." She quivered, just a little, as he drew it up and off.

"Yours, too." Easing it up his body, she sighed.

His hands moved, a sort of glide, up her back, down again.

"We should sit down a minute."

"Sit down?"

"And take off our shoes."

"Oh. Right."

They sat, hip to hip, on the side of the bed.

"A little rusty," she said.

"Not from where I'm sitting."

She tossed back her hair. "Maybe a little nervous."

"We'll take care of that."

And, sitting hip to hip, he cupped her face in his hands and kissed her.

Need smothered nerves. As she shifted to him, everything took on such focus, such clarity. The feel of his skin against hers, the taste of that wonderfully lazy mouth, the big, hard-palmed hands on her face, the scent of flowers, and him.

The smooth, crisp sheets when he laid her back made an arousing contrast with the weight of his body on hers.

He never broke the kiss, but took it deeper. Slow, slow, slow, while his hands began to move again. Under those hands, her heartbeat thickened; under those hands, she luxuriated in being touched.

And used her own.

Lean muscle, hard planes, strong shoulders. So long, she thought, since she'd explored a man's body, felt him respond to her touch.

Testing now, both of them, gauging those responses.

What do you like? What moves you? What excites you?

When he released the hook of her bra, her pulse hammered; anticipation spilled through her like wine.

When his mouth took her breast, she arched, urging him to take more.

Arching again, her hands fisted in his hair, she demanded more.

When he gave and he took, she tugged at his belt. Everything in her shot to urgent. He murmured something as he slid her jeans down her hips, but she couldn't hear through the pounding of her own heart.

When, she wondered, had the ache of need burned into fire?

Slow, he'd thought, this time, this first time. But she trembled, and heat pumped off her skin. Murmuring still, his lips pressed to her throat where her pulse hammered, he cupped her.

At the press of his hand to her center, she broke in one long, hard wave. Her body rose to his, shuddered, then fell. The hand she'd clutched at his shoulder slid away.

He might have soothed, might have tossed control aside and devoured. Before he could do either, she rolled. And took him over.

First his mouth in a wild, greedy kiss that shot into his system like a live wire. Then his body as she straddled him and took him in. Took him deep.

He saw Sonya in the firelight, moving over him, her skin glowing, her arms lifted as she rode another wave. Then she took his hands, pressed them to her breasts.

Even the thought of control snapped. He rode the next wave with her.

Soft, sated, satisfied, she melted down to him. She wondered if her sigh sounded like a prayer of gratitude. As he stroked his hand down her hair, over her back, she sighed again.

"Better than fine. Like . . ." She managed to lift an arm in the air. "Up there better than fine."

"Glad to hear it." She felt his lips curve against the side of her throat. "I planned to take it slower."

She raised her head, pushed back her hair as she looked down at him. "Was I too fierce for ya?"

"Just fierce enough. But I missed a few spots." He trailed a finger down her cheek. "I'll catch them next time."

She lowered her forehead to his. "I need to tell you something."

"If you can't tell me something when we're naked in bed after sex, when?"

"It's actually about getting naked in bed after sex. My personal rule is a minimum of four dates before I get to that event. Four, because three's become a clichéd general rule, and I don't like to follow clichés."

"Or general rules?"

"Actually, I'm fairly reasonable about general rules."

"So you broke your personal one with me. Flattering."

"Not exactly. See, I decided to consider the day you and Owen moved the furniture and stayed for dinner a kind of date."

"Interesting." Lazily, he twined her hair around his finger. "I usually know when I'm on a date."

"Well, my scale. Then the whole Gold Room incident, followed by dinner at the Lobster Cage. I considered that date number two."

"That actually was a date."

"Then on that our scales agree. After some debate and a lot of justification, I deemed the pot roast dinner a date, which makes three."

"It appears all our dates involve food."

"Dates so often do, right? And tonight, you brought pizza, so —"

"Fourth date. You didn't break your rule for me."

"No. I just worked it out my way so it came out to four. So, essentially, we've been dating for weeks."

"Looks like I need to catch up."

"I'd say you have." She gave him a quick kiss, then sat up. "You know, I didn't turn on the fire, light the candles on the mantel, or turn down the bed." Suddenly, she gripped his hand. "And I just had a very disturbing thought. Do you think they, um, watch? All the time? Like when we were celebrating our fourth date?"

His gaze shifted to the fire, the candles. "That is a disturbing thought."

"More when you consider one of them is my biological grandmother."

"I'd rather not think about it. I'm not going to think about it. Let's give her — and them — the benefit of trusting they respect privacy."

"I can do that. I think I really need to do that."

"Since you can, and you will" — he sat up, then tumbled her down again — "let's take care of those spots I missed."

She didn't give ghostly voyeurs another thought.

And he stayed.

At three, the clock sounded and woke him. Beside him Sonya stirred, but didn't wake. He slipped out of bed, pulled on his jeans. Since both dogs watched him, tails thumping, he shook his head.

"Stay." He whispered it. "Stay with Sonya."

To be sure they did, he closed the door on his way out.

There was a table clock in the front sitting room that chimed the hour, he remembered. But it chimed a soft, musical sound. That's not what he'd heard.

The old grandfather clock, he thought, second parlor. The one Collin never wound so it wouldn't sound the hour because he'd found it annoying. Particularly at night.

Sonya might have started winding it — but that didn't explain why he hadn't heard it any other time since she'd moved in.

He made his way downstairs and to the room Collin had called the Quiet Place because of its position in the house. It had only one window, facing north. The sound of the sea or the wind through the pines didn't reach here.

He turned on the light and studied the old clock with its carved cabinet and moon-faced dial. The brass pendulum hung still, and the room quiet as always.

But the hands on that moon-faced dial stood at three.

Had they always? he wondered. He couldn't remember, but he'd clearly heard the trio of bongs — slow-paced, almost funereal.

As he walked to it, a wave of icy air hit him.

He'd felt it before, in the Gold Room.

"So it's you," he murmured. "Good to know. Next thing I'd like to know. Why three a.m.?"

He heard piano music from the music room, stepped back.

"Midnight's supposed to be the witching hour, right?"

"Yeah. I thought —" He turned, expecting to see Sonya.

And looked at her grandmother.

"Man. All right." His heart gave two hard beats before it settled again. "It's you. I saw you once before."

"Sure. You were such a cute little guy. You had good hands on that guitar. You grew up."

"Yeah." You never got that chance. "Did you make the clock chime?"

"Not me, baby. You're right, that's all that bitch. Every freaking night, bong, bong, bong."

"How come I can see you now?"

She smiled, a pretty teenager who'd never grow old. "Because you're here, and she's here — Sonya — and you guys did the it."

She shrugged. "Cool with me. Free love. I missed most of that. Things were just happening when I, you know, died. Bummer. But I loved Charlie. We really had it together. I'd have loved my babies."

"I'm sure you would have."

"We were going to live here, start a commune. Art, music, poetry." She did a little spin. "Lots of spiritual stuff, too. But."

She lifted her shoulders, let them fall. "I had a ring, too."

"I'm sorry."

She lifted her left hand, tapped her ring finger with the other. "That fucking witch took it, so you watch out for her, got it? Then that old bitch — Charlie's mom — she took care of the rest. He shouldn't've done what he did, kill himself like that. I mean, wow, I didn't have a choice, but he did. And that's how she got her hands on my babies, my little boys. I was pretty pissed at him for a while. But, well, shit, I love him."

"Is . . . Is he here, too?"

For a ghost, he thought, she had a smile like the summer sun.

"Well, yeah, what do you think? Lots of us here. It's the freaking curse. So, that's it for now. You need to help Sonya — it's so far out I've got a granddaughter. I mean, far *out*! You need to help her get those rings back."

She smiled again, sweet as spun sugar. "You were real good to my boy. It's weird calling him a boy because he got to be an old man. Anyway, coming out like this really fries me after a while. You should go back to bed."

"Wait. I've got questions."

But she was gone, and the music left with her.

Deliberately, he opened the glass cover on the face of the clock, moved the hands, at random, to twenty after four.

He checked the music room anyway, then did a long circuit around the main floor, and another on the second before he went back to Sonya's room.

She slept still. Both dogs opened their eyes to watch him as he went back to the bed. He pulled off his jeans, slipped into bed with her.

In sleep, she turned to him. Because she shivered, he drew her close.

He woke in the morning to see her pulling on a sweatshirt.

"Early riser."

"Oh." She turned and laughed. "Yeah, sorry. I thought I was quiet."

"You were. I have to be an early riser. I've got court this morning."

"Court? Do you really wear a tie with your flannel shirt, or an actual suit?"

"Yeah, an actual suit. It's court."

"I bet you look good in one. I'm going to let the dogs out, make coffee."

"Right there, you've earned undying gratitude."

"I'll take it. There's spare toothbrushes in the bathroom. Either you guys stocked them or Collin had them. Help yourself."

"I will. Okay if I grab a shower? It'll save me time at home."

"It's all yours. Come on, boys, let's go outside."

The *outside* had them both scrambling up and out, with her hurrying after.

She looked good in the morning, he thought. But then, to his eye, she always did. He thought it a shame he couldn't talk her into the shower with him. But besides court, he needed time to tell her about three in the morning.

He could've spent a year in that shower, and gave Collin full marks on it.

When he'd dressed and walked downstairs, he found coffee waiting while she put pizza on plates.

"You want it warmed up?"

"Why?" He went for coffee first.

"That's what I say. What's wrong with us?"

"I've got time to sit down here with it. Do you have time?"

"Sure." She sat at the counter with him. "When I go up, the bed'll be made as perfectly as in the best hotel. I've gotten over the oddness of that, and appreciate the time saved."

He jumped right in. “Do you know the old grandfather clock in the second parlor.”

“The second parlor is . . . Right, that one. With the big clock. I haven’t really used that room.”

“Have you wound the clock?”

“No. I should do that? I hadn’t thought about it.”

“Don’t. I’m conducting an experiment. Have you ever heard it bong? Because that’s the word for it. On the hour, once for one, twice for two, and so on. One bong on the half hour.”

“No, I don’t . . . maybe.” She frowned. “Maybe.”

“Three bongs, at three a.m.”

“I didn’t dream that, or imagine that?”

“Not unless I did, too. And I didn’t. You slept through it last night. Collin never wound it either because who wants to try to sleep with that thing going off every hour? It woke me up, so I went down to take a look.”

She took a moment, ate some pizza. “I’m going to see your ‘call me’ and raise it with a ‘why didn’t you wake me up?’ ”

“Maybe you’d just wound it, and it seemed wrong to wake you up at three in the morning to ask.”

“If I’d wound it, we’d have heard it while we were eating, while we were having sex.”

“That’s a point. Blame three in the morning and fuzzy thinking.”

She took a moment for coffee while she studied him. "You're probably good in court."

"That's what they pay me for. It wasn't wound, and the hands stood at three — on the dot. If you haven't used the room, you probably didn't notice where the clock stopped."

"No, but I'll pay attention now."

"I moved them — the experiment. Before I did, the piano music started. 'Barbara Allen.' I was going to check, and when I turned around? Hot babe."

She nearly choked on breakfast pizza. "You saw her? Lilian Crest?"

"I'd say in the flesh, but that's not really accurate."

He told her, recounting the conversation.

"Lots of them," Sonya repeated. "I thought I'd accepted that, but . . . I'd have to consider that confirmation. She had a ring. I thought she must have, since the number seven keeps coming up. But damn it, if she knows Hester Dobbs has them, why not tell you how to find them, how to get them back?"

"Not in evidence, but it might be she — they — just don't know. I'm stuck on the clock, on three. Okay if I come back, after work? I could pick up something for dinner."

"I'd like you to come back whether you pick up something or not. But that's a plus."

"How do you feel about Chinese?"

"Fondly."

"Check the online menu at the China Kitchen, and text me what you want. I've got to move. Judges dislike a lawyer who's late for court. I can drop Mookie at the office. Or I can leave him with you."

"Oh, leave him. We'd love it."

"So will he." He cupped her face, kissed her before he got up. "Unless you say no, I'm tossing a change of clothes in a bag before I come back. And staying."

"I'm not saying no."

"Good. I'll see you, probably about six again, depending."

"Good luck in court."

Alone, she rested her chin on her fist and thought just how much her life, her world had changed. As part of the change, she got up to call in the dogs and give them breakfast.

Chapter Twenty

Since Yoda had company, she got a spare chew bone so both would have something to gnaw on while she worked.

As they started up, her iPad greeted her with Adele's "Lovesong."

"It's lust and like at the moment, thanks, Lilian."

The music shifted almost instantly to "Crimson and Clover."

"Okay then, Clover." The dogs took their bones by the crackling fire — one she hadn't started. "I've got to knuckle down to work. I've got a job to finish, two to start, and a major proposal to get going. And my mother's coming for the weekend, so no making up time there."

She pressed her fingers to her eyes, drew a deep breath. Then booted up her computer.

An hour in, and she *would* get the catering job to testing stage by midday, her phone signaled a text.

Which reminded her she had to look up

the menu and text Trey.

She read the text from Bree.

This scallop and pasta dish is quick, simple, and delish. IF — listen up! — IF you don't overcook the pasta or the scallops. Got that? Pay attention.

"I got it, I got it." She scanned the recipe. "It doesn't sound so simple — and you didn't need to use all caps on don't-overcook reminders. It's intimidating."

Your cook time's about ten minutes, so don't start it until your mom's there and you're ready to eat. Sometime during the day, you're going to make some — quick, easy — beer bread.

"I am? Bread. Jesus, that's crazy. I'm not making bread."

But she read the instructions.

"Okay, that actually does sound easy. I can do that."

I assume you can make a salad. If not, text me, and after I get finished mocking and judging you, I'll send instructions. Finish off the meal with a raspberry sorbet. I could give you a recipe for that — basic — but you'll buy this at the store so you don't feel overloaded.

Bon appetit! Bree

It required another steadying breath.

Thank you. My mom may collapse in shock, but thank you. I do know how to make a salad — it's a house specialty — so no mocking or judging required. I swear by all that's holy I won't overcook because I sense the scope of your wrath. Much appreciated, Sonya

Bree signed off with an emoji of a smiley face wearing a chef's hat.

Sonya set the phone aside. She'd take it when she went into the village to shop. And she wouldn't think about it until.

By midday, the catering site was ready for testing. And the dogs ready for a walk. So, she realized, was she.

The dogs bounded through and wrestled in the snow. She thought, if she looked hard enough, she could see tiny patches of anemic grass on the south side of the house.

The bounding and wrestling meant she had to mop both dogs up. They got a treat, and she got a Coke, a bowl of pretzels, and a tangerine.

At nearly four she surfaced. Cursed when testing showed her an error. After some adjustments, she ran it again.

And something that had simmered in the back of her mind on the Ryder job popped out.

"That's good. That could be good. Bold. Fun. Movement."

She got up, got her tools, and started a fresh mood board.

At her desk, she did some quick sketches just to give herself another visual.

Caught up, she shifted back and forth between the testing and refining her vision.

And jumped when a dog stood on either side of her wagging.

"Oh! God, it's almost six. I didn't mean to work this late. Sorry, boys, sorry. Let's shut it down and go — no saying the word yet."

After she backed up everything, shut down, she jogged downstairs with them. Since they dashed to the door, she went after them. She'd let them out, come back for a jacket.

And opened the door just as Trey started to ring the bell.

"Oh! They didn't bark."

"Mookie knows when it's me. I guess this one does now, too." He handed her a takeout bag before he gave the dogs attention. "Hi, guys. Good day for you?"

"I should've let them out again an hour ago, but I got involved. I just shut down. You're still wearing a suit."

A deep, dark gray with a pale gray shirt and a maroon-and-navy tie.

She all but felt her mouth water.

"You look good in a suit. I figured you would."

Since the dogs ran out and rounded the house, she stepped back to let Trey in. "I took a walk with them about noon, then I completely lost track of time."

"They're fine. You look a little dazed. Everything okay?"

"Yes. The work — it just started rolling. This smells great."

"You made good choices." He hung up his coat.

"I try."

It felt nice, just nice, to walk with him back to the kitchen.

"Why don't you sit down? I'll pour you some wine." He kissed her, several levels up from a casual hello. "You put in a long one."

"So did you, but I'll take the wine. How did court go?"

Since she'd gone for shrimp, he pulled a white out of the cooler. "Divorce case, not pretty. The now officially ex-husband made a scene, an ugly one, right in the courtroom."

"I'll bet judges don't like that even more than lawyers who are late."

"You win that bet. After two warnings from the bench, he got cited for contempt. He's lucky it's just a fine because he was heading for a night in jail until his lawyer finally got him to shut the hell up.

"Okay if I grab a beer?"

"You don't have to ask, Trey."

"Then I'll grab one and get the dog food. I

picked up more food there — it's still in the truck."

"You didn't have to. I'm going to the store tomorrow."

"Cross that one off your list. Mookie eats more than Yoda." He dished out their food and straightened at the woof at the door.

"Speaking of. I'll dry them off."

"Not in that suit you won't." She waved him back.

"Then I'll set the human food out."

And nice again, she thought, to share Chinese food in the kitchen, to talk about normal things.

"I'd like to see the mood board and sketches on Ryder."

"Sure. It's just preliminary." She smiled when he loosened his tie and flipped open the top button of his shirt. "And that's why women often like men in ties."

"Because they like to see them wearing a noose?"

"No, because when they do what you just did, it's sexy. I don't know why, but it is."

"I've got to wear another one on Saturday. Wedding. A cousin in Kennebunkport. You've got your mother this weekend or I'd talk you into going with me."

"Don't you already have a plus-one?"

Shaking his head, he speared one of the shrimp off her plate. "Wedding dates are dicey. Then you've got your great-aunt Marilyn giving your plus-one a significant look, telling you what a lovely couple you make before she beams, and says, *When are we going to dance at your wedding, Trey?*"

Shaking his head, he went back to his moo shu pork.

"Once a single guy hits thirty, you spend half your time at a family wedding dodging the when's-your-turn question."

"For women that comes once you pass twenty-five. Do you actually have a great-aunt Marilyn?"

"I do, who's married to my great-uncle Lloyd, who'd guffaw — he's the only person I know who actually guffaws — as he ogled my date, telling me I'd better snap this one up quick. She looks like a keeper."

"Now I'm sorry I'm going to miss it. For me it's my maternal grandmother, particularly, who'll give me a long, piercing look while reminding me having a career is fine, but a job doesn't warm the bed at night and won't put a baby in my arms."

"Ouch."

"Yeah, Grammy always manages the two for one — marriage and babies. Her first comment when I got engaged? It's about time."

"And when you ended it?"

"I can thank my mother — with the full backing of her sister — for warning Grammy off. Apparently Tracie got a stinging lecture, and I got a warm, sympathetic call."

"Grammy's okay."

"Yeah, she is. But if I took you to a wedding, I'd get that long, piercing look."

They let the dogs out while they dealt with the dishes. Just as Sonya wondered how long the normal would last, she saw that all the cabinet doors in the butler's pantry stood open.

"Oh well."

She walked in to close them.

"Did anything happen today?"

"Nothing new or noteworthy. I looked at the clock whenever I came down. It's where you put it. Four-twenty. Otherwise, Casper the friendly housekeeper was on the job."

"Casper?"

"I'm considering the name gender neutral, even though I think female. She made my bed, lit the library fire, washed and folded the dog towels. And Clover provided my office music, as usual."

His smile spread. "You're calling her Clover."

"She told me to — musically. Crimson and clover," Sonya sang, "over and over."

Instead of the slow smile, he shot her a quick grin equally appealing. "Got it. And you can sing."

"Carrying a tune isn't singing."

"You can sing," he repeated. "Something you kept under wraps after pot roast. You won't get away with that again. So nothing from the third floor?"

"Not today, and every day there isn't is a good one. How do you feel about watching a movie?"

"Do you want to use the media room?"

"Actually, I don't think I'm quite ready for an evening down there. I use the library."

"Works for me, depending. What kind of movies do you go for?"

"I can go for a rom-com now and then, but I also like action movies, thrillers. I've benched horror flicks for now."

"You like horror movies?"

"A lot, but like the media room, not ready to watch one here. I'm also a fan of the Marvel Cinematic Universe."

"Are you really?"

"I will confess," she said, "Iron Man is my superhero boyfriend. It used to be Spider-Man, but I've aged out and it just doesn't feel right to lust after a high school kid."

" 'Nuf said."

"Okay, another Stan Lee fan. Between one thing and another, I haven't seen *The Marvels* yet."

"Then we have a winner. Got popcorn?"

"Duh."

"I'm going to get my bag out of the truck and change."

Normal, she thought, even ordinary could equal just lovely. Dinner and a movie at home, popcorn and a couple cold Cokes? For now, this minute? Perfect.

With the dogs once again dried off, they trailed her up to the library.

Trey stood, now, like her, in sweats, studying her board.

He took the tray she carried with popcorn, Cokes, dog treats, and set it on the desk.

"I like it. The colors are going to catch the eye. Dynamic colors. Even a guy who just gears up for some touch football after Thanksgiving dinner likes to think he's dynamic. The font you have for *Sports* in the company name has movement."

"I just tweaked what we'd done before. Boosted it a little. So it looks . . . faster."

"It works. This sketch." He tapped one. "I like the way you've piled and arranged sports equipment on a field. Could be any kind of playing field. Football helmet, baseball bat, cleats, running shoe. You've got your lacrosse stick, basketball, swimming goggles, part of a dirt bike, a hockey puck, golf club. A belay rope, right?"

"Yeah. Maybe it's too crowded."

"But it's not. I don't know how you figured it out, but it's balanced. The tag under it — it's a tag, I think. *Game On.* That's a challenge. You got game? Come to Ryder Sports."

Every professional inch of her relaxed and warmed.

"That's just what I was aiming for, so if

that's what you see, it's a good start."

"What else have you got in mind?"

"I don't want to change the infrastructure of the website. It's user-friendly, but I'd like to add a gallery. Photos of regular people using Ryder gear — clothes, equipment. Like a woman on a bike, a guy swinging a golf club, kids playing basketball, that sort of thing. I have to think it through, but it could add a bang, and double as ads, since they want a full campaign. Digital, TV, in-store posters. Like whatever your game — if I stick with that tag — Ryder Sports gives you the edge."

"You sold me."

The dogs followed them up the curve of stairs, then settled down to munch their dog biscuits. With popcorn, Sonya and Trey sat on the leather sofa, feet on the coffee table.

After the movie, the sofa seemed the perfect place to tangle together while the dogs snoozed.

Later, in bed, they tangled again.

As she drifted off to sleep, Sonya thought if this was the wide-open sexual energy of beginnings, it really, really worked.

In the second parlor, just before three, the old grandfather clock's pendulum began to tick.

Back and forth, back and forth as the hands on the moon-faced dial revolved.

And the clock struck three.

The first gong woke them both; the dogs leaped up and snarled.

"It's louder." Sonya gripped Trey's arm. "Is it louder?"

"Than it was last night, yeah." He rolled out of bed, then grabbed his sweatpants. "I'll go check it out. The dogs'll stay with you."

"Please." She found her clothes in the dim light of the fire. "All of us."

"All of us then."

When they reached the door of her sitting room, piano music drifted up.

"Just another three a.m. in the manor," she murmured.

"It has to mean something. The time. It's too consistent not to." As they came down the stairs, he looked toward the portrait. "And the song. She always plays the same one."

But when they reached the music room, it stopped.

"You saw Clover, but whoever's playing — and I still think Astrid — either isn't ready or can't . . . I guess it's materialize."

"Your guess is as good as mine."

They continued down the hall. The dogs stopped at the door to the second parlor and snarled again.

Sonya's breath backed up in her lungs until she had to push it out. "The hands moved to three." She stepped in because he did. "And it's cold, Trey."

Even as she spoke, the keys on the piano in the music room crashed with crazed chords. The pendulum on the clock began to sway again, and each second ticked off like a fired bullet. With the hair standing up on the back of their necks, the dogs barked frenzied warnings.

Doors flew open; doors slammed shut. The light Trey had flipped on flickered and went out.

In the dark, something brushed by her. Something so cold it burned.

"Something's in here." Breathless, she groped for his hand. "I felt it. It touched me."

"Next time we bring a flashlight."

Something hit the front door like a battering ram.

On those wild barks, the dogs flew out of the room and toward the sound.

"Come on." Trey pulled her from the room.

"You're going to open the door. Jesus. Listen to that wind, the waves. Look, look, it's ice hitting the windows."

"So, she can pull out a nor'easter." When he reached the door, he pulled it open to a still night and a swimming moon. "But it's an illusion. Damn good one."

"Oh, the dogs."

"They're fine. She's not out there. I think she's done for the night. I think that's all she's got."

"That was plenty."

Because she shivered, he stepped back to put an arm around her.

"We can go to my place if you want to get out of here."

"No. Absolutely not. She's not going to win this, not going to chase me out of my own home. But something was in that room, Trey. I swear it touched me. Brushed by my arm."

She shoved her sleeve up. "Look, there's a mark."

The pale pink mark, smaller than her palm, marked her skin just above her left elbow.

"It's an ice burn — a mild one."

"An ice burn?"

"Let me get the dogs in. We'll put a warm compress on it, see how that does. It's barely pink, and the skin's not cracked or broken. Hold on a second."

While he called the dogs, locked back up, she stared at the brush mark on her arm.

"It touched me." Something . . . someone who'd lived and died had touched her. "It did feel like a burn, but cold."

"Let's do this in the kitchen. Does it hurt?"

"No. Well, a little sore, I guess. But, Trey, the lede is, it — she — touched me, and I felt it. I felt her. Just for a second. But . . . look. It's already fading."

He stopped to take a closer look. "Okay, yeah, it is. We'll make the compress in case. But it looks like she doesn't have as much punch as she'd like."

"That was punch enough." In the kitchen, Sonya dropped down on a stool. "I mean, holy shit!"

"The house is quiet now. All that didn't last more than five minutes." He put a shallow bowl of water in the microwave to heat it. Then poured her a glass.

She took it, drank. "Serious question. Do you ever get rattled?"

"I was a little rattled. But it's interesting, isn't it, that she pulled out so many of the stops to scare us."

"Interesting." She drank again. "There's a word."

"The thing is, it didn't work."

She shot him a look. "I was scared. Really scared."

"But you're still sitting here."

After testing the water, he soaked a clean cloth, wrung it out. "You can barely see it now, but safer's better than sorry. We'll just hold it on there."

"I don't like being scared." She muttered it. "It pissed me off."

"Says the woman who likes horror flicks."

"And novels. That's a different kind of scared. I want her out of my house. If it takes finding the rings to get her the hell out of my house, I'll find the damn rings. Somehow. The rest? I'll give the rest *interesting.*"

Holding the compress against her arm with one hand, he brushed her hair back with the other. "Finding something just means looking in the right place."

"Oh, is that all?"

Now he pressed his lips to her forehead. "We're not going to let her win."

When the cloth cooled, he took another look.

"It's like it was never there. And it's not sore, at all," she added.

"Not much punch." Lifting her arm, he brushed his lips where the mark had been. "Are you going to be able to sleep?"

"I hope so. And I hope she's done for a while. I don't want my mother going through that, then trying to haul me back to Boston."

"I'm betting you got some of that stand-your-ground from your mother."

When they reached the second parlor, where the light glowed again, he went in, opened the clock face.

"Might as well make her work for it." This time he turned the hands to seven-ten. "Owen and I could move the clock out of the house."

"I don't think that would stop it, and it's kind of a warning when it sounds. I wonder if Collin heard it. He didn't wind the clock, but he kept it here. Not up or down in storage."

"If you change your mind, we'll take it out."

He slid an arm around her waist as they walked back to the staircase.

"She was in there with us, Trey. I've felt cold spots before, but not like that, and not like the Gold Room. It's a mean cold when it's her. I guess that's a warning, too."

"Maybe you get rattled, Sonya, but you don't stay rattled. My money's on you."

In bed, she curled up against him.

"I'm really glad you're here."

"So am I."

Closing her eyes, she let the steady beat of his heart lull her until she slept.

■ ■ ■ ■

Part Three: Spirits

■ ■ ■ ■

Let us have a quiet hour, Let us
hob-and-nob with Death.

— Alfred, Lord Tennyson,
"The Vision of Sin"

Chapter Twenty-One

On Friday, after Yoda stopped sulking because he didn't have Mookie, Sonya cheered him up with a trip to the village for scallops, angel hair pasta, and something called unbleached flour.

She hadn't known they bleached flour.

A quick run left her plenty of time to arrange the tulips she'd bought for her mother's room. And start her first attempt at making bread.

"We're not afraid, are we, Yoda? We're not afraid of some flour and beer and butter and whatever. Not when we live in the haunted manor.

"Maybe a little afraid — but if we fail, we dump it, and she'll never know."

After following Bree's instructions to the letter, she stared at the raw dough in the loaf pan.

"I guess it looks like bread dough. How would I know anyway?"

Fingers mentally crossed, she slid it into

the oven, set the timer.

And decided it wasn't obsessive not to leave the kitchen. Instead, she rearranged the fruit bowl a couple of times, paced, played a quick game of tug.

"Look! It's sort of plumping up — it's the beer, I looked it up. And it's browning some, too. Can you smell that? I can smell it."

When the timer — finally — went off, she remembered she was supposed to tap the bread and see if it sounded hollow. It made no sense to her, but she tapped.

"I guess it does. Anyway, I can't stand it."

After shaking the bread into her oven-mitted hand, she turned it onto the cooling rack. Stepped back.

"Now, I'm asking you, Yoda, is that or is that not the cutest little loaf of bread you've ever seen? And made by these hands."

Her iPad played John Lee Hooker's "Don't Be Messing With My Bread."

"You got that right."

As the bread cooled, she took the flowers, a polishing cloth, and polish up to the second floor with Yoda at her heels. She'd come back to the linen closet for fresh sheets and towels.

When she got to the room she'd chosen, she smelled the fresh polish on furniture that shined. Fresh, fluffy towels hung in the en suite — which also shined — and more towels stood carefully rolled in a basket.

"Well, thank you. It's perfect." She set

down the flowers. "She'll love it. She'll like the view of the woods."

She noticed the pretty purple bowl that matched the violets on the wallpaper above the wainscoting and the little crystal clock — with the right time — beside it.

She couldn't swear they hadn't been there before, but either way . . .

"They're nice touches. Thoughtful."

As she walked through the spotless house, she decided whoever made it spotless must love it as much as she did.

And since everything looked perfect, she went back to work.

"She's going to text when she's thirty minutes out, so meanwhile we'll get some work in."

With no Mookie, Yoda contented himself by curling up under her desk.

When she got the text, she shut down, hurried to the kitchen to make the salad. She had a moment of shock when she saw neither bread nor rack.

"Oh, no, I —"

Then saw the loaf shape wrapped in a clean white cloth.

"I guess I missed that part of the process."

She considered the timing perfect when she tucked the salad in the fridge, and Yoda ran barking to the door. Rushing after, Sonya threw open the door and wrapped Winter in a hug.

From the tablet in the kitchen, Taylor Swift sang "The Best Day."

"I missed you!"

"I missed you, too. Oh my God, Sonya, this house! Oh, this dog. Look at that sweet face, look at that handsome boy!"

Yoda instantly collapsed, exposed his belly, and looked up at Winter with pure love.

Obliging, Winter crouched down, rubbed, and cooed.

"You came straight from work."

Trim in her dark suit, Winter gave Yoda's belly a last rub. "Took off early, as planned, and put my bag in the car this morning. And Cleo's stuff's in there, too."

She straightened to give Sonya another hard hug. "I didn't want to waste time getting here. You look good! FaceTiming isn't the same as real timing. And that goes for the house, too. Holy jumping Jesus, Sonya. My jaw literally dropped. It's so you."

"It is?"

"This is always what you wanted. Well," she qualified as she looked around the foyer. "Maybe more than you imagined — or I did. That staircase!"

She wandered forward, stopped. "These rooms. A piano."

"One of two. Why don't we go up, see if you like the room I chose for you. I'll give you a quick tour — a full one would take too long. No, I've got your bag."

"Thanks, baby. You told me it felt like yours." They crossed to the staircase, started up. "Now I can see it. But there's so much of it. What are you doing with all this room?"

"I have my spots." She gestured toward the library. "Such as."

"Oh, well, wow. How do you ever leave this? It's like something out of a movie. And look at Xena thriving."

Turning a circle, Winter studied Sonya's mood boards. "Doing good, interesting work while you're at it."

"I think so, and I'll fill you in on all that." And everything else, Sonya thought.

"Collin Poole must have loved this house to preserve and maintain it so well. I've been a little worried about that part with you. Now I'll worry a lot less. Everything just shines, baby. You must've found a hell of a cleaning service."

She decided on: "It's kind of miraculous. We'll talk about that, too. We're in the north wing."

"Listen to you." On a laugh, Winter elbowed her daughter. "North wing."

With Yoda prancing between them, Sonya led her mother toward the bedrooms.

"I'm at the end of the hall."

"You know I have to look. And it's just lovely. Oh, seriously lovely. Lady of the manor. Do you watch the sunrise from your terrace doors?"

"I do. I gave you a different view — but you've got your pick. You're a park walker."

"I suppose I am."

"So I put you down the hall, and on this side, facing west. It's quieter, too. I think."

She opened a door. "Let's see if it works for you."

"Oh! This is beautiful! Like my own suite in the world's classiest B and B. Look at the wallpaper. It's so sweet. And my own little fireplace. I'm going to feel like a rock star sleeping in that bed."

Winter brushed her fingers over the tulips. "Thank you, sweetheart, for knowing me so well. I'll love looking out at the woods."

"If you want to unpack, I can help. Or, after working most of the day, and driving from Boston, we can have a glass of wine."

"See? You know your mom. Let's have some wine."

On the way down, she showed Winter Cleo's room, then the secret door.

"Is it safe?" Frowning, Winter peered down the steps. "Do you go in there?"

"It's the most direct way to the gym — down — and the attic — up. I'm trying to use the gym three or four mornings a week. I'll show you around in that part tomorrow if you want."

"Maybe. Did you hear that? I thought I heard bells."

Sonya echoed Trey's words from her first

day. “You’ll have this.” She shut the door.

“Music room,” she said as they continued.

“Is that a hurdy-gurdy? I’ve never seen one outside of a museum. The painting? She’s lovely.”

“Johanna, Collin’s wife. He painted it.”

“Talented, very talented. Like your dad.”

“Yes. She . . . died a long time ago. He had his office over here, where he hung Dad’s painting.”

“You told me, but I . . . Yes, that’s Drew’s work.” Moving into the room, Winter studied the painting. “Did he come here at some point, or is that really from his dreams? Some twin connection?”

“I thought you might want it.”

“Oh.” Still looking at the painting, Winter reached for Sonya’s hand. “Thanks for that, but it feels like it belongs here. I wonder how and when Collin Poole acquired it. I like knowing something of Drew’s — besides you — has a place here.”

At the distinctive sound of a door closing, Winter glanced around. “Is someone else here?”

“Depends on your definition of someone.” To lead her out, Sonya put an arm around her mother’s waist. “I told you the house is haunted.”

“Yes, but . . .”

From the kitchen, Billy Joel sang, “Bottle of white, bottle of red.”

"We're going with white because I'm making scallops."

"My always rational daughter's telling me, very seriously, that her house is haunted *and* she's making scallops? How much shock do you think my system can handle?"

"That's why wine first."

"Then this kitchen," Winter said as they reached it. "This gorgeous cook's kitchen, this great room, and again this view. They managed to keep the integrity of the house but ditched the labyrinth feel with this space, opening up instead. Now I have kitchen envy."

Running a hand over the island, Winter shook her head at Sonya. "I failed to interest you enough in cooking, only managed to teach you the bare basics."

"I made a pot roast dinner for eight," Sonya reminded her as she chose a bottle.

"And the photo you sent was cookbook worthy. Baby of mine, you actually believe you have ghosts in this house?"

"I don't just believe, Mom. I know."

Sonya uncorked the wine as the iPad played Paul Simon's "Mother and Child Reunion."

"Such as that." Sonya poured the wine. "You need to stop now, and give me a chance." When the music cut off, Sonya handed her mother a glass. "Sit down, Mom. That was Clover. She died in 1965, after giving birth to Collin and dad."

"I'm sitting down."

"There's a lot more. I told you about her, from the book I have, from what Deuce — Oliver Doyle II — told me. At some point, I'm going to try to talk to Gretta Poole. The woman Collin thought was his mother but was actually his aunt. She has dementia."

"Yes, you told me. You're saying Drew's birth mother is here, in this house. You've seen her?"

"No. She just makes herself known with music, to me. Trey's seen her. Twice now."

"Trey Doyle — the third Oliver."

"Right. We're dating."

"More surprises." Winter took a moment to sip some wine. "Why aren't I meeting him tonight?"

"That's such a mom thing — going straight there when we're talking about the ghost of your mother-in-law."

Winter tipped her wineglass toward Sonya. "Priorities."

"First, because he didn't want to intrude. Plus, he has a family wedding tomorrow. You're going to like him."

"Cleo did. She mentioned him, and that he had his eye on you, and you had yours on him. So I'm not surprised."

"Trust Cleo. You'll like him," she repeated. "He manages to be rock steady and easygoing at the same time."

"The point is, you like him. I'm glad you've

found someone you like. I'm glad you look happy, you sound happy."

"I am happy. It's been strange, okay? Getting used to the move, then the haunted thing. When we go up after dinner — which I'm going to start in just a minute — we're going to find your bed turned down, your fire lit. Mom, I haven't hired a cleaning service because apparently I inherited one."

"I see."

"Do you?"

Winter drank wine, rubbed Yoda when he planted his front paws on the stool. "When I finally got you to sleep the night after the horrible day your father died, I didn't know how I'd cope. How I'd get through the next hour, much less the next day, next week, next year.

"And I saw him. I went into our room, and he was there. He told me we'd be all right, that he'd loved me every minute of every day since we met."

"You never told me that."

"No, I never did. I thought it was grief. But it wasn't, not only. Sometimes I'd feel his hand on my cheek as I fell asleep. I still do now and then. Or hear his voice inside my head when I'm struggling with a decision or problem. 'Trust your gut, babe, then check in with your heart.' "

Smiling, she set down her glass, reached for Sonya's hand.

"If I believe there's an after, and I do, why not believe that whatever made that person who they were, the essence of them, could linger?"

"Is that why you never remarried? Because you felt he was still here?"

"It might have played a part, but no. What your dad and I had, it was . . . magic." On a sigh, a loving one, Winter laid her free hand on her heart. "Right from the start, we had magic. I never felt that with or for anyone else. Why would I settle for less?"

She squeezed Sonya's hand. "Still, you're so much alone here. Excluding you," she said to Yoda. "Are you afraid?"

"Sometimes. And I'm glad Cleo's moving in. Because Cleo, and it'll be nice to have someone here. Add we'll use more of the house, because Cleo. I have to remind myself not to burrow in the library.

"There's a lot more. I'll tell you while I make dinner. You're not helping."

"I'm topping off my wine, and will sit right here, a fascinated observer."

Because she did know her mother, Sonya built her way to the more frightening incidents. Maybe toned them down, just a little.

When the water boiled for the pasta, she slid it in. And set a timer before continuing as she prepped the scallops.

Set a second timer there.

"You saw the mirror. The one your father

dreamed of."

"I can't say for absolute, but I believe I did absolutely. And I know I saw Astrid Poole's murder, I saw Catherine die in a blizzard. I saw Marianne deliver twins and die. And each time, I saw Hester Dobbs."

"Since you seem to have the cooking miraculously under control, I'm going to set the table."

"The small one there. The dining room's grand and glorious, but intimidating unless you've got a group."

As they worked together, she told Winter about the night Trey saw Clover again. As she began, the tablet played "Whatta Man," and made her laugh.

"She can't help herself."

"And that really doesn't give you a chill?"

"Not anymore. I'm telling you all this because I don't want you to freak if anything happens while you're here. And because I want you to know I've got a handle on it. There's a salad in the fridge.

"I hope this works, hope this works."

She heated the skillet on low, dumped in the carefully measured lemon juice, added salt and pepper — no measurement given — then spread the drained pasta on a pretty platter.

"It smells terrific, Sonya."

"It does smell good, and in about half a minute, we'll find out if it worked. Did I thank you for letting me give Corrine Doyle the pot roast thing?"

"You did, and she sent me a very nice handwritten thank-you."

"She did? That sounds like her. I've only met her once, but it sounds like her. Here goes."

With the care of a diamond cutter and a rare gem, she ladled the scallops and sauce over the pasta. Added Parmesan and a sprinkle of chopped parsley and basil.

"Artistic eye. Presentation was never your problem. You could make a takeout meal look like dinner at a five-star. I want you to know I appreciate you making me dinner."

At the table, Winter dished up a little salad, then the main. "And I'm going for the scallops first because I have to."

After forking one in half, then half again, she wound a little angel hair with it. Sampled.

And sat back.

"Sonya, it's absolutely wonderful."

"Is it really?" Bypassing the salad, Sonya tried it herself. "Oh, it's good. I didn't overcook it. Bree put the fear of God in me on that."

"Now, who's Bree?"

"Oh, Trey's ex — high school ex — and friend. She's the head chef at the Lobster Cage. A really good restaurant in the village. It's her recipe."

"I want it. I'm making this the next time I

have friends for dinner. Now tell me the rest. The ghostly rest."

"It's the clock — there's a grandfather clock in the second parlor."

Sonya told her.

"Sweetie, that's terrifying. That's Shirley Jackson territory. She burned your arm. Let me see it."

"There's nothing to see." But to placate, Sonya shoved up the sleeve of her sweater. "I'm not going to pretend it wasn't scary, or that I haven't jumped out of my skin more than a few times, but —"

"You're determined. I know your face."

"It's my house, Mom. It should've been Dad's. He should've grown up here with his brother."

"If he had, I might never have met him. We might not have had you."

With a smile, Sonya shook her head. "Magic," she reminded Winter. "You had magic. You'd have found each other, and this would still be my house. I'm going to have one more scallop because they're really good. And I'm going to find those rings. Don't ask me how, don't have a clue. But I'm going to find them."

"I could take a leave of absence, move up here for a few months."

"You'll do no such thing. Not because I wouldn't love to have you, but because you have a life, a home, a career in Boston. I'm not letting some dead witch beat me."

"Determined face," Winter murmured. "It's always a bride, a new wife or mother. You and Trey aren't thinking about marriage, are you?"

"Mom, we've barely started dating."

"And I know what *dating* means for a couple of unattached adults. Maybe he'll spend the night more often."

"I have the faithful Yoda and soon the fierce Cleo."

"Which eases my mind. Some."

"You're still taking this better than I thought you might."

"I remember your father's dreams, how real they were to him. I guess I was predisposed to this."

"What would Dad have done if, like Collin, he'd found out about his family history?"

"He'd have come here." Winter said it without hesitation. "He'd have done exactly what you're set on doing. He also had a determined face. So I'm going to do what I always did for him, always tried to do for you. I'm going to stand by your determination."

"I love you, Mom."

"Sonya, you're the most important thing in my life. Whatever's here, you're happy. I can see how happy you are. And energized. My energy girl lost some of that zip in Boston."

"It wasn't Boston."

"I know, and I know you've got it back.

Plus, to my genuine amazement, you've now cooked two very impressive meals, so I know you won't rely on pizza and Chinese. Tomorrow, I'm going to show you how to make another meal."

Before Sonya could protest, Winter held up a hand. And put Sonya's determined face to shame. "You've got beef and seafood. I'll show you how to make — as I once failed — a simple chicken dish.

"But now, let's deal with these dishes. We can pour one more glass of wine and take it with us while you show me more of the house."

"Yoda needs to go out. How about we take him for a walk, then come back for the dishes and the tour."

"Your house, your rules."

They enjoyed the breezy walk with the landscape lights glowing, the stars shimmering. When they rounded back, the kitchen was whistle clean.

"Well, my God!"

"I wanted you to see. If I don't get to the cleanup right off, someone else does. Now, let me show you the solarium from inside."

The weekend flew by, and with nothing more than what Sonya had come to feel was normal for the manor. Welcoming fires in the hearths, open cabinet doors.

Though the hands on the clock read three

again, she heard nothing in the night, and no disturbances on the third floor.

She learned — maybe — how to make a chicken and potato dish in a single skillet, and pleased Winter.

And since the whole deal, start to finish, took under an hour, she thought she could handle it in a pinch.

At the door on Sunday afternoon, her bag at her feet, Winter embraced her daughter.

"Cleo will be here in a few days. Next time I visit, I bet I have her mom with me."

"I hope so."

"Your aunt misses you. Is it all right if I bring her up sometime?"

"I love Summer, you know that. Of course it is."

"Good, that's good. Tracie gets no points from me, but she did you a favor, Sonya. Because you're happy."

Taking Sonya's shoulders, Winter rubbed gently. "As happy as I've seen you in way too long. And you were losing that zip before you booted Brandon to the curb."

Shakira's infidelity song, "Don't Bother," sang from the phone in Sonya's pocket.

"Oh, I agree." Winter laughed with it. "My girl will be just fine."

"I think you and Clover would've gotten along."

"Enough that however strange it is, I like knowing she's watching out for you. You take care of yourself. You're my favorite daughter."

"You drive safe, and text me when you get home." They hugged hard, swayed with it. "You're my favorite mother."

"Bye, sweet doggie." Bending, she gave Yoda rubs and kisses. "And you tell the guy you're dating I expect to meet him the next time I'm here."

"I will. And, Mom? I love knowing you and Dad had magic."

"The magic made you. Stay happy."

Sonya watched her go as Yoda danced in the doorway and whined.

"I know, but she'll come back. And if I visit there, I'll take you with me. But we're good here."

She looked down at him as they both stood in the open doorway. She felt spring creeping into the air.

"I was going to wear you out with a game of tug — though that takes some doing. Then I was going to work until I had leftover chicken for dinner. You know what?"

Obviously riveted, he angled his head and stared up at her.

"Screw work. It's Sunday afternoon. I'm going to grab a jacket — don't need more today — and that ball I bought last time I was in the village. We're going to take a walk, and play ball. When we're done with that, we're going to come in and snuggle right up with a book — unless we feel more like a movie."

She bent down. "What do you say to that?"

Since he raced in circles, she decided he felt fine about it.

"You hang on a minute."

She got a jacket, the little red ball.

They worked on fetch — he resisted bringing the ball back — in the slushy snow.

As they played, the shadow moved across the window. Watching.

Glancing up, Sonya shielded her eyes with the flat of her hand. On impulse, she raised her other in a wave.

And saw the shadow move.

She had no doubt in that moment, it waved back.

"All right then," she said aloud, and nodded. "Okay."

When she heard a bang, she looked to the third floor. She watched the windows in the Gold Room fly open, slam shut.

Yoda let out three snapping barks.

"I agree," Sonya told him, and shot up a middle finger.

Deliberately, she turned her back to the windows, threw the ball for Yoda again.

"Watch how much we give a tiny damn about you."

By the end of the fetch session, the windows stopped banging, and she'd managed to train Yoda to not only bring the ball back, but drop it in her hand.

"Such a good boy, such a smart boy. You deserve a treat."

In full agreement, he swung into his happy circles before racing her back to the house.

Clover greeted her with Fogerty's "Wicked Old Witch."

"Bet your ass she is."

And yet, Sonya thought as she went back to the kitchen to get Yoda his treat, other than ringing the bells, moving the hands on the clock, the house had stayed mostly quiet during her mother's visit.

After making herself some tea, she settled down in the library with her book while Yoda napped.

Clover played a medley of artists and eras, and Sonya read about the hunt for a serial killer who collected the eyeballs of his victims.

"Gruesome," she said as she closed the book. "I loved it."

As she gave some vague thoughts to dinner and a movie, Trey texted.

> Why do weddings suck up an entire weekend? Wedding brunch this morning, then I'm pulled into a post-wedding drinks and dinner where I'm limited to one beer as DD, driving my grandparents home. If we ever leave.
> Hope your weekend with your mom required

less energy. Can I take you to dinner tomorrow?

Weddings are a once-in-a-lifetime event. Everyone hopes, anyway. Had a great weekend with my mom, wherein I stunned her with my success with Bree's recipe. I owe the chef major thanks. And you can absolutely take me to dinner tomorrow.

Congrats. I'll shoot to get to you by seven.

How were Great-aunt Marilyn and Great-uncle Lloyd?

Marilyn and Lloyd were, and are, in their usual form. Only sharpened by the fact Anna and my cousin Liam's wife, Gwen, are both pregnant. I've got to get back to the table. See you tomorrow night.

Too soon to sign off with a heart emoji, she decided. After some internal debate she admitted fell on the silly side, she settled on a smiley face with red lips and long eyelashes.

When you had to fret over emojis, she thought, your dating skills needed honing.

Down in the kitchen again, she fed the dog, warmed up some leftovers. When the I'm home text from her mother came through, no need to fret over emojis.

She treated herself to a face mask, opted to

go all in with a hair mask, then a long, indulgent shower.

By nine, in her pajamas, she snuggled down on the second floor of the library with Yoda. After the serial killer, she leaned toward something light as a palate cleanser.

With some regret, she scrolled past several horror movies and settled on a comedy.

And by ten, she'd drifted off to sleep. Shortly after, into dreams.

Chapter Twenty-Two

The mirror glowed. Its glass blurred with color and movement. Around its frame, the predators' eyes seemed to gleam.

Dimly, she heard music, voices, a quick, bright laugh.

She stepped through.

And stood in the ballroom under the brilliant light of a trio of chandeliers.

Rather than shrouded furniture crowding the space, divans and chairs in deep colors ran along the walls, and the floors shined under that sparkling light.

An orchestra played. Harp, violin, flute, what she thought might be a piccolo. And yes, she recognized the piano from the music room.

Men wearing waistcoats and high collars danced with women in long gowns, many with elaborate sleeves, bell-shaped skirts. Some women wore feathers in their hair, or elaborate pins.

Jewels glittered as the dancers circled the

room in a waltz.

Others sat in the seats tucked back against the walls. More stood with drinks in hand by tables laden with food.

Crystal flutes of champagne sparkled under the light that showered from the chandeliers.

She saw the bride, regal in her white gown, the satin, the lace, the tiara crowning her black hair.

A man — tall, dark blond hair, sharp jawed, Poole-green eyes — took her hand, kissed her knuckles.

She handed her champagne glass to a servant, then glided onto the dance floor with him.

They made a striking couple as they turned, twirled. He, smile content, looked at her face. But she, Sonya noted, shifted her gaze to take in the room.

To see who watched, to see who admired.

Rather than the radiant smile of a new bride, hers seemed smug, haughty.

When the dance ended, he kissed her hand again.

"Shall I take you down to supper, Mrs. Poole?"

"Not yet, not quite yet, Mr. Poole. We'll have a ball when the holidays come, shall we? Perhaps a masquerade ball at the turn of the year. How fine it all looks."

"It pales before the beauty of my bride. Will you sit, just a moment or two, with my sister?

It would mean much to her, and to me."

"Of course. Did I not vow to obey my husband?"

"And I to cherish my wife." He escorted her to the red-and-gold love seat where a woman, very pregnant, sat. She wore a gown of pale pink, with her hair, deep blond like her brother's, worn high and smooth.

"Shall I sit with you a moment, Jane?"

"Oh, please do, Agatha. What a happy day."

"I'll fetch you champagne, Agatha. Shall I bring you some, Jane?"

"Thank you, no, Owen. I'm very content. The baby likes the music. He's dancing." Her face glowed as she said it. "George went to look in on the children. It was kind of you, Agatha, to open the nursery for them."

"It wouldn't do to have bored children underfoot. They have their nursemaid to tend them."

"Of course, of course. But I wanted to just take a peek, and George wished to spare me the steps."

The music changed to a country dance as Sonya watched Hester Dobbs slip into the room. In her black dress, her hair loose and free, she walked to where a servant arranged some little cakes on a plate.

She added another to it, frosted in dark red with a gold crown topping it.

Turning, she smiled at Sonya as the servant walked to Agatha and offered her the plate.

"You can't stop what was, what is."

Maybe not, but she could try.

Even as Sonya rushed across the room — why did it feel like she swam through syrup? — Agatha lifted the red cake to her lips.

Sonya struggled her way through the dancers. She felt the heat from their bodies, caught the scent of perfume. One of the women stumbled a bit as Sonya pushed by her.

But Agatha was already on her feet, a hand to her throat as she fought for air.

Beside her, Jane levered herself up, called for water.

Water wouldn't help, Sonya thought. Agatha slid to the floor, eyes wild. Her body shook; the heels of her wedding shoes drummed on the floor.

Owen ran to her, dropped down to pull her into his arms.

No, she couldn't stop it, Sonya thought as she watched the life begin to drain out of the bride's eyes.

Women screamed; one fainted.

In the confusion, Hester Dobbs pulled the wedding ring from Agatha's finger and slid it on her own.

"With my blade I took the first, then by my blood this house was cursed. One by one they wed, they die, because they seek to take what's mine. And with their rings of gold, my spell will hold and hold."

Once again, she smiled at Sonya. Then she lifted her hands, flicked her fingers. And vanished.

Sonya woke standing beside the sofa. She shook — not from fear but rage.

She'd watched another woman die, and had been helpless to stop it.

Could she change what had already happened? Agatha Poole died in . . . how the hell could she remember? But the fourth bride had been dead over a hundred years.

And yet, Sonya had been there, in the ballroom, at that time, in that place. She'd witnessed what had been another murder.

Yoda whined and shivered. She sat, let him jump into her lap.

"Where do I go? Is it an actual mirror, or just something in a dream? Maybe some kind of . . . subconscious device rather than an actual mirror."

And it was too damn late to worry about it now.

"I'm sorry, baby. I fell asleep and didn't let you out. It's okay. We'll take care of that immediately."

She let him out through the mudroom, stood drinking a glass of water while she waited for him to come back. Though tempted to write it all out then and there, she knew she wouldn't forget the details.

Morning would do fine, especially since it

wasn't far off.

With the dog, she went upstairs. He got into his bed and she into hers.

In the faint glow of the fire, she lay taking stock.

No, she wasn't afraid. If her mother had been there, Winter would have recognized her daughter's determined face.

Over coffee in the morning, she wrote it all out, added a number of sketches. Then put it aside.

With the caterer's job completed, she shifted her focus to the Doyle project. Since she wanted photos, she contacted Corrine Doyle.

Enlisting her as photographer proved as simple as asking.

"Check that off." She made a check mark in the air.

For the rest of the morning, she worked on the design, the structure.

And fell nicely into routine. Work, walk, work.

Because she didn't want to get too deeply into it before she had the photos, she moved over to the florist.

New photos there, too, which the florist had already sent — following Sonya's vision. They'd work, she thought as she studied them. And save the client the cost of a photographer.

Clover blasted out with "Devil with a Blue Dress On."

"Hey, volume." Sonya started to turn it down herself, then saw the time.

"Okay, I get it. Nearly six. Time to knock off and change."

She found the red dress laid out on her bed.

"Still no. Eventually, it'll be the right choice, but tonight . . ." She studied her closet, pulled out a navy blue dress with a belted waist and pencil skirt.

"This is better for dinner in the village."

Because she continued to drag her feet on a hairstylist, she opted to sort of bundle it back, clip it up.

As Yoda raced downstairs and the bell rang, she took one last turn in front of the mirror.

The dogs greeted each other as if it had been years. And the generally easy-moving Trey surprised her by pulling her straight in for a long, blood-stirring kiss.

"I missed that. I missed you."

"That's really nice to hear." More than a little off-balance, Sonya stepped back to let him in. "I need to get my coat."

"I'm going to let them run around outside for a couple minutes. In case."

She went to the closet, took a moment to breathe out. When she came back, he turned, smiled at her.

"Nice coat."

She glanced down at the black leather that

swung to mid-thigh. "I bought it for myself as a You've Got This present when I quit my job to go freelance."

"Looks like it worked. How about I call the dogs in from the mudroom, get them wiped down?"

"Good idea." She breathed out again. "Trey?"

He glanced back at her.

"I missed you, too."

"I was hoping."

As she stood, waiting, Clover wound up with the Beatles' "If I Fell."

"Just ease back. Not ready yet."

"Clock's back at three," he commented as the dogs raced back ahead of him.

"Every morning. I've got a story for you. Tell you on the way. You boys behave. Stay out of the liquor and don't make any prank calls."

"Now you've given them ideas."

When they went out, she looked at the gunmetal-gray sedan next to her car. "That's not your truck."

"No, but it's my car."

She slid in. "It's nice. So, recovered from the wedding?"

"Mostly. Then today, my mother ambushed me for pictures. No headshots, no posing. That's from you, I take it."

"It is. Your job's top of the list now."

"What about Ryder? We can wait, Sonya, if

you want to work on that."

"It gets an hour a day." Because she had a plan, and a schedule. "Which is enough until I pull it more together."

"Just so you know, if you want to take more time for it, we're not in a hurry. Now, what's the story?"

"I went through the mirror again. Wait." She held up a hand as he started to speak. "I didn't call you because I wasn't afraid. I wasn't. By the end, I was just furious, but not scared."

"All right."

"I sense you're not convinced, so let me start at the top."

When she finished, he glanced over. "She ended with poetry?"

"Yes, but like a spell or a charm? I think. I need to ask Cleo about that. But the fact is, someone I bumped felt it. Like I felt Dobbs that night.

"That's interesting, to use your word. And it felt like I was wading through mud when I tried to run, to stop Agatha from eating that damn petit four."

"Her death's listed as choking, but sounds like poison."

"It was anaphylactic shock. I'm nearly sure. I knew a girl in college with a peanut allergy. We were all out one night, and something she ate. It was really scary, even though she had an EpiPen. This reminded me of that, only it happened so fast, so maybe some poison with it. Hester Dobbs put something in that cake that caused the reaction."

As it played back so clearly in her head, Sonya shifted in her seat to face him.

"She couldn't breathe, Trey.

"She knew I couldn't stop it — Hester knew. And that just infuriated me. Then I started thinking."

He parked at the Lobster Cage.

"Is this okay for dinner?"

"Oh yes. I'd like to thank Bree in person for the recipe."

"Hold on to what you started thinking."

The same lovestruck hostess seated them in the same corner booth. He ordered wine, then nodded at her. "You were thinking."

"It's not her. I mean I don't think it's Hester Dobbs jump-starting these dreams or experiences."

"Why?"

"Why would she want me to see, to have the details? It doesn't give her any advantage. But it gives me one."

He gestured to her when the server brought out the wine, chatted with her — an older woman this time — about her new granddaughter.

"Give us a few more minutes, will you, Dana?"

"You bet — but take my word, the lobster risotto is tops tonight."

When she left them, Trey didn't miss a beat. "Did you do sketches?"

"Yes."

"I want to see them. And you've made a good point. I don't see any benefit to her letting you see what she did, or how she did it."

"How's murky," she said, but Trey shook his head.

"You're an eyewitness, and you see and remember details. So I'm saying you're right. Why would she want a witness? Do you want the risotto?"

"I really do."

"That works. I want crab cakes."

Once they'd ordered, he slid right back in. "I think it's Astrid."

"Why Astrid?"

"She's the first. She was there, obviously, from the start. And since we accept she's been in the manor since, she'd have seen the rest. She's a witness, too."

"That's logical — in this illogical situation." And it helped, so much, to have someone who could be logical, someone she trusted, to talk through it all.

"One of the details? I don't think Agatha was in love with Owen Poole. Not like crazy, deeply. And she struck me as . . . I don't think she was a particularly nice woman. More just a snob. I think he cared about her, but same goes — not the snob. He seemed warmer somehow. But I think it was what they called a good match, if you follow."

"He remarried, under two years later. Pretty sure it was less than two."

"About a year and a half — I checked. And he and his wife, Moira, had six kids and nearly five decades together. I don't know if that matters, but apparently second brides aren't in the danger zone."

"One a generation."

"Which means me. Or I guess any bride of my generation who gets married in, or lives in, the manor. It has to be there because Dobbs is stuck there, too. After my mother left Sunday? I went out to play fetch with Yoda. He's getting the hang of it. The shadow I've seen, at the library window? I waved. It waved back."

Because it made him laugh, she grinned.

"And right after? Hester started slamming the windows in the Gold Room. Very pissy. I gave her the middle finger salute."

The way he looked at her, in just that moment, had her heart doing a slow roll.

"You're one in a million, cutie."

"I don't know about that, but I know how to get pissy right back."

When Dana served the mains, Sonya looked at her plate, then up at Dana. "I can tell you were right."

"Never wrong." She winked and left them alone.

"Tell me about the wedding. The one that

didn't end with a dead bride."

"Please don't make me. Fill me in on your weekend instead."

"What's one thing — no, two," Sonya amended. "Two things that stick out, then we'll close the door on your weekend adventure and move to mine."

"The bride's uncle Jerry got shit-faced, jumped onstage with the band, and belted out AC/DC's 'You Shook Me All Night Long.' "

He waited a beat.

"While stripping. They managed to stop him before he lost his pants — there were children present — but it was close."

As she laughed, he tried some of her risotto.

"And for the second, I found the best man and the bride's brother in an extremely compromising situation in the men's room."

"You walked in on them?"

"Lock the door, man." He pressed his fingers to his eyes. "Use a stall. Rent a room. Before I could back out, they told me to congratulate them. They're engaged."

"Aw. Did you?"

"Congratulate them? Yeah, while my retinas were bleeding because I'd seen entirely too much of both of them, things I can never unsee. I said congratulations and got the hell out of there."

"I hope those crazy kids make it. Your family has exciting weddings. I wish I'd been there."

He studied her over a sip of wine. "You actually mean that. I worry about you."

"I like weddings. They're full of color and drama and joy."

"And drunken relatives."

"The best ones are."

"Your turn."

"My weekend can't compare to yours. But there is my mother's reaction to spending hers with ghosts. Which was surprisingly steady."

She told him.

"It sounds like I had it right. You got a lot of your steady from your mother."

"I didn't realize when my father died how much she had to take on. You don't think of things like that when you're twelve. And by the time I grew up enough to realize it, it just was. She gave me stability."

"It says something that she senses your dad with her."

"What does it say?"

"That love, the real deal, lasts. The real deal gives you strength."

"You must be right because I don't know anyone stronger than Winter MacTavish. By the way, since she immediately and correctly interpreted my term *dating*?" She pointed a finger at him, then at herself. "She demands to meet you the next time she's here."

"I'll look forward to that." He glanced over. "Here comes Bree."

This time the chef scooted Trey over to look directly at Sonya. "I can't look in your eyes with a text, so tell me again you didn't overcook the scallops or pasta."

"You scared me enough on that. I set timers. My mother was so shocked and impressed she forced me back to the kitchen on Saturday and whipped me through a chicken dish. So my thanks is qualified by fear and annoyance, as she told me she's going to teach me a different dish whenever she visits."

"Didn't she ever teach you growing up?"

"She tried. I'd chop and stir if cornered. But I was slippery, and I stand as one of her few failures."

Bree nodded, considered. "I still like you. Rock Hard's back in Ogunquit next week," she told Trey. "I'm going next Monday. You should come. Bring her. I gotta get back."

She hopped up, took off.

"So." Sonya picked up her wine. "She and Manny have solidified their thing."

"Looks that way. Do you want to go hear some music next week?"

"I would. Rock Hard and Manny live bold in my imagination. But Cleo's coming in a few days. I don't want to ditch her for an evening so soon."

"Does she like music?"

"She does."

"Owen will definitely be up for going. We could make it a group thing."

"It sounds like fun. I'll ask her. But then there's Yoda."

"My parents take on Mookie if I'm going to be gone more than a couple hours. They'll take Yoda.

"Think about it. Ask Cleo."

She would, and did some of that thinking on the drive home.

"I should get Yoda a doghouse. The weather's breaking, and he'd have somewhere to chill when he's outside."

"You should ask Owen to build him one."

"Owen builds doghouses?"

"Not for everybody, but Owen can build anything. You should see the one we built for Jones. It's a dog palace. It's got Wi-Fi."

"Get out of here."

"It's heated, with a circulating fan to cool it in the summer, two bunks, in case he has a pal over like Mookie last weekend. It's got a frigging porch, windows — with screens."

"You said 'we built.' "

"I'm just the free labor. He's the genius."

Which explained his workingman hands, Sonya thought.

"Does Mookie have one?"

"Mookie's is more of a playhouse. He's still a kid, really, and he lacks Jones's taste for the finer things."

"Does it have Wi-Fi?"

"It does not." He pulled up at the manor. "Mookie also lacks Jones's spookily superior intellect. I'm not sorry about that. But it has its amenities."

"Yoda wants one."

"Discuss it with Owen," Trey said as they walked to the door. "He believes in the barter system."

After the dogs greeted them, and everyone had a walk around, Trey took her hand at the door.

"I'd like to stay."

Her answer was to pull him inside with her. "Did you think you were going somewhere?"

He woke when the clock struck three, and beside him she stirred. Pulling her close, he pressed his lips to her hair.

"Not tonight. Just sleep."

If she dreamed, she didn't remember, and fell smoothly back into routine.

By midday she had a selection of photos to consider for the Doyle project. Asking Corrine, she decided, had been the perfect move. Not only good photos, but the woman knew all the subjects, and it showed.

She didn't think twice about which to use of Trey.

His mother caught him leaning back against his desk, his phone at his ear. Untucked shirt, dark jeans, scarred boots crossed at the ankles.

It captured his calm energy. A contradiction in terms, she thought, but that was Trey Doyle.

Just as she'd captured her father-in-law, in his three-piece suit, glasses at the tip of his nose as he pulled a law book from the shelf.

"These are good, they're damn good. Let's make them work."

She spent the rest of the day on it, and most of the next.

And in her opinion, it did work, and well.

In anticipation of Cleo's arrival the next day, she took Yoda into the village for some supplies and flowers.

On her way out again, her phone rang. She tapped the button on the steering wheel to answer.

"This is Sonya."

"Hey, Sonya, Anna. I'm right behind you."

Sonya glanced in the rearview. "Oh, well, hi."

"I don't suppose I could talk you into turning around. I'll buy you a cup of coffee. I was going to text you. I'd like to talk to you about a couple of things."

"I'd turn around, but I've got the dog with me. Why don't you come up? I'll buy you the decaffeinated beverage of your choice."

"Love it, thanks. I'll see you in a few."

While Sonya chose happy daffodils for Cleo's room, Cleo pulled up in front of the manor.

As she didn't see Sonya's car, she considered the wisdom of her one-day-early surprise. With a shrug, she decided she'd just haul some of her things to the front door, then send Sonya a text.

She muscled out a suitcase, pleased that spring teased the air instead of winter biting it. If Sonya planned to come back soon, she'd wait. If she planned not, well, she'd just drive down to the village and do some exploring until.

After dragging the suitcase to the door, it opened.

"Hey. I didn't think you were home, I . . ."

Sonya didn't stand there. No one did.

She hesitated, then squared her shoulders. She'd live here, so she'd better get used to it. When she walked in, the music pumped. Neil Young and Crazy Horse's "Welcome Back."

"I'll take that as a good sign."

As a precaution, she propped her suitcase against the door. It weighed a ton because she had a ton of clothes. And wasn't sorry.

She hauled her second one, then her weekender, then the last of her boxes before shutting the door.

She looked at the staircase, looked at her suitcases. Sighed.

She still wasn't sorry.

She'd pulled, yanked, carried the first to the landing when the banging started.

And the servant's door creaked open.

She heard the bell, dim but insistent. She stepped toward it.

Chapter Twenty-Three

Sonya spotted Cleo's car when she made the turn, and everything in her lit up bright.

She pulled up, jumped out. She expected to see suitcases, boxes when she peered in.

"Either you bought a second car or you already have company."

Anna walked over to Sonya.

"It's Cleo's. I didn't expect her until tomorrow."

"The friend who's moving in. What a nice surprise. Listen, I'll take off, leave you two alone to get her settled in. We can do this later."

"No, come in." From her car, Sonya grabbed the flowers and grocery bags. "You should meet her. Wherever she is. She must be inside. I don't know how because I always lock up when I leave."

They walked to the house together.

"See?" At the locked door, Sonya took out her key. Yoda raced in first and sniffed at the suitcases.

"Her things. Cleo!" Her voice just echoed back. "Hell with that." Taking out her phone, she texted.

Where are you?

The response took a minute.

Brt.

"Be right there from where?" Sonya muttered. "That's another of her bags up there. Maybe she —"

She broke off as the servant's door opened.

Cleo stepped out. She shoved a hand at her hair, then lifted her arms in the air. "Surprise!"

"You scared the *crap* out of me."

"Sorry. I got everything done, and thought why the hell should I wait until morning? So here I am," she continued as she walked down the stairs.

"How did you get in?"

"The door opened. Just like that one did." She pointed up. "But manners first as my Mama says. Hi, I'm Cleo Fabares."

"Anna Doyle."

"I know. I recognized you from your website. Wonderful work, by the way. The site and the pottery. And would you look! It's now five-oh-two. Give me some wine, Son. I've had my first solo adventure."

"Sit in the parlor with Anna."

"Anna doesn't need to sit in the parlor," Anna said. "The kitchen's fine. I'd like to hear about the solo adventure. You don't seem worried about it."

"Got some chills, literally, but no, I'm not worried. We have this fierce guard dog." She crooned to Yoda, gave him some loving rubs. "You're even more adorable in person."

She straightened, and continued as they started back, "And I've got one of my grand-mère's charms in my pocket."

"Her grandmother's a Creole witch. Maybe."

"You've got my full attention."

"You get the drinks, Sonya; I'll put the groceries away."

"What would you like, Anna?"

Still studying Cleo as if fascinated, Anna said, "Ginger ale if you have it."

"Okay. To start," Cleo said to Anna, "a friend's taken over my apartment. A friend I'm fond of, but grew less fond of every day since she moved in. She's not easy to live with. Sonya is. So when I realized I had everything done, I ran. Since I'm also fond of the surprise, I didn't give Sonya a heads-up. That's on me."

"I would've been here."

"Yeah, but then I wouldn't have had my first solo adventure. You got Toaster Strudels! She knows I have a weakness. So, when I didn't see Sonya's car, I realized my surprise might have been a little ill-conceived, but what the hell. She'd be back. I hauled one of my ridiculously heavy suitcases to the door. And it opened."

She picked up the wine Sonya set in front of her. "I came in."

"I don't think of myself as a coward." Anna considered as she sipped her drink. "But I don't think I'd have done that."

"She would."

"And did. And the house sang 'Welcome Back.' Or I should say Clover played me in."

"Clover?"

"You haven't filled her in?"

"I guess not."

"Then over to you for that."

Sonya picked up her wine. "Let's sit at the table."

She filled in some gaps.

"And you knew that, and still came in?"

"I think Clover and I will get along fine. We'll see about the rest. So, I dragged the first suitcase up those awesome stairs — I love clothes."

"Me, too!"

"We'll shop. I dragged up the suitcase, and the secret door opened."

"And you walked in there, too?"

"I thought about it for a second, since I heard those bells? The call bells downstairs?"

"I remember those, sure. They were actually ringing?"

"One was. I started down, and the door slammed behind me."

Shaking back her hair, she lifted her glass.

"I admit, without shame, that scared the shit out of me. But the lights came on when I found the switch, so that was better. When I got down there, the bell for the Gold Room's banging, doors are slamming. The TV in the media room came on, top volume. A lot of screaming seeing as it came on with the latest *Halloween* movie.

"I love Jamie Lee Curtis."

"Jesus, Cleo."

With a shrug, Cleo topped off her wine. "I wasn't what you'd call sanguine about it at the time. Then everything stopped. The slamming, the banging, the screaming. And I felt this cold, a whoosh of it. Did you see my hair when I came out? It blew right through it.

"Then you texted. So either Grand-mère's charm or you coming home, or both, shut her off."

"I wish I could have some wine," Anna murmured.

"I dedicate this glass to you and your adorable baby bump. I'm going to white sage down there," Cleo decided. "I don't think that's nearly enough, but I'll do it anyway." Already at home, she put her feet up on the empty chair, turned to Anna. "So how many weeks along are you?"

"Almost twenty."

"Halfway." Cleo lifted her glass in toast. "Do you know the variety?"

With a laugh, Anna patted her baby belly. "We just found out yesterday. Think pink!"

As easy as that, Sonya thought, they transitioned from hauntings to babies. Engaging others stood as one of Cleo's top skills.

"Who runs the world?" Cleo sang. "Got a name?"

"The middle name's easy. My mother-in-law's first name and my mom's middle is Kate. For the first name, we've got our list down to, oh, about a dozen. We're hoping to tighten that up before she starts preschool. But now that we know, decorating the nursery's top of the list.

"And since I happen to know an artist or two, I may hit them up for advice."

"I'm there!"

Now Sonya laughed. "Cleo's a baby magnet, or babies are a magnet for Cleo. Was helping with nursery decor what you wanted to talk to me about?"

"Oh no, that one just came to me. It was some other things. One was about work. They can wait."

"Now's fine. Did you want something changed on the website?"

"Not a change. Bay Arts is having their May Day open house in a few weeks, and I'm one of the featured artists. I wondered if we could do something to promote it on my site."

"Not only could but should." Sonya took out her phone to take notes. "Dates, times?"

"Second weekend in May, ten to eight on Saturday, noon to six on Sunday."

"It's annual?"

"They do a weekend every year, second weekend in May, and for the holidays, the second weekend in December. Featured artists, some demonstrations, specials, refreshments, door prizes."

Nodding, Sonya got it all down. "They'll do their own promotions, flyers, but we can do a flash on your social media. Do they include online sales?"

"Absolutely."

"Okay, we'll do a card to include in the sales off your site, hyping it up."

"That's good. I wouldn't have thought of that."

"That's my job. I can send you some options tomorrow."

She set her phone aside. "What else is on your mind?"

"The other was . . . well, it's personal."

"I'll just go haul another suitcase upstairs."

"No, don't leave," Anna said as Cleo started to get up. "It's clear the two of you are close, so you'd know Sonya and Trey are seeing each other."

Cautious, Sonya trailed a finger around the rim of her glass. "He told you."

"No, and he wouldn't unless I asked directly. But you've had dinners together at the Lobster Cage, and he's made the turn on Manor Road several times lately."

She smiled, shrugged. "News doesn't travel in Poole's Bay. It sprints."

"Do you have a problem with Trey and me?"

"Oh God, no." In a pushback gesture, Anna lifted her hands. "The opposite. Polar opposite. I love my brother, even when I want to kick him in the balls. He's so damn reasonable. You can't win a fight against his unwavering reasonable. It's frustrating. But I love him anyway."

"Reasonable," Sonya agreed. "And the calm. The absolute calm. It's both annoying and admirable. It's annoyingly admirable."

"There, see? You get him."

On the table, Sonya's phone sang out: "Whatta Man."

Easing back, Anna crossed her arms over her baby bump. "Do you ever get used to that?"

"Somehow, you do."

"Not sure I would, and it makes me really miss wine. But in any case, I'm happy Trey's with someone who gets him. I caught the carefully contained sparkage between you when we all had dinner, but I'm surprised he moved on that before Christmas."

"I might have nudged the timetable up a bit."

"And again, there." Reaching over, she squeezed Sonya's hand. "It's not as if either of you need my approval, but you've got it anyway. And I have to go. I didn't intend to stay so long.

"This was really nice," she added as she rose. "My best friend moved to Montana last summer. I miss her even more than wine, margaritas, and a second cup of coffee."

"Is she looking for a cowboy?" Cleo wondered as they walked to the door.

"In Lena's case that would be a cowgirl. Since she's working on a ranch — childhood dream — I bet she finds one."

"Come back," Sonya told her. "You don't need a reason."

"I will." Carole King's "You've Got a Friend" played from the tablet in the library. "Despite that. Welcome to Poole's Bay and Lost Bride Manor, Cleo."

After Anna walked to her car, Sonya shut the door. "And here we are."

With a "Woo!" Cleo threw her arms around her friend. "I'm officially living in a haunted house. Talk about living the dream."

"I say it's not official until you're unpacked."

"Then let's get to it."

Sonya took the weekender and one of the boxes while Cleo dragged the second big suitcase.

"Considering your wardrobe, I realized the closet in your room — You still want the same room?"

"It's *my* room. The box goes up to the studio. Just set it down there."

"Not enough closet space in your room, so I thought you could use the one in the room across the hall for spillover. Maybe separate by occasion or season."

"You have the best ideas. I'll start with the occasion system. It's not like I'm going to wear a lot of date night and cocktail wear, at least for a while.

"And here's my room! My wonderful room."

"Actually, Trey has a friend, a drummer with a band. He used to play with Trey and Owen's band."

"What? Wait. Trey had a band?"

"Did I forget to tell you?" Together they muscled the first suitcase onto the luggage rack Sonya found in a closet. "I'm so glad you're here so I won't forget to tell you everything. High school, garage band, but Manny kept up with it."

"Are you fixing me up with a drummer in a rock band before I've even unpacked? You are the goddess of friends."

"I want that title, but no. Manny and Trey's ex — I told you about her."

"The chef."

"Right. They've started a thing. So Rock Hard's playing in Ogunquit next week."

"Rock Hard's the band name? I'm even sorrier I won't have a shot at Manny."

"Bree — the chef — is going next Monday, and wanted us to go. Could be fun."

"Should be fun," Cleo agreed as she opened her suitcase. "But I'm not fifth-wheeling it with you and Trey."

"Trey said Owen would probably go, and we'd make it a group thing. And Yoda would have a chance to hang out with Mookie at Trey's parents'."

Cleo looked down at Yoda as she started sorting clothes. "Now you're using that sweet dog. Okay, if everyone's in, I'm in."

"Excellent. You know, I'm not sure two closets are going to work."

"I'll make it work."

They gave the first round of unpacking an hour before going down to feed the dog and toss a frozen pizza in the oven.

"Tomorrow, I start cooking dinner. And anytime Trey wants to join, just let me know. Same with anytime the two of you want to go out to eat."

When they let Yoda in after his post-dinner outing, Cleo looked around the kitchen, nodded. "This is all good. I have a plan. Let's give the Great Unpacking another half hour — that'll be official enough if we don't get it completely done. Then we could haul the stuff up to my studio. I'll set that up in the morning."

"I like your plan."

They carried the last of the studio boxes to the second floor and, setting them down, turned toward the bedrooms.

"A major step up from the apartment we rented our senior year."

"With the tiniest shower in the history of showers," Sonya remembered, with the fondness of distance. "And the tub drain that actually went glug-glug-glug."

"Good times."

They walked into Cleo's bedroom. No clothes lay on the neatly turned-down bed. No suitcases sat on the floor.

"Okay, wow. Yeah, some getting used to." Cleo opened the closet. "There's not only more hanging in here, it's organized by type and color."

"She does that with mine, too. It has to be a she."

Nodding, Cleo walked to her dresser, checked drawers. Nodded again and moved into the bathroom.

"Shampoo, conditioner, shower gel, my poof, all there. Skin care in the top left vanity drawer," she noted. "High octane skin care below. Makeup on the right, organized by category, and hair stuff in the middle cabinet. Efficient."

She stepped back. "I appreciate this, very

much." Then turned to Sonya. "I'm going to check the other closet."

In the second bedroom closet, the suitcases were stacked on the floor under the clothes.

"I think she likes being useful," Sonya said. "And yeah, has to be a she."

"I wish we knew her name."

"So do I. I think she must have been a servant. I started to make one up for her, but that seems wrong."

Her phone jumped out with Little Richard's classic "Good Golly Miss Molly."

"Molly!" they said together.

"You know what else that means?" Cleo said.

"They know each other. Clover either knew Molly when they were alive or . . ."

"They got acquainted after. Thank you, Molly, for saving me so much time. I don't see my spring and fall jackets in here."

"I bet we find them in the coat closet downstairs. Efficient. She — Molly — does like to play with things. Perfume, pretty things."

"She can play with mine all she wants. Are you up for carrying the rest to the studio?"

"That's the plan, and Molly saved us half an hour."

They carted the first load up. The minute she stepped into the studio, Cleo set her box on the desk, did a turn.

"Oh *God*! I love this space. It's absolutely

perfect. Look, the moon's up, over the water."

From the Gold Room came the pounding.

"Oh, fuck off," Cleo snapped. "You can't spoil this for me."

After setting her box beside Cleo's, Sonya looked around. "It is perfect, and the view slays, but are you sure you'll be all right up here?"

"Bet your ass. I'm going to get the last box."

"Trey put what you sent with Mom marked for the studio in the closet. What the hell was in that big box? It weighed a ton."

"Mostly canvases and paints, more tools. I'm going to take time between jobs — and make more time between jobs — to paint. For me. Be right back."

When Cleo dashed off, Sonya did her own turn. The pounding lowered to a few angry slams.

She had to admit, it already felt like Cleo. She walked to the closet to drag out the big box.

And saw the painting propped on top of it.

The bride wore a ring of flowers over straight blond hair that rained past her shoulders. Her simple white dress fell to the ankles of bare, narrow feet. Its empire waist circled below full, high breasts. Between, the dress covered the dome of belly.

She carried a nosegay in her right hand and wore a gold band with two entwined hearts on the third finger of her left.

She'd seen pictures. If she hadn't, with the loving details of the portrait, she'd have recognized Clover. Her father's birth mother.

She'd passed the shape of her nose, the wide bow of her mouth to her son. And so to her granddaughter.

Emotion, unexpected and poignant, flooded through her.

"The last and final," Cleo said as she came in. "So it's officially official — What is it?"

Sonya just pointed.

When she joined her, Cleo put a hand on Sonya's shoulder. "I'm going to take a wild guess. That wasn't there before."

"No. The closet was empty when Trey put your supplies in there. It's Clover. It's my father's birth mother. And, Cleo, my father painted this. I know his work, and if I didn't, there's his signature."

Reaching up, she laid her hand over Cleo's. "How did he paint her — the woman who died giving birth to him? How did it get here, in the manor? Did he dream of her, the way he did the manor, the mirror, his brother? I think that must be it."

"You should take a picture of it, send it to Winter, ask if she's seen it. Either way, I'm betting you're right about the dreams. And a twin thing again?"

"Like the painting of the manor. Collin saw it somewhere, somehow, bought it."

"It follows, doesn't it?"

"I need to sit a minute."

When she did, on the floor, Yoda crawled into her lap, and Cleo crouched down.

"I'll get you some water."

"No, I'm okay. Just wobbly for a minute. It just fills me, and hollows me out at the same time. Dad painted her; Collin brought her here. They connected."

"Now you have her, and that connects you. Sonya, it's beautiful work. She's . . . well, she's adorable. We should take her downstairs. Nobody puts Clover in the closet."

With one hand stroking Yoda, Sonya leaned her head toward Cleo. "You're right. We'll take her to the music room, with Johanna."

"I've got her. I vote we take her down, you get that picture, send that text, and I get us both a last glass of wine."

"I say aye to that."

In the music room, they propped the painting against the wall under Johanna's portrait.

"I love the still lifes in here," Cleo began. "But what do you say we switch that one out, hang her there?"

"Yes. She'd have come right before Johanna."

"Text your mom. I'll get the wine. Then we'll put her where she belongs."

Stepping back, Sonya studied the portrait again. So, so young, she thought. And that young face simply glowed with happiness. And despite the mound of belly, an innocence that touched her heart.

She took a careful photo, then sent the text.

I found this portrait. It's Dad's work. Have you seen it before?

The answer came in under a minute.

No. That's his birth mother? I can see him in her face. Is Cleo there? Is everything all right?

Yes, it's Clover. Cleo's right here, and everything's fine. We spent most of the evening hauling up her half ton of suitcases and unpacking her massive wardrobe. But when we found this, we thought we should ask. I think Dad must have dreamed her, and painted her. As a bride.

He often painted his dreams. She's lovely, and there's a sweetness. She looks kind.

Yes, she does. I know she was and is kind, so don't worry. Cleo and I are going to have a glass of wine, then go to bed. We're all good here.

Stay that way. Love to Cleo, love to you. Night.

After signing off with a heart emoji, she

turned as Cleo came back into the room.

"She never saw it before."

"You know, he might have painted it before they were married. Or he just had his reasons for not showing her. Let's put her up, Sonya, then have this wine."

They switched out the paintings, then stood back, arms around each other's waists.

"She looks right there."

"She does. And you know, Son, your father's in there, too. Your dad and his brother are in that painting. It's very special."

In her pocket, Sonya's phone played "Mother and Child Reunion."

With a laugh, Cleo picked up the wine, handed Sonya hers, and clinked her glass to it. "To Clover, the music master."

"Absolutely to Clover."

"You know what else? Johanna would've been her daughter-in-law, your mother's sister-in-law. Your aunt."

"It's just so weird."

"I think it's wonderful. To Johanna."

"To Johanna. What a strange day. Just another day in the manor."

"And my first official one."

"And so we drink to that. Yoda needs to go out."

"We'll take care of that. Then I don't mind calling it for the night. I want to get an early start on setting up my studio.

"You said Yoda was fostered with cats."

"That's right. You really want one?"

"When I find the right one. The thing I really disliked about my apartment was the no-pet clause."

They grabbed jackets — and Cleo's were, indeed, inside the coat closet.

"Oh God, the view. It's just everything. Please tell me you don't get used to it."

"No." With the last of their wine, they walked with the dog. "It still catches me. And it makes me wonder how I ever lived anywhere else. And I'm already wondering how I lived here all these weeks without you here."

"Now you don't have to."

Later, when she slid into bed, Sonya thought again: a strange day. But a good one. Yoda curled on his bed, Cleo slept down the hall, and the sound of the sea against the rocks lulled like music.

Later yet, when the clock struck three, she muttered in her sleep. But she didn't stir, and she didn't rise.

Chapter Twenty-Four

Bonus points came in the morning when Sonya walked into the kitchen to the scent of coffee and Cleo. A Cleo dressed in jeans, a sweatshirt, sneakers. She had her burnt-honey curls scooped back in a bouncy tail, and her day-at-home makeup on.

"You are up early. This is not usual."

"I honestly can't wait to start on the studio." Her quick hip wiggle proved it. "Got your coffee covered. I'm having a Toaster Strudel. Want one?"

With a head shake, Sonya took out the second half of yesterday's bagel before she let Yoda out the mudroom door.

"I find that sad. I put out fresh water and food for our boy."

"We both appreciate it."

Cleo propped on a stool while Sonya toasted her bagel. "Listen, if you want, when you take a break, come up and see how I've set things up. You've got a good, efficient eye."

"I will. Basic routine for me? I'm trying to

work out three days a week — I shoot for morning, mostly. Which is not this morning. Work until Yoda lets me know he has to go out, or I realize I need to get up and out. Walk around. Work. Toss something together for dinner, or if Trey's coming over, he'll bring takeout. I try to get into the village one day a week. Flower shop, maybe the bookstore, grocery."

"Groceries are on me now."

"And I'm happy to give that to you."

"I know your rhythms, Son, and you know mine. We'll find the new ones here. If I'm going out — I really want to explore the village, see that lighthouse, find some outdoor painting spots — I'll text you if it's during work hours. Let you know."

"Same goes."

"And we're good. No, I've got him." At Yoda's let-me-in bark, Cleo rose. "There's that boy, there's that very good boy. Breakfast is ready."

Yeah, Sonya thought, they'd find the new rhythm.

She worked straight through until noon, making progress on the Doyle job, designing three options for Anna's needs. After she let a very anxious Yoda out the front door, she walked back for a Coke. Before she could grab a jacket and join him, he was barking at the mudroom door.

"Okay, we'll walk later. But since it's break

time, let's go see Cleo."

Apparently, her very brilliant dog already recognized the name, as he raced for the stairs.

Before she reached the studio, she heard Cleo's "Did you come to see me? Did you come to see Cleo? Yes, you did!"

"We both did. Oh, Cleo!"

Paints — acrylics, oils, watercolors — lined the shelves, along with brushes, palette knives, all the artist tools carefully organized.

Spare sketchbooks, drawing pencils, colored pencils, charcoals, pastels joined them. And canvases stacked, varying sizes, beside Cleo's old, paint-smeared artist case.

She had a blank canvas on the easel, an old table she must have unearthed from somewhere beside it. She'd set a palette there with a single brush crossed over it.

On her desk sat her computer monitor, an open pencil case, a large sketchbook, some of her crystals, and a small glass dragon in deep orange.

"What do you think?"

"Still taking it in."

Sonya wandered. A pretty dish centered on the sofa table along with a pair of squat white candles in dark blue holders. A suncatcher sparkled with light in the south-facing window, cream-colored pillows plumped on the sofa with the mermaid lamp standing beside it.

"I saw this chest when I found that little table. It looks like it came off a pirate ship. Nothing in it, but it's got weight. Maybe your big, strong man can haul it in for me."

"I'm sure. Just like I'm sure you don't need my help here. It's all you."

"It won't stay so organized, but it's nice to start that way. I was thinking of getting a small dorm fridge for drinks."

"Good idea."

"The better one, I thought, since I don't like structured cardio, is using the stairs when I'm thirsty. I am grateful there's a bathroom down the hall. I put toilet paper, some soap and towels in there. I'll fuss it up some, but I like having that close by."

"Any problem with you-know-who?"

"Oh, she banged and bitched for a while." Cleo shrugged that off like she might a cloud breezing over the sun. "I've got my labradorite and black tourmaline here, and Clarence." She patted the dragon.

"Clarence, who's new to me."

"I just found him last week. Carnelian dragon. Courage and creativity. Plus, dragon."

Sonya walked over for a closer look.

"Cleo! The mermaid book?"

"Yeah. I'm working with acrylics. I wanted hand drawn rather than using software for these. I've got a few scanned, but I'm not ready to send them on."

Sonya studied the work in progress. "Can I see what you've already done?"

A mermaid swimming, long length, head lifted, eyes closed. Her gilded hair streaming back, and her tail a glittering symphony of color.

In another, a pair of them perched on rocks, facing each other, with the sea swirling under a full moon. Another speared out of the water, hands cupped, with water flying around her.

Color and movement, Sonya thought. And magic.

"You know I'm a fan of your work."

"I do, and I hear a but coming."

"You do. But I've never seen you do better work than these. Honestly, you've caught something here, Cleo."

"Oh, thank God." Sitting back, she pressed her hands to her face. "Because I really thought so, and I really respect your eye. I love this job." She let out a breath. "I don't want to miss with this job."

"You should send these to the editor so they know they've got a winner. Oh, I love this one, in the mists, and the one cradling a merbaby. They're so powerfully female."

"You need to come up more often. I'm obsessed with this one, and that makes me worry I'm too close."

"Let me turn that around on you and say being obsessed and close is inspiring your best work. And now, I need to let you get back to it."

"You definitely have to come up regularly. I'm going to take your advice and send these to my editor." Lifting both hands, she crossed her fingers. "I thought I'd make ham and potato soup for dinner. Do you want to ask Trey?"

"I'll check with him. How come I didn't know you could make ham and potato soup?"

"Because I couldn't up till a few weeks ago. But it's easier than you think."

"I can make bread."

"You cannot."

"I can, and I can show you so you can take that over next time we want it. Meet you in the kitchen at, say, about five-thirty?"

"It's a date."

On the way back to work, she texted Trey. He responded he had a man date with Owen for burgers; would Friday night do? And to say hi to Cleo.

"I've got your rhythm, too. You're giving me some time to settle in with Cleo. And that's nice. Nice, sweet, and pretty damn intuitive."

At just past five, Cleo stopped outside the library. "I'll go away unless you're about done for the day."

"I'm about done for the day. It's just you and me. Trey's having burgers with Owen."

"He could've brought Owen."

"I think he wanted to give us a little girl time. He's coming tomorrow."

"Okay then. I showed you mine, let's see yours."

"I'm working on Doyle Law Offices. I told you Trey's mom's a photographer. I got great stuff to work with."

As Sonya toggled back to the home page, Cleo came around the desk. "That's their offices? You said it was a Victorian, but wow. It's beautiful. It looks so not stuffy attorneys-at-law. I like your color palette, picking up the tones of the house, not overwhelming it. Nice clean font on the text, clear info.

"That has to be Ace!" Delighted, Cleo pressed her hands to her cheeks. "Talk about adorable. Natty! That's the word. How often do you get to use *natty* in a sentence?"

Nodding, she scanned the bio. "Impressive. Harvard man, could've retired fifteen, twenty years ago, but there he is in his natty three-piece suit with the law books.

"And next?"

"Deuce."

"Mmm. Handsome, kind eyes, tie loosened. Why is that so sexy?"

In full agreement, she slapped Cleo's arm. "I know, right?"

"I like how she took him making notes on a legal pad. Handsome, kind-eyed man at work. Oh, well now, and here's Mr. Third Generation. All long and lean and yummy. It's a great shot. He's relaxed, but he's listening."

She went through the staff.

"Mrs. Deuce is damn good, as is my BFF. I really like the way you've got this easy flow going, and — Oh Jesus, Sonya!"

She laughed and laughed.

"Mookie Doyle, Legal Consultant."

"I don't know if they'll go for it, but I couldn't resist when I saw she'd taken his picture, too. And the way he's holding his head, that look in his eyes."

"*I'm here for you. Trust me.* Oh, they have to use it. It's genius. If I needed a lawyer, I'd be at their door."

"We'll see. I've nearly got it to the point I can show them the layout. I'm shutting down. Workday is done."

In the kitchen, Sonya watched in some amazement as Cleo chopped garlic, peeled and chopped potatoes, a carrot.

"This is serious cooking."

"I've been practicing," Cleo said. "Since I'm living the dream, my contribution will not suck. We'll eat reasonably decent meals under my watch. Let me get this going, then I want to see you make bread. Doesn't that take hours?"

"Not this." After walking into the butler's pantry, Sonya came back with a bottle. "The secret's in the beer."

And as they spent the evening in the kitchen, at the table, Sonya realized Trey had been right. Some girl time did the trick.

Now and again, Clover joined them with a musical interlude. And now and again, doors opened or closed.

When they came back from walking the dog, all the kitchen cabinets stood open, and the counter stools were stacked on top of each other.

"I wonder if a kid died here." Cleo started closing doors. "This is silly stuff, kid stuff. Pranks."

"From what I've read so far, not all the children lived to adulthood. You could be right." Sonya set the stools back in place. "Yoda plays with somebody sometimes."

Even as she spoke, the ball she kept in the mudroom bounced out into the kitchen, where Yoda gave immediate chase.

"Like that?"

"That's new, but yes. And I just realized how much you're like Trey."

"Please." Cleo gave her hair a haughty toss. "I'm like no one."

"You didn't even blink. It's the calm." She followed Yoda when he raced to the mudroom, dropped the ball, and wagged.

Nothing happened.

"Not ready to have us watch yet," Cleo decided, and tugged Sonya back into the kitchen. The ball bounced out again. "See?"

"I guess I should just let them play."

"Why not? Want to watch a movie?"

"I could watch a movie."

"And after, can I borrow the Poole book for the night? I'd like to read some of it."

"Fine with me."

A few minutes into the movie, Yoda came up to join them and fell asleep almost immediately. Tuckered out from playing with his ghost pal, Sonya thought.

When she let him out the last time, the ball sat on the shelf over the washer. Apparently Yoda's invisible friend wanted to keep it handy.

As she got ready for bed, she decided she couldn't be afraid or annoyed with a spirit that liked playing with her dog.

When the clock woke Cleo, she got up quickly. No need to wake Sonya, she thought — but grabbed her phone in case. She'd just run down for a look. Maybe this time, she'd see something.

What she saw was Sonya walking past her room.

"Woke you up, too. I was just going to — Hey, wait for me."

She caught up, took Sonya's arm.

For a moment, her friend stood, face blank, staring straight ahead. Then she jerked.

"What?" Sonya shuddered once. Then her head swiveled, and her breath caught. "What's going on?"

"I think you were sleepwalking, or dreaming or something. The clock. I heard the clock, got up, and you were walking past my room."

"I don't remember getting up. I don't remember hearing anything. Where the hell was I going?"

"I don't know. I didn't realize you weren't . . . awake until I took your arm." To soothe, Cleo rubbed her back. "Are you okay?"

"Yes. I'm fine. I feel like — I feel like I just woke up. The way you do when you just half surface, then roll over and go back to sleep. There's the music."

"I hear it. I'm just going to run down and look."

"I'll go, too. I'm fine," she insisted. "Just a little groggy."

They went down together, and the dog, wakened by their voices, went with them.

Even as he raced ahead of them, the music stopped.

"Damn it, always too late."

Still, Cleo led the way to the music room.

"Everything just as we left it."

"The paintings. The wedding rings aren't there."

Cleo turned her head. "Yes, they are. You don't see them?"

"I — yes. But . . . Groggy," she said again. "I didn't see them for a second. Since we're down here, we should check the clock."

The hands stood at three.

"No point in changing them," Sonya decided. "Something happened at three in the morning. Why else would it only sound then? But I don't think it's Hester Dobbs, Cleo. Or not her getting me walking in my sleep, taking me to and through that mirror. I talked to Trey about that. Why would she want me to see, want me to know details?"

"That's a good point. But I still don't like you wandering around in a daze, in the dark."

"I'm not crazy about it either."

"We'll go back up. I'll tuck you in. I can stay with you."

"I'm fine, really." If she didn't count feeling light-headed and heavy in the limbs. "Just stupid with tired. And the moment's passed for tonight."

"I think you're right. The house is quiet. It just feels quiet now. All settled down."

Still, when they got upstairs, Cleo sat on the side of the bed. "No wandering without me."

"Definitely don't plan on it."

"I'll see you in the morning."

But she sat in her sitting room for another ten minutes, then crept back. When she saw Sonya sleeping, she relaxed enough to go back to bed.

A quiet house surrounded Sonya in the morning. Grateful for it, she went through the breakfast routine — hers and Yoda's. Clover greeted her with "Good Morning Starshine."

"Good morning to you."

She wondered, if she made it to the afterlife — a very long time in the future — if she'd manage the perpetual cheerful as it appeared Clover did.

By eight-thirty, she settled at her desk with Yoda under it.

An hour later, she heard Cleo shuffling toward the staircase.

"Hey!"

Still in her pajamas, hair everywhere, Cleo looked in with sleepy eyes. And grunted.

"Just wanted to say thanks for having my back last night."

"I've got yours, you've got mine." Yawning, Cleo bent down to rub Yoda when he darted out to greet her. "Who can be a morning grump with that happy face? But I need coffee. Must have coffee."

Yoda watched her go, then decided to spread out by the fire.

After good progress on the Doyle job, and a few tweaks to the basic design for the flower shop, Sonya started on the Ryder presentation.

One hour, she reminded herself. Then a break, and back to Doyle.

At the end of the hour, she gave herself ten more minutes.

Satisfied, she started to turn to call Yoda. "Let's go outside."

But he wasn't by the fire, or under her desk. Thinking he'd gone to hunt for Cleo, she turned off her music.

And she heard the distinctive sounds of the ball bouncing downstairs and the dog scrambling after it.

"I guess Cleo's taking a break, too. Maybe we'll all take a walk."

She started down as the ball came bouncing back with Yoda giving chase.

"Hey, Cleo, how about we play fetch outside, since we've timed our breaks?"

But Cleo didn't stand in the long hall. No one did.

Yoda dropped the ball, turned his head one way, the other. Then he picked it up again, and raced to her.

"Cleo's not taking a break to play fetch, is she? Sorry to interrupt the game."

She picked up the ball and had Yoda racing in circles as she started down the hall.

In the kitchen, she found the cabinet doors open, and the box of dog treats on the island. Open.

"Did they give you some of these, or is this my cue to do that? I can't be too freaked by a ghost who likes dogs. Just one," she told Yoda. "Then we'll go outside."

When she dug in for one of the little squares, Yoda sat, eyes gleaming. Then he reared up on his stubby back legs and waved his front paws.

After a surprised laugh, she rewarded the dog.

"Did he teach you that? I'm guessing boy, young boy. I don't know if you can go outside or not," she said as she closed the cabinet doors, "but if you can, you're welcome to join us."

She grabbed the old jacket she left in the mudroom and went out into the brisk April air.

Warm and balmy might be weeks off, but she saw more patches of ground. She decided she'd survived her first winter in Maine.

To her delight, she spied a few crocuses popping purple on the side of the apartment. And as she walked, she saw a few brave stems of green pushing out of the ground.

Daffodils, maybe. She'd find out soon.

"It'll be so pretty," she told the dog, then threw the ball for him. "I'm ready to say goodbye to the drama of winter, and hello to the happy of spring."

Wandering around the house, she hunted for other signs that spring was on the way while the tireless Yoda chased the ball.

She decided the wind off the sea didn't feel as sharp as it had even a week ago as she walked to the stone wall.

"Oh, oh, look! I think it's dolphins!" Thrilled, she watched one — no, two — no, three! — as they jumped and dived. Caught, she gathered up the dog, pointed. "See? Can you see them? I think they're playing."

Apparently more interested in her, he licked her chin.

"I'm going to put some chairs on the widow's walk when it's warm enough. Invest in a pair of good binoculars. Maybe I have them already somewhere in the house. Or a spyglass. I definitely want a spyglass."

After setting the dog back down, she lifted her face, breathed in.

She heard something scream, whirled. The window on the third floor stood open, and something flew out.

The bird, black as midnight, long talons curled, screamed once more, and dived.

Instinct had her grabbing Yoda again, hunching over him. Her body braced for the bite of those talons as she ordered her legs to run. But when she risked a look up, she saw nothing but the blue of the sky and some gray-edged clouds that threatened rain.

As she caught her breath, a window in Cleo's studio opened. "Did you hear that? What was that?"

"A bird," Sonya called up. "I don't know if it was real, but it's gone now. We're coming in."

"I'm coming down."

Jogging toward the house on shaky legs, Sonya looked at the now closed window of the Gold Room. "Did it scare you?" She nuzzled the dog. "It scared me."

Still carrying Yoda, she went in. "I'm going to the kitchen! We'll get you dried off, that's right, doggie. Everything's okay. I've got you."

Cleo found her as she rubbed Yoda down in the mudroom.

"I never heard a bird sound like that," Cleo began. "It was almost human."

"It flew out of her window. A black bird, too big, I think, for a crow. Way too big. It just dived toward us."

"I didn't see anything. Not by the time I jumped up and ran to the window. But . . . when I opened it to call down to you? I thought, for a minute, I smelled something. Something like sulfur."

"She wanted to scare us, and mission accomplished. But if she wanted to hurt us, I don't think she could."

"Not enough power outside the house, maybe. I swear, that scream chilled my blood."

"There were dolphins."

"Really? I want a Coke. Do you want a Coke? I'm getting us a Coke."

"I was watching them, and thinking how wonderful it was. I guess she couldn't let that stand. And before I went out, Yoda was playing fetch with whoever likes to open the cabinets."

"You saw them!"

"No, but Yoda did — does. I thought it was you, bouncing the ball down the hall to the foyer for Yoda. But when I came down, just the dog and the ball. Then — wait, I'll show you."

She suspected Molly rather than the boy had put the box of treats away again, so she got them out.

Yoda sat.

"Watch this."

When she held up the treat, he reared and waved his paws.

"Aww. That much adorable may be illegal in some states."

"I didn't teach him to do that."

"That just proves there's more good here than bad. We're okay, Son, and we're going to stay that way."

"Don't go near that room, for now. Please." Insistent, Sonya gripped Cleo's arm. "Promise."

"I promise, but sooner or later, we'll have to."

"I vote for later, after work."

"After work you'll find me here, making dinner. Trey's coming, right?"

"Last I heard."

"We're having chicken and dumplings."

"Get out! You can make dumplings?"

Cleo took a determined swig of Coke. "We're going to find out."

When Sonya went back to work, Clover met

her with "Don't Worry Baby."

"Trying not to. Think fetch-playing kid, not big, ugly bird."

She documented both, then went back to the Doyle job.

At the end of the day, she contacted Corrine Doyle.

"I'd like to talk to you about another job, maybe ask your advice, and hire you and your camera. Can we set up a meeting?"

"I'm free tomorrow morning. Since I'm going to be out anyway, I can come to you. About ten-thirty?"

"That would be perfect."

"Why don't you give me some broad strokes?"

"I'm working on a presentation. Ryder Sports."

"I know Ryder."

"I want to do some sports photos, but I don't want to use professional models. I want real people," she began.

By the time she got downstairs, Cleo was indeed in the kitchen. "I think I've got this. I hope I've got this. Chicken and dumplings, peas and carrots. It sounds homey. How hard could homey be?"

"Don't ask me." Sonya looked at the chicken in the skillet. "It looks sort of homey, and it's starting to smell good. I'm going to buy you a really cute yoga outfit."

"For making dinner?"

"No, so you can wear it, have Corrine Doyle take your picture — for my presentation. You like yoga, so you'll look like you yoga."

"This is for the Ryder deal? I have a yoga outfit from Ryder. I look awesome in it."

"That makes that easy. I have to talk Trey into doing this — working out or playing ball. I need somebody who has a bike. And the intern at Doyle's — he's gorgeous — I want to talk him into doing one of the shots. I want different ages. At least one kid, at least one over fifty. I just want a sample. If I get the job, I'll do more."

"Say when, not if. Intention counts. Like I intend to make these dumplings and rock your world. Stay out of my way. Go put on some makeup."

"He's seen me without it."

Cleo simply sent her a long, long look.

"Fine."

She did what she was told, and started down again just as the doorbell bonged.

He brought flowers, pretty pink baby roses.

"Cleo gets the flowers," he told her. "You said she was cooking."

"Only fair," she said as Mookie and Yoda reunited. "How about I take one of these?"

With a hand on his shoulder, she leaned in for a kiss.

"You can have all of those you want."

"Maybe just one more, for now." Then she

waited while he hung up his coat.

Playing ball, she decided. Reaching up to field a baseball. She could see it.

She hooked her arm through his. "I have a proposition for you."

"What sort of proposition? Personal, business, sexual, political?"

"You really are a lawyer. I'll get to that, and after dinner, I want to show you what I've got going on your website. Over dinner, we'll tell you about our latest incidents."

Cleo's voice carried out from the kitchen. "You boys can have some leftovers when we're done."

With the dogs watching her hopefully, Cleo looked up, dumpling dough on both hands. "A man bearing gifts. My favorite kind."

"You get the roses, but I'll put them in a vase for you. Those are dumplings?"

"They will be."

"It smells great in here," Trey told them.

"That's all Cleo. I'm meeting with your mother tomorrow morning."

"Oh?"

"Mmm." She chose a vase from the butler's pantry. "About doing photos for the Ryder job. I told you what I had in mind. The different action shots, real people. Cleo's signed up for that. You're next."

"Oh, well, I —"

"You've got a ball glove, a ball cap?"

"Sure, but —"

"I think we want the shoes, too. One foot on base, maybe stretching up to catch the ball. I'll see what your mom thinks. Do you have a bike?"

"Not since I could drive."

"I really want a shot on a bike."

"Eddie's a serious bike rider."

Sonya smiled. "Good to know. I want a gym shot, I think. A guy, maybe a little sweaty, curling."

Without a minute's hesitation, Trey threw his closest friend to the wolves. "Owen got his weights from Ryder."

"Perfect. A couple kids playing basketball — a girl and a boy — an older woman jogging, or a couple jogging together. I'd like a football shot."

"John Dee. He played in high school, and college."

"Great. I'll talk him into it. This is a solid start."

"Good. Tuck work away," Cleo told her. "Pour us some wine, set the table. I've got this dumpling thing going on."

It turned out she did. When they sat, had the first bite, Sonya just shook her head.

"Where was this talent all our lives?"

"I cooked some decent meals before."

"Few and far between."

"It's my job now. I'm kind of getting a charge out of it. What do you think, Trey?"

"Sorry, did you say something? I'm pretty busy here."

She grinned at him. "Consider it payment for taking me to see Rock Hard. It'll be fun to get out of the house for a few hours."

"You practically just got here."

Cleo gave Sonya's hand an absent pat. "I was thinking more of you, Son. My girl tends to burrow."

"I do. I can't deny it."

"Did you tell Trey about last night?"

"Not yet."

That pulled his attention away from dumplings. "What about last night?"

"I guess we'll start with that."

Chapter Twenty-Five

She told him about Cleo finding her walking at three a.m., then backtracked to finding the portrait, wove in Yoda's ghostly companion, and ended with the bird.

"You forgot about Molly. Clover let us know, musically, the name of our housekeeper."

Without asking, Cleo dished up a second helping for Trey.

"Thanks. That's a lot for a couple of days."

"Before I lived here, I'd have said it's more than enough for a lifetime." Sonya lifted her shoulders. "It's not that you get used to it, but it's more expected."

"I'd like to see the portrait."

"It's beautiful. Since you're the only one who's seen her — I guess in person — you can tell me if my father's caught her."

"He captured the manor. I wonder why, if Collin bought the portrait, he never said anything. I know it's not in the inventory."

"Which begs the question, where the hell was it?"

"I have a theory."

Sonya looked at Cleo. "Uh-oh."

"I don't think it's that far out based on, we'll say, the rules of this particular road. You said it's as if you go through the mirror and into another time. There's a school of thought that hauntings are just people out of their own time. Like a slip in time. Maybe this is a combination. And maybe the two portraits — Johanna and Clover — were, basically, on the other side of the mirror."

"That's interesting."

Sonya rolled her eyes toward Trey. "Don't encourage her."

"It's interesting," he repeated. "A slip in time? Those portraits weren't in the house, unless there's a place in the house I don't know about, Dad doesn't know about. And regardless, both ended up in the studio. And now, the last two lost brides are in the music room. Collin painted one, your father — his twin — the other."

He scooped up more chicken and dumplings. "It's interesting. The bird flying out of the Gold Room's another matter. Could you draw it?"

"I didn't get a really good look. It happened fast. I just grabbed Yoda and ducked. Then it wasn't there."

"I didn't see it, but I heard it, too. And

when I opened the window to call to Sonya, I smelled sulfur."

"I know Cleo's theory on that, and I guess it makes sense — considering the rules of this weird road."

"What's the theory?" Trey asked her.

"She conjured the bird. Hester Dobbs. But once it was outside for more than a few seconds, poof. Because she's limited, that power's limited. And yet . . . I know she lured Catherine — the second bride — out into that blizzard."

"She bespelled her," Cleo said easily. "Catherine walked out under a spell, and by the time it broke, it was too late."

"Maybe."

"Or . . . she had more power then. It's been a couple of centuries."

"She tried to lure me out, that night. I heard the pounding at the front door, saw a blizzard out the window."

"But when you opened the door," Cleo pointed out, "no blizzard."

"I see where you're coming from," Trey said. "Still, if Sonya had stepped outside, and hadn't been able to get the door open — it would've been a long, cold night."

"I think Dobbs would have enjoyed that. But I didn't have Yoda or Cleo then. Or you. And now I'm going to sound like Cleo, but I think Clover's looking out for us, too, as best she can."

Her phone played "I'll Be There for You."

"See?"

"Okay if I go take a look at the portrait?"

"Let's do that. I want to know what you think."

The three of them walked down together and into the music room.

"That face," Trey murmured. "That's Clover. It's beautiful. She looks happy but . . . serene."

"You've seen her twice. But she isn't pregnant."

"No, not like this."

"I've thought about that."

Sonya looked over at Cleo. "Theory time again?"

"Clover died, and never got the chance to rock her babies, nurse them, cuddle them, sing to them." Cleo sighed. "If there's a choice, I wouldn't want the constant reminder of what I wanted so much and never really had."

This time Sonya didn't roll her eyes, but took Cleo's hand. "And still she plays music, and comes off as happy. At least content. I think she'd have been a wonderful mother."

When her phone played "Let It Be," Sonya laid a hand over it in her pocket.

"They look good there, right there," Trey commented. "Together. I wonder . . . I wonder if you'll find the others, the ones after Astrid and before Clover."

"I looked this morning." Cleo shrugged. "I kind of hoped, but since Sonya found both of these, I guess that's for her. If and when."

"And I wonder, if I'd kept walking last night, if I'd have ended up . . . somewhere else for a while. I think next time, don't wake me up."

"Oh, Sonya."

"It's not Hester Dobbs doing that. I'm as sure of that as any of this. Breaking the curse — and I can hardly believe I'm saying *curse* — means finding the rings. The more I see, hear, feel? It seems it matters."

"If it happens when I'm not here, call me," Trey said to Cleo. "And stay with her. I need a key. I need to be able to get into the house."

"Oh."

Because her knee-jerk remembered doing just that with Brandon, she shoved it aside.

Trey wasn't Brandon. He wasn't anything like Brandon.

"All right. Yeah, that makes sense, too. I'd as soon not go wandering at three a.m. to a . . . slip in time. But I feel better about it knowing the two of you would be here."

She shook her head. "And I have to think about something else. Like doing the dishes and taking the dogs out."

The kitchen, not unexpectedly, sparkled when they went back.

"Should've known. Molly's fast. I'd feel better walking Yoda until I'm sure that bird doesn't come back."

"I'll get my jacket."

"And," Cleo said when Trey walked away, "I'll make myself scarce."

"You don't have to do that."

"Please. I'm going to take an hour to paint, then maybe go watch something on my tablet or read. And try not to be jealous you have a man to curl up with. I'll see you tomorrow."

"Dinner was so good, Cleo."

"It damn well was."

The humans walked; the dogs romped.

As they circled the house, Sonya looked up at the lights in Cleo's studio.

"It's so nice knowing she's up there. All that goes on in the house barely fazes her."

"It's good you have someone steady with you."

She tilted her head to look up at him. "A lot of people — most, really, at least at first — don't think of Cleo as steady. But she is. Her mind's wide open to everything, which makes an interesting combo with the steady. I got lucky being assigned as her roommate in college."

"From where I see it, you both did."

"I'm going to agree with that. When I walked in, the first day, she'd already set up her side of our very tiny room. Some of her artwork on the wall, a little shelf with crystals and photos and books, and a pillow on the fluffy red duvet that read: IMAGINE.

"I'd never shared a room before," she added as they herded the dogs into the house. "So I was nervous about it, and how we'd get along. Both art majors, so I knew we'd have that. But I grew up in Boston and she came from Louisiana. Who knew? Then I saw her art and I knew we'd definitely have that."

After wiping off the paws, Sonya straightened. "And she gave me Xena."

"The plant in the library."

"She was just a little thing back then. Cleo's grandmother had started her from another African violet, and told Cleo to give it to her roommate. That she was good luck. And to be sure I named her. When I said Xena, Cleo lit right up. By the time I'd unpacked, it was like we'd known each other forever."

The dogs raced up the stairs ahead of them.

"You did get lucky. My first college roommate was . . . let me think of the right word for him. Oh yeah, *prick*. A sanctimonious prick."

"This surprises me. You strike me as someone who finds a way to get along with everybody."

"I was white, straight, from a solid family — and tax bracket — he assumed were his type of Christians. He figured I was one of his group — that is, opposed to anyone who wasn't all of the above. After several weeks of trying to ignore, argue with, or block his bullshit, I told him I was bi, an atheist, my great-grandfather was Paiute, and my parents had an open marriage. He moved out, and that's how I got along with him."

Fascinated, Sonya paused at the door of the library. "You lied to him."

"It was that or punch him in the face. Seeing the shock on that face was nearly as satisfying as punching it. Anyway, I got another roommate, and we got along fine."

"Do you know where he ended up? The sanctimonious prick?"

"Never gave him another thought."

"I believe that. I believe you have that power. Okay, come see what you think of how I've built your web page. It's not ready to go live," she told him. "I still have some additions, some tweaks, then testing, but you'll get the feel."

She brought it up on her screen, stepped to the side.

"It's already a big step up, and a major change in that feel. You were right about using the offices, the house. And the colors, the font. It's not fussy, but it's not bland.

"I like that you've put the year the firm was established right up front."

"When you've got a half century in business, you flaunt it. Try the Attorneys tab."

When he clicked on it, he smiled. "Look at Ace."

"Your mom's in danger of becoming my

go-to photographer. I had others to choose from, but this was my favorite. If there are any changes needed to the front-page text or any of the bios, just send them to me."

"I don't see anything so far. And here's Deuce. It works, the casual shots. You were right again. I guess that includes me," he said when he scrolled down.

"All three of you look relatable, accessible. The backdrops, the law books, the desk, and so on say professional. Corrine is really good."

"I always thought so."

"Check out the staff."

He clicked, grinned. "Jesus, Sadie looks like she could stand on one foot and juggle. Which is what she does every day. These are great. And just enough personal details in the bios. Eddie looks so damn earnest, which he is. And . . ."

He stopped, roared with laughter that had the dogs racing over.

"You put Mookie on here. Look at this, Mooks, you're a Legal Consultant."

"I thought it added something, well, relatable again. But if it's too much — sorry, Mookie. You'll need to see how Ace and Deuce feel about that."

"The ayes on it are going to be unanimous. It's sweet, funny, and it's also genius. You even gave him a bio."

His reaction gave her a lift on both the

personal and professional levels.

"I got the details from Lucy, since I wanted you to see it fresh."

"There's another word for it. *Fresh.*"

"You've got a tab for the intern program. I haven't finished there, but I have the framework up."

"Huh. You've got, what, a solid dozen previous interns, with their current situations."

"I'm waiting on a few more. I didn't realize you've had the program for nearly twenty years."

"Started before my time. This is excellent, Sonya. Seriously blew right past my expectations."

"That's what I like to hear."

She showed him the design for stationery, business cards.

"Consistent, you said, and delivered."

"Actual delivery will take another week or two, but if we get approval from the other Olivers on the letterhead and cards, Sadie could order them. And that concludes this evening's consultation."

She shut down her computer, then slid her arms around his waist. "I'm hoping you plan to stay."

"I put a bag in the car, in case."

"Why don't you get it? Later."

"Later works."

And when he kissed her, the day fell away.

■ ■ ■ ■

Eventually he went out for his bag, undressed again, and slid back into bed with her.

"Cleo's right to be jealous."

"Sorry?"

She tangled her legs with his. "She doesn't have someone to curl up with. Like this."

"Nobody back in Boston?"

"No one special. Her grandmother told her that lovers will come and go, but she'll have only one love, and he'll be her anchor in every storm. That's right up Cleo's alley."

"Her light's still on."

"She's a night person, mostly. You rarely have a Cleo sighting before nine a.m. Ten's more likely."

"I won't see her before I leave then."

"Highly doubtful. Trey, if I start to get up tonight, you know, like before? Will you stop me? I don't want all that tonight."

"I'll keep you here." He brushed a kiss over her hair. "You haven't done any of that before when I've been here. But you talk in your sleep."

That brought her head up. "I do? What do I say?"

"I can't make it out, not yet anyway."

"I never did that before."

"How do you know? You're sleeping."

Laughing, she cuddled closer, let herself

start to drift. "The room Cleo and I shared freshman year was far from palatial. She'd have heard me, and she'd have told me. Plus, as a woman fast approaching thirty, I'll confess I've shared a bed with others. Nobody ever said I talked in my sleep."

"New then. Connected."

"Mmm. I don't want to go through the mirror tonight."

"I've got you," he murmured, and stayed awake as she slipped into sleep.

When the clock woke him, she sighed, and turned. He heard her say, "All right. Yes. I'm coming."

Before she could get up, he gathered her close. "Stay with me tonight."

She started to shift away again, but he held her. "Just stay with me."

He thought she said Lizzy or Lissy before she went still.

"She waits."

"She'll wait a little longer."

In the quiet, the piano music floated up. He heard a woman weeping before, somewhere, a door closed.

In the morning as he dressed, he told her.

"Lissy," she said. "It must be. Owen Poole remarried just under two years after Agatha, and his oldest daughter was Lisbeth. So, I guess, Lissy. She married and died the same day. It's listed in the book as multiple bites from a black widow — 1916."

"You remember all that?"

She tapped her temple. "I have the names of all seven dead brides imprinted now, and how and when they died. I still have to read more, but I know that. I'll get the book back from Cleo, but I'm sure of that name. Lisbeth Anne Poole. I can't remember the name of who she married."

"Let's move, Mooks. Listen, I have this Saturday meeting, but I'll come back. I'd like to go through the storage areas again."

"Yeah, I think we should do that."

"I can pull Owen in for it. More eyes."

"I'd appreciate it, Trey, I really would. At the same time, I don't think we're going to find the mirror until and unless it wants to be found."

"Whatever it is, it's an inanimate object."

"Is it? I'm starting to wonder. Do you have time for coffee before you go?"

"I absolutely have time for coffee."

He took the coffee, and half a bagel, while the dogs headed outside, headed back in. Mookie wolfed down his breakfast, and Trey was out the door by nine.

Twenty minutes later, Cleo walked in, dressed, day-at-home makeup and hair in place.

"Did you forget it's Saturday?" Sonya asked.

"No, and while I usually object to being up before ten on any given Saturday, I started a painting last night. I like where it's going, so I want to give myself the morning to see how far I get. Trey and his faithful hound?"

"Morning meeting, but he's coming back, maybe with Owen. He wants to go through the storage areas again."

"Excellent." Cleo got herself some coffee. "Not only because I want to do the same, but they can haul that chest down to the studio for me. How'd you sleep?"

"I asked Trey to stop me if I tried to get up at the usual hour. I did, and he did. Plus, he said I talk in my sleep."

"No, you don't. I'd have heard you."

"Well, I do now. And last night I told somebody I was coming. And said Lissy."

"Lissy for Lisbeth?"

"I think it must be. She's next in line."

"What did she die of?" Eyes closed, Cleo held up a hand before Sonya could answer. "Wait, I'll get it. Spider bites!" She stopped, shuddered. "Why do spiders have to have all those legs?"

"Because spiders?"

"Anything over four is just creepy."

"As opposed to a house inhabited by numerous ghosts and a dead, vicious witch?"

"Damn right. I'll take ghosts over spiders all day, every day. Multiple bites. I remember this now."

"Like a dozen? I think that's right. I just remember she died from black widow bites."

"Thirteen bites — they found them when they took off her wedding gown and the rest. The spider or spiders had already scurried off on its/their too many legs. It appeared it had somehow gotten into her dress or the underpinnings. I mean, today they'd have antivenom. She'd have probably gotten sick, but wouldn't have — probably — died. Although, maybe, with that many. But early twentieth, a lot of people died from poisonous spiders. I looked it up."

Cleo downed coffee. "She was dancing. It was about time for her to go down and change into her going-away outfit. She never got the chance. The groom was bereft, but I read up some on him, and I think he was most bereft because she was an heiress."

"Cynical."

"It's how I read it."

Restless, hands in her pockets, Sonya wandered to the window and back. "I should've had Trey follow me instead of stop me. I just didn't want to go through it last night."

"Son, you're entitled. I'd have a hard time knowing I was going to watch another woman die on what should've been the happiest day of her life. If you want a break, you take it."

"I guess I did take it. I thought you wanted to explore the village today."

"That was the plan, but the painting's got me. Maybe tomorrow. I'm going straight up to see if I've got what I think I've got. You're okay?"

"I am. I've got a bunch of Saturday stuff. Starting with a workout. No, scratch that. Corrine's coming." She checked the time. "Shortly. And I don't know what time Trey's coming back."

"I'm facing the front so I'll see him. Maybe. Or hear him. Probably. If not, send someone up to get me. I really want that chest, and to go through things again."

Sonya tossed some laundry in the washer, made herself presentable.

Not just a photographer she hoped to hire for a project, she thought, but Trey's mother.

At ten-thirty sharp, Corrine rang the bell.

Like mother, like daughter, Sonya thought, as Corrine looked Saturday-morning stylish in black pants with a hip-length, pinstriped vest over a flowy white shirt.

"Thanks so much for coming out."

"You've got me intrigued."

"Let me take your coat. I'd like to explain everything to you upstairs so you can see some of what I have in mind."

"Collin would love the way you're living, making good use of the manor. Trey said your friend moved in."

"Yes. Cleo's up in the studio. It's the perfect space for her, and I hope he'd appreciate she's not only making good use of it but loves it."

"Now you have this good boy and your good friend. And . . . Trey."

"Ah."

"He's a grown man." After giving Yoda a final pat, Corrine straightened. And looked Sonya dead in the eye.

"I believe I raised him to make good choices. As his mother, I certainly think you've made a good one, let's say, spending time with him. We'll leave it there."

"He's very kind."

Now Corrine's eyebrows shot up. "So's this puppy."

With appreciation, Sonya laughed. "Trey has other attributes, but like you said, we'll leave it there. Come on up."

"Aren't you clever?" Corrine said the minute she stepped into the library. "Collin — and I'll apologize for bringing him up again, but he was a very cherished friend. He would so appreciate this. The creativity, and the practicality."

She turned, looked at the mood board. "Ryder Sports. Yes, yes, yes, I see what you're after."

"I found action shots. Of course, some of these are models, posed, but I got some from articles. The high school track meet, the yoga class, and so on. That's actually Cleo doing the warrior pose. The studio where she practiced in Boston took that for their site."

"She's gorgeous, isn't she? And limber."

"She's both. I want movement, I want the effort or the satisfaction or the sweat, depending, to show. Let me share with you the basic design I've started."

They sat together at the desk as Sonya ran it through.

"As I said, you're clever."

"I hope clever enough. I have a list of names, and the sports or equipment I think works best for each. I've got Cleo and Trey on board so far."

Turning, Corrine gave one slow blink. "You got Trey to agree to do this?"

"He likes baseball, so I've squeezed him into fielding a ball. And he said Owen uses a gym, so I thought I could get him lifting weights."

Rather than her son's slow smile, Corrine had a lightning grin. "I can't wait. Who else?"

As Sonya told her the rest, Corrine added in suggestions. People she knew, locations.

"I was sure you'd have ideas that would fill this out."

"Oh, ideas I have. Why don't you let me contact the people I know who you don't? I can be persuasive."

"Trey mentioned that. Since you're here, why don't I show you how I've incorporated your work into the Doyle Law Offices' website."

As Trey had, she scrolled through, then she nodded.

"I admit I didn't think we needed this. Now that I've seen what this is? We did. This reflects the firm and the people in it. And we work well together."

"I think so. You wouldn't take a fee for Anna's job or for the law offices. This is different."

"It is, and I'll expect to be paid."

"Why don't we go down, have some coffee, tea, whatever you like, and talk terms."

"I've seen what you can do," Corrine said as they started down. "I know what I can do. If you don't land the Ryder job, it won't be your fault or mine. I'm firm on that. It'll be because they lack good sense."

"I'm going to hold that thought."

"Oh." Corrine stopped outside the music room. "Another bride. Is that . . ."

"Lilian Crest. Clover. I found it where I found Johanna. My father painted it."

"I see. Of course, I don't see at all. It's your father's work, and you found it here. His and Collin's birth mother. I've seen her photo, the book Deuce made, but they weren't good shots. This is . . . it's wonderful. I used to joke Collin had the sexiest mouth. Now I see where he gets it. And you."

She laid a hand on Sonya's arm. "And it's wonderful, too, that the brothers who never knew each other have their paintings side by side."

Sonya's phone played "He Ain't Heavy, He's My Brother."

"It seems she agrees. Well." Corrine gave Sonya's shoulder a quick rub. "I'll take that tea now."

Chapter Twenty-Six

Once they came to terms that satisfied both of them, Corrine sat back, looked around the kitchen and great room.

"More little touches. The copper jar on the shelf, and that — is it rose quartz? — the raw hunk of crystal. Little pots of herbs on the windowsill. I especially like the blue ball hanging in the window. I think they call them witch balls."

"That's all Cleo. She actually made that ball."

"Really?" Fascinated, Corrine rose to take a closer look. "Hand-blown glass? I didn't realize she did that."

"She knows someone who does, and opens up a few times a year to give classes. She took one, made that."

"Apparently you're both clever."

"I can guarantee if Anna ever has a lesson day, Cleo would be first in line."

"That's an interesting thought."

"Corrine . . . could I ask you about Johanna?"

"We were friends, close friends. More than that," she said as she walked back to the table to sit. "She was a sister to me. I think our bond was like what you have with Cleo, so you understand what I mean."

"I do."

"I introduced them, Johanna and Collin, and watched them fall in love. God, we were all so young." On a wistful smile, she closed her eyes. "I can see us so clearly. Jo helping me shop for my wedding dress, and a few years later, me helping her find hers."

She looked back at Sonya. "Good memories — you should always bank those good memories. She was a teacher, and oh, she loved children. She and Collin talked about filling the manor with them."

"Everything Trey's told me says they'd have been wonderful parents."

"I'm sure of it." Her mind in the past, Corrine turned her teacup in its saucer. "She was smart, funny, very, very independent, and more than opinionated on certain issues. Women's rights, physical and emotional safety for children at the forefront. She and Collin fell in love gradually, a slow dance, and both of them were content to stay single. Deuce and I, it was bang, there you are, let's get started."

Laughing, she shook her head, sipped some

tea. "But when they got there, it was solid and strong. The wedding was in late June, in the gardens. Everything blooming and beautiful. I didn't realize she'd gone inside, gone upstairs. I'll never know why she did. If I'd gone with her . . ."

"No." Sonya reached out, laid a hand over Corrine's. "You couldn't have known."

"We didn't believe in curses. The hauntings? They simply were, and fascinating by and large. No one saw her fall. She was just . . . gone."

"I'm so sorry."

"It broke something in him, in Collin. In me, too, for a while. Then I saw her."

"Here, in the manor?"

"Yes. In the music room where you put her portrait. I'd come to bring Collin some food, a week or so after her funeral. I went into the music room — we'd had good times there. I sat and cried for her, for Collin, for myself. And there she was, in the wedding dress I'd helped her pick out.

"She said, 'Don't cry anymore, Corry.' She and Deuce are the only ones who've ever called me that. 'I had love, and I still have love. Don't let him stop living. Be here for him.'

"I said her name, and got up to go to her, but she was gone."

"Did you ever see her again?"

"No, but I sometimes catch a trace of the

perfume she liked, or just get a feeling. I know she's here."

Corrine sat back, lifted her hands. "I'm not a fanciful woman, but I know she's here. Knowing that helped mend what broke in me. You finding her portrait, then putting it in that room, in that place? I have to believe that was meant."

"I feel the same there. About both portraits. And now you've helped me really see her."

"I think you'd have liked each other." Corrine gestured toward the glass ball, the vase of flowers. "I know she'd have liked the little touches you and your friend bring to the manor."

"I love this house. So does Cleo."

"It shows."

"Can I get you more tea?"

"No, but thanks. I'm glad you asked about Johanna, because you should know more about her. Now, I have to run a few errands before I head home. And," she added as she rose, "I have some calls to make, a few arms to twist, and some planning to do."

"If — Cleo says to say when. When I get this job," Sonya said as she got up to walk Corrine out, "it's going to be in very big part due to your photos."

"Your concept, your design, but I'm not going to disagree the photos are going to matter." She waited while Sonya got her coat. "So I'm going to make them damn good. I'll be in touch."

After she closed the door, Sonya did a quick happy dance that inspired Yoda to race in circles.

"I'm not going to jinx it, but I think our chances just went way up."

As Clover played a happy tune from the library, Sonya grabbed a vest and a scarf to take Yoda for a walk.

No shadow today, she noted, and wondered who often stood there looking out.

Johanna? One of the other brides? Molly?

She could see Johanna now, beyond the portrait. She could see a woman who believed in herself, in looking out for others. She saw a woman who comforted a friend, and wanted the man she loved to go on living.

More good than bad, she thought again.

Looking over, she could see the back of the easel in Cleo's front window. She kept Yoda close as she took a long look toward the Gold Room.

Nothing right now, she thought, but no doubt she planned something.

When she heard a car coming, she told Yoda to sit. "No running toward the truck. I think Mookie's back. Sit, sit, sit," she insisted, as when they both spotted Trey's truck, Yoda popped up. "You just wait, just wait, and go!"

While the dogs greeted each other, the Gold Room window slammed three times.

Nothing flew out, but Sonya kept an eye on it.

"You just missed your mother."

"Passed her on her way down. So, she's in."

"She is." He had a look in his eyes, she realized, and a hard set to his jaw. "Is everything okay?"

"Yeah, yeah. Just work. Can't actually talk about it."

But clearly it troubled him, she thought. That something in his eyes, something caught between mad and sad.

"If you want to put this off —"

"No. No, I could use the break." He chin-nodded toward the window. "Has she been acting up?"

"Just now. Nothing much."

Turning their backs on the window, they walked around the side of the house and toward the mudroom.

"Your mother gave me some really solid input."

"Yeah, about that, the baseball thing. I was thinking you might want to use a kid."

She offered him a guileless smile. "Are you worried you can't catch a line drive?"

"I can catch a damn line drive. I played second right through Little League and into high school."

"Second." Holding on to guileless, she opened the mudroom door. "I would have thought first given those long arms and legs."

"Manny played first, Owen played short. But —"

"Oh, so it was Poole to Doyle to . . ."

"Garcia. We made our share of double plays. But a kid —"

"I want to use kids for basketball, and your mom suggested using another, with Mom or Dad holding on to the back of a bike. Just lost the training wheels sort of thing. Speaking of Owen, is he coming today?"

"He should be here pretty soon."

"Let's make a deal." She finished wiping paws, then cupped Trey's face. "If, after your mother takes the shots, you honestly don't like yours, I'll think of something else."

"I strongly dislike that's fair."

"Good. Now, where would you like to start?"

"Why don't we head up, work our way down?"

She hung the vest and scarf on the mudroom hooks.

"We should wait for Owen . . ." Both dogs barked and took off toward the front of the house. "And I think the wait's over."

The minute she opened the door, Jones strutted in. He accepted the greetings, sniffed at Sonya's shoes, and appeared to approve.

"Thanks for doing this, Owen."

"Hey, who doesn't like a treasure hunt?"

"No jacket?"

"Got one in the truck." He stood in jeans

with a flannel shirt open over a black tee. "It's April."

"We're going to go up, work down," Trey told him.

When they started up, the dogs charged ahead.

"Looks like we've got a whole crew," Sonya commented.

"Where's Lafayette?"

"In her studio. I should get her."

Owen looked ahead. "I'll do it. Attic first?"

"Meet you there," Trey told him as Owen peeled off.

Owen made his way down the hallway to the small turret, then stopped in the doorway.

She had her back to him as she faced the easel, a paintbrush in one hand, a wooden palette in the other.

She'd set the place up, he thought, pretty much as he'd expected. Not really fussy, but definitely on the girly side of things.

She'd shoved her ton of hair mostly on top of her head and wore a faded, oversized shirt — as a smock or whatever, he assumed.

From her desk, her computer played whale song.

Then she stepped back, angled her head. And he saw the painting.

He could see it wasn't finished, but what was went straight to his gut.

The mermaid sat on a rocky shore, half

turned to sea, half turned toward shore. Her tail — it wasn't green or blue or gold or red, but all of that and more — swept through the water.

He could see it move in his mind, trailing through the churning blue water and white foam.

Her hair, not quite brown, not quite red, showed streaks of pale blond as it tumbled down her bare back.

He saw something serene in her face, though the artist hadn't finished her. But something serene as she looked out toward where what he thought might be a blue whale when completed sounded in the symphonic light of the setting sun.

He said, "Hey," and she whirled around, the brush now held like a dagger.

"Jesus! You scared ten years off me."

"You looked more armed than scared. They're starting in the attic." But as he spoke, he walked closer to the painting. "I thought you did drawings and stuff. Kids books, like that."

"I do, and other things. I'm working on a book of mermaids — a coffee table book."

"Right, you said that. You paint them first?"

"Yes, sometimes, but no. No, not like this. I have time to paint here, and she, well, came to me."

"Blue whale?"

"Eventually. I'll just clean up and —"

"What's she holding? The way you have her hands, she's holding something."

"I'm not sure yet. I think a shell. Maybe a jewel. Probably a shell."

"How much?"

"How much what?"

"How much do you want for her?"

"I haven't thought about it." Cleo shrugged as she cleaned brushes.

"I'll buy her, so how much?"

Startled, Cleo looked back at him. "Are you serious? She's not even finished."

He shot her a look that wavered between impatience and amusement. "Have you ever sold a painting?"

All of a sudden, she felt he crowded her space. "Yes, but —"

"So how much?"

To flick him back, she grabbed a number out of the air. "Five thousand."

"Okay."

"Okay? No, stop. I just made that up. That's gallery price — and inflated some at that."

"What's the difference? Gallery price?"

"If you show and sell at a gallery, they take a chunk. About sixty percent."

"So direct sale's more like two grand? Let's call it twenty-five hundred."

When Cleo just stared at him, Owen stared back. "I want her. I've got a place for her. Make a deal, Queen of the Nile."

Cleo looked back at the canvas. She knew

the instant sorrow of the sale. She'd felt it before, and knew it would pass.

"A deal. How much to build me a Sunfish?"

A different sort of interest flickered in his eyes. "You sail?"

"I've never had my own, but I rented a sweet little Sunfish a few times in the summer in Boston. I thought I'd do the same here, but I'd like my own."

"You could buy a ready-made or used cheaper."

"Then it wouldn't be a wooden boat built by Poole for me to sail in Poole's Bay, would it?"

Considering, he looked back at the painting. In his mind the mermaid was already his. "We can make a trade. I couldn't start on it for a few weeks."

"You haven't asked me when I'll finish the painting."

"Will you finish faster if I bug you about it?"

"Absolutely not. In fact, I'd add time on just to spite you. I have a feeling you work the same way." She held out a hand. "When the painting's done, you can take her. When the boat's done, I'll take it."

"Deal." He took her hand, shook. "It's a good trade."

In the attic, Trey and Sonya removed any sheeting still in place.

"Do you think they got lost?"

She glanced over at Trey. "Cleo was painting, so it might take her a couple minutes to pull out. But maybe I should go check. It has been a while."

"Let's give them another minute. It's quiet. The dogs are settled."

"You mean you don't think we're going to find the mirror up here either."

"Still gotta look." When he reached the side wall, he tapped his way along it. "Maybe there's a space."

"Like a hidden door. Like the servant's door. I did the same thing in the music room." Willing to try again, she wound her way to the opposite side to tap.

"You said you remember standing in front of it. Nothing else?"

"Not about the where. I could see through it, through the glass. Movement, like shadows at first, then clearer. But the rest is blank, and frustrating. Because I notice details. It's part of what I do. Does that sound hollow?"

"No."

"I didn't think so either." She reached for another sheet. The dogs' heads came up, in unison. And she heard footsteps, then Cleo's voice.

"We're moving right along here," Trey called out.

"Sorry." Cleo brushed her hair back as they stepped into the attic. "We were making a deal. Apparently, Owen's an art collector."

Trey just frowned at him. "Since when?"

"I've got some art. Cleo wants a boat."

"You do?" Surprised, Sonya bundled the sheet aside.

"I want a sweet little Sunfish to sail Poole's Bay on summer Sunday afternoons. The chest I want is over in that section, by the way. You can't miss it. It's Davy Jones's locker. Davy Jones!"

Laughing she bent down to rub Jones. "Now I get it."

"Yeah, well, sometimes you just have to be obvious."

"Why don't the two of you take that section?" Trey pointed. "If we spread out, we'll cover more ground."

Cleo gave Trey a sorrowful look. "So said every soon-to-be-slashed-to-ribbons character in a horror movie."

"This ain't no movie." So saying, Owen headed left.

"Oh well." Cleo followed.

They went inch by inch, foot by foot. Cleo got her chest, and Sonya found a pair of teak chairs she wanted for the widow's walk.

They found mirrors — wall mirrors, hand mirrors, cheval glass — but they didn't find *the* mirror.

In the ballroom section, Cleo started a pile of take-downstairs items.

"This is like the best antiques shop ever. I

mean, look at this little lamp."

A nude goddess in bronze formed the base. The hard candy–pink shade dripped with crystals.

"It looks like it came out of a whorehouse," Owen commented.

"I *know*! I love it. She's going to sit on a table in my sitting room. Unless you want her, Sonya."

"She's all yours. Antiques shop, bordello, fun house. I swear, every time I come up here I see something I didn't see before. I should've taken all the sheets off first round. Eventually I should move some of this to some of the third-floor bedrooms. They're not all furnished, and it seems wasteful to have so much stuck up here.

"Eventually," she added. "Because I don't see using any of those rooms in the near future."

"You're going to give up that whole wing because of one bitchy dead witch?"

"Owen, you haven't been here when she gets going."

With her head bent as she pulled another sheet, she didn't see the look Trey and Owen exchanged.

"Dogs need to go out. Why don't you and Cleo do that," Trey suggested. "Owen and I can grab the chest."

"Wouldn't mind a cold one."

"Cokes now, alcohol after." Cleo clapped

her hands for the dogs. “Okay, gang, time for a pit stop.”

Trey waited until the sounds of barks, footsteps, and women’s voices receded. “So?”

“Let’s go. I don’t remember the rooms in that wing. Never had a reason to spend time there.”

“I know where it is.”

He led the way.

“You know, I have to say there is something creepy about this section. The light’s off,” Owen commented. “Not turned off, just not quite right. The air’s colder.”

“It wasn’t, at least not that I noticed. It’s noticeable now.”

“You’re worried this is where she comes when she does the mirror walk.”

“I’ve had some moments there. But she’s got a point when she says it’s not Dobbs with the mirror. A lot colder here. Right here.”

They stood in front of the Gold Room door, and could see their breath come out in streams of fog.

Owen reached for the door handle, then jerked his hand back. “Shocked me, not just a little jolt either.”

Something hit the door.

“The fucking wood bowed out. Did you see that?”

Trey nodded. And it struck again.

“Is she trying to get out, or trying to keep us out?”

Trey pulled the sleeve of his sweater over his hand. "Maybe both. Bang on the door."

As Owen pounded his fist, Trey grabbed the door handle, twisted.

The door flew open. The wind that slammed it back against the wall blew like a gale. Yet nothing moved. Even the curtains at the windows hung straight and still.

The windows behind them shot open, banged shut. In the hearth a fire kindled and blazed without wood to feed it.

Once again, the walls bled.

"I gotta say," Owen began, "this is kind of cool."

But Trey felt his temper click up when he thought about Sonya opening the door.

"This is bullshit."

Trey stepped forward. As his foot hit the threshold, something struck him with enough force to lift him off his feet and fling him back until he hit the wall.

The door slammed.

"Hey, hey!" Owen dropped down beside him. "Take it easy, easy. You hit hard."

"Knocked the wind out of me. Shit. Shit!" he repeated as he heard running feet.

"Pal, you just got tossed in the air by a dead woman. I think you can handle your girlfriend. Just stay down a sec."

"Oh my God, what are you doing? What were you thinking?"

And Trey found himself warding off a trio

of dogs and two women.

"You're hurt. There's blood. Cleo, call nine-one-one."

"Stop." Because he felt the blood trickle from his nose, he swiped at it. "I don't need an ambulance. Come on, Mooks, back off."

"He's okay." The two men gripped forearms, and Owen pulled Trey to his feet.

"Did you hit your head? Are you dizzy?"

"Yeah, I rapped it some, and no, not dizzy."

"You sent us outside so you could do this. That's out of bounds, both of you. Completely out of bounds."

Scared and pissed, Trey thought, and took Sonya's hands. "You're right, it is. Sorry."

"Listen, Trey could probably use an ice pack. How about you be mad at us downstairs?"

"All right, I think we're done with the hunt for the day, and I can be mad anywhere."

"I really am sorry." Though she tugged at it, initially, Trey kept her hand in his. "I should have told you I wanted another look. I felt it made more sense for you to be out of the house when I did, but that's no excuse for not being up front about it."

"I see exactly what Anna means."

"About what?"

She shook her head. "I'll get you an ice pack and a beer, and you can explain all this."

Because he felt Cleo hanging back, Owen slowed his pace to hers. "You're pissed, too?"

"For Sonya, I am. My problem is I was working my way up to doing exactly what you did, so I'm saying as little as possible."

"Smart move. Don't try it alone. Just don't."

"I have some things that might help if I can get in there."

"I just watched Trey get hit by something I couldn't see, hard enough to send him flying about eight feet until he hit the wall like he'd been tossed by the Hulk. Don't try it alone.

"I really want that beer now."

In the kitchen, Sonya, coolly silent, got an ice pack, wet a cloth.

"Hold that to your nose."

"It stopped bleeding."

"I can see that." Despite her anger, she trailed her fingers gently over the back of his head. "You've got a small knot, but that's not bleeding."

She handed him the ice pack. "Hold that there."

"Got it. Thanks. Sonya, you can't leave the room closed off forever."

"I don't know. I'm thinking of having a steel door installed over the existing one."

She got two beers and opened them. She set trays in front of him then offered the other to Owen when he came in with Cleo.

"You were hurt, and it could've been a lot worse."

"But it wasn't."

Cleo patted Sonya's arm. "I'll get us some wine. The windows in that room started slamming. Hard enough I don't see how the glass didn't break. The dogs went crazy."

She pulled the stopper from an uncorked bottle, poured two glasses.

"The dogs went crazy, and we all ran to the house. They're barking and snarling and racing upstairs. We heard banging and crashing. You were shouting."

Owen took another long pull of beer. "Was I?"

She nodded. "Your turn."

"It was mostly my fault. I've gotten everything about that room and Dobbs secondhand. So, you know, let's have a look."

"Nice try. Commendable." Steadier now, Sonya sipped her wine. "But Trey's a big boy, and — obviously — he can take his lumps."

"Just saying. So, the light's off in that wing — got a dingy look to it — and the air's cold. Did you notice?"

"No." At her look at Cleo, Sonya got a headshake. "But we were a little distracted seeing Trey crumpled on the floor."

"I wouldn't say *crumpled.*" He added.

He picked up the story, careful not to leave out any details. Not fair to her, and he had to admit, he hadn't been fair to her.

"A lot like before then." The anger faded, leaving just a shade of resentment.

"A lot like," Trey said. "But not altogether. This time I saw her."

"You saw her." Instantly Cleo dropped down into the chair beside him. "And you didn't lead with that?"

"Just for a second, but I saw a woman, black dress, black hair, and one who looked a lot more pissed off than either of you." He looked at Owen. "You didn't?"

"I was pretty busy watching you go airborne. And the door slammed shut."

"Sonya did some drawings of her. Like I said, I only caught a glimpse — while airborne — but I didn't have any trouble recognizing her. Or recognizing that most of what we saw in there was bullshit."

"So you said before you flew," Owen reminded him.

"The curtains weren't moving. The room's full of wind, but the curtains don't move?"

Frowning, Owen sat. "You're right. You're right about that."

"Illusions. Trickery."

"The bloody nose and the lump on your head aren't illusions."

"No." Because he thought they could both use it, he rose, put his arms around Sonya. "But she couldn't, or wouldn't, come past the door. Like the bird that vanished a few feet out of the window."

He kissed her forehead. "We'll figure it out."

"Any way we can figure it out with food?"

Owen wondered.

"Damn it! I forgot to get anything out for dinner."

"You could do that thing you did last time. With the vodka and the pasta. I want to see how you do it."

"I could do that."

"We're about finished upstairs. We can do the basement tomorrow. Can you manage that?" Trey asked Owen.

"After what just happened? You couldn't keep me out of it."

"No more side trips while the little ladies are tucked away."

He gave Sonya a solemn nod. "No, ma'am."

"You're welcome to stay if you like. God knows we have enough bedrooms — discounting that wing."

"I don't have any gear, but . . . I've never spent the night in the manor. I've got some work clothes in the truck. Got a spare toothbrush?"

"And plenty of them. Pick a room."

"I'll do that. What do you all do about breakfast?"

"That's strictly fend for yourself," Cleo told him. Firmly.

"Even on Sunday?"

"Even. And I'm down to my last Toaster Strudel, so don't even think about it."

"The apple ones with the white stuff on the top?"

"Don't even think about it."

With a shrug, he opened the refrigerator, checked some cabinets. "I'll make breakfast."

"While we're taking a moment, Trey says you work out, lift weights, and such?"

He gave Sonya a shrug. "Sure. Yeah, you've got that gym downstairs. Can I use that?"

"Help yourself. And that brings me to a project I'm working on, a possible job, for Ryder Sports."

"Okay."

"I need photos, which Trey's mother is going to provide."

"She's good at it."

"She is. I want one of you, maybe doing the classic biceps curl."

"Me? Why?"

To help the cause, Cleo reached over, tested his biceps. "Oooh." She batted her lashes. "That's why, stud."

When he laughed, Sonya went in for the kill. "It's a big job, and I've got one shot at it. I want to show ordinary people — not professional models — using Ryder equipment in their daily lives. You do biceps curls, so, that's you. Cleo's going to represent yoga. Trey's baseball."

He laughed again. "She got you? First the lawyer shot, now this? He hates having his picture taken."

"*Hate*'s a strong word," Trey said.

"But . . ." Lashes batting again, Cleo ran a

hand down Trey's cheek. "So handsome."

"Yeah, she's got you. Me? I'm fine with it. Come on, Jones, let's go pick out our bunk for the night. Don't start that vodka thing without me," he told Cleo. "I want to watch."

"An interesting man, your friend."

Trey sent Cleo his slow smile. "He's many-layered. Like Shrek."

Chapter Twenty-Seven

As Trey walked toward the kitchen in the morning, he smelled bacon and coffee. The duet of siren calls.

Owen, the sleeves of an ancient denim shirt rolled up, the front open over an equally ancient T-shirt, whipped something in a bowl.

"Dogs beat you down. They're having a meeting outside."

Nodding, Trey headed straight to the coffee.

"Heard the clock," Owen added. "Three in the a.m."

"Yeah. Sonya slept through it. And the music after."

"I heard somebody crying, it sounded like down the hall from the library. I walked over, then downstairs. Nothing and nobody there. Except. You know I've got twenty-twenty, but when I walked into the music room, just for a second, I didn't see rings on either portrait. Wedding rings. Then I did."

Eyes narrowed, Trey leaned against the

counter. “That happened to Sonya. She mentioned it last night.”

“Yeah? Maybe it’s a Poole thing.”

“Maybe. And maybe it means she’s not the only one who can find the rings. Wherever the hell they are.”

“Or — maybe again — take a walk through that magic mirror. Wherever the hell that is.”

“Have you talked to any of the cousins about this?”

“They’re not interested. Collin didn’t leave them the manor for good reason. They’d have sold it in a heartbeat.”

“But not you.”

“No. I don’t know what the hell I’d do with it, and there’s another reason he left it to Sonya. But it’s been in the family for more than two centuries. That shit matters. The business matters, same reason, and that they get. Even if it’s only, or at least mostly, for the income.”

“But not you,” Trey said again.

“Hey, I’ve got nothing against making money. We play to our strengths, and that works. Clarice may not know how to build a dinghy, but she’s got an eagle eye on the business of the business. Connor could sell sand to a man wandering the desert. Mike could build if he wanted, but he’s best at design. Cathy and Cole, they’re both settled in Europe, got family there, and handle that end of things.

“And Hugh,” Owen added, speaking of his younger brother, “he’s grateful for the share Collin left him, and he’d do whatever I asked him to do. But what he wants is to live in New York, wear fancy suits, and work in finance. He’s good at it.

“Do you figure the women are coming down before lunch?”

“Sonya’s up. She wanted to check something in her office first. I don’t know about Cleo.” Trey looked in the bowl. “French toast?”

“It’s Sunday.” Owen got out two skillets. “Somebody else is doing the dishes. How many slices do you want?”

“I can smell the bacon. Are you making eggs, too?”

“It’s Sunday.”

“Then two.”

When Sonya walked in, Owen added more soaked slices of bread to the skillet. Then poured beaten eggs into the other.

“You meant a serious breakfast.”

“It’s Sunday. How many do you want?”

“Just one, thanks.”

“That’s sad, but your choice.”

By the time he’d piled everything on one big platter, Cleo joined them. He shot her a look.

“Do you wake up looking like that?”

She just smiled. “Now, that’s a Sunday breakfast.”

"I made extra in case you decided to show up."

"It's Sunday," she said, and made Trey laugh.

As they ate, Sonya turned to Owen. "So, Trey tells me you build doghouses."

"Not really. A couple."

"You did that duplex for Lucy."

"A few," Owen corrected.

"Yoda really needs his own house. I mean like right now, he has guests. Maybe they all want to hang out, watch some ESPN. Or *Paw Patrol.*"

Owen scooped up some eggs, eyed her as she smiled at him.

"What'll it take?"

"Don't know. Haven't thought about it. Right off, you need a design, dimensions."

"It just so happens." She popped up, retrieved the sketchbook she'd brought in with her. "I have that."

"Did you get this going?" he asked Trey.

"Inadvertently."

Owen continued to eat as he studied Sonya's sketches. Ones she'd carefully drawn to scale.

"Mansard roof, a turret, arched windows."

"It needs to honor the Victorian style of the manor. It's Yoda's manor."

"Uh-huh. Interior, tray ceiling, with a fan, heated floor. A freaking trundle bed."

"For sleepovers."

"An electric fireplace."

"Between that — I found a really small one — and the heated floors, it would be warm in the winter. What do you think?"

"She wants a boat." He pointed his fork at Cleo. "And we already made the deal. But I can think about it. If I do, you're slave labor," he told Trey.

"No problem. Speaking of dogs, I'll let them in, feed them."

"I'll handle the dishes." Cleo rose. "I suppose we need to get started. Why don't we take the downstairs?"

Within the hour, they were deep into it, removing more dustcovers, hunting through the warren of rooms. When she uncovered a big rolltop desk, Sonya searched through drawers and pigeonholes.

"Needs oiling." Owen ran a hand over it. "Solid mahogany, got the S-shaped tambour front, original carved handles. Late Victorian probably."

Sonya thought she knew him well enough now to recognize the tone.

"It's yours."

"No, no way. This piece has got to be worth —"

"A custom doghouse?"

"Shit. Damn it. Done."

She surprised him by throwing her arms around him and giving him a noisy kiss.

He shot Trey a smug look. "You're doomed

now, pal. You know what happens when I kiss a woman."

"She kissed you," Trey pointed out.

"I can fix that." But he turned back to the desk. "It'll be interesting getting this out of here."

As they worked their way through, the bell began to ring.

"There she goes," Sonya muttered.

Trey walked over, put his hand on the bell, stilled it. Under his hand, it began to vibrate.

"You're just pissing her off." But Cleo crossed over, put a hand over his. "Insistent. And cold, right?"

"Yeah, getting colder."

He removed his hand and the bell swung wildly.

"We could take it off the board."

"I thought of that." Joining them, Sonya shook her head. "But it's kind of an early warning system. Plus, ignoring it's like flipping her off."

"Any of the others do that?" Owen asked.

"Not that I've noticed. Cleo, look at this desk. The slant top. That's mahogany, too, isn't it? You should take this."

"I already have a desk."

"For work, for art. You should set up an office. We have all these rooms. And the more of them we really use? It just feels like sticking a thumb in her eye."

"When you put it that way."

"It's looking like we're just the muscle," Owen commented, then pointed. "What about down there?"

Sonya looked at the basement door. "I don't go down there. Ever."

"Can't skip the basement."

He went to the door, and it creaked just as Sonya imagined it would when he opened it. He hit the switch. "Lights work," he said, and started down the steep, narrow stairs.

"We'll do a quick sweep," Trey said. "You can stay here."

"I'm not staying here." Cleo looked at Sonya when Trey went down. "Are we staying here like helpless damsels?"

"Oh hell. You go first."

The stark lights only added to the gloomy shadows and corners. The concrete floor showed a dull, unhappy gray. It held another labyrinth of rooms, low-ceilinged, bare walled.

There should have been cobwebs, Sonya thought. But the basement proved as clean as the rest of the house.

"Molly keeps busy." Sonya stuck close to Cleo.

"If you didn't watch so many horror movies, you wouldn't be thinking of Freddie or Jason or, who is it, Michael Myers."

"Don't say the names!"

She heard the men talking about tankless water heaters, furnaces, support beams. And headed in that direction.

At the top of the stairs, the door slammed shut.

And the lights went out.

"Oh shit, oh God. Jesus. Cleo?" She groped for Cleo's hand, gripped it.

"I'm here. Where —"

Since Cleo's voice came from the left, and the hand she held was on her right, Sonya didn't even think about stopping the scream.

Whirling, she ran into someone — something — screamed again.

"It's me! It's me!" Cleo held tight, and they heard feet running. Saw dim light bouncing.

"Sonya!"

"Something's in here."

When Trey reached her, he wrapped one arm around her, held his phone with the flashlight in the other. Beyond the door, the dogs barked like maniacs.

"Are you hurt?"

"No, no, but —"

"Got your phone?"

"Yes, sorry, yes. The door. The lights."

She fumbled out her phone as Owen moved past her and toward the steps. "Locked, from the other side."

"There were tools in the back."

"Why don't you get those? We'll take it off the hinges."

"We're fine," Trey told Cleo. "Just give me a minute."

"Wait." Cleo held up a hand as the lights flickered. "Try the door again."

"I just did."

"Again," she snapped. "Look at the lights. She's either finished or she can't keep it up. Try it."

When the knob turned in his hand, he glanced back at her. "You're right."

The lights came on full as he opened the door. The dogs jumped, wagged, shivered. Since she didn't consider pride an issue, Sonya took the stairs two at a time.

"I'm sorry. I panicked. But she can have the Gold Room and the basement. When the lights went out, I took someone's hand, and it wasn't Cleo's because she was on the other side of me.

"I'm going up," she added. "It wasn't Cleo's or either of yours. I took someone's hand. I held it."

Hers still shook when she reached the kitchen and got a glass of water.

"I panicked."

"Who wouldn't?" Owen said.

"What did it feel like?"

"A hand, Trey."

"I mean, a man's hand, a woman's?"

"Oh. I . . ." She gulped more water, tried to think. "I honestly thought it was Cleo's, but I was expecting Cleo's."

Closing her eyes she took herself back to the moment. "A woman's, or girl's. God, it was probably hers. Hester Dobbs."

"I don't think so." Cleo stroked a hand down Sonya's hair. "You didn't say cold. The hand."

"I didn't notice."

"You would have, I'm sure of it. The bell, Trey, it got icy."

"True enough."

"You said you reached for my hand, and took a hand. It got cold when the door slammed, and the lights went out, but not like the bell. I think it was one of the others. And she let you take her hand to reassure you."

"Didn't work that way. I screamed."

"Again," Owen said, "who wouldn't?"

She sent him a wan smile. "Thanks for that."

"Just fact. Let's try it again," he said to Trey.

"Oh. Do you have to?"

"Just give us a minute." Trey bent down, kissed the top of Sonya's head.

"I'm not going back down there, Cleo."

"Why should you? Let them check it out. They'll feel better. And I don't think she can play that trick again so soon anyway."

Sonya's phone played the Eagles' "Take It Easy."

"Trying to."

"It might have been Clover, or even Molly." Cleo wandered as she spoke. "But someone who cared enough to let you take her hand.

An opposing force. I know it scared you. It would've scared the hell right out of me, too. But I don't think that was the intent."

"You're right. You're right. When I brushed up against Dobbs, I got an ice burn. This wasn't like that. At all.

"But I'm not going back down there."

When the men returned, Trey sat beside her, took her hands. "Nothing down there now that shouldn't be."

"Good. I'm putting it on my never-go-there-again list."

"Why don't we do this? We'll see what it takes to get those desks up here, and anything else you want, then we'll call it. We'll go out, grab some dinner."

"Why don't we do just that?"

Everything settled back to normal. Even Clover backed off her musical interludes as if she understood Sonya wanted the quiet. She worked through Monday morning without interruption until Cleo came to the doorway.

"Sorry, but I wanted to tell you I'm going to the store. Unless you want me to wait until you can go with me."

"No, that's silly, go ahead. I'm fine here,"

"I won't be too long. Rock Hard's tonight."

"How could I forget? I checked with Bree. She said sexy club wear."

"Is there any other kind? See you later."

"I'll walk out with you. It's time for Yoda to

have a round."

The quiet and normal held, for the walk, back at work. This, she thought, was what she wanted. The big, beautiful house around her, the restless sea outside, the dog napping by the fire.

And her work.

She tried not to worry that if she didn't get the Ryder job, she'd have an empty schedule very soon.

Something would come, she told herself. Do good work, and something would come.

When Yoda barked and ran down to greet Cleo, Sonya realized she'd worked another three hours. So much for Cleo's *won't be long.*

She shut down and found Cleo in the kitchen, putting away groceries.

"I love Poole's Bay! I figured you'd text if you needed me, so once I got there, I just had to poke around. The little shops! All so cute."

Sonya glanced at the shopping bags. "You had some fun."

"I did. And when Gigi of Gigi's — that fun little store with clothes and soaps and lotions, made locally — found out I was your friend, she said she'd been thinking about contacting you. She's seen Anna's website."

"Really?"

"Naturally, I told her you were the GOAT, and that with all her lovely things, you'd build her something fantastic. I'd expect a call from

Gigi this week."
"I would love to get a call from Gigi."
"Gigi's daughter once dated your cousin."
"Owen?"
"No, one of the other ones. Cole."
"He lives in London, I think."
"And Gigi's daughter lives in Bangor with her husband and two daughters. And a Saint Bernard named Milly."
"You always get the dish."
"Yes, I do. Anyway, I had a great time.
"Unless something irresistible comes my way, I may take a few weeks off this summer. Paint and sail and sail and paint, and just wander."
She tucked the cloth market bags away. "How about a salad with grilled chicken before we get our sexy club wear on?"
"Sounds perfect."

It didn't surprise Sonya when she went up to change to find the red dress once again laid out on the bed.
"You know what? Tonight I can make that work. Unless."
She walked to the hall, called out, "Cleo, are you wearing red?"
"No. The black dress with the silver."
"Oh, that's a good one. Okay."
Now Cleo stepped out. "You're wearing that killer red."
"This is like the third or fourth time Molly's

laid it out for me."

"She picked the black for me. So, let's make her happy."

Maybe not normal in most parts of the world, Sonya decided, but normal enough for the manor.

For the first time since she'd moved in, she pulled out her curling iron. She was going for it.

It took her a full hour, but when she stood in front of the mirror, she thought: Yes. Worth every minute.

She walked down the hall in heels she hadn't worn in months, and into Cleo's room.

Her friend had let her hair go wild, and paired the black dress with silver heels that picked up the thin, raised glittery stripes in the dress.

Cleo turned, and her lips, painted vivid red, curved.

"We are so hot it burns. Let's go down."

"Trey's dropping Mookie off, then picking us up, then dropping Yoda off, then picking Owen up. It's a lot."

"What about Jones?"

"Jones has Wi-Fi in his doghouse."

"Right. Forgot."

Yoda announced Trey before he rang the bell.

When they answered, he gave them a very slow, very satisfying blink. "Well, wow. I got nothing but wow."

"We'll take it." Cleo stepped out.

"Really big wow."

Sonya shut the door behind her.

In the village, Yoda reunited with Mookie, and minutes later, Trey pulled up in front of a Cape Cod near the bay with an enormous garage.

One toot of the horn had Owen walking out.

"Nice house," Cleo said.

"Needs work, but it's coming along."

"A family of four could live in the garage."

"It's not a garage. It's a shop. You look good," he said. "Both of you. Manny let me know Bree let him know we were coming. He got us a table. Old times' sake."

No one brought up ghosts or ringing bells, so the drive to Ogunquit continued the normal tone of the day. Maybe it was just a lull, Sonya thought, but like Cleo with the *wow,* she'd take it.

When they walked into the club, she realized she'd missed this.

The movement, and the heat of bodies in motion, the crowded bar, the pounding music.

When she looked toward the raised stage, and the drummer, she realized she wouldn't have pictured Bree with Manny, with his Buddy Holly glasses, goofy smile, floppy brown hair.

But the chef stood beside a table, hips

twitching to the beat. And Sonya saw the goofy smile was aimed straight at her.

"Bree's holding the table," Owen shouted. "I've got the first round. Want your first and only lonely beer?"

"Yeah. I'm DD, lost the coin toss."

"How's the wine here?" Sonya asked.

"I wouldn't know."

"I'll go with him. Got you covered."

Cleo moved off with Owen as Trey led Sonya to the table.

"Woo! You made it. They're killing it tonight."

The chef wore skintight leather pants and a sleeveless top that showed off some midriff and a pierced navel. She had a tattoo of a dragonfly skimming up from her elbow to shoulder.

"Looking hot, Sonya."

"I've got to say the same back to you."

"Just you two?"

"Owen went to the bar," Trey told her. "Cleo went with him. Nobody trusts Owen to order wine."

"You're right about that. I gotta dance."

Bree ran out to the dance floor and joined a group of four who didn't seem to mind.

"Do you want to dance?"

"Observe first, dance soon." After sitting, Sonya turned to Trey. "Either they're really good or I haven't heard live music in much too long."

"Could be both." He trailed a hand along her hair. "This is new."

"Takes work, trust me."

He leaned over to kiss her. "Thanks for the effort."

Cleo set a glass down in front of Sonya. "They actually have a very solid wine list."

"One lonely beer."

Once Owen set the beer down, Cleo grabbed his hand. "We're dancing."

On a laugh, Sonya took a quick sip, then grabbed Trey's. "We're dancing."

She danced with Trey, with Owen, with Cleo, with Bree, with a few complete strangers. And forgot everything but the movement and the music.

When the band took a break, she met Manny, who turned out to be both nerdy and sweet. And when he squeezed into a chair with Bree, the nerd and tattooed chef looked perfect together.

When Rock Hard started the next set, Sonya turned to Bree. "Okay, Manny's adorable."

"He totally is. And he's a monster in bed."

"Bree, Jesus."

Bree waved a dismissive hand at Trey. "Oh, shut up. You were no slouch. He's no slouch," she said to Sonya as Cleo laughed like a lunatic.

"He's no slouch," Sonya agreed.

To cut off the topic, Trey grabbed Sonya's hand. "We're dancing."

After midnight, Trey pulled back up at the manor. Mookie and Yoda curled together on the back seat of the truck with Cleo.

"That was a night. I could become a Rock Hard groupie. You coming in, Trey?"

He glanced back at Cleo, then looked at Sonya. "I've got an eight o'clock. But —"

"You go home." Before Sonya could lean over to kiss him, Cleo touched her fingers to her lips, then his cheek. "Yoda and I will say good night and thank you. Loved every minute."

" 'Night, Cleo."

"I loved every minute, too." Now Sonya leaned over to kiss him. "I like your friends."

"I like yours."

"That's a nice bonus, isn't it? Go home, get some sleep."

"You're sure you're okay for the night?"

"We're all good. We've got a nice lull going." But she kissed him again, lingered over it. "Don't get out."

"Sleep's not really that important."

Laughing, she nudged him away. "Go get some," she said, and opened the door. "You, too, Mookie."

He waited while she walked to the door, let herself in.

Cleo walked back down the hall. "All the

cabinet doors open in the kitchen and butler's pantry. And this time, the doors on the buffet and server in the dining room, too. I think someone was unhappy we took the dog for so long.

"Someone," Cleo added, "Yoda greeted by running in circles, then actually dancing a little on his hind legs. I think all is forgiven."

"Good. Because I danced my ass off, and I want bed."

"I'm there with you. In my own bed. That was so much fun," Cleo added as they walked upstairs, arms linked.

"I almost forgot what it was like to just let go and dance my ass off." She stopped outside Cleo's door. "You're the best friend anyone could ask for."

"Who'd know better than you?"

"I mean it. You really didn't like Brandon at all." She drew back, met Cleo's eyes. "I can tell, because you really do like Trey."

"I really do like Trey."

"Me, too. Good night, Cleo."

In her room, she managed to clean off the makeup, slap on some moisturizer. She stuffed the red dress in her dry-cleaning bag, then pulled on pajama pants and a T-shirt.

Yoda already snored lightly in his bed.

She got into her own.

"Please, everybody, just one more night. Just a full twenty-four hours of quiet. I just want to sleep. If there's more, save it for tomorrow."

And closing her eyes, she dropped straight into sleep and stayed there.

Whatever passed through the room, whatever wandered the halls, did so quietly. After so many years, one night wasn't long to wait.

Chapter Twenty-Eight

She knew the lull couldn't last, but it stretched through the next day, and into the following. She worked while a spring snow shower whisked tiny flakes outside that melted the moment they hit the ground.

And midmorning, she accepted an offer to design another book cover. That called for a celebrational Coke and a bowl of pretzels.

While she ran final tests on the Doyle project, she thought about her years with By Design. At this point in a project, she'd have other eyes on the work, and now she only had her own.

There would have been coworkers or bosses to bounce around ideas with or discuss solutions to problems.

Now, again, she had only herself.

She supposed a part of her would always miss the office camaraderie, but the trade-off? Trusting herself, her eyes, her instincts?

It balanced it all out.

"I'm sending this to the three Olivers, Yoda.

Then we'll take a walk before I come back and do a round on the florist."

She composed the email, attached the files, and sent it off.

And sat back.

"Amazing what you can get done without distractions. From coworkers to ghosts."

She started to turn off her music — she'd given the tunes over to Clover — rising as she did.

Yoda wasn't napping by the fire, or curled under her desk.

With the music off, she heard the sound of the ball bouncing downstairs, and Yoda's scrambling race over the wood floors.

She slipped quietly out of the room, and began to creep down the stairs.

Yoda ran after the ball, snagged it at the front door. He raced in two circles before he trotted back down the hall.

She heard it, faint but clear. Laughter, a young boy's laughter.

The ball came bouncing back her way as she neared the bottom of the stairs.

And a tread creaked under her feet.

With a silent curse, she dashed down the rest, and caught a glimpse of a figure. A boy! Yes, a boy who sprinted away, fleet of feet down another hallway.

Ball clutched in his jaws, eyes alive with the game, Yoda chased after. Sonya did the same.

"Wait! Please. I'm not going to hurt you.

How the hell would I hurt you?"

She followed the sound of the dog, running past sitting rooms, toward the solarium, beyond that to the morning room. When she neared the formal dining room, she heard the cabinet doors slamming, and slowed.

"Okay, all right."

More than a little breathless, she stepped into the kitchen, where Yoda sat, head angled, the ball at his feet.

"There's no need to be mad." Briskly, voice even, she went around closing cabinet doors. "I'm glad you're playing with him. He's a really nice dog, isn't he?"

Talking to a ghost, she thought, but since she talked to Clover routinely now, it didn't seem all that strange.

"Sometimes I get caught up in work and forget he needs some playtime. I know he has fun with you. Honestly, I just wanted to say thanks."

"Who are you talking to?" Cleo asked.

Sonya jolted so hard she nearly stumbled back and fell on her ass.

"Jesus! Make some noise! I saw him."

"Saw who?"

"The boy. I knew it was a boy. Playing with Yoda, opening the cabinets. I saw him, Cleo."

"Here?" Cleo looked around. "Do you still see him?"

"No, and not here. In the main hall. I heard the ball bouncing and Yoda chasing it, so I tried to sort of sneak downstairs. But he heard me and took off. I caught a glimpse though."

She grabbed a paper towel and a pencil, began to sketch.

"I'm going to say eight, nine, maybe ten. In there. Short-ish brown hair. About my color, I'd say. I didn't really see his face, just a quick snapshot of his profile. He was wearing like — what do they call them — knickers? Brown pants that stopped below the knee, a white shirt."

She set the pencil down. "That's all I've got."

"But you actually saw him, Son. When you were wide awake. That's progress."

"Is it? He ran. I actually chased him. I don't have any idea what I intended to do if I caught up to him."

"Have a conversation, like you were trying to do when I came in."

"He's so sweet with Yoda, I just wanted to . . . Oh well. Why did you come in?"

"Need my midday boost." Turning to the fridge, Cleo got out a carton of yogurt.

"I don't understand the correlation between yogurt and a boost. I wonder who he was," Sonya murmured. "And what happened to him. Just a kid."

"I don't know when kids wore knickers. It might help to get a ballpark on when he lived here. He must've lived here."

"He sure as hell died here. I'm taking Yoda out for a walk. You're welcome to join us."

"Are you talking to me or ghost boy?"

"Either or both."

"I'm just here for the boost, then it's back to the drawing board. Literally. See you at dinner."

Sonya didn't know if the boy joined them, but he didn't make himself known. The walk convinced her despite the snow shower April meant business. Those brave bulbs poked up higher; the sun spread just a bit warmer.

The days, she thought, were getting noticeably longer.

And she was more than halfway through what she'd considered her three-month trial.

"I'm not going anywhere." She glanced up at the third floor as she spoke. "I'm sticking."

When she went in through the mudroom, Yoda's box of treats stood on the kitchen island.

"You should give him one. I'll go back up to work, and you give him one."

Since Yoda didn't follow her, she decided the boy made himself known there at least. By the time she settled back down to work, she heard the ball bouncing.

"What's his name, Clover? Do you know his name?"

"Jumpin' Jack Flash" rocked out of her tablet.

"Jack. Well, if you get a chance, maybe you

could let Jack know I'm happy to share Yoda with him, and Cleo and I are happy to share the house."

Not as if she had a choice, Sonya thought, but it made sense to keep the peace wherever possible.

She worked until five. Sometime during the work, Yoda made his way back upstairs and, clearly tuckered out by the play, snoozed by the fire.

When she rose, looked over at him, she saw the Poole family book on the table, open.

Yoda blinked his eyes when she walked over, thumped his tail.

She saw the facing page listed the children of Owen Poole — Agatha's Owen — and his second wife, Moira.

Michael and Connor, twins.

Charles, born a year later.

Lisbeth, born the following year. Died at eighteen on her wedding day.

Alice, born three years after Lisbeth, married and moved to Virginia, where she lived until the age of sixty-nine.

And John (Jack), born a year and a half after Alice, who died at the age of nine. Scarlet fever.

Poor kid, she thought.

Yoda rushed out; the doorbell bonged.

As she went down, she thought of the boy, suffering, maybe delirious. His desperate parents, his frightened siblings. For more than a hundred years he'd lived this . . . could it be called a half life?

And now he played with her dog.

She opened the door to another dog, and Trey.

"There's Mookie. You've got a friend, Yoda. And you've got a key," she said to Trey.

"For emergencies, not drop-bys."

Nothing, she thought, just nothing like Brandon. And wrapping her arms around him, held hard.

"Is everything okay?"

"Yeah, just feeling down, I guess. I read about Jack Poole — the boy who plays with Yoda and opens the cabinets. I saw him this afternoon."

"Saw him?" Trey drew her back to look into her eyes.

"What you'd call a fleeting glimpse. Come on, you can have a beer while I tell you."

Cleo, already in the kitchen, smiled at Trey. "Excellent, another victim. I'm doing this pork thing and trying my hand at scalloped potatoes. Is it glass-of-wine time, Son?"

"It could be. Did you bring the Poole book into the library today?"

"No."

"Somebody did. His name's Jack. He died of scarlet fever. Nine years old."

"Oh." Cleo's eyes went damp. "Poor little guy."

"I need to backtrack for Trey."

Once she had, Trey picked up the history. "I'm nearly sure it was Michael Poole who married Patricia — your bio great-grandmother. She's the one who refused to live here. Michael was the oldest twin. She basically closed the place up."

"And her son, Charlie, opened it up again, moving in with Clover and friends?"

"That's the story I know," Trey agreed. "Charlie wanted the place, his parents didn't, so his father deeded it to him. In trust, if I'm remembering right, until he hit eighteen. He would've inherited it anyway, as Michael Poole's oldest son, and I think Michael Poole died before Charles hit eighteen. Or soon after that. It would be in the book."

"So Jack would be my great-great-uncle? It's confusing. I've put off reading more of the history and lineage, and I shouldn't. I need to get back to it."

She looked over at Cleo. "Anything I can do here?"

"We're all going to hope I have this under control."

"It looks like I timed a drop-by on the money. I wanted to let you know we all went over the files, and it's perfect."

"You're good with it?"

"More than. Sadie actually grunted twice, which is effusive praise."

"I can have it up live first thing in the morning. This is awesome. Every time I think

I miss the office vibe I realize how much more I like my own vibe."

The ball came bouncing into the kitchen. Both dogs gave mad chase.

"Even with that, I like my own vibe. And I guess I should pick up another ball."

After dinner, Sonya pointed at Cleo. "You had it under control."

"I did. I'm sort of into it. How about I take the dogs out and you guys deal with cleanup?"

"Fair trade," Trey agreed.

"Then I'm thinking about movie-time. I'll use the library if you're not interested. If you are, it seems like the right moment to break in the media room."

"Oh." Her stomach knotted. Knee-jerk, Sonya thought. Time to move on from that. "You know, you're right. What's the point in having a media room if you never use it?" She turned to Trey. "Are you up for a movie?"

"Can there be violence, maybe nudity, and harsh language?"

"We're good with that." Sonya rose to clear the table. "Scratch sophisticated comedies, dramas, bittersweet romance. We're all about the action. I insist on strong, potentially kick-ass female lead. Now, let's narrow that down. Classic or released in the last two years?"

"I love the classics," Cleo said. "You know what I've never seen, commercial free and on a screen bigger than my desktop monitor?

The original *Terminator.*"

"That clicks all the boxes." Sonya gave Trey a hip bump as they dealt with the dishes. "You get a vote."

"I vote the next time we follow up with the sequel. Collin's got the full set of DVDs."

"Let's go, boys." Cleo grabbed a jacket from the mudroom, then stuck her head back in the kitchen. In her best Schwarzenegger, she said, "I'll be back."

It was fun. Fun, Sonya thought, to settle down in big, cushy chairs with popcorn. Yes, the bell rang — or more accurately banged — as they did just that. She liked to think ignoring it as the ominous opening music filled the room was a middle finger raised in Hester Dobbs's direction.

About the time Kyle Reese told Sarah Connor to come with him if she wanted to live, the lights flicked on and off like a strobe.

"She doesn't like it that we're having a good time," Cleo observed.

No, no, Sonya agreed, she really didn't. When the lights stopped flashing, the banging started. It echoed through the room as the walls shook, and her heart beat hard in her throat.

"It's pissing her off," Trey murmured. He took Sonya's hand. "Just the fact we're sitting here like this."

Restless, the dogs huddled near the chairs.

When the doors flew open, their hackles

rose on a series of warning barks. They slammed shut again with a crack like a gunshot.

"Just give it a minute." Trey spoke quietly as Sonya started to rise. "Let it play out."

Framed posters fell off the walls. Beneath her feet, she felt the floorboards quake. The booming reached a pitch where she wanted to press her hands to her ears and scream for it to stop. Just stop.

As she neared her own breaking point, it did. Just stop.

She realized she gripped Trey's hand on one side, Cleo's on the other. Cleo's trembled in hers; Trey's was rock steady. And for whatever reason, both helped ground her.

On-screen, the heroes ran from the machine whose only purpose was to kill.

Like her hand, Cleo's voice trembled. "I guess that's all she had for tonight."

Maybe, Sonya thought. Maybe. But like the terminator, she'd be back.

It made a point, though, she decided, that they finished the movie. And rehung the posters. They dealt with popcorn bowls, let the dogs out. All the normal, ordinary things people did in normal, ordinary lives.

Cleo went up first. After they brought the dogs in for the night, she and Trey followed.

"You said you've watched movies down there before."

"Yeah. And no, nothing like that. I'm finding it hard to believe she didn't hassle Collin, at least off and on, but he never said much about it."

"I think it's me. She was done with Collin, wasn't she? If she managed to find a way to kill Johanna, get her ring, he didn't really matter. I'd be next in line. Or Owen, any of the Poole cousins if he'd left the house to them."

"You're not a bride."

"No, and maybe that's why she doesn't like me being here. On the other hand," she said as they walked the long hallway, "we know of at least two others — Molly and Jack. No, three, with the cigar smoking man. Non-brides, and still here. There are probably more."

"A house this old? It's held a lot of life, and death. I've spent a great deal of time here, and sure, there have been things — I told you about a couple — but nothing like that show tonight, or in the basement, in the Gold Room."

"And what's changed?" As they walked into her room, Sonya turned to him. "I'm here. Living here, working here, determined to stay here. I'm not what she wants."

"Maybe not, but I think it's more than that. You're what the others want, and need."

"To find the rings."

"That's the recurring theme. Find them, break the curse, get rid of Dobbs. And no more dead brides."

"But when I've seen her — on the other side of the mirror — she's wearing them."

"All seven?"

"No." She paused to consider. "So far, I've seen them in order. Astrid, Catherine, Marianne, Agatha. Four rings total, so far. Do you think something could change when I see her with all seven?"

"I wish I knew." He ran his hands down her arms, then back to her shoulders. "I wish there was more I could do to help get you through this."

"You've helped a lot." She leaned into him. "Like this helps. It's nice to know that when I really need it, I've got somebody to lean on."

"Anytime."

"You kept me from jumping up and screaming during the movie."

"Why give her the satisfaction?"

"That's exactly right, but I was close to giving her plenty of it." Tipping back her head, she rose on her toes enough to meet his mouth with hers. "Now I'd rather give you plenty of it."

"How about some give and take?"

When he ran his hands under her sweater, up her back, she boosted up to lock her legs around his waist. "You have the best ideas."

Tonight, she wanted the heat and the movement, the fun of being able to give and to take. His hands on her body, his lips on her skin, lingering, lingering until everything in her ached and burned.

For more. Still more.

All hunger and greed, she rolled with him, urging him to take more, still more, even as she did.

She was like a brush fire under him, over him, around him. Hot and quick and dangerous. He told himself he let her set the tone, the pace, but he wasn't sure he had a choice. Tonight, she consumed.

Urgency elicited urgency. He, breathless as she shuddered under him, gripped her hands with his. As he drove into her, he watched her face, watched the shocked pleasure flash over it. Watched her eyes go opaque as her breath caught, then released on a moan.

Though she shuddered, she moved with him, beat for beat on a fast, reckless climb. At the crest, their entwined fingers vised together, and held tight.

At three, the clock sounded, and Sonya slept on. Trey lay awake beside her listening to the music drifting up the stairs.

And from somewhere deep in the house, the sound of a woman weeping.

It surprised her when Cleo stopped in the library doorway before nine the next morning.

"You're up early for Cleo."

"I want to give the painting some time today, so gotta get started. Trey's already gone?"

"He'll soon be taking his first appointment of the day. Meanwhile, the Doyle Law Offices website is going live in five, four, three, two, one."

"And the crowd cheers," Cleo said, and stifled a yawn. "Need coffee."

She came back in ten minutes with a mug.

"I just texted with Corrine Doyle. She strikes me as a woman who lines up her ducks."

"Yeah, I'd say that's accurate."

"It looks like this duck is posing in her Ryder yoga outfit tomorrow."

"Tomorrow. She moves fast. Is that good for you?"

"Suited both of us. She's arranged to use the little yoga studio in the village, and I can run some errands after."

"Should I go with you? I should go with you."

"You should not, because then you'd be all, maybe you should do this, do that, look this way, look that way."

"I would. I couldn't help it, but —"

"She'll send you the best shots. Go back to work."

"We should talk about what you're doing with your hair."

"No, we shouldn't," Cleo called back, and kept walking.

Sonya considered different pitches for changing Cleo's mind. She even debated the chances of insisting — and killed that thought in its infancy.

Still, she fretted about it until, shortly after her midday walk, she got files emailed from Corrine Doyle.

In the first she found a dozen photos of Eddie on a bike. He wore a suit and tie, a backpack. She'd blurred the background enough he might have ridden on any street anywhere.

Young man riding to work, she thought.

The second file held another dozen, this time of Owen. Sweaty and sexy, she thought, sleeveless black tee, heavy weight curled toward the shoulder, biceps popped, face set, and eyes focused.

She studied ones of him standing, but thought: Nope, the close-up of the curl said it all.

"This is going to work."

Immediately, she switched over to play with her two choices and the layout.

At the end of the day, she jogged into the kitchen.

"I'm making a salad," Cleo told her. "We've got enough pork and potatoes for another meal if it's just us, plus salad."

"Fine. Look at this."

She showed Cleo the evolving layout on her tablet.

"Ooh, a very handsome bike rider — love the suit and tie idea. And biceps. Mmm-mmm-mmm."

"I know, right? Sexy."

"You've already got a man."

"I can still appreciate the mmm-mmm-mmm."

"True. I pity the woman who can't."

"Picture you in your yoga pose, a couple kids playing basketball, Trey reaching for that line drive or fielding a bouncer, and so on. I think when I get them all, I'll do a poster. Like, *In sports, in life, Ryder's got you.*"

"You've got it going, Son."

"I'm going to hit it for another hour or two after dinner, keep it going."

"Works for me. I'm giving my mermaid — well, Owen's mermaid — a little more time tonight." Stopping, Cleo huffed out a breath. "Well, Jesus, Son, when did we get so boring?"

"Boring, my ass. We're driven, creative, professional women. We forge our own path."

"Damn right."

"Besides, we went clubbing just a little while ago."

"We did. We did that, but you know, maybe we should think about having a party. A gathering. A get-together."

"A shindig?"

"A shindig. You know, something with food and drink and conversation. We know people. There's the Doyles, and Owen — you could open it to the other cousins. There's Bree and Manny."

"John Dee, maybe the rest of Rock Hard."

"Maybe add in your Poole's Bay clients, the flower ladies, Gigi."

As an idea struck, Sonya plucked a crouton out of the salad bowl and popped it into her mouth. "Not a shindig so much as an open house. You've got your High Street merchants, the mayor, and like that."

"Keep it very informal. People come, people go during a, what, maybe three-hour period."

"I'm liking this. People will come. They're curious. Besides the Doyles, hardly anyone's really been inside the manor for years, if ever."

"It'll take some planning."

"We're good at planning."

"Nobody better," Cleo agreed. "I can do an illustration of the manor."

"Which I can use to create invitations."

"I'm seeing Corrine tomorrow. I bet she'd know who should go on the guest list."

After dishing up the meal, they sat at the kitchen counter, working on the details.

"Late May," Sonya decided. "Early June. We'd have some green, some blooms. We'll do some planters. People would be able to use the deck, the gardens."

"If this shapes up the way it looks like it could, there's no way our meager talents can handle the food."

"So, we use every restaurant in the village — spread it out. Something from the Lobster Cage, from the pizzeria, from the hotel kitchen, from the bakery, the China Kitchen, the Village Pub. A little bit from all."

"Smorgasbord, and excellent community relations. It's genius. We'd need servers."

"We tap Bree, Anna's husband, get some help figuring that part out."

"We're beyond shindig, Son. We're having An Event."

Thrilled, Sonya bounced in her chair. "Who says we're boring?"

"Not me."

They went back to work, both full of ideas and enthusiasm.

Before she settled into it, Sonya texted Trey.

News! Cleo and I are hosting An Event, sometime late May/early June. An open house at the manor, to include invites to friends, relatives, local luminaries, politicos, merchants. Looking for help making up the guest list.

Major undertaking. Sure you're ready for that? Answer must be yes. I can help, but my mother or Seth are more tuned in for this kind of thing. Fair warning, you won't see many declines or regrets.

We've got weeks to plan it out, so we'll be ready. Cleo's seeing your mom tomorrow, and will enlist her. We're both putting in a little extra work time tonight. How about you?

The same. Mookie thinks I'm boring and misses Yoda. I miss you.

Cleo worries we're boring. And I miss both of you.

If I can break away tomorrow, why don't I take you both to dinner? We can try the Tavern at the hotel.

I'll check with Cleo, but I'd say that's a yes. A definite yes from me if this includes you staying for breakfast.

Pick you up at seven. Don't have to leave until maybe eight-thirty the next morning, so we'll share a bagel. Don't work too late.

Same to you. But it's been pretty quiet around here, so I'm taking advantage. See you tomorrow.

He signed off with a heart emoji, which had

her deciphering the meaning for the next several minutes.

"Oh, stop. What is this, high school?"

Tabling it, she opened her file on the florist.

In her studio, Cleo stood poised in front of the canvas. She knew now what her mermaid held cupped in her hands. Not a gem, not a shell. She'd hold a clear glass ball. Inside the ball, another mermaid sat on the rock, looking out at sea, a whale sounding, with a glass ball in her hand.

And in that, yet another.

The trick would start with the scale, the tiny details, then the way the light should strike the glass, and the glass within the glass.

She worked to the music of flutes and strings, a soothing sound as she created the main sphere. She wanted the light from the brilliant sunset to glow over the ball, and in turn the light from the inner ball to illuminate the interior.

A hint of gold, a touch of red, a blush of purple.

She mixed paints, worked in small dabs, minute brushstrokes to slowly build that light.

When her fingers cramped, she set down the brush, stepped back. Flexing her fingers, she studied the result.

Good, she thought. Pretty damn good.

Still flexing her fingers, she stepped out to walk down to the bathroom. She'd go back, take another fresh look. Maybe put in a little more time. Her contracted work was right on schedule, so if she spent another hour or so on the painting, she could sleep in a bit in the morning.

Too bad the world wasn't geared for night owls, she thought as she relieved her bladder.

Humming to herself, she washed her hands, and glanced in the mirror over the sink.

Hester Dobbs stood behind her.

Throwing up her hands in defense, Cleo whirled. Though the air had chilled, no one stood there. One hand over her pounding heart, she pressed her back to the wall.

"I saw you." Sonya's sketch had been on the mark with the wild black hair, the fierce dark eyes, the sharp chin, full mouth. "I saw you."

Maybe her voice shook, just a little, but she squared her shoulders. "And you can fuck right off."

Water exploded out of the tub faucet. Eyes wide, she watched the hot water knob on the sink turn, and water pour into the bowl. When she tried to turn it off, she had to snatch her fingers away, as the metal burned.

She grabbed a towel to protect her hand, but the knob wouldn't budge. As steam filled the room, something pounded at the door.

As she looked around frantically for a weapon, she saw something written in the mist of the mirror.

In the steam-drenched room, the air turned to ice.

At her desk, Sonya heard nothing as she prepared to shut down for the night. While she saved the evening's work, Yoda stirred under the desk.

And growled.

Scooting back, she reached for him. "What is it, baby?"

In the hearth, the low, simmering fire rose to a roar. Upstairs, the wall screen erupted with the sound of a woman screaming.

The library's pocket doors slammed shut; the lights went off.

The light from the fire glowed red and eerie, smearing the shadows, burning against the glass of the windows until the room she loved became a hellscape.

Through the screams and the dog's wild barks, she heard pounding that had the chandelier swaying like a pendulum.

Third floor, she thought. Cleo.

She ran to the doors, tried to drag them open. She managed an inch before they slammed shut again.

"Come on, come on!"

Straining, she widened the opening. Yoda wiggled through before it slammed shut again.

"No, no! Yoda, wait! Goddamn it, don't you

hurt my dog, you bitch!"

Mustering every ounce of strength, fear, fury, she pulled the door apart enough to squeeze through. Calling for Cleo, she ran for the third floor.

Cleo, Yoda bundled in her arms, sprinted down the hallway.

"I couldn't get out. I couldn't get out." Shaking, Cleo huddled against Sonya as the dog lapped at both their faces. "The bathroom. She was in there with me. I saw her."

"Dobbs?"

"She was in there, then she wasn't. But she was. Then she turned all the hot water on, and I couldn't open the door. And I panicked. I freaked. I completely lost my shit."

"Did she touch you? Did she hurt you?"

"No, no. God. She left me a message on the mirror. Leave or die. Well, fuck you, Hester! Sorry, Son." Easing back, Cleo swiped at her eyes. "I just fell apart. I always thought when and if I came face-to-face with anything like this, I'd handle it. I'm so pissed at myself."

"You did handle it. You have handled it, right from the start. That's why she went at you so hard."

"You think? Maybe. Hell. She won this round, but that's it."

"She hit the library, too. Roared up the fire, blasted the TV, shut off the lights, and slammed the doors. Then I heard the pounding from up here. Let's go down. Yoda needs to go out, and we could use some fresh air."

"I need to clean my brushes. I was going to go back for a while. Scratch that now, but I need to clean up." After expelling three long breaths, Cleo eased back. "I'm not going to let her chase me out of my studio. No more wins for her."

"We'll do that, then take the dog out." Sonya hugged her again and murmured in Cleo's ear, "And talk outside."

With a nod, Cleo led the way back to the studio.

"Oh, Cleo! She's spectacular!"

"Got a ways to go yet."

"But she's so clearly glorious. Oh, the globe. I see what you're doing. That's magic."

"I hope so. And Owen better have a really good place for her, because she's going to deserve it."

Once she'd set her studio to rights, they walked down to the bathroom.

"Like nothing happened. But it did."

"It did," Sonya agreed, and gripped Cleo's hand. "And we're still here."

The house held quiet as they walked down. In the library, the fire simmered low.

Sonya tugged her jacket closer when they walked out in the night air. "I think she saved it up. You know how quiet it's been for the last few days. I think she needed to, like, store it up so she could pull all this off tonight."

"Recharging the batteries. It's energy of one kind or another, so yeah, that makes sense. The fierce and brave Yoda saved me. I heard him barking, and I automatically reached for the door again. The one I couldn't open before. And it opened. There he was. I just scooped him up and ran."

"He shoved through the doors when I got them open a few inches. Which scared me more because now I had to worry about both of you. I can't believe I'm going to say this, but do you think your grandmother has something that might block some of this? Or defuse it? Something."

"I'll sure as hell ask her. Meanwhile, how do you feel about a sleepover?"

"I feel good about a sleepover. Say my room, since Yoda's bed's already there."

"You bet."

"And, Cleo? If I get up, start to walk? Don't stop me. Follow me."

"Are you sure? After all this?"

"Positive. Especially after all this. Follow me. Call Trey. There have to be some answers there. Right now we only have questions."

"You won't be alone." Cleo took her hand. "I promise."

Chapter Twenty-Nine

1916

On this, the happiest day of my life, I become Lisbeth Anne Poole Whitmore. Today I marry my dear and darling Edward. Oh, the sweet little village church can hardly hold all who come to see us take our vows and become one.

My dearest friend Dina, my maid of honor, looks so lovely in her gown. The robin's-egg blue suits her so well. I do hope she and my cousin Hugh make a match! And it's such fun to have Edward's little niece toss rose petals down the aisle in her pink organdy.

My heart beats so fast as I take my dear papa's arm. I've dreamed of this moment all of my life, but now it is here. In my head, I hear angels sing as I begin this final walk as a maiden down the aisle strewn in rose petals.

I want to be a beautiful bride. I know the dress is a dilly, the white silk charmeuse, the lace inserts on the bodice and sleeves, the dozens and dozens of wax pearls. I trust the slender silhouette, one accented by the braided satin belt, is flattering, as Dina, Mama, and the dressmaker all assured me.

My hair is arranged high under my veil with curls falling down the right side nearly to my shoulder. It took so long to perfect it, but I so wish to be fashionable for my dear and darling Edward.

There are butterflies in my stomach as I see him, so very handsome, waiting for me. I see tears in Mama's eyes, but know they are happy ones. Then I see nothing but Edward.

Papa lifts my veil. He kisses my cheek and says, very softly, "I love you, Lissy." Then he places my hand in Edward's.

I know I am a beautiful bride by the way Edward's eyes gaze into mine. The dream I've dreamed so long comes true in the sweet little village church.

I can hardly see through the blur of my own happy tears as we walk back down the aisle, husband and wife. And oh, everyone is so frightfully cheery as they toss rice.

We ride to the manor in Papa's Model T with villagers applauding us on the way. As we turn up Manor Road, Edward gathers me into a kiss, and the butterflies are back as I think of the wedding night to come.

Mama had the private, frank talk with me. Of course, I knew what the marital bed entails. I am eighteen, after all. But I am somewhat anxious and hope Edward will be gentle and patient as he makes me truly his wife.

But now is for celebration! Though it is quite warm, I can't mind. The manor is decked with flowers, the halls ring with laughter. The food is plentiful. The champagne sparkles.

Edward and I, our parents, the wedding party, all sit for formal pictures. I find it hard to sit so still when my heart is giddy and my feet want to dance and dance and dance. But this is duty, and, as Mama says, I will treasure the pictures in years to come.

The orchestra plays in the ballroom. Waltzes, of course, but we have the lively with fox-trots and the turkey trot, the grizzly bear.

It's all so gay and bright, and I find myself wishing the day would never end.

I feel a quick prick of pain near my heart, as if a needle stabbed into me. The anxiety again, I think, and press a hand there as if to calm it. But another stab, and another, and I hear myself shriek as something crawls over my skin.

The heat is suddenly unbearable as if I'm on fire. My stomach cramps, my chest is tight. And oh, they are crawling, crawling, pricking, stabbing all over me!

I think I faint, for it seems I am outside of myself, watching my body on the ballroom floor, shaking, convulsing.

I see her, a woman in black, a hard smile

on her face, walk toward me. She stands over me, somehow alone as my Edward holds me.

No one sees her, no one, as she looks down at me.

She says, “It will be over soon.” Then she takes my wedding ring from my finger, and what is in me and outside me fades away.

In the morning, Cleo rolled over when Sonya got up.

“I nearly forgot you sleep like the dead. Though maybe that’s the wrong term to use in this house.” Cleo snuggled into the pillow. “I didn’t forget you get up way too early. I’m going for another hour.”

“Help yourself. Maybe you slept through it if I got up, but I don’t remember anything if I did.”

“Because you didn’t. I heard the three a.m. alarm; you didn’t.”

“Maybe the business with the mirror’s finished. I don’t know how to feel about that. Oh, and with all the uproar, I forgot. Trey’s coming by around seven to take us to dinner.”

Cleo flopped over again. “I have to get a man so I can stop horning in on your dates.”

“You’re not horning in. And we plan to finish up our date without you.”

“In that case, I’d love to go out to dinner. Good night.”

Sonya went downstairs, got coffee, let the

dog out.

What was it, she thought, about daylight that made everything that went bump — and bang — in the night seem distant?

Foolish really, because plenty of things bumped and banged in the manor in the clear light of day. But for the moment, she'd take that foolish distance.

She got back to work on the florist job, and made personal notes for what she now termed The Event on where she'd want flower arrangements.

She looked up as Cleo rapped knuckles on the doorjamb.

"I'm off to my photo shoot."

"God, you look gorgeous."

"I do, don't I?" She'd tossed an open white shirt over a boldly red sports bra and yoga pants with a muddled black-and-red pattern. She'd worked her hair into a thick braid and added the sparkle of studs to her ears.

"I really should go."

"You really should not. I'll see you later."

"Have Corrine send me shots as you go." Popping up, Sonya rushed to the head of the stairs as Cleo walked down. "Don't look directly at the camera. You're doing yoga poses, but you're not posing."

Cleo just waved a hand in the air as she turned to get a jacket out of the closet. And kept going.

"Don't forget to —"

Cleo closed the door behind her, decisively.

Clover countered Sonya's muttered curse with the Eagles' "Take It Easy."

"Fine. Fine. It's all fine." Irritated, she went back to her desk, plopped down. Then popped up again when she heard the front door open.

"Hey! I just want to say you should —"

She broke off. The door stood open, but no one stood there. And she clearly heard Cleo's car driving down the road.

As she watched, the door swung shut again. The doorbell rang. Yoda raced down, his barks echoing.

"Nobody's there. Come on back upstairs."

Doors slammed up and down the halls, quick bullet cracks. The servants' door shuddered and creaked. Though her heart tripped, Sonya strode downstairs to scoop up the dog.

"We're going to ignore her, okay?"

As she passed it, the servants' door opened so she heard the distant ring of the call bell. On a spurt of temper, Sonya shoved it closed before she turned into the library.

Her tablet played "Evil Woman."

"I've got that."

As the doorbell rang again, she considered closing the library doors, but decided it struck too close to hiding.

Instead, she sat down, soothing Yoda in her lap.

"Go ahead!" she shouted. "Waste your time

and energy. I'm not going anywhere. This is my house. You're just a pest that needs to be exterminated."

The wind streamed through the room, icy and fierce. It sent Sonya's mood boards toppling, sketchbooks sailing. Overhead the ceiling pendants swayed like boats in a stormy sea. She clutched Yoda with one arm, gripped the edge of the desk with her other hand as her chair started to lift off the floor.

It trembled inches above the floor as her muscles screamed and strained to hold it in place.

Then it dropped with a rattling thud, and the air went still.

Gathering the dog even closer, Sonya rocked to soothe them both. "That pissed her off, and I'm fine with it."

Maybe she couldn't quite catch her breath, maybe the chill over her skin seemed to dig straight into her bones, but she would be fine with it.

Stroking the dog, she sat back, closed her eyes.

"Am I crazy? Am I just freaking crazy to stick through all this? Wouldn't a sane person just tuck tail and go back to Boston?"

Clover answered that with Helen Reddy's anthem "I Am Woman."

Her laugh came out a little shaky, but it was a laugh.

"Okay. Let's straighten up this mess and

get back to work."

The ordeal distracted her so the photo shoot slipped out of her mind. When the first file came through, it was a surprise. Especially when she opened it.

Cleo sat on a navy yoga mat, body twisted into a pretzel and a goofy, cross-eyed grin on her face.

"Funny. Ha ha. You won't think it's so funny if I use this one."

But it told her Corrine and Cleo had joined forces smoothly.

In another hour she started the first round of tests on the florist job. Yoda wiggled out from under her desk and ran downstairs.

"Now? Give me ten minutes. We'll go out in ten."

Then she heard the sound of the ball bouncing down the hall.

Even better, she decided. She had a built-in dog sitter.

She took fifty instead of ten, then remembering how the boy had run from her, announced herself.

"I'm going to take Yoda out for a walk now."

She found Yoda sitting as if waiting for her. Then he rose up on his hind legs and took several steps forward.

"Look at you, puppy! You guys are an awesome team. Thanks, Jack."

No, not crazy, she thought as she walked outside with her dog. She'd accept stubborn, preferred determined. And now that she could actually feel spring shoving winter aside, only more determined. She had daffodils waiting to bloom, and the witchy-looking weeper on the side of the house held its buds tight. But they'd burst free before long.

What snow still lay slept in shadows.

She heard a window open behind her and turned, expecting something ugly from the Gold Room.

Instead, she saw Cleo's window opened, and the ones in her own bedroom as well.

Airing them out, she realized. Letting the first breaths of spring in.

No, not crazy, she thought again, and felt her heart lift as she watched a whale sound. She'd had to adjust her entire perception of how the world worked, but that didn't make her crazy.

She heard the car coming. Yoda ran to the walkway, then spun in two circles when Cleo's car made the turn.

She'd buttoned her shirt, but had her jacket over her arm.

"What a gorgeous day! It's even warmer down in the village. I saw daffs blooming, and some hyacinths."

"How did it go?"

"Super, seriously super." She bent to rub Yoda. "We finished nearly an hour ago, then grabbed some lunch so Corrine could get me started on our guest list."

"An hour ago?"

"She's good; so am I. Terrific natural light in the studio. I might try some classes there. And how was your day?"

"Eventful, initially. Our resident bitch went off before you'd headed down the road. Slamming doors, ringing the doorbell. Nothing very creative until she blew a gale through the library. It actually lifted my chair off the floor, with me in it."

"God, Sonya."

"It was her clapback for me calling her a pest. She's been quiet since. Clover's hung with me, and Jack played with Yoda. All in all, a typical day at the manor. Oh, and Molly's airing out our bedrooms."

Cleo looked up. "What a good idea. A perfect day for it."

"Now tell me why I don't have the files from the shoot."

"Because we decided she'd wait to send them until I got home, so we could look at them together. And I'm texting her right now that I am, and we will."

"Are you sure you got enough? Hardly an hour at it?"

"Nearly an hour and a half," Cleo corrected. "And yes. We looked them over in the studio. I know what you want, and so does Corrine. Slick, professional, but with a casual, just-living-your-life feel."

"Well, yeah."

"Let's go see if we pulled that off."

"I'm grabbing a Coke," Sonya said as they went inside.

"Good idea. I'll take one."

In the kitchen, the box of treats sat on the counter. But this time a note sat beside it. In very formal, careful cursive, it read:

Toss it.

"Cleo." Sonya tapped a finger on the note.

"Well, just wow. Messages from the beyond? Toss one and see."

Yoda sat, butt wiggling. After digging out one of the little biscuits, Cleo tossed it in the air. Yoda leaped, snagged it, landed.

"Oh, well done, Yoda." Cleo applauded. "Well done, Jack. Let me do one. You're a champion dog."

"He wrote a note," Sonya murmured. "I was afraid I scared him, but he wrote a note."

Cleo put an arm around her shoulders. "There's an awful lot of good energy in this house. Let's go up."

Yoda settled by the fire as Cleo pulled a chair over to join Sonya at the desk.

She opened the file.

"Okay, you did get plenty, and I can already see you're right about the light. It's perfect."

She started clicking through, enlarging when one struck her.

"You can probably tell I started out with a basic Vinyasa, to warm us both up."

"Added a Tree Pose, which is perfect, and really lovely. But, I think, too typical."

She continued on.

"Oh, this. Reverse Warrior, the curves, the light. Top contender."

She flagged it before going on. Then flagged another, Warrior Three, before shifting to floor poses.

"Show-off," she said as they viewed Cleo in a split-leg fold with her torso flat on the floor. "But this one, this bridge, the curves again, and that light doesn't quit. Scratch that, this one. One-Legged Bridge, the leg extended up. Curves and angles. How do you manage to look relaxed holding that pose?"

"Because it relaxes me."

Sonya went through the rest to the final cross-legged, hands in prayer, eyes closed.

Namaste.

"These are absolutely right in every way. I'll go over them another, oh, five dozen times, but it's going to come down to the Reverse Warrior, Warrior Three, and that One-Legged Bridge. I've got multiple shots of each after I settle on which.

"Thanks, Cleo. Big, giant thanks."

"I had fun, and I like Corrine. She's elegant without being stuffy. Now I'm going to put my nose to the grindstone. Makeup and hair's done, so I'll probably work till six. If you knock off earlier, come up and drag me away."

She sent Corrine a thank-you text and gave her the top three current picks, then settled down to work, with Yoda napping and Clover playing quiet classic rock with some pop tossed in.

Just before five, she got another file from Corrine.

Too perfect a day to miss doing some outdoor shots. It took some persistence — of which I have a deep well — but I think I got what you were after. Owen volunteered to hit a few, which stirred up that sense of competition I wanted. Let me know what you think.

She opened the file, said, "Oh, oh, oh!" Then literally jumped out of her seat and danced.

There was Trey, worn jeans, blue T-shirt, fielder's cap, stretching for that line drive with the ball inches from the sweet spot of a Ryder's ball glove.

Sonya spun into a pirouette, then another before she managed to sit again.

Trey digging for a grounder, that long line of motion, eyes focused, and another snapping a throw toward — she assumed — home plate.

And unexpectedly, one of him all but

horizontal to the ground, the ball pinched in his glove.

She went through them all, flagged her favorites. And answered Corrine.

> I'm thrilled. I'm speechless. I'm not paying you enough. Forget I said that. These are beyond perfect. Thank you for your persistence and your talent and your incredibly handsome son.

She shut down, grabbed her tablet, and ran straight up to Cleo's studio.

"I'm here to drag you away. Can you stop? You have to see these."

"Nearly ready." Cleo sat at the workbench with a tabletop easel, finishing an illustration in acrylics.

Knowing how it worked, Sonya walked down to the sofa, sat, and went over the file she'd copied to her tablet.

When Cleo sat back, Sonya bounced up.

"What do you think?" Cleo asked.

Walking back, Sonya studied the painting. "Lovers meet, under the sea."

"Mermaids need mermen."

"And it's lovely, their movement toward each other, arms reaching, fingers nearly touching. The yearning."

"That's what I wanted. Not just sex, but emotion, yearning. It's human. Now, what do I have to see?"

"Another version of poetry in motion."

"Oh, she said she was going to try, but not to mention it in case Trey's schedule didn't allow. And may I again say, mmm-mmm-mmm."

"You may."

"I know you had this one as your vision, but this one — where he's basically hovering above the ground? It's awesome."

"And I'm going to frame it for him, but I think, like your split-leg fold, it's too good. Intimidating for regular people. And in the first, you can clearly see the Ryder logo on the mitt. The client will like that."

"You win the point. I guess we should go change so Mr. Baseball can take us to dinner."

"I've got to push it, grab a shower." She glanced at the time. "Why is it always later than I think it should be?"

She hustled back downstairs, jumped in the shower. Wrapped in a towel, she decided to twist up a ponytail, clip it, and consider her hair done. Looking forward to an evening with Mr. Baseball, she fell into her fifteen-minute, night-out-makeup routine while she tried to figure out what she should wear.

She came out to find the choice already made.

She studied the long, flowy white shirt, the stovepipe-gray pants, the cap-sleeved, open-weave red sweater.

"I think Molly has a thing for red, Yoda. But you know, it works."

After she dressed and considered jewelry choices, her phone rang. She saw Trey on the readout.

She wouldn't bring up all that happened over the phone, she decided. She and Cleo could detail everything later, over dinner.

That would sure as hell keep things lively.

"Hey. It's the all-star."

He let out a weak laugh. "Yeah. Listen, Sonya, something's come up. I won't be able to make it tonight."

"Oh, I'm sorry. Are you okay? You're upset, I can hear it."

"I'm okay. I'm sorry for the late notice."

She heard voices in the background, what sounded like a call over a PA. Her heart jumped.

"Are you at the hospital? Are you hurt? What —"

"It's not me. I'm fine."

"Your family."

"No, no, everybody's fine. It's a client. She . . . Jesus, Jesus, he beat the hell out of her. The divorce, I handled the divorce just a couple of weeks ago. He got drunk, nothing new there, pushed his way into the house, and went at her. A lot of good the restraining order did her."

Not just upset, she realized. Furious and fractured.

"I'm sorry. I'm so sorry. Do you want me to come? I can come. Can I help?"

"No. No, thanks, but . . . They're working on her right now, and they say she'll be okay. The kids ran out to a neighbor, he called the police, went over, managed to stop him before it got worse.

"Goddamn it, I've known these people for ten years."

In that moment, all she wanted to do was put her arms around him.

"Are the kids all right? Do the police have him?"

"Kids are pretty shook, but they're fine. They'll be okay. They can stay with the neighbors. And yeah, he's in custody. I need to stay with her. I don't want her to be alone when she comes out. Her mother and sister are flying in, but they won't get here until ten or eleven."

"If there's anything we can do, check on the kids, pick up Mookie, just call."

"Thanks. Owen swung by to get the dog. I just need to stick here until her family comes, and I want to talk to Hal again."

Chief of police, Sonya remembered.

"I'll get back to you tomorrow."

"All right. We'll talk then."

When she hung up, Cleo spoke from the doorway. "I heard enough of that to know something bad happened."

"One of Trey's clients is in the hospital.

Her ex-husband broke in and attacked her. He beat her, Cleo. It sounds horrible."

"Because it is. How bad is she hurt?"

"I don't know exactly, but he's staying with her until her family can get there." Because it knotted, Sonya pressed a hand to her stomach. "A few hours, so she won't be alone."

"Trey Doyle's not just a pretty face. He's a really good man."

"He was so upset. You just don't hear him get really upset, not easily."

"I've noticed."

"But he was, upset and worried and frustrated. And really, really angry. I've never heard him really angry."

"Come on. We'll go downstairs, throw together something to eat. We'll light a candle for her."

"Yeah, that's better than standing here feeling helpless. I think I know who it is — not who by name," she qualified as they started down. "But Trey handled a divorce and mentioned how the husband went off in court, got slapped down by the judge. Then he had that early meeting on the weekend, remember? And I could tell he was worried when he got back. He said something about a restraining order on the phone just now. I bet this is all the same person."

"Poole's Bay looks idyllic, and mostly it is, I think. But bad people live in good places."

Cleo looked toward the ceiling as she spoke.

"We sure as hell know that for a fact. I'm sorry this happened to her, I'm sorry her ex-husband's a vicious motherfucker. And I'm going to say she's lucky to have somebody like Trey looking out for her. Making sure she has someone with her when she needs it most."

As they turned into the kitchen, Sonya nodded. "You're right about that." But she couldn't get the furious and fractured sound of his voice out of her head.

"If he's free tomorrow, let's not go out. We could make dinner. I could make the pot roast deal. He really liked it. And he sounded so down."

"You'd make him a pot roast dinner?"

"I did it before. It should be easier this time. Maybe. What's that smile?"

"This smile, as I get us some wine, is due to me seeing my best friend move over the arc of serious like into the next phase."

"Maybe," she said again. "Oh, crap, I can't help it. He just has a way of . . . He just is. But let's take it easy. A year ago, I was engaged to an asshole."

"A year ago was a world ago. Pour that wine while I light a candle. Then we'll see what we've got in here that's easy."

"Mom told me what she had with Dad was magic."

Cleo glanced back. "And you want that?"

"Yeah. Don't you?"

"Damn right I do. I think everybody in the world wants that, and the lucky make it. Because you don't find magic, Son, you make it."

"You make it. I like that idea."

"Not an idea, a fact."

After lighting a candle, Cleo set it in the center of the island. "A little light so she recovers, in every way. And knows she's not alone while she heals."

Every knot in Sonya's stomach loosened again.

"You make magic, Cleo, just by being you."

"Light always wins. Sometimes it takes way too long, but it always wins."

"I'm going to believe that. I haven't told Trey about anything that's gone on the last couple days. I thought we'd do that at dinner tonight."

"Good call. He's got enough on his plate. And we dealt with it. Well, after I lost my shit, momentarily, we handled it. You'll tell him later."

"That's what I thought. I don't want him worried about us. And most especially right now."

Cleo sent out another knowing smile. "So you can worry about him now." Holding up a finger, she got another candle. "This one's for Trey," she said as she lit it.

"It works. I don't know why it works, but it works."

"How about grilled ham and cheese sandwiches, and we toss some of these frozen fries in the oven and say screw the vegetables tonight?"

"I say yes." Already comforted, Sonya got up to deal with the fries. "I'll feed Yoda, and I further say let's eat in front of the TV."

"And watch a tear-jerking, heartrending, but happy-ending romance."

"Took the thought right out of my brain. But this means jammies."

"Required. So, feed our boy? Then make a quick dress-code change?"

"There's the plan. Yoda can take a bathroom run while we cook this up, then we all snuggle in."

"Teamwork," Cleo said as they bumped fists.

Chapter Thirty

Because they needed the emotional hit with the romantic glow at the end, Sonya and Cleo watched a double feature. It included over half a box of tissues and a jumbo bowl of popcorn.

As the credits rolled on the second movie, they both sighed in utter satisfaction.

"This was great. This was all that and more." Cleo dried her eyes again. "Honestly, you forget how cathartic a good cry is until you have one."

"Especially when the final tears are after love conquers all. And you just can't watch and fully appreciate movies like this unless you're with a girlfriend."

"Men don't get it." Cleo gave another satisfied sigh. "I mean at the end, when she's walking toward the lake, and there he is, holding that single daisy?"

"It killed me!" Sonya grabbed another tissue for each of them. "Oh, that was so perfect. And the kiss, the long, slow kiss with the sun setting over the lake?"

"You're getting me going all over again. Here's a pact. Once a month, girls' movie night in the manor. No boys allowed. Except for Yoda."

"I'm there. Okay, Yoda, last run for the night."

"You get the dog, I'll get the dishes." So saying, Cleo blew out the candles they'd brought up with them from the kitchen.

"I hope Trey's client's okay, and her family's with her by now."

"As horrible as it is, Son, maybe this is the start of a happy ending for her. She and the kids will get away from him. Be safe."

"I hope so."

They dealt with the dishes, the dog, then started upstairs, shutting off lights as they went.

"Are you okay sleeping solo tonight?"

Sonya nodded. "Are you?"

"I expect to be out like these lights in one minute flat. After what she did last night and today while I was gone, I think she needs some recharging time."

"We can hope, because I really don't want to lose this romantic movies buzz. But you know where I am."

"And you know where I am. 'Night," Cleo added as she turned into her room.

" 'Night."

It took Sonya barely longer than Cleo's one minute flat to fall asleep.

Shortly after midnight, Trey pulled up in front of Owen's house.

Exhausted in every possible way, he sat a moment, scrubbed his hands over his face.

Poole's Bay spread quiet, serene, safe around him. But the hard and mean, he thought, could manage to carve a place even there.

He knew Marlo couldn't be in better hands, knew her mother and sister would take turns sitting with her through the night. But he'd never get the image of her bruised and battered face out of his head.

Could he have done something differently? Something more, something less, to somehow avoid what happened? Just one damn thing to stop the pain and viciousness before it started?

Now a woman lay in a hospital bed, a man sat behind bars. And their children . . . they'd carry the scars.

He'd gone over it countless times in the past hours, searching for that one damn thing. And found nothing. Yet.

He eased himself out of the truck, crossed to the porch, then let himself into Owen's house.

The TV played some old black-and-white where the men wore fedoras and the women had snappy comebacks. No doubt, at all, Owen had seen it at least a couple dozen times before.

Since he wasn't sprawled on the sofa, Trey knew Owen had it on for the background noise, and to amuse himself with the dialogue he could, most likely, recite verbatim.

Instead of the sofa, Owen sat at the kitchen table he often used as a drawing board. He'd helped Owen demo the wall so the kitchen opened to the rest.

Owen liked his elbow room.

When Trey walked in, the dogs curled by the fire barely glanced up.

"You didn't have to wait up."

"Working on something." But Owen rolled the drawing up, tucked it in one of the slots he had for that purpose beside the fridge.

And hit the remote on the TV to shut it off.

"How's Marlo?"

"Jesus, Owen." In one frustrated move, Trey shrugged off his jacket, tossed it on the back of the sofa.

One look at his friend's face had Owen getting up.

"Hold that. I was going to say get a beer, but you look like you need a whiskey and a bunk for the night. Sit."

"Thanks. All around."

"Now I've gotta play Mom. Did you eat anything?"

"Something fairly disgusting from the vending machine."

"I got Hot Pockets."

"No. Seeing a woman beat to shit kills the appetite. The whiskey'll do."

Owen got them both a short glass and left the bottle on the table. "So?"

"She gave a statement to the cops. Hal ran it all through for me so I didn't have to ask her to go over it again. He pushed his way into the house, knocked down the oldest boy — the eight-year-old — when the kid opened it. Marlo came running, and he punched her in the face. She went down but yelled for the boys to run. And he kept right on pounding."

"Kids right there makes it even worse. Is Zane hurt?"

"He's got some bruises." Digging for his calm, Trey took a slug of whiskey. "Eight years old, and he has to grab his little brother and run while his father's calling his mother a whore and beating on her."

"Motherfucker. How bad is she hurt?"

"Three cracked ribs, dislocated shoulder, concussion. She's got two black eyes. They were worried about a detached retina in the left, but that's okay. Busted her nose, fractured her cheekbone. Gut punched her plenty, but they've ruled out internal injuries."

Steadier, he took another, slower sip.

"He tore at her clothes, grabbed her tits,

her crotch. If the kids hadn't gotten out and got Bob Bailey, he'd sure as hell have raped her. And I think he might've killed her, Owen. I swear to God.

"I knew it was bad. That's why I convinced her to get the TRO, but I didn't see this in him. I didn't see it."

"What the hell were you supposed to do about it that you didn't?"

"I don't know. But I didn't see it."

"Neither did any-damn-body. I'll go see her tomorrow, if you think that's okay. If she's up to it."

"Yeah." Trey downed some whiskey. "I think she could use all the support she can get."

"Wes did good work when he was sober." Owen spoke carefully. "I can't say he was ever the cheerful sort, but he did good work, kept his head down, collected his pay. The last few years, he didn't stay sober. Did half-assed work, picked fights, came in when he damn well pleased."

Shaking his head, Owen studied the whiskey in his glass. "He got belligerent when I tried to talk to him. I had to let him go."

Catching the tone, Trey met Owen's eyes. "This isn't on you. None of it."

"No, not on me, not on you either. It's on him. But firing him pushed the cycle, I'd say. How long you figure they'll give him?"

Trey closed his eyes. He'd had a beer with

Wes Mooney at the Village Pub over the years, enjoyed a potluck cookout in their backyard, watched the oldest play a Little League game or two.

And now?

"Felony assault, and domestic adds to it. Add the breaking in. They'll go for at least sexual assault if not the attempted rape. The extent of her injuries adds to it. In front of the kids adds to it, and the door bashed the kid in the face when he shoved it open. Bloodied his nose. We had a restraining order on him because he came by drunk to pick up the kids and threatened her when she wouldn't let him have them. Took a couple swings at Bob, so that's another charge."

"Drunk and stupid, seeing as Bob's twice his size."

"Which he found out. Property damage. Resisting arrest. He's looking at ten to twenty."

"He earned it."

"Yeah, he did. Her family wants her to go back to New Hampshire with them when she's able. I think she will." After downing the rest of the whiskey, Trey poured them both another.

"She wants full custody of the kids, so I'll work on that. She'll get it."

"Fucking A."

"Not always a slam dunk."

"Should be."

"Should ain't is. But he bloodied the kid's nose, put Marlo in the hospital. I'm going to make damn sure she gets full custody and clearance to move out of state. What were you working on?"

"Cleopatra's barge. The little Sunfish." Owen shrugged. "Had a little time, had an idea."

"Such as?"

"She likes mermaids, doesn't she?" Rising, Owen pulled the drawing out of the slot, opened it. "So how about a pair of mermaids swimming up port and starboard toward the bow? Add some carving. It'll be fun to work on."

Trey scooted his chair for a better angle. "And seriously cool. You're trading her this for a painting?"

"Have you seen the painting?"

"Got a glimpse when we hauled that chest in there. It's a beauty. So's the artist."

"Yeah, they've both got the looks. And it's a fair trade. Anyway, she might not want the fancy work. She'd be stupid not to," he considered, "and she doesn't come off stupid, but we'll see. I'm just playing with it, spare time."

"I'm taking my spare time and crashing. Thanks for the drink, and the bunk."

"Always here."

Owen's spare room had started as an office, but Owen had deemed it too closed in.

No elbow room.

He preferred the kitchen table or one of the workbenches in his shop.

So in its current state, it held a bed, a nightstand he'd built himself, and a dresser no one used that he'd refinished.

The walls, a sad beige, bore a few stripes of paint Owen tested and had yet to decide on.

Trey stripped down to his boxers, dropped down on the bed, and was asleep almost before he yanked up the covers.

In the manor, Cleo barely stirred when the clock sounded. Rolling over, she snuggled into her nest of pillows and floated in that netherworld between wake and sleep.

The piano music drifted up, and used to it, she drifted back off.

Somewhere, deeper in the house, a woman wept. Somewhere, deeper yet, one cried out in pain.

"Everybody quiet down," she muttered.

Then she shot straight up when she felt a hand on her shoulder, when she heard a voice whisper, urgently:

Sonya.

Pulse racing, she fumbled for the light. Alone in her room, she rubbed a hand between her breasts so her heart wouldn't just leap out. No panicking, she ordered herself. Absolutely not again.

Probably dreamed it, she thought, probably

dreamed it, but . . .

Wide awake now, she hurried to the door. Sonya stepped out of her room and started to walk down the long hall. Burying her instinct to rush to her, Cleo raced back for her phone.

"Please let this be the right thing."

The phone pulled Trey out of a dead sleep. For one terrible moment, he could only think Marlo had taken a turn for the worse.

"It's Trey."

"Cleo. Sonya's walking. She said if she did, I should follow her and call you. I'm following her and calling you."

"I'm on my way."

"I'm close behind her, but . . . Maybe hurry."

He grabbed his pants, yanking them on as he went to bang on Owen's bedroom door.

"What the fucking fuck?"

"Sonya's sleepwalking or whatever the hell it is. Cleo's behind her. I'm going."

"Getting my damn pants on."

They were out of the house along with the dogs inside two minutes.

At the manor, Sonya approached the staircase. And stood as if undecided, swaying a little, while the piano music stilled, and the house ticked and settled.

Then she turned and walked past the library, continued on toward the stairs to the third floor.

"I'm with you," Cleo murmured. "I'm right here."

She heard the weeping woman now, and stopped as Sonya did outside the door to what had once been the nursery.

When Sonya opened the door, the weeping became more distinct, and tears gathered in her eyes.

What do you see that I don't? Cleo wondered. *What do you see in the dark?*

She held her phone up to use some light, saw the shadows of the antique crib, the cradle, the dresser, the rocker she remembered.

Then she heard it, under the grief of weeping. The rhythmic creak of a rocking chair. And as she watched, she saw it move, slowly, back and forth, back and forth.

"Night after night," Sonya murmured, "year after year, Carlotta grieves for the son, so small, who came into the world too soon, and left it only hours later."

Quietly, Sonya closed the door and moved on.

As they approached the stairs, Cleo sent another text.

Going to the third floor.

The return text came fast, and brief.

5 mins.

"That's fast, all right. Trey's coming, Sonya, and I'm right here."

Cleo braced herself as the walls shook, the floor trembled. On the third-floor landing, Sonya again paused. Down the hall to the right, the outline of the door of the Gold Room glowed red. To Cleo's eyes it seemed to pulse like a heart. Tendrils of smoke curled out from under the door to crawl along the hall.

The scent of it, fetid, carried and soiled the air.

"Don't go that way, Son. We're not ready to go that way."

The pulsing took on sound, the drum, drum, drum of a heartbeat.

"She exists to feed," Sonya said, "and her feed is fear and grief. Night after night, year after year, she gobbles the weeping, she drinks the tears. She feasts on every shiver and shudder of the living for the dead."

"Are you awake?" As Cleo started to reach out, Sonya turned left toward the servants' quarters.

Now she heard that cry of pain again, and the moans and sobs that followed. Dark closed tight here, and though Sonya walked on, Cleo switched on her phone flashlight to help her see.

They went up the short flight and through the door that kept this wing separate. Cleo's skin prickled from the colder air, but Sonya seemed unaffected as she walked, barefoot, toward another door.

When she opened it, Cleo caught the smell of sickness, of fever and sweat and vomit. She heard the creak of a bed as if someone in it tossed restlessly.

"Can't help." Sonya sighed it. "What was and is. Can't help poor Molly O'Brian. She traveled from Cobh, away from family and home, but found one here. She took pride in polishing the wood and the glass. Help came too late to save her."

A tear slid down Sonya's cheek as she closed the door.

"Can't help young Molly. Only bear witness."

When Sonya turned, walked back the way they'd come, Cleo's heart sank. But Sonya turned toward the ballroom.

Cleo followed and texted again.

I think we're going to the ballroom.

On Manor Rd, nearly there.

With the dark so deep that her phone couldn't help, Cleo took a chance and groped along the wall for a light switch.

If Sonya woke, she woke, but she wouldn't risk either or both of them taking a fall in the dark.

She found a light switch outside one of the

anterooms, and when she flipped it on, Sonya simply continued toward the massive ballroom doors.

When she threw them open, stepped into the shadows, Cleo switched on the first of the chandeliers.

It showered light over the mirror that stood amid the furniture they'd undraped, searched through, shifted. Its glass tossed back that light as the predators framing it seemed to snarl as if guarding what centered them.

"What should I do? I don't know what to do. What do you see in there? All I see is us. But . . . God, if it's some sort of portal, I'm not letting you go alone."

The cold cut to the bone, and she could hear the pound, pound, pound of that heartbeat from the Gold Room. Beyond the mirror, the shadows danced, but she feared stepping back far enough to turn on more light.

Then she heard the rat-a-tat of Yoda's barking. And the deeper answer of another dog. Trey, finally. She nearly called out, but she could already hear the racing footsteps.

"Please wait, Sonya. Just wait."

They came up with a racket that steadied her nerves. Risking a glance back, she saw Trey hadn't brought only his dog.

"Thank God. It's here. The mirror. It wasn't, but it's here. She made some stops along the way. It's been a journey." Shivering, Cleo hugged her elbows.

"It's a meat locker in here." Owen stripped off his jacket, handed it to her even as Trey shrugged out of his own.

"Thanks. Should we wake her, Trey? I don't know if we should. She saw things, she said things."

As Trey started to drape his jacket over Sonya's shoulders, she said, "I'm awake."

Instead of the jacket, Trey draped himself around her. "You're freezing, cutie."

"I wasn't. I don't think."

"Were you awake this whole time?" Cleo demanded.

"Just now. Standing here. I was dreaming. And I . . . don't know. I don't remember. I feel sort of out of it. Do you see the mirror? Is it real?"

"It's real."

With one hand in Trey's, Sonya reached out to touch the frame. "I'm not dreaming, and we all see it."

"Maybe" — Cleo rubbed a hand on Sonya's back — "you woke up because we do."

"Do you see what's in it?"

"Mirrored glass," Trey began. "And all of us."

"No. No. I see . . ."

"Colors, movement. Light, shadows."

With a kind of desperate relief, Sonya turned to Owen. "Yes. You see it?"

"Yeah." He looked at Trey, at Cleo. "You don't?"

"You're both Pooles, we're not." Cleo lifted her hands. "That must be it."

"My father saw it, Collin saw it. Maybe others, too. There are people, dancing. I hear music."

"Way old-timey," Owen confirmed. "Bad acoustics," he added, "like in a tunnel. It's getting brighter," he added. "And the music's louder."

"It's here, the ballroom, but it's full of flowers and people. Everything shines and glistens." Charmed, Sonya put a hand on the glass. Her fingers slid straight through. "Oh. It's warm on the other side."

"Sonya." Trey took her wrist, drew her hand away.

"I'm supposed to go. It pulls at me. I need to see. It's part of my inheritance. Do you feel it, Owen, the pull?"

"No, but I see it, and I hear it. So." When he put his hand on the glass, it went through to the wrist. "That's a kick in the nuts."

After pulling his hand out, he turned it, studied it. "Still intact, and yeah, it's warmer over there."

Sonya gripped Trey's hand, and Cleo's with her other. "I'm awake. I'm aware. I need to go. I can't explain, but I want to go. I'd rather go when I know what I'm doing, when it's my decision, and when you're all here."

Trey pressed his hand to the mirror, felt only solid glass. Over Sonya's head, he shifted his gaze to Owen's.

"Yeah, I got it."

Understanding, Sonya turned to him. "You don't have to do this. It doesn't pull at you."

"Don't be stupid." Owen took her hand from Cleo's, linked fingers. "I'll go first."

With a hand on Owen's shoulder, Trey bent down to kiss Sonya. "Don't keep me waiting long."

"Wait. Wait. Take my charm pouch." Digging in her pajama pocket, Cleo pulled it out, pushed it into Sonya's. "Wait!" she said again as Owen started to step forward.

"What now? Silver bullet, wooden stake?"

She grabbed his face in her hands, kissed him. "Bring each other back."

"Wouldn't have it any other way." With a firm grip on Sonya's hand, he waited for her nod.

As he stepped through the glass, she glanced back, then followed.

The mirror swallowed them.

"Oh my God, oh my God."

Cleo pressed both hands to the glass as Yoda whined and pawed at it.

"They're just gone. What the hell do we do now?"

Trey stared at the mirror as if willing himself to see the other side.

"We wait."

The heartbeat from the Gold Room stilled, and silence fell over the manor.

ABOUT THE AUTHOR

Nora Roberts is the #1 *New York Times* bestselling author of more than 230 novels, including *The Becoming, Legacy, The Awakening, Hideaway, Identity,* The Dragon Heart Legacy trilogy, and many more. She is also the author of the bestselling In Death series written under the pen name J. D. Robb. There are more than 500 million copies of her books in print.

The employees of Thorndike Press hope you have enjoyed this Large Print book. All our Thorndike Large Print titles are designed for easy reading, and all our books are made to last. Other Thorndike Press Large Print books are available at your library, through selected bookstores, or directly from us.

For information about titles, please call:
(800) 223-1244

or visit our website at:
gale.com/thorndike